HAWK HUNTER FLEW HIGHER—UP TO 40,000, AND INTO THE MIST OF A BILLOWING CLOUD.

A faint ringing began in his brain. Within seconds he could feel a distinct buzz throughout his body. It meant only one thing.

Aircraft!

A lot of them. Out toward the east. Two, maybe three hundred miles away.

He checked his fuel supply. It was at 85%. He checked his weapons. Four Sidewinders and a maximum load of cannon shells—all okay.

The sensation grew stronger. The hair on the back of his head was standing up. *Trouble.* He knew it. He had to check it out. No time to call for the scramble jets. He had to act *now!*

He booted in the afterburner and steered due east. . . .

WINGMAN

#2
THE CIRCLE WAR
BY MACK MALONEY

PINNACLE BOOKS
KENSINGTON PUBLISHING CORP.
http://www.pinnaclebooks.com

PINNACLE BOOKS

are published by

Kensington Publishing Corp.
850 Third Avenue
New York, NY 10022

First printing: July 1987

Printed in the United States of America
10 9 8 7 6

Chapter One

The sky was on fire . . .

Brilliant reds, yellows, golds, blues, and greens streaked across the horizon. Waves of color darting in and out, appearing and disappearing like phantoms in the crystal-clear night. The ghostly lights reflected on the ice and tundra below, doubling their intensity. Flying eight miles high and heading due north, Major Hawk Hunter relaxed for a moment to appreciate the mysterious beauty of the *Aurora Borealis.*

The cockpit of the U-2 was cramped—odd for an airplane designed to stay aloft for 10 or more hours with a single pilot at the controls. Compared to this, the cockpit in Hunter's F-16 was as big as a living room. But creature comforts and sightseeing were the furthest things from his mind right now. He was only reaching the midway point of his long recon mission. He still had a long way to go.

The U-2 was a spy plane. Long and pencil-shaped, it sported a pair of gooney-bird sized wings—the better to fly high and farther with. Normally the airplane was unarmed. But these weren't normal times. Hunter had jerry-rigged two Sidewinder missiles under the jet's wings in case of the unlikely possibility that he'd meet up with an unfriendly airplane somewhere over the frozen wasteland. He had also installed two 20mm cannon in the ship's nose, though at this high latitude and height, the muzzles tended to freeze up unless he test-fired them occasionally.

A sophisticated camera of his own design peeked out from the bottom of the airplane. It was a combination heat sensitive/infra-red video set up, complete with a small TV screen in the cockpit. Should he see anything strange or threatening on the ground, with the push of a button, its shape and "heat signature" would be captured on special videotape instantly even if the ground was obscured by smoke or snow or darkness. The spy plane was also jammed with eavesdropping equipment, designed to pick up the faintest radio or TV transmission for 50 miles around. But right now, all was quiet across the miles of cold, bleak, barren, uninhabited arctic landscape.

That was fine with him . . .

This was the 50th—or was it the 51st?—arctic recon flight he'd made in the past six months. His course never varied. Taking off from his base in southwest Oregon, he would climb to 40,000 feet over what used to be the state of Washington. Then he would skirt part of Free Canada, then straight up—over the Wrangell Mountains, over the abandoned city of Fairbanks, across the Arctic Circle through to the top of Alaska.

His mission was simple. He was looking for Russians.

Off Point Barrow, Alaska, a pre-set indicator light blinked on; it was his signal to enter a course correction into the flight computer. Then he put the U-2 into a long arching sweep to the west. Within an hour, he would be over the coast of Soviet Siberia.

It was a lonely but necessary vigilance. He knew any sign of Soviet ships, aircraft or even arctic ground troops could be the advance units of a large invasion force. And if the Russians were coming, they'd be coming through this arctic backdoor. And only Hunter had eyes in this part of the world. He was the sentinel. But so far, in his 50 previous flights, he hadn't spotted a thing.

Hunter had come to both love and dread the long recon flights. He loved them simply because he was flying. The utter starkness of the arctic landscape below fascinated him. But each long journey alone also gave him time to think—too much time. The long hours were a blessing and a curse.

He thought about his country . . .

The United States were victors in World War III's battles against the Soviets, but losers in the deception that followed the ceasefire. All it took was a traitorous vice president, who arranged the assassination of the president and his cabinet, then let the Star Wars shield down long enough for a flood of Russian missiles to come over the North Pole and obliterate America's ICBM force while it was still in the ground. The vice president—who was later revealed as a Soviet mole—then "negotiated" the peace. The result? Now there *was* no more United States. It was broken up, decentralized and, in the years since, frequently at war with itself.

This was America under "The New Order."

The devastated middle of the continent—the location of the destroyed-in-place U.S. ICBM force—was now a nightmare of neutron radiation, poison gas and a swirl of strange hallucinogenics that were spread everywhere when the Russian missiles hit. This was The Badlands, the schism that stretched from the Dakotas to the northern border of the new Republic of Texas.

These events gnawed at Hunter—he was obsessed with hate for those who had had a hand in the destruction of the country he loved. The Russians. The vice president. The turncoat National Guard troops who carried out the New Order to the letter while the regular U.S. forces were overseas fighting real battles.

He hated the air pirates—renegades who now roamed the skies, preying on innocents and attacking the huge air convoys that were the only contact between the relatively civilized portions east of the Mississippi and the West Coast. Ditto the Mid-Aks—the corrupt, fanatical leaders of the Middle Atlantic Conference which grew out of the Mid-Atlantic states. Then there was The Family, the super-criminals who had operated out of New Chicago. Their armies had attacked Football City—formerly St. Louis. But the free-wheeling, independent gambling territory refused to knuckle under to the threats of blackmail and extortion from their unfriendly neighbors to the north. It was Hunter and the air force of rescued pilots he organized, who helped Football City's army and thousands of Free Forces' volunteers defeat The Family's 80,000-strong invading force in a series of spectacular battles.

Both the 'Aks and The Family relied on Soviet help—Hunter was certain of it. Defeated on the European battlefields and elsewhere, the Russians had a great interest in keeping America fractionalized and unstable. Hunter was a stumbling block in these devious plans. His goal was to reunite the continent—reestablish the democracy that was once the United States. If this dream was to come true, the destabilizing elements in New Order America—and there were plenty of them—would have to be defeated.

After the big war, Hunter had joined a bunch of his ex-Air Force buddies in a group known far and wide as "ZAP." The *Zone Air Patrol* was the crack air force for the Northeast Economic Zone, the area once known as New England that had become its own country after the New Order went down. But as good as ZAP was, they couldn't prevent the Northeast Economic Zone from falling to the Mid-Aks. That's when Hunter became a fighter pilot for hire, only later did he get revenge by defeating both the 'Aks and The Family.

Now he was part of the newly-formed Pacific American Air Corps, or PAAC. He and a number of other ex-Air Force and ZAP pilots had established a new air base near Coos Bay, Oregon. They were allied with the Republic of California, a democratic government sometimes known as The Coasters. Together, their charge was to protect the western flank of the continent as far east to the Rockies and up through Alaska. It was a huge responsibility, but they were relatively well-equipped for the job—especially in air power. They had to be. Because once the Soviets recovered from their wartime losses, Hunter and many other freedom-loving people were certain they, or possibly some puppet army, would invade America for real to complete the job they failed to do in Europe.

And that's why he flew these long missions . . .

His country, its enemies, his past—all these things haunted him during the long, solitary flights. But there was another memory—more personal, that deep down inside him also refused to let go.

Her name was Dominique . . .

Hours passed. The night got darker. He was over the tip of Siberia when he switched on the plane's eavesdropping equipment. Just like 50 times before—he heard nothing, saw nothing. He stayed on a southerly course for a while, soaring over the Chukchi Peninsula. Then he turned back to the east. The sun was coming up. Soon he was over northern Alaska once again, heading for home.

Suddenly, it happened. *The feeling*. His sixth sense that told him that trouble—usually trouble on wings—was nearby. He hadn't felt it this intensely in a long time. Now, his body was ringing with it.

He checked his instruments. He was over Seward's Peninsula, about 100 miles north of Nome, Alaska. Below him were banks of frozen clouds. He knew an arctic storm was brewing, but the inhospitable conditions made no difference—something was down there. He put the U-2 into a dive to get a closer look.

The airplane bumped and bucked as he passed through the turbulent cloud cover. Snow started to swirl around him and accumulate on his cockpit windshield as he lowered his air speed. Suddenly a trio of flat panel warning lights buzzed and flashed in succession on his control board. His heat-sensitive infra-red camera sensors were confirming his sixth sense. They had detected telltale signs of heat—a lot of it—somewhere on the ground below.

Another pilot might have just set the cameras rolling and passed over the area at a safe height, waiting until he got back to base to check the "heat" film and see what it revealed. Not Hunter. He instructed the flight computer to take the craft to the source of the heat.

The U-2 was being buffeted by very high winds and the snow made visibility close to zero. Once he got to a reasonably low altitude, Hunter switched on his ground radar and waited for an image to appear on the screen. Slowly, the hazy forms of the ground contours materialized. He was about a half mile above a valley that was surrounded by mountains on three sides. The sensors indicated the heat source was located at the southern end of the valley.

He finally broke through the cloud cover only to find he was still flying blind. A blizzard was raging through the valley, and it was all he could do to keep the aircraft level. He slowed his airspeed down to almost a crawl. His visibility was now absolutely zero. He was flying on instruments and instincts.

He switched on his TV "heat screen," the read-out from his special video camera. At the end of the white fuzzy patterns of the valley walls, he could see a large red form indicating heat. What the hell could possibly be giving it off? There certainly couldn't be any people or settlements surviving in this frigid wilderness.

Unless . . .

It was now straight ahead of him. He brought the plane down even lower—to 500 feet. The mysterious source of heat would soon be just below him. He dropped to 200 feet—near suicidal for a pilot of lesser caliber in the blizzard winds—but fairly routine for him.

"5 . . . 4 . . . 3 . . . 2 . . . 1 . . . Now!"

He flipped on the infra-red/heat sensitive camera and watched as the image below him materialized on the cockpit TV screen. He knew that whatever it was, the camera would also record it on the airplane's internal videotaping system. Slowly the image took form . . .

"Jesus Christ!" he yelled. He couldn't believe it. The images were fuzzy and unfocused, but unmistakable. Up ahead—lined up in two neat rows—were no less than 50 jet fighters! Their engines were on, to keep them from freezing, creating ghostly auras around each one. Even though he was at 200 feet, he sank even lower, dispatching his landing gear to get his speed down to a crawl. All the time the special camera whirred.

As he drew closer, he saw the images of more than just jets. There were also heat outlines of buildings—igloo-type affairs scattered about near the fighters, plus a radar dish and antenna. He could even see a few human forms moving in the blizzard around the jets.

Even though his camera was picking up everything, he had to try and get a visual sighting on one of the airplanes. He *had* to find out who owned these airplanes. Still being banged around by the blizzard winds, he dropped down even lower, and tipped the jet to its port side. Through a freakish break on the gale-force snowstorm, he was able to catch a split second glimpse of one of the jets. Then, in an instant, the "hole" in the storm was gone and he was flying blind once again.

Suddenly a buzzer sounded in the U-2's cockpit. Two bright red lights started to blink on the flat panel control board. He didn't have to look at the controls to know what all the commotion was about. Someone down below with their finger on the launch button of a SAM had acquired a radar lock on him. Within seconds the buzzing noise switched to a continuous alarm sound. The light stopped flashing and stayed on, burning even brighter red. The missile had been launched and was zeroing in on him.

No matter. He had enough in the camera anyway; it was time to leave. All in one motion he flicked the landing gear up, pointing the U-2's nose skyward and booted in the airplane's afterburner. The airplane seemed to hang suspended in the air for a moment. Then a great burst of energetic fire shot out of the rear. In a split second, the U-2 was gone. The missile tried to keep up but it was too much. It ran out of fuel and crashed into a snow-covered mountain four miles away.

Hunter headed south, his throttle open on "full military" power the whole way. The missile fired at him confirmed it; those were not "friendlies" down there. He had to get back to his base, organize an air strike and return as quickly as possible.

What he had just barely seen was unbelievable but unmistakable. He was soon 20, 30, 40 miles away, but the image was still burned onto his retinas and in his brain. He had only seen the jet for a split-second, not nearly long enough for him to ID its type. But emblazoned on the side of that one jet was an emblem. A red star with a yellow border. The insignia of the Soviet Union. The Pacific American Air Corps had a bunch of Russian jet fighters right in their backyard.

But not for long . . .

Chapter Two

One hour and 20 minutes later, Hunter was leading a strike force comprised of eight PAAC aircraft back to the site of the Soviet base.

He had had no time to explain; no time to review the infra-red tape in the U-2's cameras. He had kept strict radio silence all the way back to the base, but once he landed, he virtually leaped out of the U-2 and into his F-16. He called to the two "scramble" jets—aircraft that were always armed and warmed up and ready to go at a moment's notice—to get airborne, while at the same time, sounding a red alert at the base.

Within minutes, five more airplanes were gassed, armed and taxiing for take-off. Hunter allowed himself a tinge of pride at the speed and professionalism of it all, though it wasn't all that surprising. The majority of PAAC pilots were, like him, veterans of the old ZAP . . .

The strike force was made up of a potpouri of aircraft. The two scramble jets were A-7 "Strikefighters" bulging at the wings with napalm cannisters. There were also three T-38s, converted training jets that he knew were carrying four 1000 pound bombs each. Two A-10 "Thunderbolts" were also along for the ride. They too were carrying napalm, and each plane had two Vulcan cannons in its snout. Hunter's famous souped-up F-16—the highest performance jet left on the continent—was carrying its standard "six-pack" of Vulcan cannons, plus a ordnance dispenser attached to its belly. This device would drop up to 800 "bomblets" on the base—small hand-sized explosive charges that were well suited to destroying parked aircraft and landing zones.

Hunter swung his F-16 in and out of the formation, checking with each airplane's pilot that their craft were ready for action. He then checked his own instruments. He was within 10 miles of the location of the base. The snow was still falling but it had let up slightly. He knew that whoever was at the base would probably be expecting some kind of an attack, especially after they had taken a shot at the U-2. He had to be prepared to see a few of the Soviet jets airborne, flying protection over the base, that is, if they were able to take off in this weather. Luckily both his F-16 and the A-7 Strikefighters were carrying Sidewinder air-to-air missiles.

He slowly brought the formation down low—they would come in right above the deck. He and the A-7s would go in first, lay down their bombs and then climb up to 2000 feet and serve as the air cover while the T-38s and the A-10s did their work. If no Russian jets were there to challenge them, each plane would return and strafe targets of opportunity.

He recognized the mountain just ahead of him as the one that formed the southern edge of the valley's border. Just beyond it was where he had spotted the Russian planes. He checked his instruments a final time, and increased his throttle slightly. The F-16 responded and pulled a little ahead of the A-7s. The trio of T-38s were slightly behind and the A-10s brought up the rear. Hunter would be the first over the target—if any SAMs were coming up, they'd be aimed at him. He gave a thumbs-up signal over his head for the A-7 pilots to see. Then he bore down over the mountain and prepared to unleash his bombs on the Russian base . . .

But there was nothing there.

He streaked down the mountain valley only to find that where he had seen the Soviet jets less than two hours before was now nothing more than a snowswept landscape. The jets, the huts, the antenna, the radar—everything was gone. He quickly re-checked his coordinates; he *knew* this was the place. But where the hell were the Russians?

The other pilots came over the mountain and shared the same surprise. Quickly, each pulled up and threw their arming switches to the Off position. Soon the eight planes were flying in formation once again. While the others orbited above, Hunter streaked low through the valley. He couldn't even see so much as an oil spot to indicate the Russian base had been there a few hours ago. He put the F-16 on its tail and climbed to join the others.

Hunter was the first to break radio silence. "Sorry, guys," he said with the puzzlement much evidenced in his voice. "I guess we're shooting at ghosts again."

"That's okay, major," one of the A-7 pilots, a guy named Mick, radioed back. "Alaska's pretty this time of year."

"Well, you guys enjoy the scenery on the way back," Hunter said, checking his fuel. "I'm going to look around a little more."

"Gonna need help, Major?" It was Max, one of the A-10 pilots.

"Thanks, Max," Hunter replied. "But I'll go this one alone. Go buy yourselves a round of drinks and put it on my tab."

"Aye-aye, sir," Mick radioed back. "Good luck."

With that, the seven attack jets turned southward and streaked off. Alone again, Hunter began searching . . .

The conference room at the PAAC base headquarters was filled to capacity. More than 60 pilots plus base support personnel were squeezed into a room that was built to hold 50 people, tops. Around the round conference table—its top strewn with empty and full coffee cups, wrappers from sandwichcs and countless liquor and beer bottles—sat the principal officers of the Air Corps. The atmosphere was tumultuous as the pilots talked among themselves. Finally, the man they had been waiting for—General Dave Jones, commander of the Pacific American Air Corps—strode into the room. The assembled men snapped to attention as one, and barraged their commanding officer with an orgy of salutes.

The general, small, craggy faced and wiry, instinctively returned the salute. These guys are real pros, he thought. The PAAC had done away with all but the most barebone rules and regulations between the ranks, yet Hunter and his guys never failed to catch the old USAF officer in him.

"Sit down, gentlemen," Jones said, walking over to shake hands with a few of the officers within reach.

"Relax . . ."

Hunter, standing at the head of the conference table and in front of a large video screen, greeted Jones. For Hunter, seeing Jones was like seeing a ghost. The man was the identical twin brother of the deceased hero, General Seth Jones—Hunter's one-time commanding officer and mentor. Seth Jones had died bravely in the opening rounds of the Mid-Ak coup in the Northeast. Before he died, he told Hunter and the other ZAP pilots to head west and join up with his brother Dave. Eventually, they did.

"Good flight up, sir?" Hunter asked him. Jones's HQ and the main base for PAAC was located at the old Naval Air Station in San Diego.

"Sure, no problem," Jones said, taking off his trademark baseball cap and undoing his leather flight jacket. "Any coffee or whiskey left?"

"Both," Hunter said, retrieving a bottle from the table while another pilot handed a mug of coffee to the general. Jones splashed a healthy slug of whiskey into the coffee cup and took a gulp. "Okay. It's good to see everyone. As you all know, I've been out of touch for a while. Without going into detail, we've got a secret project working and I was locked up in a laboratory—me and a bunch of eggheads—for several weeks. Now I hear there's been somse strange stuff happening. So what the hell *is* going on up here, Hawk?"

Hunter looked around at the soldiers in the room and especially at those seated around the table. This was the first council of war called since the new PAAC base was established at Coos Bay, Oregon. Anyone who was anyone at the base was on hand. At the far end of the table sat Ben Wa and J. T. Toomey, Hunter's friends who had served with him in the Thunderbirds before the war and in his F-16 squadron during it. They had also been with him at ZAP. Next to them sat four officers known as the Ace Wrecking Company, the two-plane F-4 fighter team for hire—and commanded by the swaggering Captain "Crunch" O'Malley. They had helped Hunter win the Battle of Football City and had accepted employment with PAAC when Hunter headed west.

Beside them sat two officers from The Crazy Eights, the eight-aircraft chopper team that once formed the equally famous Zone Air Ranger brigade back in the days of ZAP. The Crazy Eight Rangers were now doubling as the new base's airborne security force.

Captain Frost, an officer in the Free Canadian Air Force and another friend of Hunter's, was on hand as the liaison officer for PAAC. Next to him, and sitting at Hunter's right hand, was Captain John "Bull" Dozer, the tough Marine commander who had been with Hunter all through the war with The Family.

These men made up the war council, the group which, by agreement, was called to a meeting any time a crisis threatened the security of PAAC or the territory it protected.

Now Hunter had the floor.

He flipped a switch and the video screen came to life in a burst of static. He waited until a fuzzy image appeared on the screen then froze the picture.

"This is the videotape shot from the U-2 two days ago," he started. "Before I roll it, let me just say that

I'm glad what's on this tape proves that I am not losing my mind—there were Russians out there—and that the tape will clear up a little of the mystery as to how the Soviets were able to disappear so quickly and take fifty jets with them. In a blizzard yet."

He paused briefly, "this is just one of a number of strange things that have been happening around here. Before I run this tape, let's just hear what you guys have run into lately, then maybe somehow, we can try to figure out what the Christ is going on."

He turned to Ben Wa and Toomey. "Ben, you first."

Ben Wa, the Oriental fighter pilot, stood up and began his story.

"About three weeks ago, J. T. and I were on TDY down to Nellis Air Force base outside of Vegas. As you know, we've been using the Nellis as a refueling station and target practice area lately.

"Anyway, we were drinking in town one night—there are a few barrooms still open in Vegas—and the locals told us they had heard strange stuff out in the desert a month or so earlier."

"What kind of strange 'stuff?' " Jones asked.

"A loud explosion, sir," Toomey, the perpetually sunglassed pilot jumped in. "Like an atomic bomb went off, one guy told us. Louder than a sonic boom or jet aircraft or things like that."

"But that area is practically deserted," Jones said.

"Yes," Wa continued. "That's what was so strange about it. The people were scared, sir. They said the explosion—or whatever it was—shook the city for ten minutes. Then they saw a lot of smoke and flame, out on the eastern horizon.

"We decided to stick around and try to track it down. We flew around the area where they said they saw smoke and flames. It took us a while, but then we found it."

"And what was 'it?' " Jones asked.

"A crater, sir," Twomey said. "The biggest God-damn crater you'd ever want to see. It *looked* like it was made by a nuke. Easily a mile across. It was still smoking when we got there."

Jones took a swig of his spiked coffee. "Meteorite, maybe?"

Toomey shook his head. "We landed, then drove out to the place, sir. It was definitely an explosion. There were bits and pieces of metal everywhere. Plus a few threads of clothing. Even a few fresh bones—they still had some, well, muscle on them."

Jones took off his hat and ran his fingers through his hair. "A mile wide crater?" he asked. "That's a lot of bomb, if it was a bomb . . ."

"Whatever it was," Wa said. "It shook up the civilians pretty bad. Some of them left town; others are chipping in to buy an anti-aircraft battery, just in case."

A murmur rose up and subsided among the assembly.

Jones shook his head and took a swig of his booze-laced coffee. "What else?" he asked.

Hunter nodded to Captain Crunch, commander of the Ace Wrecking Company.

Crunch stood up and started his story. "We were flying routine sea patrol, General, a few weeks before Ben and J. T. were down in Vegas. We were about one hundred fifty klicks off what used to be San

Fran when we started picking up some strange radio clutter."

"What kind of strange?" Jones asked.

"Well, it sounded like a lot of different kinds of traffic. Routine stuff—like weather, wind direction, but also the kind of transmissions you'd hear between ships. Course headings, fuel loads, these kinds of things. Some of the voices were in English, others, well . . . not English."

"Russian?" Jones asked, looking up.

"I don't speak it, sir," Crunch said. "But it could have been."

"So what happened?" asked Jones as he refilled his coffee cup.

"Well, we alerted the base and vectored to the area," Crunch continued. "That's when we made contact with the Coaster intell ship that was coming back from a long-range patrol."

"That was the Liberty Two ship, General," Hunter interjected.

Now a collective shudder went through the room. Everyone there knew what happened aboard the Liberty 2 was downright spooky.

"Right," Crunch said. "We talked to them. Reported that we were hearing all this strange stuff and it seemed to be coming from a point close to their location. They said they were picking the stuff up too, and that they were getting a little jumpy. They also said they were in the middle of a first-class fog and to them, the radio traffic sounded like a whole Goddamned fleet of ships was bearing down on them.

"We told them to sit tight, that we were about

fifteen minutes away. We radioed the base again and requested back-up and also a air-sea rescue chopper, just in case. Then we lit out toward the Liberty. We were still getting a lot of noise on the radio, so much so we had trouble raising and maintaining contact with them."

Crunch stopped and took a chug from his coffee mug. It wasn't holding coffee. He continued, slowly: "Well, we finally got to within twenty miles of the Liberty's coordinates and sure enough, there was the biggest Goddamn fog bank I've ever seen. It went on for miles in every direction. Thick as hell. We got a good lock on their receiver and we started sending like crazy. At first we got no answer, then . . ."

Jones looked up. "And then, Captain?"

Crunch took another slug from his cup. "Then we had one more transmission with them, sir. We were talking to the skipper."

"What did he say?"

Crunch reached out to the tape recorder which sat in front of him and pushed the PLAY button. "Here's what we picked up, sir."

The room was completely silent as the tape crackled to life. First, a burst of static could be heard. Then noises, like hundreds of voices, were clearly evident. Then, one voice came through. It was the Liberty 2 skipper. His voice was shaky: "Get here, quick, Phantoms! Get here quick! They're all around us! Jesus, there must be a hundred of them! Phantoms! Do you copy? May Day! May Day! May . . ."

The tape abruptly ended in a burst of static. The whole room shuddered as one again. Even Jones shook off a chill.

"We searched the area up and down, sir," Crunch said, caution evident in his voice. "We were twenty five feet off the deck in that God damn fog and we didn't see a thing."

"So what happened?"

"We waited for the chopper and that's when they found the ship," Crunch answered.

Hunter took it from there. "The chopper dropped two divers, General," he said. "They climbed aboard the ship and found not a single soul on board."

"The engines were running, the radio was still on, the coffee was still hot on the stove," Hunter said. "But there wasn't anyone to be found."

"Any blood?" Jones asked. "Any signs of a struggle?"

Hunter shook his head. "We sent an armed tug out and they towed it back. We went over it with a fine tooth comb. Didn't find a thing. It's like they vanished into thin air."

"Goddamn it, what happened to those men?" Jones said, lightly pounded his fist on the table.

Absolute silence fell upon the room.

"I'm afraid the worst is yet to come, sir," Hunter said. He turned to one of the officers from the Crazy Eights. His was the strangest story of all.

The officer, a lieutenant named Vogel, stood up and slowly, clearly told his tale:

"We were sitting in the scramble house one day when we got a call from the frontier guardsmen's post out in the Hell's Canyon area," Vogel began. "It seems that one of their patrols was on a week-long mission and they passed through a small town named Way Out.

"They had planned to bivouac there, as they had in the past. But when they arrived, they found the town was . . . well, gone, sir."

"Gone?" Jones asked. "Don't tell me the whole Goddamn town vanished, too . . ."

"No, sir," Vogel continued. "Gone as in dead, sir. Wiped out. All of the townspeople killed. Mutilated."

There was dead silence.

"There were more than 300 people," Vogel went on. "So many the guardsmen couldn't bury them all. They headed back for their post and that's when they called us."

"Then what?" Jones asked.

Vogel continued: "I took *Crazy Two* and *Crazy Four* out with seventy five men. By the time we reached the outpost, there was no one left there either. It was burned to the ground. No one around except this one guy. He was beat up pretty bad, lost a lot of blood. The medics tried to fix him up, but he was fading fast. But he kept saying one thing, over and over . . ."

"And that was . . . ?" Jones said.

Vogel paused, then said: " 'Horses,' sir. That's all he could say, was 'Horses.' "

" 'Horses?' What the hell does *that* mean?" Jones asked, looking at Hunter. All the pilot could do was shrug his shoulders.

"Then what happened, lieutenant?" Jones asked.

"Well, I set up a defense perimeter, sir," the officer continued. "Then I took twenty five men with me in *Crazy Two* and flew out to Way Out.

"It was just as the guardsmen said. Bodies everywhere, horribly cut up. Some missing arms, legs, heads. They were in really bad shape. So bad even the timber wolves wouldn't eat them. Just like the guardsmen, we couldn't bury them, so we burned them instead."

Vogel paused for a drink from his coffee cup.

"Then we flew back to the outpost," he went on. "By that time, our guys had found the rest of the guardsmen. Or what was left of them. They were all thrown into a pile about a half mile from the place. They were also badly cut up—no arms, heads. Disembowelments.

"We burned them, too. Then it started snowing, so we had to pull out."

Jones took a healthy swig from his whiskey-laced coffee.

"Any of your guys see any tracks out there, lieutenant, horses or otherwise?" the general asked.

"No sir," Vogel answered. "But, like I said, it was starting to snow pretty hard. Anything would have been covered up."

Jones thought for a moment, then turned to Hunter. "Raiders, Hawk?" he asked.

"Could be," Hunter answered. "But I doubt it. Too messy. The ones we've dealt with like to come in quietly and fade away. The less commotion for them, the better."

"Could be someone new to the neighborhood," Dozer said, speaking for the first time.

"Anything is possible, I guess," Hunter said, swigging his own laced coffee.

"Well this beats the shit out of me," Jones said, refilling his cup with both java and booze. "Okay,

Hawk, your turn."

Hunter turned back to the frozen video frame.

"As you all know, this is the video I shot the other day," he began. "For my own peace of mind, I'm glad to say that it *does* show something was out there."

He pushed a button and the video started rolling. It began as Hunter's U-2 descended through the storm clouds and into the blizzard-swept valley. The heat sources could clearly be seen at the end of the fuzzy outline of the gorge.

As the U-2 drew closer, the heat source started to become defined. Soon it was clear the heat was coming from many separate shapes. The two lines of fighters, plus the igloo building and the radar dish came into view. Then, two figures could be seen, the heat sensitive video giving them the look of garish red ghosts. Two more figures could be seen running out into the snow and aiming a SAM launcher at the jet.

Then, just as the camera passed over its closest to the jet fighters, Hunter hit the video's SLO-MO button. He zoomed in on the image. Sure enough, everyone could see the side of a bluish jet, with the unmistakable red star with yellow boarder emblem of the Soviet Union.

"Now that's the best image that we have so far," Hunter told the group, freezing the frame on the video. "We have some guys at the photo recon lab working on it with computer enhancement. But it's a slow process. So they tell me it will still be a few days before we can reach any conclusions on what type of Soviet jet we're dealing with here."

Jones looked at the screen and then spoke the

words that were on everyone's lips: "Amazing," he said.

The meeting broke up after a short time later. Hunter and Dozer saw Jones back to his airplane. The General would return to his PAAC San Diego base and brief his top officers there. But before he left, both he and Hunter agreed that the incidents that were discussed at the meeting should all be considered top secret for the time being.

After Jones's airplane took off, Hunter and Dozer retreated to the base bar for the first of several rounds of drinks.

"This is bugging me," Hunter confided in the Marine captain. "Here I am, flying all over the Goddamn North Pole and the Russians somehow land 50 jet fighters right on top of us, then somehow get them to disappear. Some watchdog *I* was."

"Hey, Hawk, knock it off," Dozer told him. "You were doing your best. There's a lot of weird shit happening these days. This is just another one of them."

Hunter downed his drink and poured another.

Dozer continued. "Ghost, spooks. Mysterious explosions. Those swabbies vanishing like that. Someone icing those frontier guardsmen. I mean, those guardsmen ain't just out there playing soldier. They're tough guys."

"I hear you," Hunter agreed. "But these Russian jets are what really bothers me. We're lucky they didn't come down here and nail us. I mean, we would have shot them up pretty bad, but still, we would have been on our ass, too."

"Well, I know we have plenty of eyes up there now," Dozer said.

"True," Hunter said. "I've got two-plane missions flying up there around the clock. Frost told his people, of course, and the Free Canadians are patrolling up there, looking for something—anything—that could give us a clue as to where those jets went."

"Well, when you find them and the weather ain't for flying," Dozer said. "Me and my boys will go in and take them out on the ground."

Hunter smiled. His "boys" were the 7th Cavalry—a battalion of Marines that fought for Dozer in the big war in Turkey. They won their name after being surrounded by an overwhelming force of Soviets only to survive and escape, thanks to Dozer's leadership. When the war ended soon after, the Marines had no way to get home. Dozer rallied them, "hijacked" two airliners and flew the battalion to Scotland, (where they first met Hunter) and where they all caught a ride back to America aboard the aircraft carrier, JFK.

"We need intelligence," Hunter said. "Not just here, but from back east too."

"Heard from Fitz or St. Louie lately?" Dozer asked, referring to two close friends and allies of Hunter, both of whom operated back east.

"No," Hunter answered. "But I think a meeting with them is long overdue. Besides, the photo lab guys tell me they are still two days away from a positive ID on those jets."

He drained his drink, then stood up to go, saying to Dozer, "Ever been to MacIntosh, Idaho?"

Chapter Three

The formation of five helicopters descended on the small, abandoned Idaho town.

The two Crazy Eight Chinooks went in first, landing beside a rusting grain elevator at the side of a railroad track. As soon as the first chopper touched down, the side doors were flung open and three squads of Dozer's best Marines jumped out. They quickly formed up on the railroad tracks and marched into the town barely an eighth of a mile away.

Meanwhile the rest of the choppers had set down, one by one, on a moist field nearby. The second Crazy Eight was carrying a portable Roland SAM air defense system and radar set. As soon as the big chopper's blades stopped turning, two more squads of 7th Cavalrymen emerged and went about setting up the small SAM launcher and radar warning system.

The third large helicopter was a converted U.S. Navy chopper called a Sea Stallion. Hunter and Dozer emerged from the machine and went over to talk to the pilots of the two helicopters known as the

Cobra Brothers. The Brothers, flying the small but lethal, bug-like choppers, would provide air cover over the small town, just as the Marines would secure the town itself. The precautions were needed. The hills surrounding the place were undoubtedly filled with bandits, raiders, and God-knows-what kind of New Order outlaws.

"Sir!" one of the Roland operators called out. "We're picking up something."

Hunter and Dozer walked back to the Roland set and watched over the man's shoulder. Sure enough, five blips appeared on the SAM's radar screen. "Looks like four Hueys and a Blackhawk," the operator told them.

"That'll be St. Louie's guys," Hunter said. He could *feel* the aircraft coming long before they appeared on the radar screen. The electronics just confirmed his sixth sense.

Five dots soon appeared over the eastern horizon, gradually getting bigger. Within two minutes, the formation set down directly on the railroad tracks, the Blackhawk first, then the four Hueys.

The doors to the Hueys burst open and soldiers of the elite Football City Special Forces leaped out. They were clearly recognizable in their futuristic one-piece combat outfits, complete with their Football City emblem patches.

The highly trained troops quickly dispersed through the field and took up positions along a tree line 100 yards away. As planned, these soldiers would be responsible for the perimeter defense while the conference was taking place in the town.

The doors of the Blackhawk opened and two

familiar figures stepped out. The first one was a tall, distinguished looking man, clad in a three-piece, all-white suit. His clothes and his great shock of snow white hair gave him an evangelical look. This was Louie St. Louie, the creator, leader, and president of Football City. Formerly known as St. Louis, the city had become a "super-Las Vegas" after the New Order came in. St. Louie—who despite his name was really a true-blue Texan—hired Hunter to retrieve a valuable diamond shipment of his, and later convinced the pilot to raise an air force and help defend Football City against a takeover attempt by the criminals known as The Family. Football City was nearly devastated in the war that followed, but its rebuilding programs—including revival of the year-long, open betting football game from which it took its name—were well under way.

The second man was shorter, with a mass of brown hair, wearing brown combat fatigues and a green beret. This was Hunter's old Thunderbirds' buddy, Mike Fitzgerald. The perky Irishman was now the top man at the Syracuse Aerodrome, the well known and notorious airplane "truck-stop" located in up-state Free Territory of New York. Fitz, a fiercely independent businessman, had made a fortune servicing jets moving across the convoys routes between Free Canada and the West Coast. For this occasion, Fitzgerald was carrying two cases of scotch.

Hunter and Dozer walked over to greet their friends.

"Howdy, pardner," Hunter said to St. Louie, shaking his hand.

"Good to see you, Hawk," St. Louie said, a wide

grin revealing a perfect set of white teeth. "Been too long, boy."

St. Louie went to greet Dozer as Hunter approached Fitzgerald. "Hey, Fitz," Hunter said, kidding the Irishman, "Only two cases of booze. Think it will be enough?"

"Now stop with ya joking and take one of these, will ye?" the man said in a brogue that couldn't be cut with a buzzsaw. "Good scotch weighs a lot . . ."

Hunter took one of the cases from him. The airman had to laugh. Here were two of his closest friends, both, who despite the New Order chaos across the continent, had still not only managed to survive, but had made millions of dollars in the process. At least capitalism was not MIA in the post-World War III age.

"So, Fitz," Hunter said as the four men walked toward the town "You have that hundred bucks you owe me?"

Fitzgerald, well known for his frugality, blanched. "I'm not here to talk over old debts, Hawker, me boy," he said. "We have work to do."

The old saloon was a mass of cracked veneer and plywood, dirt, dust, mud and broken windows. A smashed jukebox sat in one corner. Chintzy decorations hung ragged from the ceiling. The barroom's booths had long ago succumbed to age. Yet the old place still had a quality of sleazy charm to it.

"Looks like it was a good place to get lost in, in its day," Hunter said as the four men walked into the saloon in the middle of the small town.

Dozer and Hunter retrieved a semi-sturdy table as Fitzgerald opened a few bottles of his scotch. St. Louie was heating a bucket of his famous Texas stew over a dozen cans of Sterno. A set of semi-clean plates and glasses were found and once everything was ready, the four sat down to eat and talk.

Hunter filled in St. Louie and Fitzgerald on all the strange happenings PAAC had run up against in the past few weeks. Both men sat nearly open-mouthed as they listened to the stories.

"Dear mother of God," Fitzgerald exclaimed. "I believe the whole damn continent is haunted . . ."

"You've been having odd things happen, too?" Hunter asked between mouthfuls.

"Aye, we have," Fitzgerald said. "Lights. Strange flying lights. Over the Lakes. We were getting calls from people out there every night."

"Flying lights?" Hunter asked. "Like in 'UFOs?' "

"I guess," Fitzgerald said, refilling his glass. "The people who see 'em, claim they are different colors. Floating. Way up in the sky. Hundreds of them. Coming in from the northeast and heading southwest. They make no noise."

"Have you check them out?" Dozer asked.

"Sure have," Fitzgerald said. "Scrambled jets eight nights in a row, we did. They found nothing. And believe me, it's an expensive proposition, to fly four jets out to the Lakes and back for no good reason."

"How about radar?" Hunter asked.

"We haven't seen them," Fitzgerald replied. "We sent a portable unit out there finally. Those guys sat on the edge of Lake Erie for three days and nights, freezing their asses off. No lights. No nothing. We finally called them back in and the very next night, we get two hundred reports that the sky is filled with them."

"Whew, boy!" Dozer said. "This gets creepier by the minute."

"Well boys," St. Louie drawled. "You ain't heard nothing yet. I got a story that will beat any of yours."

The ruddy faced Texan pushed his empty plate aside and took a stiff belt from his whiskey glass. Then he began his story:

"A few weeks back, one of our long range patrols went out on an extended mission. These patrols are our eyes and ears on the western edge of our territory, which, as you know, borders the southern Badlands.

"These guys are the toughest, meanest bunch of troopers you'd ever want to meet. Well, forty-two guys went out. Only one came back. And he'll be in the loony bin for the rest of his life."

"Jesus Christ," Hunter said. "What the hell happened?"

St. Louie paused, then said: "We don't know exactly. We talked to the one survivor, but believe me, he's gone around the deep end and he ain't coming back.

"But this is what he said—or mumbled—about what happened:

"They were on the fourth night of a twenty-one-day mission. Now according to their orders, they could skirt the 'Bads, but if they actually went in, they had to maintain radio silence, as part of their training.

"Anyway, they *did* go into the Badlands. That

much we know. Apparently on that fourth night, someone—or something—crawled into their camp and stole all their food and water."

"Weren't there any sentries?" Dozer asked.

"Oh yeah," St. Louie answered. "They found them, six of them, cut up terrible. Butchered. Now remember, these recon guys are the highest trained force we have. But still someone greased six of them very quietly, then came in and stole the food.

"So now my guys are hopping mad. They start to track whatever it was. Soon they're more than a hundred miles inside the 'Bads, which has got to be the furthest anyone civilized had gone in before.

"Well, they get in there—and the survivor said it was like being on another planet, no trees, nothing growing, poison everywhere. Fog covering everything. Very, very strange.

"And in the middle of all this, what the hell do they find? *A nuke station!* And the Goddamn thing is working!"

"What?!" Hunter couldn't believe it. "That's got to be impossible . . ."

"That's what *I* said," St. Louie replied. "But, I'm telling you, this guy swears it's true. They spot this place with three cooling towers. Steam coming out of them and lights blazing all over the plant.

"Anyway, at this point, it gets fuzzy. But, for whatever reason, they decide to head back home. They were three days into the return trip when they were walking in a ravine. It was around midnight, as by this time they were sleeping during the day and moving at night.

"So they were in this ravine, when all of a sudden,

the guy said they heard this tremendous noise. Like thunder. They turned around and . . . and it gets really strange here, boys . . . they see thousands of guys coming at them. *On horseback!* Screaming, terrible. At full charge.

"They came up on my guys so fast, they couldn't get to defensive positions. They must have formed up in tight groups, but it didn't make any difference. These . . . horsemen ran them right over. Trampled almost all of them to death and kept right on going!"

Hunter shook his head as if the motion would drive away the very strange story. Dozer and Fitzgerald looked like they were in a state of shock.

"Only three guys lived through it," St. Louie said slowly. It was evident the loss of the men had hit him pretty hard. "Two of them were really badly broken up. They died on thc way back. This one guy stumbled across the border eight days later. We found him and got him on a medivac chopper but it was useless. He was out of it. Delirious. Still is. Whatever he saw out there—horses or whatever—his brain is gone."

The four men were silent for a long time, absorbing the frightening tale. Fitz reached for another bottle, opened it and took a long healthy swig. Hunter could see the Irishman's mind working. He knew his friend was seriously superstitious. And Hunter had to admit to himself, that right now, he was getting more than a little spooked too.

Chapter Four

The departure from Mac Intosh went off without a hitch. Just as the five PAAC choppers lifted off, a PAAC C-130 tankerplane appeared right on schedule over the small town, its four-ship T-38 fighter escort in tow. Two at a time, the PAAC helicopters hooked up to the orbiting C-130's in-flight refueling probe and drew fuel from the mother ship. Their tanks thus filled in mid-air, the small air armada headed for home.

But it was a long, troubled flight back for Hunter. He sat alone in the Sea Stallion's spare navigator's seat, everyone on board knowing enough not to bother him. The intelligence meeting was a success from an operational point of view, but he had a million things running through his already overloaded mind. The disturbing stories from Fitz and St. Louie had only added to his worries about the similar strange events happening on his side of the continent.

The tale of the recon troops in the Badlands was

particularly haunting him. He felt a shiver in his spine when he thought of the brave soldiers walking into the gates of hell like that. St. Louie said he doubted if the lone survivor would be able to leave the psychiatric ward—ever. Right then and there, Hunter had vowed to find out what really happened in that ravine that night.

But Fitz and St. Louie had given him other information as well. Both men had spies everywhere, especially entrenched in the Northeast and the old Atlantic States' region where the Mid-Aks once ruled with a brutal iron fist. Things had changed dramatically since Hunter, along with Dozer and a special strike force, rescued a bunch of ex-ZAP pilots the occupying 'Aks were holding prisoner in a Boston skyscraper. Not only had Hunter and his small, airborne army freed the pilots; they blew up a liquid natural gas facility close to the city which torched most of the Mid-Aks' military supplies that were foolishly stored nearby. The daring rescue mission and the destruction left behind more or less ended the 'Aks military domination in the region. Right now, the once-thriving Northeast Economic Zone—the territory that ZAP once protected—was pretty much abandoned. The 'Aks retreated southward to be closer to the home territory; the citizens had fled northward into the relative safety of Free Canada.

But now Fitz had told him that some of the Mid-Aks were itching to become a force to be reckoned with once again. Or at least share that power. Right after the Battle of Football City had been won—at a terrible loss of life and property—Hunter had heard that a new, more sinister alliance was forming in the east. Apparently made up of representatives of the air pirates, the Family, the 'Aks and other scum, the shadowy alliance—known as The Circle—was now gaining momentum.

According to Fitzie's spies, the group was being run by a mysterious figure named Viktor Robotov. They said that although he was probably as Russian as his name indicated, where he came from was still a mystery. One rumor had it that he was a major in the Soviet KGB before the war. Another said Viktor was part of the so-called Peace Committee that had imposed the bogus New Order on the hoodwinked American populace. Either way, it made him a mortal enemy of Hunter's.

Now this Viktor character was said to be calling the shots and that the other members of The Circle were listening. One thing that gave him his power was money. Apparently Viktor had a lot of it. One of The Circle's first actions was to put a bounty on Hunter's head. But the group also had amassed great quantities of military supplies, spending freely on the wild and dangerous arms black market in South America and in parts of Soviet-occupied Europe.

But what was worse, Fitz had told Hunter that The Circle was actually starting to *manufacture* weapons. This was very disturbing news. In the past, since The New Order came to force, the warring factions on the American continent relied on armaments left over from the pre-war days and not destroyed in the similarly bogus "disarmament" frenzy that swept the continent after "peace" was restored. Because a lot of equipment *was* destroyed, there was a limited amount to go around—a blessing really, as it imposed a kind of finite cap on the number of weapons available on the continent. The costs of these weapons also made buying them on the black market an expensive proposition. But now, if The Circle started *making* new weapons, this delicate "arms control" balance would be dangerously upset. According to Fitzgerald, the weapons being made by The Circle were presently limited to imitation M-16s and ammunition. But he knew, as did Hunter, that it was only a matter of time before The Circle moved into making more sophisticated armaments.

So Hunter saw two problems: the bizarreness that seemed to be sweeping the countryside and the obvious rise of the dangerous Circle. Maybe St. Louie was right. *Maybe the whole fucking continent was becoming haunted . . .*

But even with all of these reports troubling him, it was a more personal matter that, deep down, bothered him most. Before St. Louie and Fitz flew off at the end of the confab, to leapfrog into Free Canada for their refueling stop, Hunter had asked the Irishman if his spies had any word on Dominique. Ever since she had disappeared in Free Canada after a flight Hunter had put her on landed safely in Montreal, Fitz had assigned two of his best men to try to find the woman. Nearly two years had passed since, and they had come up with complete dead ends in all that time. Sadly, Fitzgerald had to report to Hunter once again that he had no news. Dominique was nowhere to be found.

These troubles wrapped Hunter in a mental cold blanket that lasted the entire flight back. Dominique. Always his thoughts were absorbed with her. Hunter was a strikingly handsome young man; his looks, fittingly hawk-like in youth, were now more like an eagle as he reached his mid-20s. He was tall—taller than most pilots—and sported a shock of golden, sandy hair, usually worn long. He was a genius (first certified at the age of three), an athlete, had a sense of humor, though usually taken as quiet on first meeting. He had never experienced any trouble attracting women—from his days at MIT (where at 15, he was the youngest student ever admitted into that institution's aeronautical doctorate program) and before, all the way through his USAF and Thunderbird days. But no woman—before or since—had ever affected him like Dominique.

They had met in a deserted French farmhouse where both had sought shelter during the wild days after the war had ended in Europe. They had spent one night together; he woke in the morning to find her gone. But later, she had come looking for him and found him at the ZAP base on Cape Cod. In what seemed to be a dream to him now, they had lived happily together at the base. But it was only for a few weeks. When a Mid-Ak attack on ZAP was imminent, Hunter put her on a flight to safe Montreal. Then she disappeared.

He was never the same. The yearning never stopped. There had been plenty of other women since for him. Sexual playmates all. But the thought of Dominique had stayed with him—a very private haunting since he last saw her.

Once the helicopters and escorts landed back at

the Coos Bay base—which was known by all as PAAC-Oregon—Hunter immediately headed for the photo recon unit's very elaborate development lab. Although it was close to midnight, Hunter was glad to find the technicians still working on the infra-red video image of the mysterious Soviet jets. It was a painstaking job. Working with a computer that Hunter had helped design, each enhancement of the image took several hours of calculations and programming. And each program produced another, more defined video image which had to be electronically "cleaned up," also a long process.

The techs showed him what they had so far: they had been able to zoom in on the clearest image of the jet so much that they would soon be able to count the number of rivet spots on the jet's midsection. Once this number was established, it was a matter of calculating the overall size and weight of the plane, then using the additional information from Hunter's infra-red camera to determine the heat displacement of the aircraft. The techs hoped to match up these figures with previously stored data on Soviet fighter aircraft and come up with a reasonable guess as to what kind of jet Hunter photographed that day. It was intelligence work at its best—long, arduous, but in the end, hopefully fruitful.

The work looked promising but the technicians told him that a final determination was still about a day and a half away.

He finally headed home. Though exhausted, he couldn't sleep. He found himself wandering around his huge log cabin—a place he'd built himself. The house sat on a hill which overlooked both the base's runways and the Pacific Ocean. A twin-.50 anti-aircraft battery was located to one side of the structure, the spinning dish of one of the base's operations radar sat on the other. The lodge itself was crammed with radios, electronic gadgetry, a larger, fixed antenna capable of pulling in signals from all around the northern hemisphere when atmospheric conditions were right. Some nights Hunter would sit and listen to the radio traffic for hours, searching for any clue—like a sudden burst of radio chatter—that might tip an impending attack on America from the Soviets to the west.

The house had no kitchen; he ate and drank at the base. But a well-stocked bar sat in the main living room. Close by was a huge fireplace that heated the structure all too well in the often-damp Oregon climate. Two of the rooms were filled with his books, their topics ranging from advanced aeronautical design to theories on setting zone defenses in basketball. Another room was reserved for weekly poker games at which he hosted the likes of Dozer, The Cobra Brothers, the Ace Wrecking Company pilots, Captain Frost and anyone else with a week's pay to lose. Still another, more private, room featured a waterbed whose dimensions approached those of an aircraft carrier, plus a single control switch which dimmed the lights and activated a continuous tape loop of sweet, electronic music.

On top of the house he had built a turret in which he installed a moderately powerful telescope. On clear nights he could be found studying the cosmos through its lens. It was usually an exercise in wishful thinking for him. The most ironic day in his life was the Christmas Eve he arrived at Cape Canaveral to begin training as a pilot for the Space Shuttle, only to find that the Soviets had launched a devastating nerve gas attack on Western Europe and that his F-16 squadron was being activated. Although he had missed the chance to pilot the space ship—just one more thing he blamed on the Soviets—he never gave up his dream of flying in space one day.

Hunter lived alone but that didn't mean he slept alone. He had two frequent houseguests. Mio and Aki, two bisexual Oriental beauties who had first lived with him when he worked for a short time for Fitzgerald at The Aerodrome. They had moved west with him when he joined PAAC. The two girls—Mio was 21, Aki 19—lived in a smaller log cabin he built nearby. But they spent most of their time at Hunter's, serving in every capacity from his maids to his mistresses. They kept his house neat and his bed warm. They instinctively knew when he wanted to be alone and when he wanted company. They also knew of the woman Dominique, whose name he had once whispered while he slept.

The house was strictly functional; it had very few decorations other than his aircraft design drawings cluttering up the walls. However, over the fireplace encased in a heavy glass and metal picture frame hung his most valuable possession. It was a small, now-tattered American flag. He had first come upon it in war-torn New York City right after the war. Trying to make it across town to the relative safety of Jersey, Hunter (who was traveling with Dozer's 7th

Cavalry at the time) saw an innocent man shot in the back by a sniper. The man was Saul Wackerman, a tailor who had been caught up in the battle that raged in Manhattan between rival National Guard troops trying to claim the island. These days New York City was a pit of anarchy, murder, street wars, drug dealing and black market arms sales. But Hunter never forgot Saul Wackerman or the look on his face when he died in Hunter's arms. He was holding this very flag in his hands at the time and Hunter took it from his body.

One of the rules of the New Order made it illegal to carry the stars and stripes—a crime punishable by death. It was a law Hunter detested and habitually broke. In fact, during the ZAP days right through the Football City War, he had kept the flag folded up and in his pocket at all times, drawing strength from it almost daily. To him it represented his major goal, his dream, his reason for being. That was that some day, this country would be reunited again. Some day, there would be the United States again. He had vowed to make it happen. Or die trying. The flag was the symbol of that crusade.

He finally fell asleep for a couple of hours, but was up again and at the base before the sun had fully risen. He had work to do. Jones had placed the base on a Code Three Alert, meaning they were two notches away from a war or "attack-imminent" situation. As overall commander, it was Hunter's duty to make a status check on PAAC-Oregon's aircraft as well as the base's ground defenses.

Requisitioning a jeep, the pilot methodically worked his way down the flight line. When he performed similar duty at ZAP's old Jonesville base, the task would take all of 15 minutes—as famous as ZAP was, the corps never had more than 18 aircraft on hand. Now, thanks to the bulging coffers of PAAC, the Oregon base had more than three times that many.

At the southern edge of the base sat the PAAC support fleet which consisted of four C-130 Hercules tankerplanes and two C-141 Starlifters—huge jets used for dropping paratroopers as well as carrying supplies. Moving on, Hunter reached the 12-aircraft PAAC Ground Attack Support Group. This unit, primarily dedicated to supporting the ground operations of the base's 12,000-man infantry division, had four more C-130s, modified to carry up to six GE Gatling guns apiece. These frightful weapons, capable of firing more than 100 rounds *a second*, were all installed on the planes' port side. In action, the aircraft—known as "Spooky" gunships—would slowly circle the battle area, tipped to the left and deliver an incredible barrage.

The ground support arm also flew six A-10 Thunderbolts, the famous "tank busters" that were the scourge of every Soviet commander during the war in Europe. The unusual-looking 'Bolts—more flying weapons platforms than graceful jet fighters—had wings strong enough to carry tons of varied ordnance, as well as two Vulcan cannons in their noses. The Cobra Brothers' helicopters were also assigned to the ground support arm, its pilots shared duty as the unit's operational commanders.

Stationed beside the center-strip runway was the base's Bombardment Group. There were 18 aircraft in all, including ten massive B-52s, four nearly-antique B-57s, two A-3 "Whales," plus a cranky, old B-58 "Hustler," left over from the Football City War.

Next to the bombers sat the fighter-interceptor squadron—among them four F-104 "Starfighters," two F-106 "Delta Darts," six souped-up A-7 "Strike-fighters," six converted T-38 "Talon" trainers and two F-105X "Super Thunderchiefs." Two of these airplanes were always in the scramble mode—armed, fueled-up and ready to go up and intercept any perceived threat to the base. And, with proper configuration, each of these airplanes could be converted to a fighter-bomber role.

Further along the flight line sat the "oddball" unit. The twelve airplanes—known throughout the base as "The Dirtiest Dozen"—were favorites of Hunter. PAAC had come upon them in a variety of ways—some were thrown in free when the base purchased other high-end aircraft, others were found abandoned at air bases throughout the west. Still others were liberated from a small air museum in old Utah. There was the F-84, a veteran of the Korean War; an F-94, the two-seat mid-50s interceptor that was designed with chasing UFOs in mind. And there were two A-1 "Skyraiders," hulking prop-driven planes that were already grandfathers when they were used in Viet Nam.

But these planes were youngsters compared to aircraft that the base's ground crew mechanics (known by all as "monkeys") had somehow resurrected from the Utah museum. There was one P-38

"Lightning," and a P-51 "Mustang," both heroes of America's effort in World War II. The oldest plane on the base was a veteran Curtis biplane, which carried a still-working Vickers machine-gun.

Then there were the five B-47 "Stratojets," bombers nearly as big as B-52 and nearly as old. Hunter had purchased them for duty in the Football City War and they served well, if briefly. Now the PAAC had inherited them, as well as the oddest duck of all: an enormous B-36 bomber. This airplane, built just before the Jet Age dawned in the late 1940s, had six propeller engines fitted backwards onto ultra-long wings. Hunter kept promising himself that he would take the big bird up for a ride one day, but he never seemed to find the time.

The base also maintained a small fleet of helicopters, including the Crazy Eights, and used three Boeing 727 converted airliners as cargo planes and also on convoy duty.

It was an air fleet that rivaled any power on the continent—even PAAC-San Diego could boast only six more aircraft. In free-for-all New Order America, air power was usually the determining factor in most disputes, big or small. The continent was united—for trade purposes—only by air travel. Huge supply convoys—made up of reconditioned airliners like Boeing 707s, 727s, and 747 Jumbo jets—traveled between eastern Free Canada and the West Coast. As the skies were filled with air pirates who made a living shooting down stray airliners, convoy protection—in some cases provided by free-lance fighter pilots—was in high demand.

But it was one pilot—and one jet fighter—that was

known as the best in the business. The pilot was Hunter. The airplane was his F-16. And within minutes of the status report being completed, Hunter was roaring down the base's center runway, taking his jet up for its daily workout.

Chapter Five

It was the same airplane Hunter had flown when he was part of the USAF's Thunderbirds aerobatic demonstration team. When the Soviets "won" the war and the New Order became a reality, one of the dictates was that sophisticated weapons like the F-16s—along with just about every front-line weapon in the West's mighty arsenal—be destroyed. In the wave of disarmament fever that followed—carried out for the most part by fanatical, if slightly suspicious National Guardsmen in the U.S.—literally billions of dollars of equipment was blown up, dismantled or otherwise made useless. Except for this one F-16 . . .

A year after the war, General Seth Jones, the late twin brother of PAAC's Commander-in-Chief, Dave Jones, had found the plane locked away in an isolated hangar at the abandoned Thunderbirds' HQ at Nellis Air Force Base near Las Vegas, Nevada. Why the plane had escaped the disarmament destruction, he never knew. But to be caught with the aircraft was a crime in the eyes of the New Order, punishable by death. Nevertheless, as part of his plan to draw

Hunter out of his self-imposed exile on a New Hampshire mountain, Jones risked death by firing squad and had the aircraft disassembled, then flown piece by piece back to ZAP's Jonesville base on Cape Cod where it was put back together in secret. Once Hunter got a look at the '16—probably the last one left in the world—he immediately agreed to give up the hermit's life and to join ZAP.

Jones had the plane repainted in its original Thunderbird red-white-and-blue colors, but it was Hunter who modified the aircraft to carry up to a dozen Sidewinder air-to-air missiles, instead of the usual four. He also installed a "six-pack" of Vulcan cannons, three on each side of the jet's nose. The pilot put his aeronautical doctorate to work when he disassembled the jet's GE engine and uprated it to nearly twice its power. Now the F-16 could reach speeds of nearly 2000 m.p.h. with the afterburner kicked in.

Even before the war, Hunter was well recognized as the best fighter pilot who had ever lived. Now, in the dangerous, post-war world, his fighter was well known and accorded the highest respect across the continent. Consequently, the F-16 was known as the best fighter ever built. If any plane was built with a pilot in mind, it was the F-16 and Hunter. They were made for each other.

Hunter put the F-16 into a long slow turn back over the base. At this point he knew he was serving as a "target" for the anti-aircraft crews below—these daily flights allowed the crews to test their tracking and aiming equipment.

His flight path brought him over the dozens of quonset huts that served as the base's barracks. There were about 15,000 troops in all stationed at the base—the infantry division, the Airborne group, Dozer's 7th Cavalry. With their support groups and families, the population at PAAC-Oregon reached 25,000. And just as with the old ZAP base on Cape Cod, a large community of ordinary citizens had sprung up around the installation. In the anarchaic New Order, the prime real estate was near the protection of friendly forces like PAAC. Not only did the citizens know that in times of trouble they could seek refuge inside the base, but living next to the installation also provided them with work in the many support operations needed to run the huge operation.

Once he received radio confirmation that the AA crews around the center of the base had completed their exercises, Hunter steered the fighter toward the outer defense perimeter of the base. Below him he could see the acres of farmlands, tilled by citizens, that supplied the base with its food. Just as the small fleet of fishing boats docked near the base provided the servicemen with fresh catches daily, these farms put the vegetables on the mess tables. The neat squared-out patterns on the ground were broken occasionally by an anti-aircraft battery or a SAM site. Corn grew right next to a string of ack-ack guns, and a Hawk missile system cohabitated with a field of carrots.

The outer defense line was located some 11 miles out from the center of the base. Its perimeter ran nearly 30 miles and was demarked by several waves of barbed wire. In front of this was a half-mile wide, heavily-mined and booby-trapped defoliated area that would discourage the feistiest infiltrator. Guard towers appeared at 200-yard intervals and the perimeter was patrolled endlessly by the base's security forces and the local civilian militia. The commanders of PAAC-Oregon were vigilant to a fault. But with good reason. Just beyond the no-man's land and the barbed wire sat the hills and forests of old Oregon. This is where the uncertainty began. The land that stretched all the way down the coast and east to the Rockies and beyond, was filled with bandits, raiders, terrorists. The PAAC-Oregon base was the exception, not the rule in New Order America, just like the old U.S. Cavalry forts in the old Wild West days. Along with the Frontier Guardsmen outposts that were scattered throughout eastern Oregon serving as the trip-wire for the main base, PAAC-Oregon was an island of sanity and civilization on the edge of a lawless, out-of-control countryside.

Finishing his patrol of the base's outer defense ring, Hunter headed due east. It was a beautiful day for flying, mostly clear except for huge cumulus clouds that waited for him at 20,000 feet off to the northeast. But great flying weather or not, he was filled with a troubled feeling he could not shake. It had clawed at him since the last recon flight. Despite Dozer's encouragement, Hunter blamed himself for not detecting the mysterious Russian fighters sooner. How could he have been so lax as to let the Soviets build a fighter base—and somehow make it disappear—right under his nose?

He flew higher.

When he had joined PAAC, he had thought of it as the best way to continue his personal vendetta against the enemies of old America. He knew it would take not only fancy flying but hard work—in intelligence, in logistics, in procurement—to continue his crusade. He knew that to be successful, he would have to keep his hand on the pulse of what was happening across the continent and beyond. He designed the role of America's sentinel for *himself*. And, until now, he was always confident that it was thumbs-up and "do-able." Now, he wondered if that confidence was just cockiness. *Some sentinel!* He had radars and radios and long, dramatic recon flights and yet he let the Russians build a base so close to him he was surprised he hadn't smelled the borscht cooking.

He flew even higher—up to 40,000 and into the white mist of the huge, billowing cloud.

Betrayal. He felt that he had betrayed his own people—the other servicemen in Pacific American Armed Forces. The butchered frontier guardsmen and the sailors missing from the abandoned patrol boat. And how about the civilians that he pledged to protect? How had he served the murdered citizens of Way Out? No doubt the time he'd spent drinking and gambling and whoring and joy riding should have been put to better use.

And if he was such a great intelligence expert, what the hell happened down near Vegas? What the hell was going on over the Great Lakes? What the hell really happened to St. Louie's recon troops in the Badlands? *And where the hell were those God-*

damned Russian jets?

Now he went even higher. 50,000 feet. 55,000, 60,000.

What the hell was he doing? Flying around, playing soldier. Harboring some stupid dream of reuniting his country. He knew he was the last of the sentimental Americans. Why couldn't he accept the reality of the New Order and just live with it? Make some money. Make a lot of money! He was once hired to retrieve some diamonds for St. Louie, a job that paid him more than $100,000. Most of it was gone now—put toward purchases of PAAC-Oregon aircraft. And soldiering was the least profitable business to be in these days. Free-lance convoy protection duty. That's where he should be. Hire out to the highest bidder. He'd been offered incredible sums to ride shotgun for "special" cargoes. Let the rest of them fight it out. Why be a soldier? Why did he do it? He shook himself out of it temporarily. *Questions.* Too many questions . . .

He needed answers and he needed them now!

A faint ringing began in his brain. His ears perked up; his eyes cleared. Within seconds, he could feel a very distinct buzz throughout his body, this one very recognizable. It meant only one thing. Aircraft. A lot of them. Out toward the east. Two, maybe three hundred miles away. He checked the time. Just past 1200 hours. He checked his fuel supply. It was at 85%. He checked his weapons. Four Sidewinders and a maximum load of cannon shells—all okay.

The sensation grew stronger. The hair on the back

of his head was standing up. Trouble. This was trouble. He knew it. He had to check it out. No time to call for the scramble jets. He had to act now. He booted in the afterburner and steered due east.

Chapter Six

It was a convoy.

Although he was still 30 miles due west of them, Hunter could see the airplanes quite clearly. He counted 11 Boeing 707s, four 727s, an L-1011 and two DC-9s—18 airliners in all. They were traveling in the standard convoy formation; six groups of three-plane chevrons, each aircraft leaving a slight, wispy contrail in its wake.

But right away Hunter sensed something was very odd about the airplanes. There was no radio chatter at all coming from the airtrain—highly unusual as convoy pilots were known to be as talkative these days as truck convoy drivers were before the war. Hunter knew it had to mean the pilots were flying "booted," maintaining radio silence. Second, the airplanes were flying low, down around 10,000 feet. This was strange because it was better and cheaper to cut through the thin air at higher altitudes than the sludge down below 15,000. So most convoys cruised at 40,000 feet or higher, just to save gas.

But it was the convoy's direction that tipped him.

The airliners were traveling due north. Every big air convoy flying these days flew either northeast-to-southwest or vice versa. So where the hell were these guys going?

As he closed in on them, he ran another check on his weapons systems. He knew he would soon be showing up on their radar screens if not already. The convoy could simply be lost. But he doubted it and he wanted to be prepared for anything. Green lights started popping up on his weapons control panel. All his armaments were in good shape. He closed to within 10 miles of the airliners and flipped on his radio sending switch.

"Convoy leader, this is Major Hunter, Pacific American Air Corps," he said slowly. "I am at two-niner Tango from your position. Everything okay with your course-direction finder?"

Silence.

"Convoy leader," he repeated, closing to within five miles of the airliners and banking to fly a course higher but parallel to the leader. "Major Hunter, P-A-A-C here. Do you need course-direction assistance?"

Again, silence.

Hunter checked his own location. He was somewhere over the southern part of the old state of Montana, technically outside of PAAC's air space. But screw it, no one bothered much about such distinctions these days. He banked again to his right and in seconds was streaking over the first three-plane formation.

Instantly, he knew there was going to be trouble. The three airliners were typical in every way except one—each had twin-gun barrels protruding from its tail. Airliners with rear gunners were a rare item—they were the Rolls-Royce of airliners. And never did one see more than one or two and then only traveling with a 50-plane or bigger superconvoys. Yet here were three, flying side by side.

He banked hard to the right and executed a 180 turn which carried him over the second group of airliners. These three airplanes also carried rear guns. He swept back over the third group and confirmed they too were carrying.

But suddenly rear guns on airliners didn't bother him anymore. He had something new to think about. Looking down toward the southeast he could see four F-101 Voodoos rising to meet him . . .

He knew the jet fighters would show up sooner or later. Somewhere in the back of his consciousness, he had *felt* their presence. No sane convoy master would assemble 18 big airliners without contracting some free-lance air cover. And, as this particular group of airliners was definitely shady, Hunter could only assume the F-101s were too. He took five deep gulps of the pure oxygen for a quick jolt, switched on his own, specially-designed engagement radar and dove to meet the Voodoos head-on.

The lead '101 fired first, followed a second later by his wingman. No warning, no radio message asking Hunter to ID himself. It was shoot first, so no questions had to be asked later. The Voodoo pilots were probably air pirates signed on to make some extra money. But they had just made a big mistake by shooting at him. They would soon know who he was.

There was only one F-16 flying around these days and everyone on the continent knew who its pilot was and what he stood for. And now they had made themselves an enemy.

The two Sparrow air-to-air missiles flew by him, both missing him by 300 feet. The Voodoos had tipped their hand, foolishly firing their Sparrows at him head-on when the missile was designed to be shot only when engaging from the rear. Hunter breathed a tinge easier. Despite the four-to-one odds, now he knew he had one advantage: These guys were shaky.

He aimed the F-16 right at the center of the four '101s and booted in the afterburner. The Voodoos scattered. He yanked back on the control stick. The F-16 stood on its tail for an instant, then rolled over on its back. A flick of the wrist and he was on the tail of Voodoos' second flight leader. The pilot tried to zig-zag his way out of Hunter's line of fire, but it was a useless maneuver. Hunter instinctively mimicked the Voodoo's movement. He quickly selected a Sidewinder and let it rip. The missile flew perfectly into one of the Voodoo's tail exhaust pipes and detonated. The blast broke the jet into two distinct pieces, both of which blew up seconds later.

One down, three to go . . .

He was already tracking his second victim, the lead flight wingman who had fired the second missile at him then attempted to flee to the east. Hunter pulled up and back and locked on to the Voodoo from long range. It was a distance shot for sure, but he fired anyway. The missile ignited and shot off out of his line of sight and toward its prey. Twelve long seconds later it hit. The '101 disappeared in a puff of black smoke a full 10 miles from Hunter's position. "That was a three-point shot," he thought as he yanked back on the control stick and climbed to meet the two remaining Voodoos.

By this time the '101 pilots knew who they were up against. The pair linked up and were now turning toward him. He let them. Would they be foolish enough to waste more Sparrows shooting at him head on? Or maybe they wanted to engage with their cannons. If so, then he'd return the favor with his Vulcan six-pack.

The Voodoos opted for the cannons, streaking close to him and simultaneously squeezing off timid bursts before diving away.

"C'mon boys," he said into his microphone. "You'll have to do better than that . . ."

The Voodoos pulled up in tandem and tried to approach him from the rear. He simply flipped the F-16 over on its back again and headed straight for them upside down. He put the jet into a slow turn to right itself, pressing the Vulcan firing trigger at the same time. The '16 shuddered as all six of the cannons opened up in a twisting murderous barrage. The lead Voodoo pilot never knew what hit him. His nose, then his canopy, shattered instantly. Smoke began pouring out of the open cockpit as the airplane started its long plunge to earth.

Now Hunter turned his attention to the last F-101. The fighter had taken a few hits and had broken away to the south. He was now intent on fleeing in earnest.

Hunter booted in the afterburner again and soon caught up with the Voodoo. The pilot knew he had no chance to shake the powerful F-16, so he took the safe route out and ejected, letting his airplane fly on unattended. The ever-conscientious Hunter deposited a Sidewinder into its exhaust tube anyway preventing the one-in-a-million chance that the jet's eventual crash would kill someone innocent on the ground. The missile obliterated the Voodoo as advertised. Off to the east, Hunter could see the pilot's parachute drifting slowly toward the mountains below.

The engagement was over. Now Hunter turned his attention back to the convoy . . .

The eighteen big airliners had disappeared in the time it took him to battle the Voodoos, but he quickly located them on his radar and floored it. Gradually, off in the distance, the distinctive contrails once again came into view. The airliners had climbed to 45,000 feet in an effort to make a fast getaway. But the deception was lost on Hunter. He was soon riding off the wing of the last Boeing 707 in the convoy.

Just then his radio crackled. Someone, somewhere in the convoy had yelled "Break!" and the airliners instantly obeyed. The eighteen airplanes started to scatter in all directions. Some climbed, others dove. Some banked left, some banked right. Soon the sky around him was a patchwork of contrail streaks. Yet he stayed right on the rear 707, intent on identifying it or following it to its eventual landing place.

Neither would happen. The rear gunner in the airliner foolishly opened up on Hunter as the plane banked to the left to cross in front of him. It was a stupid, risky maneuver. He could see the big airplane's wing flap with the strain. The way the airliner was moving, Hunter doubted many people were on board. He tried to contact the airplane's pilot.

"707, 707," he said calmly into his microphone. "Cease firing and ID yourself."

His message was returned by another burst from the airliner's rear gunner. Hunter routinely dodged the cannons shells and moved up to a position beside the big jet's cockpit. He could see the pilot inside, his attention fully devoted to flying the airplane.

"707, ID yourself," Hunter called again. Suddenly the big airplane did another quick bank to the left in an effort to ram him. Even Hunter was surprised by the desperate move, deftly pulling back on the control stick just in time to avoid getting hit by the airliner.

"This guy's crazy," Hunter thought. He was also in trouble. Hunter could see smoke trailing from the 707's port-side outer engine. The violent maneuver must have snapped a fuel line or oil feeder pump. He knew what would happen next. The engine caught fire and ignited the fuel tanks in the 707's wings. Within seconds the airliner's port wing was enveloped in flames. The big airplane started to go down. Flaming pieces of the wing were breaking off. Then the starboard engines, themselves buckling under the sudden strain, began to smoke.

Hunter could only watch as the doomed 707 continued to lose altitude. He followed it down. 10,000 feet. 8,000 feet. 5000. He knew the pilot could not pull it out in time. 4000 feet . . . 3000. Except for one stretch of highway, the terrain below was all mountainous. It appeared to Hunter that the pilot was trying to steer toward the roadway. But at 2000 feet, an entire half of the jet's portside wing broke off, trailing a long plume of black, oily smoke with it. Hunter could see the airplane shake as it involuntarily banked to the left. It never had a chance to attempt a landing on the road. Instead it hit a row of trees at the end of a small valley, bounced once, hit again and plowed up the side of a small mountain. He watched as it kicked up a great sheet of flame and earth and smoke before finally coming to a stop.

Hunter dove and flew low over the crash. He knew there'd be no survivors. Wreckage was strewn everywhere, but the main fuselage and the starboard wing were still intact, though smoking heavily. He briefly considered taking off and finding another airliner from the mysterious convoy. But on second thought, he became determined to return to this crash site and search the wreckage. He had to see who the hell these guys were.

He reconnoitered the long stretch of the abandoned highway nearby to see if it could handle the F-16. After two passes he decided to try for it.

Chapter Seven

There were only about two hours of daylight left when Hunter finally reached the crash area. The highway—a battered sign revealed it as Montana's Route 264—proved long and straight cnough for him to set down. He hid the '16 underneath an overpass bridge, and armed with his trusty M-16 and other equipment, had trudged for an hour through the forest to where the airliner came down.

He was soon at the base of the mountain, close enough to see where the huge letters "TWA" had been hastily painted over on the airliner's tail section. The big airplane carried no other identification numbers, not unusual these days. The ground was still hot and steamy as a result of the crash; the heat was melting the shallow ground snow that covered the mountain. The big fire had died down, but he knew it was only temporary. There was still fuel in the crumpled starboard wing and it was only a matter of time before it got hot enough to blow. For now though, everything around him was very quiet—the only noise coming from the dozen or so small fires that crackled in the bushes around the wreckage, plus a low hissing from the wreck itself. He knew he had about ten minutes before the rest of the airplane went up. He checked the magazine on his rifle, then scrambled up the hill to what remained of the 707.

After a climb of 300 or so feet, he reached the back of the airplane. A rear door that had twisted off its hinges and was hanging from the fuselage now by only wires looked like a means of entry. A moderate amount of smoke was still coming from inside the aircraft. For this contingency, he had kept his flight helmet on and carried his emergency oxygen tank on his back. Now he lowered the helmet's clear visor flap and strapped on the air tank's face mask. He knew the smoke was toxic, and without the visor, it would have been difficult to see. He took a few gulps from the oxygen tank, then carefully stepped up to and inside the wreckage.

He was not surprised to find the airliner was empty. A full airplane would have hit the ground much harder and destroyed itself on impact. He looked around inside the cabin. It was a typical New Order Special: an airliner converted to cargo carrier by ripping out all the seats and replacing them with spider's webs of straps and fasteners to hold the airborne goods in place. He looked to the rear of the airplane, trying to locate where the rear gunner had been stationed. But that portion of the aircraft was crushed beyond recognition. He knew the gunner's body was buried in the twisted metal.

He started to walk toward the front of the airplane. It was slow at first—the airliner's hollowed-out fuselage was pretty battered. But even in the twisted mass of ripped metal and wires, Hunter realized the airplane had not been transporting the usual kind of convoy cargo. In fact, the floor of the airplane was covered with what looked like straw or hay. He found several burlap bags that had ripped and scattered their contents around the airplane when it went down. He picked up one of the bags. Printed in black lettering on its side was the word: "Oats."

"Oats?" Hunter said to himself in surprise.

He continued to pick his way through the fuselage and eventually he reached the cockpit door. It too was smashed and twisted, but he was able to squeeze through what was left of the passageway leading to the flight deck.

There was only one pilot and he was still strapped in his seat. The body was already stiff, its hands locked into a death grip on the control column. A large gash in the man's temple looked to be the cause of death although half the skin on his face was missing and his body was perforated everywhere with shards of glass. His green coveralls were soaked through with blood now turned black and inky. Weirdly, the man's eyes were still wide open; a look of crazed horror staring out of them. What was worse, the corpse's mouth was formed into a slight, grim smile. Hunter felt a chill run through him as he stared at the deathly grin.

He looked around the cockpit. No papers, no registration plaque. He was able to read the flight distance indicator. It read 419.10 miles. He filed the number away into his memory banks. Everything else on the control panel was smashed. He moved back to the pilot. Very carefully, Hunter patted the body looking for some identification. He found a single piece of folded heavy paper inside the man's breast pocket. Gingerly he removed the paper and unfolded it. What he saw would change his life forever . . .

It was a photograph of Dominique.

Body Rushes. He knew he got more than the average person and for more and different reasons. He'd flown close to the edge of the atmosphere; he'd flown at nearly four times the speed of sound. He'd not only seen battle; he had fought in the largest, most destructive war ever. He'd been around the world several times, had seen its oceans, its peaks, its valleys. He'd known love; he'd known hate. He'd experienced rushes through his body that left him buzzing for hours if not days. But nothing equalled this rush. It exploded in his brain and traveled at the speed of light to each and every one of his nerve endings. There were sparks in his eyes.

Dominique? What the hell was this guy doing with a photo of Dominique? Hunter stared at it in disbelief. Was it really her? The young Bridgette Bardot-look-alike face was there. Her hair had grown out long and now looked lusty and blond. It was definitely the body he'd taken in person and so many times in his dreams. Who wouldn't be haunted by this? There was no question. It *was* her.

More sparks in his eyes. He couldn't believe the way she was . . . *posing*. The photograph was not a hastily snapped affair. It was in clear, crisply focused full color and almost artistic in the way it was shot. She was leaning forward slightly, her eyes staring directly into the camera. She was heavily made-up. Her clothes—what there were of them—were stunning. She was dressed in what looked to be a female version of a black tuxedo jacket. She wore no dress. Her black nylon stockinged legs were fully exposed, as was the garter belt that held them up. She wore short, black leather boots. Her blouse, which looked to be pure silk, was drastically low cut, exposing more of her breasts than not. The clothes managed to look expensive and trashy at the same time. She was wearing several diamond necklaces and what appeared to be a tiara of some sort. Even the chair she sat in had a plush look about it. It was all staged so strangely, yet beautifully. The photo looked like a cross between a pin-up and an expensive portrait sitting.

His eyes were filled with sparks now—*real* sparks. A loud bang knocked him out of his trance. There was another bang, followed by a louder, more dangerous rush of hissing. Looking out the smashed cockpit window he saw the starboard wing had erupted in flames. The hissing signaled an explosion was imminent. He had no more time to search the body or the cockpit.

His instincts began to take over. He quickly folded the photograph and slipped it into his boot. He wiped off his helmet visor and checked his air supply. But he took one last look at the pilot's face. Who was he? What was he doing? Where was he going? And what the hell was he doing with Dominique's photograph? Hunter knew one thing: the dead man could have led him to where Dominique was. But now he was cold and so was the trail. *Who the fuck were you, pal?* As if to answer him, Hunter watched as by some trick of *rigor mortis*, the grin widened into a full-toothed, grotesque smile.

"I have to get out of here," Hunter whispered.

Moments later the wing blew up, violently knocking the fuselage onto its port side. No matter—Hunter was clear of the wreck by this time, having sprinted and ricocheted himself down the cabin and out the door. He made a quick slide of it down to the base of the mountain—mucking up his M-16 in the process. The airplane exploded in one last, agonizing boom, after which it was totally engulfed in flames.

He passed 65,000 feet and was still climbing. The sky had suddenly turned dark, night was falling. As he approached 70,000 feet—nearly 14 miles high—he could see the faint twinkling of stars above him. Higher and higher he went. The F-16 was soon closing in on 80,000 feet, past the safe ceiling for its make and model.

Yet Hunter still climbed . . .

He clutched the picture of Dominique. There were too many questions bouncing around his head. So he sought refuge. At 85,000 feet the sky was like night and the stars were bright and in full view. Suddenly he saw a huge band of red light streak across his northern horizon. It was followed by another, then another. It was the *Aurora Borealis* again. But strangely it displayed just one color. Deep red. The streaks were dazzling, sparking bright crimson leaping across the sky like huge airborne waves. In all his years of flying, he had never witnessed the phenomena as intense as this.

Hunter felt a jolt run the length of his body,

bounce off his flight boots and rebound back to his flight helmet. He was transfixed by the brilliant, eerie lights and their strong, hypnotic quality. He found himself being drawn toward the display. Slowly he leveled off at 90,000 feet. The air was so thin at this height he imagined he could see it travel by him in long curling wisps.

He pointed the jet fighter north, determined to plunge into the bath of red light. Soon the entire airplane was awash in the one color. It was the color of blood. He took his hands off the controls and held them up to his eyes. Strangely, they looked white while everything else around him appeared red. His body shook again. The red became more intense. He closed his eyes.

He knew it was an omen. War was coming. A big one. To the east. He could already hear the bombs exploding and big guns being fired. He could see the smoke and the tail fires of missiles as they streaked to their targets. Highways lined with the weapons of war. He could smell the gunpowder and the cordite and the napalm. He saw huge fires. He heard people screaming—their sounds intertwined into a symphony, playing so hard in his ears they started to ache. The jet was shuddering, its engine shrieking as it streaked into the Northern Lights.

Suddenly a new, entirely different feeling washed over him. His eyes were still jammed shut. Inside, he felt the color turn from red to white. Then, everything started to clear. In an instant he knew how the Russian jets had pulled off their *svengali*. The answer had been there all along and he laughed when he finally realized the truth. So that was it! He felt a surge of power travel through his body. His fists tightened. His teeth were clenched. He gulped the oxygen from his face mask. The fuckers. They almost had him. They almost psyched him out. But now he was on to it. One mystery down, just several more to go. No more time to contemplate his condition. No more self-pity. No more doubting his resolve. He had to get to work.

He kept his eyes closed just a moment longer, drawing the last jolts of strength from *the feeling*. The last image he saw before opening his eyes was that of the beautiful Dominique. She was alive. The photo proved it. He knew it now for sure. She was out there. Somewhere. He would find her.

He opened his eyes. The Northern Lights were gone and the night sky was cold and clear. The feeling hadn't entirely vanished, however. In fact, a little bit of it would stay with him for the rest of his life.

Chapter Eight

Hunter returned to the base, shut down the F-16 and ran to the base's recon photo analysis lab. The two technicians who had been laboring over his footage came out to meet him, both anxious and glowing with news.

But before they could say a word, Hunter spoke to them. "Jump jets?" he asked.

"Bingo, sir," the senior tech told him. "Yak-38's. We narrowed it down about two hours ago."

The Yak-38 was an airplane design the Soviets ripped off from the famous British Harrier. By using a multi-direction jet nozzle, the airplane could lift off vertically, then, with the push of a button, its thrust could be redirected backward and the jet could instantly fly like a normal fighter. The Harrier was an amazing airplane; the Yak-38 an effective, if bargain basement version of it.

Now all the pieces were fitting into place. The Russians hadn't really constructed an air base in the arctic valley—they had simply cleared a landing spot, for the jets could land vertically, too. The airplanes had leapfrogged over from Siberia, probably rendezvousing with tanker planes or even preadapted ships at sea for refueling. After all, the Yak-38 was originally designed to operate off Soviet aircraft carriers. When Hunter happened to find their base, it only would take about an hour or so to get the 50 airplanes lifted off and moving.

But one mystery solved sometimes led to another: Now that he knew how the airplanes got there—and how they got *out*—he had to find out where they were going . . .

"Where the hell are they now?"

Seated around the table were the principal officers of PAAC-Oregon. One by one, Twomey, Ben Wa, the Cobras, the Ace Wrecking Company, an officer from the Crazy Eights, Major Frost, and Dozer looked at the still photographs gleaned from the infrared tape of the Yaks.

"This is not your typical Soviet stunt," Hunter was saying. "These guys were pros. It took a lot of planning and execution to jump fifty Goddamned jets across the arctic."

"And to do it in bad weather," Frost said. "And without a peep on the radio."

"Some kind of special unit," Dozer said. "Probably trained just for this mission."

"Damn!" Hunter said, pounding the table. "I would never have guessed the Russians had five of these Yaks left, never mind fifty!"

"We have to find them and take them out," Captain Crunch of the Wreckers said. "Any ideas where they went, Major?"

Hunter was quiet for a moment. "I hate to even say this but . . ." he began slowly. "My guess is they jumped themselves right over into the Badlands."

"Christ!" Twomey blurted out, expressing the feeling of every officer there. They were all unquestioningly brave men. But still not one of them wanted anything to do with the Badlands.

"Why do you figure the Badlands, Hawk?" Wa asked.

"Well, based on the maximum operating range of the Yak-38, if they flew light and conserved fuel, they could have made it in one extra jump," Hunter said, pulling out a notebook of calculations. "And these photos show they weren't carrying any ordnance under the wings. They were, however, carrying extra large wing tanks.

"This tells us something else. If they weren't carrying bombs, it could mean they were meeting up with someone who was."

"Goddamn," Dozer said. "Fifty Russian jump jets flying around the continent can cause a lot of misunderstandings to say the least."

"What are they here for, Major?" one of the Cobras asked. "Convoy raiding?"

"Well, it seems like a hell of a lot of trouble to go through just to shoot at airliners," Hunter said.

"Could be part of another disruption campaign," Dozer said. "They sent a bunch of jets over to The Family, too."

"That's true," Hunter said. "But we've got to figure

that they sent more jets than pilots that time. Pilots must be in very short supply over there, still. And so are top-shelf airplanes like these Yaks. Top-shelf to the Russians, anyway."

"You think something bigger is brewing?" Frost asked.

Again, Hunter was silent for a few seconds. He had given it a lot of thought in the past few hours, though he had to admit, some of the answers literally popped into his head from nowhere. He now had theories on most of the recent mysteries, both on the west coast and on the east—all except one.

"Okay, let's look at these one at a time," he began. "First, we have a patrol boat who reports something strange and sends out an SOS. By the time we get there, they're gone. Now, whatever it was, it had to be a ship that attacked them. Yet the Wreckers didn't see anything else floating around out there."

"True," one of the F-4 pilots confirmed.

"Okay," Hunter continued. "Maybe it was a *submarine*. Maybe it was a bunch of submarines. By the way the patrol boat captain was talking, he might have sailed right into a school of them."

"Or a wolf pack," Dozer interjected.

"Exactly," Hunter said. "They can't blast the patrol boat out of the water because they know we could probably find it and figure it was hit by a torpedo, or a Harpoon-type ship-to-ship missile, or even a deck gun.

"So what do they do? They jam the boat's radio transmission, then they board her and either kidnap the crew or throw them overboard."

"We never saw any bodies," a Wrecker said.

"Right, too messy," Hunter agreed. "So maybe those guys *were* taken alive."

He paused for a moment, then continued. "Now, how about what went down in Vegas? What the hell exploded out there and why would anyone want to blow a mile wide crater in the middle of the desert?

"Well, how about this: We assumed it was done on purpose. Suppose it wasn't. Suppose it was an accident?"

"Accident?" Twomey asked.

"Sure," Hunter answered. "Why not? Someone moving a whole lot of ammunition. Something goes wrong. Boom! Everyone is blown into smithereens and the place looks like an A-bomb went off."

The rest of the officers around the table nodded in agreement. It *was* possible.

"How about what Fitzie's guys have been seeing, Hawk?" Twomey asked. "Lights floating over the Great Lakes?"

"Not floating, really," Hunter said. "More like soaring."

"You mean . . . like gliding?" Dozer asked.

"I mean exactly that," Hunter said. "They could have been gliders, released somewhere outside the Canadian radar net. Shit, if you launched a glider high enough, with the winds over the Lakes, it could fly for hundreds of miles. Granted, it would have to be pressurized and winterized and whatever else."

"But it's not impossible," Frost said.

"But what's in these gliders?" Wa wanted to know.

"Could be anything," Hunter continued. "But my

guess is troops. At the very least, officers and advisors. Sure, a few years ago we know the Soviets could disguise one of their big planes as being 'East European,' load it up with troops and fly right into the Aerodrome. But they knew then, and they know now, that with our intelligence network, we'd be on those airplanes as soon as they touched down and we'd stay with them the whole way.

"But how do you do it when you don't want anyone to see or hear you? Sneaking in fighters is one thing. And maybe there are weapons and ammo on the subs. A sub you can dock in any number of places around the continent without a soul seeing you. But bringing in troops—raw manpower—on the QT, well, that takes some doing."

"Jesus Christ!" Dozer said, putting the pieces together. "Are you saying they're sneaking a whole Goddamned army into the country!"

Hunter nodded gravely. "They're not doing this just to harass us. They've been doing that kind of Mickey Mouse stuff ever since the armistice. This is big time. Serious stuff."

He paused. "I think what we've feared most is underway and has been underway for some time.

"The Russians are invading America."

"But, wait a minute," Toomey said. "What happened at Way Out, or the guardsmen's post?"

"You mean, 'Horses,' " Hunter asked. "I'm still working on that one. But we do know this much. Two men—the surviving guardsman and St. Louie's recon guy—both saw some kind of intense action, and although they were more than a thousand miles apart, they both remembered one thing: Horses. And I'm personally going to find out what the hell they meant."

Chapter Nine

A week later, Hunter sat in the hold of the Sea Stallion chopper, looking out at the darkened landscape below. They were heading east, over the old states of Idaho and Wyoming, over the South Platte River to where the borders of Colorado, Nebraska and Kansas once met. There was an almost full moon this night. He could see the contour of the land below him change from mountainous to hilly range land to flat open spaces. He checked his watch. 0150 hours. By 0230, the chopper would be on the edge of the Badlands. Then he would be on his own.

He had briefed the rest of the PAAC-Oregon officers on the mysterious convoy and wreck of the 707. The incident fit into his theory. If the Soviets had moved men and materiel into one end or the other of the Badlands, it would just be a matter of getting hold of some convoy jets, hiring on some fighter protection and moving freely anywhere in the midsection of the country. In all likelihood, the convoy he intercepted had strayed somewhat from its course, bringing it slightly west of the Dakotas. Again, not an unusual occurrence in these days of flying more by the seat of one's pants than by sophisticated navigational gear.

Using the 419.10 miles he'd found on the 707's distance indicator, he did some quick calculations which led to a very interesting discovery. Within the 420-mile radius of the crash site there were four airports—or former military air bases—that could handle 18 big airliners like the ones in the convoy. Three of these bases were inside the Badlands. Even the hay and the oats made a crazy sort of sense. "Horses," again. Another piece of the puzzle seemed to be falling into place.

But the photo of Dominique was another story. That almost defied explanation. He told no one about it . . .

He checked his watch again. 0200 hours. His face was properly blackened as were his clothes. He did a final check of his gear. He was carrying Dozer's smaller Uzi instead of his own, larger M-16. On his back was a satchel filled with HE (high explosive) hand grenades, several signal rockets, a long distance radio transmitter and receiver, a long, bayonet-like pack knife, and a .45 automatic. He also carried two gallons of water and six small bags of food. He knew he'd never eat any of the food—when he was this charged up, food was the farthest thing from his mind. But he took the packets along only as a favor to Mio and Aki.

He turned his attention to the contraption sitting next to him. He'd spent the last week designing and building it, yet he still couldn't come up with a proper name for it. It was kind of a combination ultra-light/hang-glider/mini-jet. He had started with a tricycle-type frame and enclosed it with a small, soapbox derby style cockpit. Inside was a seat, a main control steering column, and two mini-control panels. Located directly in back of the seat was an umbrella-like device on which was the vehicle's presently-folded triangular sail. In the rear he had installed a small, intricate jet engine. Two stubby wings projected a foot and a half out from each side of the frame. They were just long enough to hold four small dual-purpose air-launched missiles, two on each wing. The missiles were also filled with HE. A tripod built next to the steering column held a swivel fastener on which he could bolt down the Uzi. A small radio was on board. Right next to the front landing wheel was a black box housing two miniature cameras. Hanging off the starboard side was an elaborate eavesdropping device he had taken off the U-2.

The entire mini-jet was painted dull black and—except for a few of the critical engine parts—was made entirely of plastic. This way it had "stealth," meaning it wouldn't show up on radar. It would also be very quiet. He had built the airplane from scratch, robbing pieces of material here, cannibalizing other pieces there. It was basically a very elaborate hang glider. The jet would give him the thrust he needed to stay airborne, then he would shut down the engine and just glide. Fuel would be the main concern. He designed an especially small combustion chamber for the engine—one which would efficiently use every drop of gas he could carry. Still, he knew the 25-gallon plastic tank he hooked up under the mini-jet's seat would have to be used very carefully. That's why he programmed the whole firing process into one of the aircraft's two minicomputers. He didn't relish the prospect of having to look for jet fuel in the middle of the Badlands.

And that was where he was going. He had to. PAAC needed intelligence and they needed it fast. He was convinced the Soviets were infiltrating men and arms into the country and hiding them somewhere. And the best hiding place on the continent was the 'Bads.

A perpetual fog had hung over the place since the day of the Soviet bombing. The mist was so thick in places, it was nearly impossible to photograph any of the Badlands from the air. With concentrations of radiation, nerve gas, germ gas, and God-only knows what, only fools entered into the Badlands at all. Fools and soldiers.

Hunter knew very well the only *sane* way to see the forbidden place was from 50,000 feet up and traveling at top speed. But Hunter also knew the only way to get some real answers was to go in and see what was happening in the danger zone himself.

He made arrangements to contact Dozer whenever he could via a link-up with a radio on a C-130 gunship which would be on station just outside Badlands' airspace from midnight to two every morning. There was just a little comfort in Hunter's knowing that the C-130 would also be carrying 30 of Dozer's best paratroopers. But if it got to the point of his calling them in, by the time they arrived, they just might be able to recover his body and that would be about it.

Still, the trip was critically necessary and that's why he chose to do it. With him he carried two things on which he hoped to draw strength, luck and inspiration. In his breast pocket was the searing photo of Dominique and the tattered American flag.

The jumpmaster came back to the hold to tell Hunter they were approaching the drop-off point. The Wingman did a quick double-check of the chopper's position, then prepared for his jump. Several years before when he reconditioned the Sea Stallion to prepare for rescuing the ZAP pilots being held in Boston, he had installed a movable platform in the center of the chopper's belly. It was originally designed as a missile launcher, but for this mission, Hunter removed the missile tubes and adapted the platform to hold the mini-jet. Now, with the help of the jumpmaster, he fastened the small airplane onto the platform and started feeding fuel to the engine.

With five minutes to drop, he was sitting in the jet clutching the wire which operated the umbrella device holding the folded-up wingsail. He saluted the jumpmaster, who gave him the thumbs-up sign and pushed a button. The chopper's hold door opened and the platform began to lower. Slowly Hunter and his airplane descended into the black night. It was cold and the wind was blowing hard. After being lowered about eight feet, the platform creaked to a halt. Then the hold door slid shut above him. He hunkered down into the cockpit and started activating the aircraft's minicomputers. He was reassured when the control panel's lights instantly blinked on in proper sequence. But the noise! The helicopter's rotating blades were making such a racket it was practically unbearable. Although he was wearing his standard flight helmet—another good luck piece—the noise was still deafening.

The helicopter had slowed to about 30 knots. Hunter made one last check of the controls then he pushed the engine start-up button. To his relief, it fired perfectly. He slowly raised the fuel feeder level and the little jet became hot. He checked his watch. Ten seconds to go. The Sea Stallion had now slowed to a near hover about 5000 feet above the flatlands below. Hunter gave each missile a tug just to make sure it was held on securely. He pulled the wire to release the safety switch on the wingsail's spoke ring. Then he crouched back down into the small, open cockpit and started to count . . .

"5 . . . 4 . . . 3 . . . 2 . . . 1 . . . Now!"

Right on cue, three small explosive charges located where the mini-jet was fastened to the platform ignited and catapulted him into the night. The chopper then shot straight up and banked away to fly clear of him. Once free, Hunter floored the engine. A long thin spit of flame appeared from the jet's exhaust tube and the craft started to pick up speed. Then he pulled the wire which raised the umbrella and locked the bat-like wingsail into place. The minijet shuddered for a few hairy seconds, but then wind caught the sail and immediately the craft started gaining altitude. "What d'ya know," Hunter thought. "It works . . ."

He quickly slowed the engine and worked the

controls to steer the airplane. From here it was up to him which way he wanted to go. There was a lot of territory to cover over the Badlands, and he preferred to start while it was still dark. He checked the missiles' status then mounted the Uzi and connected an extra long magazine. He patted his breast pocket feeling both the sharp folded edges of Dominique's photo and the softer, frayed border of the American flag. Then he banked the tiny jet into a 120-degree turn and sped off toward the eastern horizon.

He wouldn't see anybody or anything for the next two and a half days . . .

It was hot.

The people who claimed the sun didn't shine in the Badlands were crazy. The thin, permanent layer of clouds that hung close to the ground might have blocked the view from the air but they also provided a textbook example of the Greenhouse Effect. If anything, the clouds magnified the sun's rays, giving everything—including the air—a hot and steamy feel. Another myth—that nothing grew in the Badlands—also proved false. While there were many patches of dead vegetation dotting the landscape, Hunter did see other places where trees and bushes were growing at a lusty rate.

Water was another story. Most of the rivers were dried up and the few lakes he'd seen were all of a different color—none of which was blue. The water was poison. At the very least it contained traces of deadly radiation. Anywhere he saw water, he also saw nearby skeletons of hapless animals who long ago somehow managed to survive the Soviet holocaust only to fall victim to its after-effects as soon as they got thirsty.

His search carried him back and forth over vast stretches of western Kansas, Nebraska and the Dakotas. He found nothing. He was sunburned, dirty, and carrying an itchy, three-day beard. He was now glad to have the food that Mio and Aki prepared. He ate it out of sheer boredom. More than once he looked at the picture of Dominique. And more than once he began to think that his "hidden army" theory was a bunch of hooey. Still, he pressed on.

At least his flying machine was working perfectly. He had flown long distances, but the jet was needed only sporadically. He still had more than 18 gallons of fuel left and the way things were going, that would be plenty.

That first day, he had lain low, hiding out atop a huge mesa near the edge of the Black Hills. The position gave him a commanding view of the surrounding territory. But there was absolutely nothing to see. That night, as he was preparing to take off, he saw an air convoy passing over. It was flying way up there, at 50,000 feet at least, and had more than three dozen airplanes. Its direction was southeasterly; no doubt a legitimate skytrain making its way from Free Montreal to the trading mecca of Los Angeles. The sight had given Hunter a melancholy feeling. Life goes on, he thought at the time. No matter what you do, life goes on.

He flew all the next day and the next night, stopping only for short breathers and to check in with the radio on the gunship. His first two calls simply gave his position and the codewords "Delta Diana," which meant "nothing to report." Should something turn up, he would begin his transmission with the call "Alpha Diana Romeo," and quickly follow with an coded report.

But would he would ever send that message?

He found his answer the next day. It was around noontime. He had just witnessed another myth dispelled: It *did* rain in the Badlands. A morning shower had temporarily grounded him. He was waiting it out, sitting on the lip of a small plateau somewhere in the middle of Nebraska. The rise overlooked a vast plain which stretched for miles, broken only by a north-to-south, two-lane road which started at one horizon and ended on the other. The closest it came to him was about four miles from his position.

He was just getting ready to leave when he heard a long, low rumble, somewhere off in the distance. Thunder? He looked to the north and saw rising above the road a distinctive puff of dust being kicked up by a vehicle.

He grabbed his binoculars and focused. Goddamn! Not just one vehicle—there were many. Too many.

Bursting through the cloud of dust came distinct gray shapes moving down the road at a fast clip. They weren't cars; they were too big for trucks.

Tanks, maybe? Closer they came. He shielded the spyglasses from the bright, hazy sun. The shapes started taking a definite form . . .

"Jesus H. Christ," he whispered, not quite believing what he saw. "They're SAMs. On wheels."

SAMs. Surface-to-air missile batteries. First, he could see ten, then 20, then 50, then more than 100 of the mobile air batteries. The vehicles carrying them looked like dump-trucks. The missiles on their backs were Soviet SA-3s, NATO nickname: "Goa." There were four of them per launcher. Hunter took a deep breath of the clammy air. This was bad news. The SA-3 was a very dangerous missile. It could hit a target 55,000 feet high and 18 miles away and travel at Mach 2 to do it.

He took out his notebook and started taking an accurate count. It took a full 10 minutes for the deadly parade to pass him, and when it was over, he had noted 306 launch vehicles. More than 1200 missiles. That was enough to end all the speculation as whether something fishy was going on in the Badlands or not.

The question now was: Where were the SAMs going?

He trailed the column for the next four hours, staying a good 4000 feet above the absolutely flat land, firing the engine only when needed. He could do little more than follow as the convoy of SAMs continued southward along the perfectly straight, seemingly endless highway. He knew that no one below could spot him as the Badlands haze proved to be an adequate shield and the plastic construction of the mini-jet made it all but radar-proof.

Finally, the column reached a crossroads in south-central Kansas where it found five tanker trucks waiting. As he circled high above, he saw each vehicle get a quick fill up, then head east. It was getting dark by this time. If he got lucky, the column would reach its destination just before nightfall.

Another hour passed and the trucks showed no signs of slowing down. He figured he was somewhere just west of where Wichita used to be. This was close to the area where St. Louie's recon troops ran into trouble. Off in the distance, a new moon was rising. It was full and orange and spooky. He shook off a chill and did a weapons check.

Then he saw it. Off on the eastern horizon. At first it appeared as a single, greenish light, reflecting off the perpetual Badlands haze. As he drew closer, he saw the green hue was the reflection of many, many lights. Still closer, he found the lights were coming from a settlement of some sort.

The closer he got the more ominous the place looked. It was completely surrounded by an elaborate yet medieval-looking stone wall. It was high and thick like parapets of old; yet it was complete with many turrets and towers each which held some definitely *un*-medieval looking gun batteries. Inside, he saw more SAMs than he'd ever thought was possible. But not just SAMs. There were also trucks with guns riding on the back, some personnel carriers, even a few pre-World War III-vintage American tanks. And everywhere, he could see soldiers.

It didn't take him long to figure out that he had discovered the main base for the "hidden army."

He climbed to 8000 feet. From there he wasn't surprised to see three cooling towers belching steam about 20 miles from the base. Another piece of the puzzle fit. It was the nuclear plant the recon trooper had reported. A castle-like Soviet military base being powered by a nuke plant in the middle of the Badlands. Only in The New Order.

He started to head back down to a lower altitude. The SAM column had come to a halt outside the base where its drivers appeared to be parking their trucks and setting up for the night.

The darker it got, the better Hunter liked it. He circled the Soviet castle, gradually reducing his altitude. The thermal updrafts over the city allowed him to almost hover at times, letting him work both his surveillance cameras and his eavesdropping device at will. The Soviet castle was a strange place. He felt as if he was dropping in on another planet. Many of the buildings inside the walls were topped off by spires and minarets. Every structure was painted a different garish color, and was flying one of hundreds of flags that flapped in the thick night air.

But, right in the middle of the place was the biggest flag at all. It was a huge, blood-red, hammer and sickle design. The flag of the Soviet Union, fluttering in the Kansas breeze.

Chapter Ten

The radio aboard the C-130 gunship crackled to life with a burst of static. "Alpha Diana Romeo," the distant, but familiar voice began. "Repeat. Alpha Diana Romeo."

The aircraft's radio operator immediately acknowledged the password and called back to PAAC-Oregon's communications center to alert Dozer that a message from Hunter was coming through. Once he had Dozer on the line, he patched the radio transmission from deep in the Badlands to the PAAC line, ran it through a scramble device so the two men were able to talk openly to each other.

"Hawk, what's going on out there?" Dozer asked.

Hunter replied slowly and in careful measures. "Our thinking was on track, Bull. We have trouble out here. Russians. Russian equipment. I spotted them about noon today. Been with them ever since. And they're carrying more than just popguns."

For the next ten minutes, Dozer listened incredulously as Hunter told him he'd spotted the SAM column and how it eventually led him to the Soviet's castle-like main base. When the sun was down completely, he had brazenly flown low over the city, sometimes as low as the gun turrets. No one had spotted him. He had taken a lot of photos over the walled city and especially over the multitude of military equipment located around its perimeter.

He told Dozer he spotted a few tanks and personnel carriers. But it was the SAMs that were most in evidence. The Soviet castle was ringed with them, all of them mobile like the SA-3s. Inside the walls of the base, Hunter saw many people wearing Soviet uniforms. His eavesdropping device had also picked up a number of Russian conversations as well.

"How about aircraft, Hawk?" Dozer asked over the increasingly annoying static.

Hunter's reply was distant. "I found the Yak jump jets. Ten of them, anyway. Parked just outside of the city. They've got a working airfield out there. A few Hind gunships."

"Christ, Hawk," Dozer said. "How could they have brought all this stuff into the country right under our noses?"

Hunter's reply came back even fainter. "From what I've seen—to get this much stuff in—they must have started sneaking it in at least two years ago."

Dozer tried to save the dying signal: "You mean while we were so busy screwing around with the 'Aks and The Family, the Sovs were backdooring us all along?"

He was answered by a loud burst of static, then silence.

". . . Hawk?"

The Marine never got his reply. The signal had faded away for good.

The next day, Hunter struck out to the north. He was back to flying high and quiet enough so that anyone chancing to spot him in the Badlands haze would think they were looking at a bird—perhaps an eagle or more likely, a buzzard.

Hunter was astounded. Not a mile went by when he didn't see some kind of evidence of the Soviet hidden army. He spotted 15 more Yaks at an airfield about 150 miles north of the Soviet castle on the old Kansas-Nebraska line. There were another five Yaks at an auxiliary field 20 miles north of that, near where Omaha used to be.

But it was the hidden army's SAM missiles that most worried Hunter. There were tens of thousands of them. He spotted SAMs of all types and sizes. There were more mobile units—SA-2s, SA-4s, SA-6s, SA-8s and SA-9s. He saw units equipped with the short-range, shoulder-launched SA-7s. He even spotted concrete foundations he knew would handle the long-range SA-5s, a missile that could hit a target 95,000 feet high and 185 miles away.

All the time his cameras were snapping away, capturing it all on special high speed film. For that entire day and most of the rest of the night, he flew on northward. It seemed as if on top every hill or mountain he came upon sat another concentration of Soviets. Everywhere were the SAMs. He saw rings of them around two more sizable bases and two or three units atop of isolated mountaintops. They were scattered throughout the great plains of Nebraska, and on up into South Dakota.

And every single one of them was pointing west . . .

Hunter knew what the overabundance of SAMs meant. The Soviets knew who their enemy would be: the only stable governments left on the continent—the free states of Texas to the south and the Pacific American Armed Forces Protectorates to the west. Both democracies were heavily into air power. The SAMs were here to put an end to that.

Hunter was able to reestablish radio contact with Dozer two nights later, and then was able to talk to him for three more consecutive nights. Each transmission brought even grimmer news, which Dozer would soberly report to the PAAC-Oregon officers at their daily 0600 briefing. General Jones was also getting several daily reports on the crisis via top secret courier deliveries. PAAC-Oregon and PAAC-San Diego were brought up to Code 2 Alert, just a step away from a war situation. As was the custom at PAAC-Oregon, every officer on the base was given a briefing on the situation and they in turn delivered the reports to their chain of command on down. The philosophy was that if PAAC was going to ask their troops to go to war, then they owed them at least the courtesy of being open about the reasons for it.

Reports were also being secretly transmitted to Fitzgerald and St. Louie. The situation was particularly ominous for them, especially Football City, which was right next door to the 'Bads. With their major allies—the Pacific American Armed Forces—far to the west, Football City and The Aerodrome suddenly found themselves on the wrong side of the Soviet hidden army.

By the 10th day, Hunter found himself near the edge of the Dakota foothills. Here he made another discovery. The northern anchor of the Soviet hidden army appeared to be an old abandoned air force base near Aberdeen, South Dakota. A number of convoy-type airliners were in evidence. Some of them no doubt part of the mysterious convoy he had intercepted days before. But boldly lined up on three of the five runways were also hundreds of large gliders. These had to be what Fitz's people were seeing when they reported strange lights over the Lakes.

The gliders looked like they were manufactured especially for this particular Soviet adventure. They were probably made of wood, Hunter guessed, then covered with plastic sheeting. That way they wouldn't have shown up on radar either. And he knew that correctly piloted, a glider released off the coast of northeastern Canada at a height of, say, 80,000 feet or more, could soar for hundreds if not thousands of miles. He was sure that just one Russian Bear bomber could tow six or seven of the gliders out and turn them loose just beyond the reach of the Free Canadian radar sweep. From there they would have to rely on the continent's high night winds and thermal currents to "bounce" off Lakes Ontario and Erie. With a turn north after Lake Michigan and with enough height and wind, they could make it the last 600 miles or so.

But why light shows over the Lakes? Because, while the gliders were able to run high and silent, they still needed to travel in bunches with the lead guy somehow navigating. The sky can get very crowded when you're soaring 14 miles high, at night, without an engine, in a crowd of other wooden airplanes that don't have engines either. So you kept your anti-collision lights on and hoped for the best. It was a hell of a way to fly; damned cold and at the mercy of the winds. He was sure the Soviets lost more than a few gliders along the way, especially over the Lakes. Yet somehow their more plucky pilots made the trip and lived to tell about it.

Hunter made several high passes over the occupied airfield. He was not surprised to count 10 more Yaks at the base, plus the usual orgy of SAM sites surrounding the place.

It was the morning of the eleventh day when he landed and finally rested for a spell, 100 miles north of the Aberdeen glider base. He had to change his film and collect his notes. It was not a job he looked forward to. Glumly, he sat down and calculated that just from what he had seen in materiel strength alone, the Soviet hidden army would have to have more than 15,000 troops on hand to operate the thousands of pieces of equipment. That's some infiltration! Jesus, these guys made pushing a bike down the Ho Chi Minh Trail while dodging the U.S. Air Force look like a Sunday morning stroll.

But Hunter had a question: How could the Soviets

maintain—as in "feed"—such an army? Sneaking in troops, advisors or, more accurately, technicians to run all this gear, was one thing—*continually* sneaking in chow for them was another. An army runs on its stomach and he knew there wasn't an edible piece of corn in the entire Badlands. Even if it grew there, you wouldn't want to eat it.

Another question: If war against the western democracies *was* the Soviets' intent, who would do the dirty work? The bust-ass, slogging in the blood and mud, hand-to-hand combat? A bunch of SAM techs? No way. So there was another funny thing about the Soviet hidden army—it was an army without any infantry he could find.

Question Number Three: Where was the army's rear area? Where were all the extra ammo, fuel, spare parts kept? The answer was: nowhere. As far as he could tell, the jagged line that ran 600 miles from just west of Wichita, Kansas to just north of Aberdeen, South Dakota wasn't so much a frontline as it was a self-contained forward firing zone, about a mile or two wide and filled with a lot of SAMs. There was no depth to the Soviet positions, no backups that would normally be sequestered 20 to 30 miles to the rear.

He suddenly realized what the Soviet hidden army had done. They had managed to set up another wall—like a Berlin Wall—this one made of surface-to-air missiles. Once the SAM line was in operation, no airplane—be it a fighter or an airliner in a convoy—would be safe to fly through the center of the continent. In the next breath, Hunter realized that he was peeking in on a project that was not yet completed. He was sure that if he had made this trip two months later, he would have seen a line of SAMs extending through the wilderness of Oklahoma in the south, up through the rugged Dakotas to the Free Canadian border in the north. Once this "missile alley" was complete, Texas—and all that oil—would be in a dangerously isolated position. All the Soviets would have to do is station a few hundred of their new supermissiles—like the 70-mile range SA-12s he spotted—and they could knock down anything flying above the Louisiana-Texas border. The continent would thus be split in two, and easy access between the lifeline markets in Los Angeles and Free Canada would be blocked.

Early the next morning, he ate the last of his food, took off and immediately climbed to 10,000 feet. The minijet was still operating well but the fuel was down to nine gallons. And he still had one more place to go. He would have to catch strong winds at the higher altitude and glide most of the way to his destination.

He headed south, then east. His goal was located somewhere near the Soviet castle. He decided to locate the same ravine where St. Louie's recon guys met their deaths. Since his discovery of the Soviet hidden army, he knew now that anything was possible. Yet he still had to solve the mystery of the horses.

Using the upper air currents, he made it back over

the big Soviet main base in less than 14 hours. Along the way he took many high-altitude photos of the Soviet emplacements. It was dark again when he bypassed the Soviet castle, steered clear of the steaming nuke plant, turned east then lowered down to 1000 feet. Now he tried as best he could to pick up the route the doomed patrol traveled.

It was close to midnight when he spotted a piece of terrain that seemed to match the patrol's description of the ravine. He reconnoitered the area for 10 miles around and, not seeing a soul, landed the minijet near the area.

Then he waited. The moon rose. The wind kicked up some dust and blew it across the vast, deserted plain. He walked some distance from the minijet, taking the Uzi with him. He was surprised how bright the stars were shining even through the murk of the Badlands' atmosphere. Somewhere, a surviving coyote called at the moon. At least he thought it was a coyote . . .

That's when he heard the sound of hoofbeats.

do the same much less in less than 14 hours. Along the way he took many high-altitude photos of the Soviet emplacements. It was dark again when he arrived at Snake Rock, the [illegible] of the remaining fake grass, which was then nosed down to 100 feet. Now he circled as best he could to pick up the route the doomed parrot marked.

It was close to midnight when he spotted a piece of terrain that seemed to match the parrot's description of the valley. He would circle the area for 10 minutes, and, not seeing anyone, landed the monster near the sign.

Then he waited. The moon rose. The wind kicked up some dust and blew it across the dry, deserted plain. He waited some minutes [illegible] the [illegible] taking the lift with him. He was surprised how bright the stars were shining even through the murk of the [illegible] atmosphere. Somewhere, a [illegible] [illegible] part of the moon. At least he thought it was a coyote.

Then, when he heard the sound of footsteps.

Chapter Eleven

Hunter froze . . .

Off to the west, five riders, their horses at full gallop, were coming toward him. He quickly undid the safety on the Uzi and checked the magazine. It was full. He retrieved one of his two HE hand grenades, then he slowly crouched down, never once taking his eyes off the approaching horsemen.

He was about 25 feet away from the minijet, but the riders were coming on so fast, he would be spotted instantly if he attempted to get to the aircraft. And the way the horsemen were riding, their route would carry them right past the vehicle. What would happen then was anyone's guess.

The lead rider was the first to spot the small airplane. He immediately pulled up the reins on his horse and slowed down. His four comrades did the same. Hunter heard the simultaneous sound of five rifles being cocked. That meant the horsemen weren't just out for a pleasure ride. Whoever they were, these guys meant business.

He strained to make out forms behind the five

silhouettes. They appeared to be wearing some kind of armor and metal-visored helmets. And were those swords they were carrying in the belts?

The leader slowly urged his horse toward the minijet. He withdrew his sword and used it to poke at the airplane's deployed wingsail. Hunter watched, barely breathing. If the guy started jabbing and hit the wrong connecting wire or fuel line, then the minijet would be inoperable and Hunter would be stranded.

He had to act. The chances of these horsemen being friendlies was remote. He unslung his powerful belt lantern and switched it on. Instantly a beam of light cut across the night and caught the five riders in its path. That's when he saw their faces . . .

They were Orientals. Soldiers. They were wearing armor and metal helmets. They carried AK-47s Soviet assault rifles. Swords hung from each man's belt. The horses were also elaborately dressed. Jesus Christ! These guys looked like . . . *Mongolians*?

The riders turned and pointed their rifles toward him. They started shouting at each other in an indecipherable language. Hunter knew they would be momentarily blinded by light. An HE grenade would get most of them, but would also take out the minijet. The Uzi could get three, maybe four, but the fifth would probably get him in a crossfire. So he did the only thing he could do to draw them away from the minijet: He killed the light and ran in the opposite direction.

The riders followed. He scrambled up a hill and down the other side. He heard the horse's hooves trailing him close behind, and spun around as soon as he was sure the horsemen had reached the top of the hill. That's when they started shooting at him.

Their Ak-47s were loaded with tracer bullets. He saw streaks of light whiz by close to his left, then even closer to his right. Well, enough of this bullshit. He hit the ground, rolled and threw the HE grenade just á la John Wayne. It exploded right in front of the first two horsemen, lighting up the desert plain and blowing the riders and their horses to bits. The next horseman unwittingly rode into the bomb's resulting fire, which ignited his clothing as well as his mount's. Like something out of a horror film, the man, trapped atop his flaming horse, rode off screaming into the darkness.

There were two riders left and both survived the grenade's explosion. Hunter kept rolling and spinning away from their tracer-laden-bursts of gunfire. In a second, the Uzi was in his hand and firing. A barrage of bullets ripped across one man's face; he could hear the distinct pings as the slugs hit his metal helmet. The man slumped off his saddle, only to catch his boot in one of the stirrups. Hunter squeezed off another burst, just over the horse's head and the animal bolted in panic, dragging its hapless rider with it.

Undeterred, the lone rider continued firing at Hunter. At the same time he was diving away from the tracers, the airman realized that off on the horizon he could see in the dim light of the moon, hundreds—no thousands of riders. In an instant his mind clicked and another piece of the puzzle fell into place. *Cavalry.* That's what St. Louie's recon patrol ran into. And that was one way the Soviets intended to defend their SAM positions. But *Mongolian* cavalry? Here in America?

He didn't have time to think about it. He spun around. The last rider bore down on him, AK-47 in hand. But he was so close, he couldn't get a good aim on the airman. With the rider just a few feet away, Hunter reached back to his belt, drew his bayonet and threw it. The blade ran true, slicing into the man's throat. Hunter had to step out of the way as the horse, with its rider bleeding horribly, galloped by.

He had no time to lose. The main force of the cavalry was heading his way and he was sure they'd seen the action. He was back up and over the hill in seconds, neatly side-stepping the bloody goop of the first two riders he'd dispatched.

The cavalry was just a quarter of a mile away by the time he reached the minijet. He jumped in and started punching his computers to life. He quickly opened the fuel feeder valves and watched the fuel pressure needle rise. "C'mon baby, just fire one more time . . ." He crossed his fingers and pushed the engine's ignition switch. The little jet turbine instantly came to life.

He released the brakes and steered around in a circle. He would have to take off the same way he came in. Unfortunately, that was in the exact direction that the cavalry was bearing down on him. Having no other choice, he hit the throttle and the minijet started moving. He opened it up and it moved faster. All the while, his eyes and brain were working the calculations of how close he would have to come to the on-rushing cavalry before he could get airborne. The numbers were not with him this time. He knew by the time he could get off the ground, the aircraft would be twenty deep into the onrushing horde.

With a flick of a switch, he armed the minijet's missiles. They went green just as only 300 feet separated him from the lead element of the charging horsemen. He pushed a button and his outside starboard missile was gone, spiraling toward the riders. It impacted on the fourth man in, the HE splattering over two dozen or so of his comrades. Hunter launched his outside port missile a split-second later. It became imbedded in a lead horse's body, toppling it and delaying its detonation for a moment. But when it did blow—it was big, fiery, and bloody. Twenty more horsemen were mowed down. The lead horses immediately went into a panic. Those in the rest of the rest of the column that could, quickly swerved either right or left.

Now he had the gap he needed to take off. He yanked back on the controls and the minijet lifted off the ground. He could see the startled looks on the otherwise fierce faces of the cavalrymen as he rose up and over them. Some of the riders managed to fire at him as he raced to get altitude, the tracer bullets lighting up the sky but missing him by a wide margin.

But he still had problems. The power takeoff and the emergency ascent had sucked up a lot of his precious fuel. He still had quite a distance to fly. As he turned the craft westward, he programmed the computer to give him his maximum distance at his current fuel use rate. Once again, the numbers came back bad. He couldn't climb; he would use too much fuel getting up to the higher altitudes to catch the stronger winds. Yet, if he stayed low to ground, he'd run out of gas more than 150 miles short of the nearest Sea Stallion rendezvous spot. And with all those SAMS in place, he wouldn't even think of asking that a PAAC craft come any closer than the western fringe of the Badlands.

His only solution was to get more fuel.

There was only one place he could think of that might have jet engine fuel out here in the 'Bads. With a turn slightly to the northwest, he plotted a course for the small auxiliary Yak base he'd spotted near the Kansas-Nebraska border.

It was still two hours before dawn when he reached the small airbase. It had been a cinch to relocate it; its buildings were the only things that broke the monotony of the vast midwest plain. Approaching from the south, he could see the five Yaks bathed in spotlights, sitting in the middle of a square metal take-off and landing platform. Several Hind helicopters waited in the shadows nearby. A radar dish turned lazily atop one of the four buildings surrounding the small installation. Nearby sat two SA-2 mobile SAMs—the same kind that American pilots dodged over North Viet Nam years before.

Hunter figured the Soviet fuel supply would be heavily guarded; he guessed it was like gold to the Soviet infiltrators. He knew this because despite all the airpower the Russians had sneaked in, he had yet to see any of it flying around. The reason had to be an order by the high command to conserve all the available Soviet jet fuel until it was really needed.

Two gallons would get Hunter where he had to go. The question now was: how to get it. He cut the jet engine and drifted over the base. His guess was right, there were at least a dozen soldiers on guard duty near the base's fuel dump. Another dozen or so were guarding the Yaks. No one was watching the SAMs though; apparently the Soviets weren't expecting any air attacks. He counted 26 soldiers in all, awake and armed. He had no idea how many other soldiers were sleeping somewhere on the base.

The situation called for a diversion. He landed the minijet about a half mile away from the base and started crawling—not toward the installation but rather to a point north of it. He carried with him his two remaining wing missiles, his last HE grenade and his two signal rockets and his now-empty 5-gallon water jug. The trusty Uzi was also strapped to his back.

Reaching his destination and working quickly, he fashioned two delayed-reaction bombs. Each one contained a wing missile and a signal rocket. The missile's internal fusing system would serve as the timers, the HE inside would serve as the explosive and the signal rockets would add a little fireworks. He set one timer to go off in 30 minutes, the other would tick just two minutes longer. He was hoping the first explosion would get everyone's attention at the base and that second one would bring most of them running. By that time, he would have crawled up to the edge of the fenceless base and, with luck and a lot of confusion, he could withdraw some gas, head back to the hidden minijet and be gone before the Soviets started looking in other directions.

It was a good plan, he thought. But even the best of plans go awry . . .

Chapter Twelve

Hunter had just finished fusing the second bomb when he heard a loud whining noise coming from the base several hundred yards away. He couldn't believe it; it was the sound of a jet engine coming to life. It was still dark; dawn being more than an hour away. Yet for some reason, someone was warming up one of the Yaks.

It didn't make sense. If the Soviets were flying only when absolutely necessary—if at all—who would be wanting to take off in a Yak, especially at this hour? Could it be they were going to fly out a couple of hundred miles and check on that little commotion he caused back in the ravine? He quickly discounted the theory. They'd send the Hinds for that.

Maybe it was a training exercise. He knew that Soviet conscripts—the rookies, the greenhorns—were sometimes roused early from their sleep and put to work for an hour or two before breakfast. It had something to do with testing their Marxist mettle. Would they be firing up a Yak to let these guys work on it?

Again, unlikely. But whatever the reason, it was bad news for him. The airplane would be making a racket the entire time it was running and he wondered if anyone at the base would even hear his explosions. Or a hovering pilot might spot him or the minijet or both from the air.

Then he heard a second whine start up, then a third. Now he *knew* no one would hear his time bombs going off. But maybe it didn't matter. He could tell by the pitch of their engines, these three Yaks were not just warming up. They were preparing to take-off.

Suddenly, he felt a tingling go down his spine. He turned around and looked into the still-dark, northern sky. *The feeling was coming over him.* Way off in the distance, he could see four sets of red twinkling lights. They were at about 10,000 feet and coming fast. He watched four more sets of red lights appear behind the first group. Soon they were directly above him. They were Yaks, eight of them, dispatched, he figured, from one of the Soviet zone's northern bases.

Without so much as a wag of their wings, the eight fighters streaked over their countrymen and off to the south. Their roar had not yet died down when Hunter heard a fifth Yak start up at the base nearby. The Soviets had their air units on the move. It could only mean one thing: Something big was up.

Flattened out on the ground, Hunter watched as the first Yak, then the second, rose slowly over the nearby base. As always, he found himself fascinated by VTOL jets. They looked almost unreal as they hovered on a cushion of downward jet wash. The noise was intense, the jets' vertical thrusters churning up a heap of dust around the small take-off platform. Then, with the flip of a switch inside the cockpit, the jet's powerful thrust was diverted backward. In the snap of a finger the Yaks accelerated and were gone.

Now a third Yak rose, the first lights of dawn catching reflections from its steel gray body. Hunter could see hard ordnance hanging from its wings, but no air-to-air missiles. He knew the jets were going on a bombing mission, and not an aircraft interception.

"This is too good to be true," he thought, instantly knowing he had to take advantage of the situation. Grabbing the two makeshift time bombs, he shifted gears and started running in a low creep directly toward the base.

If he was lucky, he wouldn't even have to change the bombs' timers . . .

The Soviet captain in charge of the auxiliary Yak base hadn't yet put his boots on. There was no time. He had received the highly unusual urgent message just ten minutes before, and now he was following orders and getting four of his five planes armed and into the air. There was trouble to the south. His superiors didn't tell him so, of course, as no one in the high command would stoop so low as to tell a mere captain what was going on. The Soviet officer simply deduced that if the high command had ordered 20 of the Expeditionary Force's 50 Yaks stationed in the zone to arm up and head south, then it must be a critical situation.

Did this mean he'd see action at last? the Soviet wondered. He'd already spent 14 months out in the middle of this nowhere, breathing this bad air, eating the bad food and avoiding the water at all costs. He had already suffered through three unintentional bouts with low-level radiation sickness—each episode being worse than the previous one. And he was sick and tired of fighting with the others over the now-dog-eared copy of *Playboy* they had found a year ago.

What was worse, the Russian wasn't even sure what the hell he was doing over here in the first place. When he had somehow survived the big war in Europe, he thought his troublesome service days were over. In reality, they were just beginning. Not three months after the armstice was signed, his unit began training for this American "Expeditionary" mission.

First came the survival classes on how to operate the Yaks in a foreign environment. Then he was schooled on the proper supervision needed to operate a SA-2 missile system. Then, inexplicably, his commanders put him and 80 other officers aboard a creaky wooden glider and the next thing he knew, they were all vomiting *en masse*, as the glider battled fierce Canadian crosswinds high above the Great Lakes.

That had been just over a year ago. He had heard that his commanders were using a battle being fought between two American cities as a cover to infiltrate him and his support troops. He was deposited out in the deserted American plain and told that the Yaks—being flown in via Siberia and the American arctic—would arrive any day. They came exactly one year later.

He also knew it was too simple to blame his cement-headed superior officers for the unbelievable delay; the air forces operating on the American continent were known even to the Russian infiltrators as being top notch. The Soviets needed guarantees from their turncoat American allies like the Mid-Aks and The Family, that before the Yaks—or anything else belonging to the preciously small Soviet military machine—came over, at least half the continent had to be in their hands.

Thus the Soviet leaders had watched thc battles pitting the Mid-Aks and The Family against the democratic forces with great interest. Despite the battering the Soviet puppets had taken, the power of the democratic forces had shifted to the west coast. All that was left east of the Badlands were isolated islands of democracy—The Syracuse Aerodrome, Football City, to name two. In theory, these would be mopped up once the time was right.

But even he, a Soviet captain, who had spent 14 lonely dull months shooting at jack rabbits for their fur, knew that further promises had been made. Somehow, the Mongolian People's Mounted Army became involved; most likely someone knew the American plains were well-suited to use good old fashioned cavalry. But foremost of all, the Soviets were demanding their American allies provide an infantry to do the fighting once the Soviet infiltration was complete.

That's where this man they called "Viktor" came in . . .

The Russian officer's thoughts were broken as the fourth Yak lifted off. The fifth and final Yak would stay; he had ordered the jet warmed-up only as a stand-by in case one of the first four had to return to base due to a malfunction. He would keep the Yak warm for 15 minutes and if none of the others were back by then, he'd shut it down. After all, he was under strict orders to save as much fuel as possible.

He turned to go back to his quarters and finally retrieve his boots when his attention was drawn to a long plume of black smoke that was rising from the SAM launch vehicles parked nearby.

"I'll be shot for this," was his first thought. "The SAM is on fire and will soon explode and I'll be court martialed and shot for it." He immediately started screaming orders to his troops, frantically pointing at the burning missile launcher.

Some of his soldiers were already taking action. The base had a small trailer containing fire extinguishing equipment and now a dozen of his troopers were dragging it down the hill and toward the SAM site. From where the captain stood, it appeared that only the launch vehicle's rear tires were ablaze. But he knew in less than a minute, the fire would reach the fuel tanks of the four missiles on the launcher's back and the whole fucking thing would go up.

He ordered his other troops—mechanics, guards, everyone—to grab anything they could and go and fight the fire. A second fire brigade—armed with small fire extinguishers and five-gallon water containers—ran out of the base. Now the only ones left were the captain and the pilot of the warmed up Yak. The captain was finding cold comfort in the fact that the explosion from the four missiles blowing up would probably destroy the whole base anyway, killing him instantly and thereby sparing him from the slow death of Soviet military justice. As for the pilot waiting in Yak, he was also watching the fire and thinking that now might be a good time to take off and escape the conflagration to come.

But then something else caught the captain's attention. A man—wearing black clothes, a blackened face, and what looked like an American fighter pilot's helmet—was scrambling underneath the Yak. Amazed, the Russian watched as the man attached a loose chain to the bottom of the jet then ran to its other side. What's was going on here? the Soviet thought. Who the hell is that guy?

Amid the confused panic of the blazing SAM launcher, and the awful racket of the whining jet, the Soviet officer started screaming at the Yak pilot. But it was useless; the pilot couldn't hear him for the noise and couldn't see him because he was still looking the other way, nervously taking stock of his comrades' losing battle against the SAM fire.

In desperation, the Soviet officer looked around for a weapon. An AK-47, dropped when its owner was pressed into service as a fireman, lay nearby. The officer retrieved it and took aim at the man in black. By this time, the interloper had climbed the small ladder leading to the Yak cockpit and was pummeling the unsuspecting pilot. The officer squeezed off a burst of automatic gunfire which sailed far over the top of the airplane. He aimed lower and fired again, shooting out the Yak's front tires, causing the entire airplane to shudder. Suddenly it dawned on the Soviet officer that he was firing at a fully-bombed up, fully fueled airplane. A stray bullet could ignite a blast that would make the SAM's inevitable explosion sound like a firecracker. The Russian immediately ceased firing.

It was no use anyway. The man in black had subdued the pilot and literally dragged him up and out of the cockpit. The pilot fell a long nine feet to the hard metal surface of the landing platform below. Barely conscious and battered, the Russian pilot nevertheless hurriedly dragged himself out from under the Yak. He collapsed at his officer's feet.

The Soviet captain watched helplessly as the man in black climbed into the pilot's seat and started to quickly scan the airplane's controls. Suddenly the jet's irritating low whine leaped into full roar. The Yak started to ascend. In desperation the Soviet officer began firing the AK-47 again. But it did no good. The airplane was picking up speed and moving away. The man in black was smiling down at them and saying something so distinctly, both Russians could read his lips. He was saying: "See you later, boys."

The Soviet troops fighting the fire on the SAM barely noticed the Yak taking off. Still bootless, the Soviet captain ran down the hill toward his troops, grabbing half of them and yelling at them. He was pointing at the Yak with one hand and back toward the base with the other. Quickly, a dozen of the Soviet soldiers ran back to retrieve their weapons, leaving the other 12 to battle the fast spreading flames.

The Yak was still hovering nearby. It had not sped off as the Soviet officer thought it would. Perhaps the man who commandeered it was having trouble flying it. The Russian captain could not let it escape. Losing a SAM to a fire was one thing; having one of his jet fighters stolen was quite another.

Now the Yak was very slowly moving away toward the east. The pilot had closed the canopy and brought up the landing gear. Most of the Russian soldiers had their weapons in hand again and were shooting at the jet fighter, but the pilot somehow managed to avoid the concentrated barrage. Below the airplane hung the eight-foot length of chain the strange man had fastened beneath it. A large hook was conveniently attached to the bottom end. The airplane moved even further away but then stopped and hovered over a point about a half mile from the base. Now it looked to the Soviet officer that the pilot was lowering the Yak down. All the while his troops were hurrying to the spot, stopping and firing at the airplane as they advanced.

Using his binoculars, the Soviet captain watched as the Yak descended even lower, the chain dangling just 10 feet or so from the ground. The airplane hovered for a moment, then moved forward. The hook at the end of the chain snagged something and in one motion, the Yak started to quickly gain altitude.

The SAM's blew up a few seconds later—not from the fire but from a time-bomb hidden underneath the launcher. Three of the SA-2 missiles were obliterated immediately along with most of the Soviet soldiers fighting the fire. The fourth missile actually launched itself, traveled a brief, spiraling path and impacted on the side hill less than a mile from the base.

Flaming pieces of shrapnel from the explosion started to rain down on the base, touching off many small fires. It didn't matter. Exactly one minute after the SAM blew up, a second time-bomb went off under the base's precious fuel supply. Within seconds the installation was a mass of flames, growing higher with every exploding barrel of jet fuel.

The last thing the Soviet captain saw was the stolen Yak-38 turning toward the west and accelerating, the smaller minijet hanging underneath it.

Chapter Thirteen

The two PAAC F-105 Thunderchiefs were at full afterburner when they intercepted the Yak somewhere over Wyoming. The jet fighters were on armed air patrol when the PAAC Early Warning Radar net detected an unidentified aircraft coming out of the Badlands. The Thunderchiefs were immediately vectored to the area.

When they arrived at the coordinates, the PAAC pilots observed the Yak, its landing gear deployed, its collision lights blinking frantically, plus it was flying completely upside down. The F-105s got no response after ordering the airplane to identify itself. Normally, at this point, they would have shot it down. But this airplane was flying so oddly, the Thunderchiefs decided to hold their fire and investigate.

It was a good thing for Hunter that they did . . .

Hunter had never flown a Yak before, but he had got the hang of it quickly. The Soviet-designed cockpit and controls didn't bother him; they were essentially the same as the British VTOL Harrier, an aircraft he had flown on several occasions. As long as he knew where the throttle, the up-down-forward steering controls and landing gear buttons were, he was okay.

Getting the Russian-made radio to work was another story.

For the first 50 miles, Hunter had flown the jet slowly and steadily, being careful not to drop the minijet hanging underneath. It was not for entirely sentimental reasons that he had risked getting shot down in order to retrieve the small airplane. There was a load of valuable recon film in the minijet's cameras—film that he knew would be critically important to PAAC in the coming weeks and months.

He had located an isolated stretch of roadway and set down long enough to discard the minijet's wingsail, fold up the small aircraft's irreplaceable parts, and store them inside the Yak's undercarriage. As long as he flew with the landing gear deployed, the valuable minijet would stay secured. He took the precaution of removing the precious film and keeping it inside the cockpit with him.

He was up and flying within an hour, though the wheels-down gear position prevented him from putting the Yak at full throttle. He started fooling around with the radio soon after taking off. But no matter how hard he tried, he couldn't get so much as a crackle of static on the thing. The airman spent most of the flight cursing the so typically Soviet malfunctioning radio; he was certain it was busted before he ever arrived on the scene. The trouble was he hadn't talked to Dozer via the gunship link in a while. He knew because of the information he did get to them, the base and all of PAAC's aircraft would be on a high state of readiness, which was not casually nicknamed a "shoot first" alert. All they needed to see was a Russian Yak come streaking out of the Badlands unannounced and they'd be picking him up in pieces somewhere between Cheyenne and Yellowstone. He had to somehow warn them off . . .

The F-105s slowed down and took up positions on either side of the inverted Russian fighter, their Sidewinder missiles armed and ready. They could see the pilot waving and giving them the thumbs-up sign, but it wasn't until they saw the small American flag attached to the inside of the Yak's canopy did they back off long enough to allow the airplane to do a quick flip. Only then did the Thunderchief pilots recognize Hunter as the grinning man at the controls. Heartened to see their commander again, the F-105s escorted the Yak home.

Alerted ahead of time that a "friendly" Soviet fighter was on its way in, a large group of base personnel and civilians turned out to see the airplane make a dramatic vertical descent and landing. Hunter received a half-kidding round of applause from the crowd of mechanics and others who quickly gathered around the VTOL jet.

General Jones and Dozer were waiting for him.

"Are we glad to see you," Jones told him, shaking his hand as Hunter stepped down from the Yak.

"Same here, General," Hunter said. He took off

his helmet and shook hands with Dozer.

Jones walked around the Yak, inspecting its unusual features. "Wait 'til we get a bottle before you tell us how you got this," Jones said. "Right now, let's have it. How bad is it?"

"Real bad, sir," Hunter said solemnly rubbing his sandpaper-like beard. "They have more SAMs sitting out there than in Ho Chi Minh's best wet dream."

The trio started walking toward the base saloon.

"Can we take them out with air strikes?" Jones asked, his face furrowed with concern.

Hunter shook his head. "It would take every airplane this side of the Mississippi, plus all of the Free Canadian Air Force too, just to make a dent in it," Hunter said grimly. "We'd face very heavy losses to the SAMs. Plus we'd have the Yaks to contend with—forty-nine of them anyway. Then, there's their cavalry . . ."

"Cavalry?" Dozer asked. "You've got to be kidding."

"I know it sounds crazy," Hunter said, "but not only have they moved in all those Yaks and SAMs, they've somehow managed to infiltrate at least a division of cavalry. Probably much more. Ever hear of the People's Mounted Army of Mongolia?"

"Yes," Jones said. "They were the last regular cavalry units left in the world. But the Russians disbanded them in the early 'Fifties. Gave 'em trucks instead."

"Well, they've been reactivated," Hunter said. "I tangled with a bunch of them. They're tough customers."

"It's incredible," Dozer said. "But I guess that would explain these horses we've been hearing about lately."

"But how did they do it? Did they swim over from Siberia?"

Jones asked.

Hunter shrugged. "They must have come across the Bering Straits in anything that could float, then let 'em off in the Yukon somewhere and pointed them toward the 'Bads."

"Like Hannibal and the elephants," Dozer said incredulously. "And these guys are probably experts in working their horses in the snow, over mountains, through the desert, Jesus, wherever."

"And the plains of Kansas and Nebraska are perfect for operating cavalry," Jones added.

"So is Texas," Hunter said ominously. "We know they've been flying some of these guys from a hidden base somewhere way out in northern Montana and ferrying them and their horses down to southern Oklahoma. That's what that convoy was doing when I ran into them."

"No wonder that seven-o-seven looked like a stable," Dozer said, laughing at the absurdity of it. "They've probably been flying the nags all over the Badlands."

They arrived at the base's club and quickly took possession of a corner table. The bar maid brought over their usual brand of whiskey and a plateful of bar sandwiches. Hunter began wolfing down the first of several of the saloon delicacies.

"A well-trained cavalry could do a lot of damage in

Texas these days," Jones said, pouring out the drinks. "They could drive the Texans crazy raiding along the border then provide cover for the infantry when the big push came."

"There are still two major questions," Hunter said, downing his drink and reaching for another sandwich. "One: how the hell did they get all those SAMs over? And two, who's supplying the infantry when the balloon goes up?"

"We might have both answers," Jones said, knocking back a shot of the no-name whiskey. "A lot of things have happened since you left." He reached inside his flight jacket and produced a photograph. "But first of all take a look at this. It came from the Texans a couple of days ago."

Hunter took the photo and examined it. It was a typical recon picture, taken at low-level. The photo showed a long stretch of beach, perhaps two miles worth, dotted with what looked at first to be about fifty beached whales. A closer examination showed them to be not whales, but submarines. Russian submarines.

"Christ," Hunter exclaimed. "Where the hell was this taken?"

"That's Acapulco, Mexico," Jones answered. "Two Texans in an F-4 took it about a week ago."

"The lost patrol boat. These have got to be the subs we've been looking for," Hunter said.

"Or some of them, anyway." Dozer added.

"We know they're all diesel-powered boats," Jones continued. "Russian mothballed stuff, mostly, but also a few North Korean and Indian. Most of them are old. I mean really old. Granddaddies. Some of them are lucky as hell they made it."

"Has anyone searched them?" Hunter asked.

"Yes," Jones said, swallowing a shot and lighting a massive cigar. "The Texas Special Forces choppered in a couple of squads the next day to look around. Each sub was stripped to the bone inside. No torpedos, no missles, no nothing. Not even any bunks. Every boat was stark empty. The controls were even modified so that a skeleton crew could bring them over."

"They were using them as cargo ships," Hunter said, as he continued examining the minute details of the photo. "They were hauling only very exclusive cargo. Ammunition, fuel, anything too flammable to risk bringing it in by soarplane."

"You found Fitzie's 'UFOs?" Dozer asked.

"Yep," Hunter said, pouring himself another glass of whiskey. "Just as we thought, they were very terrestrial gliders, running over the Great Lakes with their landing lights on so they wouldn't have a fender-bender at 80,000 feet."

"My God," Jones said. "You mean they skipped them over the Lakes and hoped to get a thermal around Milwaukee?"

Hunter nodded a split-second before he downed his second shot of firewater.

"Jesus, that's one hell of a trip!" Dozer said, astonished.

"Some of them must have made it," Hunter said. "There's a bunch of sailplanes—every inch of them wood and plastic—sitting out in South Dakota. I've got pictures of them. And, just like these subs, they were used strictly for a one-way mission."

Hunter turned his attention back to the photo. "But why Alcapulco?" he said, almost to himself.

Jones re-lit his cigar and ran his hand over his close-cropped head. "Let's say the Russians knew that both the Texans and PAAC do a long-range recon to the Gulf of California on occasion," he said between puffs. "They would have been sitting ducks for our anti-shipping patrols in those narrow waters."

"So they must have hired on some local help to unload the subs," Dozer said, picking up on the theory. "Then they could float the stuff right up to the Colorado River. But from there, they could have kept right on going right up to . . . "

"To Las Vegas," Hunter filled in. "Or, the desert near Las Vegas . . . "

"Then that must have been what all the commotion was about down there," Jones said. "They were carrying a load of ammo and someone dropped a cigarette butt. Bang! Goodbye cruel world."

"Could have been an accident," Hunter said, pouring himself a drink. "Could have been our patrol boat guys, letting us know where they were. If that's the case, they were probably blown up in the explosion too."

"But there's another thing," Jones said. "Although whatever went off out there made a hole big enough to see down to China, it still was probably just the cargo from one of those subs."

"Well, they're carrying some pretty heavy stuff," Dozer said.

Hunter pounded the table softly. "But it still

doesn't say how they got all those SAMs over here," he said. "They wouldn't dare fly them in. And they couldn't fit them on these subs. How the hell they get 'em in?"

"We have our theories on that," Jones said. "But, Christ, it bothers me that the Reds are being innovative all of a sudden. Gliders. Cavalry. A million Goddamed SAMSs. Supplying criticals by sub then overland. Busting those Yaks in was a feat in itself."

"Yeah, and it's not like them to be so smart," Hunter said. "That's what's got me worried."

"Wait until you see this," Dozer said. He produced a pouch that was marked TOP SECRET and handed it to Hunter. "One of Fitzie's boys flew it in late last night, up and across Free Canada. And in the shittiest Piper Cub you've ever seen."

"Typical of Fitzie," Hunter said, as he opened the pouch. "His intelligence guys are the best, but he'll have them fly cheap junk."

His smile quickly faded as he read once, then twice, the telex-type message inside. "Oh God," he said slowly. "This is very bad."

"When we asked Fitz to keep his eyes open on the East Coast," Dozer said, his voice almost weary, "he blanketed the area with recon flights from old upstate New York all the way down to Florida. Got guys on the ground too. God knows if he ever thought that this is what he'd find."

"I think that answers your question as to who will be supplying the manpower—if not the missiles—for the Soviets, Hawk." Jones said gravely.

Hunter read the message over another time:

SECRET TRAINING BASES . . . INFANTRY, SOME ARMOR FOUND IN PENNSYLVANIA. VIRGINIA. NORTH CAROLINA. GEORGIA. POSSIBLY MORE . . . HAVE I.D. FAMILY, PIRATES, AKS, MAYBE OFFSHORE MERCENARIES . . . ESTIMATE 10 DIVISIONS MINIMUM. FLYING UNDER CIRCLE FLAG. PHOTOS LATER.

"The Circle!" Hunter spat the words out.

"They're for real, Hawk," Jones said. "And in a big way. Not only is this 'Viktor' character, whoever the hell he is, whipping the Mid-Aks and The Family and God knows what other morons into a blood frenzy—the fucker is organized."

"If anyone else but Fitzie had sent this, I wouldn't have believed it," Hunter said. "But *ten* divisions! That could be one hundred fifty thousand men or more. At their best, the 'Aks and The Family couldn't field one hundred twenty thousand guys, tops."

He was quiet for a moment, letting the new information sink in.

"I wasn't all that worried about this Viktor or The Circle until this," Hunter began again. "Now it looks like everyone on the eastern side of the continent who wants to go play soldier."

"Could be some kind of cult," Dozer said. "And he's drawing in anyone who can shoot a gun and wants to eat. After losing Football City and Boston, I imagine there's more than a few out-of-work Family soldiers or 'Aks out there."

"And what's worse," Hunter said. "We know that

The Circle has the capability of producing weapons and ammunition. But if they were giving guns to only half these guys, it would mean that somehow, somewhere, there must be some major munitions factories or a large arsenal operating."

He bit his lip and was silent for a moment. "And if they can turn out one hundred thousand M-16s plus ammo," he went on, "How hard would it be for them to start manufacturing SAM components? *Russian* SAM components. I mean, you don't have to be Albert Einstein to figure out how to attach part A to part B. If someone's giving you the directions, that is."

"Russian weapons factories? Here in America?" Jones asked.

"That's crazy," Dozer said.

"So is sneaking in a Mongol horde," Hunter said, his voice going up one notch in excitement. "But that's got to be it. It's the missing piece. We've been trying to figure out how the Russians got all those SAMs into the country. The answer is: They didn't. They didn't have to. They're being made right here!"

"Using Russian blueprints . . . " Jones filled in.

"Exactly," Hunter said. "They could even have ten, twenty, Christ—a hundred little factories churning these things out. And how would we know? Look at all the abandoned territory just in New England. The microelectronics sites around Boston, Route 128. No one trashed *those* places when the New Order came down. No one used them during the good old ZAP day, but only because there was nothing there the Northeast Economic Zone could sell."

"But now there is . . . " Jones said.

"And the Russians are buying." Dozer said.

"I've got a feeling that it's more like a partnership," Hunter said. "They both have what the other one needs. The Circle has industrial savvy and now they're raising an army."

"And the Russians are providing the high-tech stuff and advisors," Dozer said.

"That's a roger," Hunter agreed. "It was a policy of theirs for years before the war—however crudely it was handled. They haven't changed."

"But what's their purpose?" Jones asked.

Hunter shook his head. "It has to be what the Russians have wanted all along. They want to control America. And we're the only ones who can stop them.

The three men were quiet for a long time. Finally, Hunter broke the silence. "But, then again, we've got a few aces up our sleeves, too . . . "

"As in 'Top Secret' aces?" Dozer asked.

"God, do we have to reach deep down into our bags of tricks so early?" Jones said. "I thought we could keep those deep-sixed for ten, fifteen years."

"Me, too," Hunter said, feeling his body fill with emotion. "But we're going to be faced with at least ten divisions of infantry, a small air force of Russians and a wall of SAMs that runs from Texas to the Dakotas."

"And not to forget the Mongolian People's Mounted Army," Jones said.

"And the lid is coming off," Hunter said. "Damned quick. Not only did I trade shots with their 'comrade' horse soldiers, they'll be missing that Yak soon. Also their other Yaks were on the move earlier today. Heading south. Loaded for bear."

Jones poured another drink. "I've called an emergency meeting of Security Group tomorrow," he said. "We'll have to get some Texans up here, and some Free Canadians. It's going to be their fight, too. Can we show the film you shot during your trip to the 'Bads? They'll need convincing."

Hunter pulled on his jacket and got up to leave. "If the Marines will help, I can have an edited print along with ballpark locations by noon tomorrow."

Dozer also got up, grabbing what was left of the whiskey bottle. "I've got a feeling we're going to spend the night watching movies," the Marine captain said.

"That's right," Hunter said. "Remind me to tell you how I grabbed the Yak later . . . "

Chapter Fourteen

It wasn't until late the next morning that they found out why the Soviet Yaks were scrambled on Hunter's last day in the Badlands.

A small, camouflaged Lear Jet, carrying markings of the Texas Air Force, touched down at the base shortly before noon. Its occupants flew in to attend the emergency Security Group meeting that Jones had called. Hunter had finished developing the last reels of his aerial recon film and as commander of the PAAC-Oregon airbase, he was on hand to meet the Texans.

He watched as the jet taxied into the visitors parking area. A squad of monkeys materialized out of nowhere and proceeded to block off the airplane. The jet's whining engines started to wind their way off as the door to the airplane opened and two Texans stepped out. Both were tall, of course and dressed in the standard issue uniform of the Texas Air Rangers—blue one-piece flight fatigues, snakeskin boots and no less than a ten-gallon cowboy hat.

Hunter met them and introduced himself. They had flown up not just to attend the Security meeting, but also to brief PAAC on a border incident early the morning before. They quickly told Hunter their story. It had a sickeningly familiar ring to it.

A dozen towns along the border of Texas and Oklahoma were attacked the night before. The populations butchered. The towns were in isolated locations, obviously selected to be hit. The pleas for help from citizens started coming in over the radios about midnight. By the time Texas Border Guards arrived in each town, it was too late.

Except once. Just before dawn, the Texans airlifted a company of Special Forces into the dot of the town of Kilcoyne, Texas figuring it might be next on the raiders' hit list. The Texans arrived just as the town was about to be attacked by cavalry. Three mounted companies. The Texans dropped down right in front of them just on the outskirts of the town. It was three-to-one against the Texans, but the choppers spooked the horses and gave the troopers the advantage they needed to kill about 50 of the raiders before the others retreated.

No sooner had the Texans moved into the town to take up positions when four Yaks appeared overhead. One by one, the jets came in low and dropped napalm. The Texans had some Stinger missiles and they hit at least one of the attacking jets. But it was of no use; the town was burned to the ground. Only 30 of 100 Texas soldiers made it—about the same number of citizens were killed.

The Air Rangers said that other towns along the border were also napalmed that same night and early that morning. The Texans rushed troops to the border and had been patrolling the area intensely since the attacks. But as yet the raiders had not returned.

Hunter felt a charge of anger well up inside of him as the Rangers told him the story. Attacking and burning indiscriminate little towns was done for no military value—it was done for propaganda reasons. This wasn't war. This was terrorism.

Hunter immediately offered the Rangers all the services PAAC could spare. The Air Rangers graciously accepted. They would return to Texas immediately after the emergency session.

Who were the raiders? The surviving Texas chopper troops had searched the bodies of the horsemen killed in the clash at Kilcoyne. The attackers carried no papers or identification, but they were men of Oriental features and they were armed with a variety of weapons including Soviet AK-47s.

Again, it sounded all too familiar to Hunter. He quickly told the Texans about his recon mission to the Badlands and his discovery of elements of the Mongolian People's Cavalry. The Texans listened intently. It *must* have been the Mongols who raided the Texas border towns. But there was one odd twist: the chopper troops had found one of the attackers was carrying some unusual items in his saddle bag. The Air Rangers produced the well-worn brown leather sack and handed it over to Hunter. He reached inside and pulled out a handful of beat-up photographs.

They were pictures of Dominique . . .

The conference room was absolutely still. The only noise was the whirring sound of a film projector flickering images on a large screen at one end of the room. Every person crowded into the darkened room had their eyes riveted to the screen. No one spoke as the hour long film ran from beginning to end.

It was the recon film Hunter had shot over the Badlands. It began abruptly with his tracking the convoy of SAMs, ran through his dramatic low-level sweeps of the Soviet's castle-like base, and then, in what seemed like a never-ending series of sequences, focused in on the hundreds of Russian SAM installations stretching across the continent's devastated mid-section.

Finally—mercifully—the film ended with shots of the glider base in South Dakota and some high-level north-to-south panoramas of the Russian missile sites. When it was over, someone threw on the lights and the projector cranked to a stop. Still the room was completely silent.

Jones finally rose slowly and stood at the end of the table. He looked out on the men seated around him. The Ace Wrecking Company was there, as were the Cobra Brothers and officers from The Crazy Eights. Captain Frost sat beside Dozer. The two Texas Air Rangers were to Dozer's left. Crowded in the back of the room were the approximately 50 PAAC-Oregon pilots, plus the senior officers of the base's security force and infantry division. Sitting apart in a far corner of the room, totally alone from them all, was Hunter.

"Gentlemen, we face a very grave situation," Jones began. "I guess all of us who fought in the war—and got screwed by The New Order—always feared that the Russians would invade America someday.

"Well, I think these pictures—plus the incidents that have been happening over the past few months—confirm that not only are the Russians here, they've got in without hardly firing a shot.

"What's worse, they've succeeded in splitting the continent in two. From the reports we get from Fitzgerald in Syracuse, the Russians apparently have allied themselves with this terrorist army, The Circle. And, if our information is correct, The Circle is not only raising a huge army, they've acquired substantial weapons-making capabilities.

"I don't think I have to tell anyone here what this all means. We have to remove those missile sites. The Russians and The Circle are in a position now that they can call the shots east of the Rockies, except for Texas, and as they so brutally displayed a few nights ago, the Texans seem to be next on their list. The most vital link on this continent—that is the free, safe and direct air convoy routes between Free Canada and the West Coast—will be shut off as soon as the Russians make their move. And that could be any day now."

The silence in the room became frightening. The situation seemed hopeless.

Jones looked at Hunter. The ace fighter pilot was in another world, staring out into space, as if he wasn't listening. Something bigger than the missile crisis was eating at him, Jones knew. Something personal. And Hunter was too distant for Jones to ask him what it was.

The general turned his attention back to the Security Group. He removed his baseball hat and ran his hand over his stubbled hair. "Gentlemen," he began again slowly. "We are in a bad situation. But all is not yet lost.

"I'm about to tell you one of our most closely guarded secrets. This information is so secret, only the president of the United States and a handful of people knew about it before the war. And, frankly, we stumbled across it when we set up the Pacific American Armed Forces.

"I see this secret—this weapons system—as being our best hope of holding our own when the shooting starts in the Badlands. But first we must get it to work. And we must use it properly. Only then will we have a chance to save what little there is left of democracy on this continent."

All eyes were on the general as he paused and drew a breath.

"Gentlemen," the general continued, "two hundred and twenty-nine miles south of here, near what once was Eureka, California, there is a top secret air base. You would never know it because it is disguised as a typical, small municipal airfield.

"There is a hangar at this base. Very typical looking. However, underneath this hangar is one of the most sophisticated weapons laboratories ever built by the U.S. Air Force. It is in this underground laboratory, my friends, that we may find the way to fight back . . ."

Chapter Fifteen

The huge elevator creaked to a stop. Its hydraulic door slid open to reveal a huge subterranean cavern lit by hundreds of flourescent lights. The members of the Security Group stepped out into the underground bunker. Except for Dozer and Jones and a few others, no one in the group was even aware of the secret installation's existence until the general made the revelation the day before at the emergency Security Group meeting.

They were more than 400 feet underground, directly below the Eureka Municipal Airport. The elevator was actually a cleverly disguised section of one of the airport's repair hangar's floors. Similar to the lift on an aircraft carrier, it was big enough to lower a large airliner into the bowels of the earth.

The cavern was immense, easily encompassing the size of three or four normal-sized airplane hangers. Its metal floor was cluttered with aircraft support equipment, most of which looked like it hadn't been used in some time. The smell of lubricants and jet fuel filled the dank air.

"This is just the beginning, boys," Jones said as he

and the Security Group walked briskly toward the far end of the bunker. Once there, they found a huge metal door—big enough to be out of a science fiction movie. Jones located the controls and pushed a few preliminary buttons. A series of buzzes and clicks emanated from the control panel, and a few seconds later the word "READY" flashed on the panel's screen.

Jones turned and addressed the group.

"Behind this door lies one of the closest kept secrets of the U.S. Government before the war," the general began in measured tones. "Back then it was called, appropriately enough: Project Ghost Rider. The Air Force never got to use it during the Big War. I guess we're lucky they didn't. Because gentlemen, what lies on the other side of this door may be our only hope in countering the Russian's missiles and The Circle."

Jones hit the button and the gigantic door rolled open. Beyond lay another cavern, completely darkened. Jones thew another switch and a bank of ultrabright lights snapped on. The glare temporarily fuzzed the eyes of the group like a camera's flash bulb going off. But as soon as each member's retinas adjusted, they saw what Jones was talking about.

"Hot *damn*!" one of the Texas Air Rangers cried out. "That's about the prettiest sight I've ever seen."

The rest of the group could only agree. Before them sat five, gleaming brand-new B-1 bombers . . .

Hunter didn't make the trip to Eureka. He was

getting ready for another journey—one he knew would take him to five dangerous locations. Uncertainty waited at each stop. Even death. He would be gone for at least two weeks. This in a critical time when a huge war was imminent and the democratic forces of the west would need every man they could get—especially fighter pilots. And most especially, the best fighter pilot ever.

Yet he had to go. First, to the west, over the vast Pacific, to a place whose name was burned into the American soul. Pearl Harbor.

Then to Wyoming, to a place called Devil's Tower. Next it would be Arizona's forbidden Grand Canyon. Then on to a particularly nasty part of New Mexico, and finally to the most dangerous place of all: New York City.

Five locations. Five secrets to be revealed. Five Holy Grails to be retrieved and brought home. If not, the west would surely lose the war that was coming.

Project Ghost Rider involved five, specially-adapted, ultra-sophisticated B-1 bombers. The swing-wing, "do-it-all" B-1 was originally built in the 1980s to replace the granddaddy of bombers, the B-52. But these Ghost Rider B-1s were birds of a different feather. They were actually five pieces of the same weapon system. They had a mutual brain—it was jam-packed into the command airplane, known as *Ghost Rider 1*. Tens of thousands of semiconductors, miles of digital audio tape, a sea of bubble memory banks—all ruled by the most elaborate artificial intelligence system ever designed.

When *Ghost Rider 1* commanded, *Riders 2, 3, 4*

and *5* obeyed. As well they should—because by following the orders of the AI brain in the command aircraft, the five B-1s became invisible to radar. Not just "hard to see" or flying with a low radar "signature." But invisible. That's what the Ghost Rider Project was all about.

Five "black boxes" held the key. Once in place in their respective airplanes, the control boxes interconnected the flight, weapons and navigational systems of the five Ghost Riders. Working together and making full use of a radar-jamming technology so complex that even Hunter was just now beginning to understand it, the five bombers could literally fly over enemy territory without showing up on radar. They could not be shot down with radar-homing missiles; they could not be tracked by radar controlled anti-aircraft guns. Radar-guided air-to-air rockets would fall to earth unexploded because no target could be found.

All this was of the utmost importance to PAAC because although the Russian SAMs sitting in the Badlands were of many different sizes and configurations, they all had one thing in common: they tracked their targets on radar. And what they couldn't "see,' they couldn't shoot down.

But the eyes of the Ghost Rider Project were missing. Dispersed by design after the war so they—and the nearly completed Ghost Rider total radar avoidance system—would not fall into the wrong hands. The black boxes were under the command of an Air Force general named Christopher Josephs when the Big War broke out. At the time the system was just a month away from going operational—but it was never dispatched to the European theater. Why? Call it a fluke of the military bureaucracy or call it fate. But when the war came, the test pilots assigned to Ghost Rider were routinely called back to their combat bomber duties. From the day they left, General Josephs was on the phone to Washington DC every hour of every day trying to get his pilots returned. Without them, the airplanes could not be tested. But they never came back. And soon no one answered the phones in Washington.

So Josephs called in his trusted right-hand man, a captain named James Travis. It was Travis's job to take the five Ghost Rider black boxes and hide them at Josephs' direction. When PAAC discovered the underground laboratory they found Josephs' personal diary sitting on the pilot's seat of Ghost Rider 1. It took months to break the computer code which held the secret of Ghost Rider and which Josephs—his fate and whereabouts unknown—had left behind to find, for anyone who was smart enough to look for it.

The black box locations were finally narrowed down to Pearl Harbor, Devil's Tower, the Grand Canyon, New Mexico, and, of all places, Manhattan. Why these locations were selected, no one knew, but at least Josephs could never be accused of not having an imagination: the black box at Pearl was supposedly hidden in the flag mast of the USS *Arizona*, the battleship that was destroyed by the Japanese sneak attack and that still sat half sunk in the harbor serving as a war memorial.

As soon as they discovered the meaning of Ghost Rider, PAAC engineers began work on all the other aspects of the system. Coincidentally, Jones was intent on discussing a recovery mission with Hunter when the current troubles in the East took precedence. Now the black box recovery mission was critical. It was up to Hunter to find the boxes and bring them back to Eureka. Only then could the five B-1s operate up to their marvelous potential. Only then could they be sent in to destroy the SAMs in the Badlands. Only then could PAAC lead the fight against The Circle armies. Only then could the battle for democracy on the American continent be won.

But for Hunter, there was more at stake in the mission. For him, there was another mystery to be solved; that of the photographs of Dominique. The pictures the Texans brought with them were variations of the same pose and dress as the photograph he'd found on the renegade convoy airplane. The horsemen's pictures were discussed briefly during the viewing of the Badlands recon film—but were quickly dismissed by Jones.

"They must have busted into an X-rated book store somewhere along the line," the general had said to the Security Group at the time. Actually Hunter had taken Jones into his confidence, telling the senior officer of his previous discovery on the crashed 707. The general was as mystified as Hunter on what the photographs meant to the overall problem. Ben Wa and Toomey were also told as the two ex-ZAP pilots were the only comrades of Hunter who knew Dominique. All three of his friends agreed that the photos were an odd twist to an already strange story. But they also agreed to keep it top secret. They knew it was a mystery—and a battle—Hunter would have to face himself. They knew he wouldn't let them help him if they tried. That was the nature of Hunter. The imminent war had taken on a new, different meaning for him. The battle against the totalitarian forces that were attempting to take over what was left of the American way of life was uppermost in his mind and in his soul. But in his heart, the whole thing had become very personal. Why they had found photographs of Dominique on the convoy pilot and the Mongol warrior, he didn't know. But he did know that the only connection between the two dead men was they were on the side of The Circle and the Russians. Hunter also knew that back east, somewhere, was Dominique. The fact that he was heading in the opposite direction didn't bother him. He felt in his gut she was being held against her will. A prisoner. Now he renewed his vow to find her. And God help those responsible when he did.

Jones had taken most of the afternoon explaining Project Ghost Rider to the Security Group. Hunter took off later that same day, heading for Hawaii. The next morning, which was appropriately May 1st, the Soviet SAMs opened fire on a convoy that was attempting to pass over the southernmost section of the Badlands. Seventeen airliners were brought down by SAMs. At about the same time, two divisions of The Circle Army were spotted heading for the Syracuse Aerodrome. Another two divisions were discovered marching from the western end of Kentucky into eastern Missouri, apparently moving toward Football City. Their lead element ran into a company of Football City's famous recon troops and a sharp firefight ensued.

By noon that day, the first shots of the Second American Civil War had been fired.

Chapter Sixteen

The F-16 had spent the past hour lazily circling the Hawaiian island of Oahu at 50,000 feet. Hunter was surveying the ground below using his topographical contour radar. The device allowed him to spy on the island below him, charting where any weapons—including interceptors, anti-aircraft guns or SAM sites—might be located.

He found none, which didn't surprise him. Although contact between the Hawaiian Islands and PAAC on the mainland was nearly non-existent, the Pacific Americans knew that the New Order frenzy of disarmament had been nearly complete throughout the 50th state and that a kind of modern royal-tribal rule had returned to the islands.

He located an airstrip on the northeastern end of the island and swept the area with his scope. There wasn't a weapon nor a breathing human around. He quickly set the F-16 down and hid it in a forest of coconut trees located at the end of the runway. The landing strip appeared to be an abandoned Coast Guard air station. He found a paved road nearby which would carry him south and he began to walk.

The sun was just coming up out of the sea on the eastern horizon. The sky was red—as red as the *Aurora Borealis* he had encounterd at 90,000 feet several weeks before. He knew a red sky in the morning was a powerful omen for bad things to come. But to Hunter, the crimson sunrise meant another thing: the fighting had started to the east. Although he was thousands of miles to the west, he could smell *war* in the air. His mission just became more crucial, possibly more desperate. He quickened his step. He had to make the 25 miles to Honolulu by nightfall.

Hunter had been to Hawaii several times while he was touring with the Thunderbirds. The Honolulu he'd remembered was a nice, clean if overcrowded city. Now he was sure that had changed. According to the reports PAAC did get from Honolulu, the city was now a sprawl of honky-tonks, drugs, hedonism and crime. Gambling, never considered a vice in the old days, had been raised to the level of science on the islands these days. Yet there was no police force or government. Hunter was glad he'd made the trip packing both an Uzi and his trusty M-16. He also carried a small backpack that was filled with some of his best tricks of the trade.

He met his first Hawaiians about five miles into his trip. They were all wearing typical Hawaiian shirts and calmly manning a roadblock set up in the middle of the highway. It was the marking of the edge of their tribe's territory. He knew from here on in, he'd have to deal with these gunmen. The one regret Hunter had was that Ben Wa, he of the island of Maui to the south, wasn't able to accompany him on this trip. They would have made a great team, but a pilot of Wa's caliber was much too valuable at the front.

Of the 10 men guarding the outpost, six were asleep. They were quickly roused when their partners first spotted Hunter, clad in a green, unmarked flight suit, baseball cap on his head, his flight helmet dangling from his belt, walking down the middle of the unused highway.

The pilot carried his firearms in full view as he approached the men. He heard the safeties click off their firearms—a variety of hunting rifles, M-16s and shotguns. Hunter walked right up to their railroad crossing-style barrier and asked the first man he came to: "Which way to Honolulu?"

The gunmen laughed at him. A man who appeared to be their leader emerged from a small hut and walked up to Hunter. He was a small, dark, obviously Hawaiian man of middle age. Tough and wiry, he carried a .357 Magnum on one hip, an extra-large machete on the other.

To this man, Hunter repeated his questions: "Is this the road to Honolulu?"

"Could be," the man said in broken English.

Hunter got right to the point. "How much to pass through?"

"How much you got?" the man said.

"I'll give you a thousand in real gold now," Hunter

said calmly. "Two thousand on the way out."

The man grinned. "Lot of money. Why don't we just shoot you now and get all three thousand?" A few of his men laughed in agreement.

"Ain't got it all now," Hunter said. "Gotta do my business in Honolulu first."

"What kind of business?" the man asked.

"Drug kind of business," Hunter answered. "As in blow. Coke. You guys get that stuff up here?"

The leader laughed again. "How much you got?"

"It ain't how much I got," Hunter said. "It's what kind I got." With that he reached into his backpack and produced a brick-sized piece of compacted brownish leaves.

"Jesus Christ, man," the leader exclaimed. "You got a brick of. . ."

"Raw coca," Hunter said, finishing the man's sentence for him. "Now unless you guys got some processing works around here, you'd better let me through, so I can sell this shit."

The leader knew Hunter was right. The chemicals needed to break down the raw coca were in short supply—ether especially. Handling a brick of raw coca would be useless—but breaking it down into pure cocaine could net them anywhere from $25,000 to $50,000 in real gold, and that was only if they were stupid enough to sell it pure. And they weren't that stupid.

Neither was Hunter. The leader thought for a moment, then said. "You go, two of my guys go with you."

"Bodyguards?" Hunter said. "That's great, my

man. You just got yourself an extra thousand."

"At least," the man said, grinning.

Twenty minutes later, Hunter was sitting in the back of the gunmen's speeding jeep, enjoying the scenery. Not only had he parlayed himself a ride for the final 20 miles into Honolulu, he also had a way to pass through the seven further checkpoints between him and the city. At each stop, the gunmen—known as the *Tau Fin*—were routinely waved through. A peaceful, if shaky, coexistence was in force among the tribal gangs, or at least the ones who controlled this roadway. Between roadblocks, his escorts remained silent, which was fine with Hunter. He sat back and let the warm late spring sunshine soak through him.

They reached the outskirts of Honolulu about an hour later. From the top of a hill, Hunter could see the island that used to be the Pearl Harbor naval station. He was too far away to see if there was any military activity at the base. His earlier radar sweep revealed nothing heavy, but he hadn't yet discounted the possibility of some kind of presence at the base.

He had to reach the *USS Arizona* Memorial, but first he had to rid himself of his chauffeurs. He didn't feel that he was justified in shooting them, although they had foolishly left him alone in the backseat of the open vehicle with his M-16 and Uzi, both fully-loaded. Instead, he would put the two to sleep.

"Stop!" he yelled in the driver's ear as they drove into the very outskirts of the city.

The passenger gunmen turned around quickly, his

sawed-off shotgun at the ready.

"What?" he yelled over the sound of the motor.

"Stop," Hunter yelled again. He had reached into his backpack and produced a small plastic bag of white powder. He waved it in front of the passenger-side gunman.

The man smiled broadly. "Coke? We do a line?" he asked as his partner slowed the jeep.

"We do many lines," Hunter said, producing a mirror and a razor blade.

The jeep had slowed down and stopped by this time. The gunmen smacked their lips as they watched Hunter expertly pour a small pile of the powder onto the mirror and start chopping away with the razor blade.

He fashioned the resulting fine powder into six long, thick lines. A straw was produced. Hunter handed the mirror to the passenger-side gunman who took a long, noisy sniff, pulling the entire stretch of white stuff up his nose in one swipe. "Ahhhhh!" he said with evident satisfaction.

His partner grabbed the mirror and repeated the process. His reaction was also one of delight. "Goooood stuff,'" he said, snorting the stuff back into his nostrils.

In two seconds, both he and his partner were knocked out cold.

"You mean 'Goooood night,' " Hunter said, jumping out of the jeep and hauling the two limp bodies out of the vehicle. Thorazine pentathol, Hunter's own concoction of sleeping powder, looked, cut and tasted like cocaine. The gunmen would sleep for almost 24 hours, he figured. That's what they get for being so greedy with their lines.

"See ya, chumps," Hunter said as he disarmed the men, got behind the wheel of the jeep and roared off toward Honolulu.

He was across a makeshift bridge and at the fence of the old Pearl Harbor base less than an hour later.

Passing through the city of Honolulu had been an experience in itself. The place had so many gambling casinos even Louie St. Louie would have blushed. There were people in the streets although it was still barely 9 AM. Every one of the men were armed and it seemed every one of the women were topless. Ben Wa would have been proud.

He had found the road to Pearl with no problem. Driving slowly long the perimeter fence, he saw little evidence of military activity inside the base. There were a few military vehicles such as APCs, half-tracks and even an old M-60 tank. But he saw very few people walking inside the base.

He reached the main gate and found it manned by a lone sailor. With his white uniform, complete from upturned hat to black boot leggings, the man looked like something out of World War II. He was also sound asleep.

Hunter climbed out of the jeep and approached him. He was precariously balanced on an old chair leaning against a small guardhouse.

"Excuse me, sailor," Hunter said in a voice that was half a shout.

The man didn't stir.

"Hey, Navy!" Hunter said, a little louder.

Still asleep, the man brushed an imaginary bug from his nose.

Hunter leaned down, cupped his hands and yelled into the sailor's ear. "Hey! Swabbie!"

The man went over like a capsized ship. He was quickly to his feet, his hand wrestling with the .45 automatic he wore on his belt. When retrieving it failed, he foolishly took a swing at Hunter. The punch wasn't even close.

Hunter's Uzi was out and against the man's nose in a split second. "Take it easy, Popeye," Hunter said, his other hand seizing the sailor's .45.

"Who the fuck are you!" the man screamed.

Hunter looked at him. He was unkempt, unshaven and, judging from the downwind, unbathed. The sailor was a disgrace to his uniform.

"Where's your CO?" Hunter asked sternly.

"Where he always is," the sailor said, trying to upright his fallen chair. "Shitfaced."

"Where?"

The sailor pointed over his shoulder to a white two-story structure. "Up in his office," he said. "Over there."

Hunter snapped out the .45s magazine. It was empty. He shook his head and returned the useless gun to the sailor.

"You know something, I *always* bet on you guys in the Army-Navy game," Hunter said angrily. "No wonder I always lost."

For the first time the man looked embarrassed.

"Hey, listen flyboy, it ain't always been like this."

It didn't matter what he said; Hunter was already hurrying toward the dirty white building.

He entered the unguarded structure and double-timed it up the stairs. He found an entire row of offices unoccupied. Then he came to a corner room and saw a man sitting with his back to him. He was turned around in a chair behind a desk, reading what looked to be a skin magazine. As far as Hunter could tell, the man was the only person in the building.

He walked in. "I'm Major Hunter, Pacific American Armed Forces. From back on the mainland."

Startled, the man took one look at Hunter and instantly sprang to his feet.

"Commander . . . Josh . . . McDermott," he said, his voice trembling as if from lack of use. "United Sta . . . I mean, United Hawaiian . . . National . . . Royal Naval Defense . . . ah, Forces."

The man's hand was shaking as he tried a salute.

While the sleepy guard was a wise-ass slob, this man was pitiful wreck. He wasn't old. Hunter figured 43, maybe 45. Yet his face, his skin and his white hair were those of a man twenty years his age.

"Good to meet you, Commander," Hunter said, reaching over the desk and surprising the man with a handshake.

The man calmed down a little. He was dressed in a tattered U.S. Naval dress white uniform that looked like he had worn it, unpressed, every day for the past five years. The office itself was shabby. Files long gathering dust cluttered the place. Paperwork lay discarded on the floor. The windows were so dirty, it was hard to see the water of Pearl Harbor that lay just a short distance from the building. Through the grime, Hunter spotted the white shape of the *USS Arizona* Memorial.

"What brings you our way, Major?"

"I'm looking for something, Commander," Hunter said, reaching into his pocket for a photo of the Ghost Rider black box. "This box is very important to me," he said, handing the picture to the man. "It's hidden on the *Arizona*."

"The *Arizona*?" the threadbare officer asked as he took the photo and studied it. "What is it, Major? A guidance system or something?"

Hunter looked at the man. He could tell that at one time, the guy must have been a savvy officer.

Hunter shook his head. He couldn't hold it back any longer. "What's happened here, Commander?" he asked looking around the disheveled office, a trace of sadness in his voice. "This is Pearl Harbor, for God's sake . . ."

The man turned away and shook his head. A whiskey bottle stood on a windowsill nearby. He reached over and grabbed it, scooping up two glasses in the process. When he turned around the pitiful look had added the new dimension of apathy.

"Have a drink, Major?"

For the first time in as long as he could remember, Hunter declined.

The man poured himself a healthy one anyway.

"We were left behind, Major," he said, bitterness evident in his voice. "Left behind after the armistice with no ship big enough to get back to the mainland."

The explanation hit Hunter like a punch in the gut. In an instant, he realized the man's tragic plight. "How about airplanes? Some must have come through," he said.

"Sure," McDermott said, downing his drink. "Plenty of them in the first few weeks following the end of the war. All unauthorized. I was the fool. I decided to be all-Navy. I didn't believe for a minute that the country—that our armed forces would go along with the New Order double-cross. I was sure the fleet . . . the real Navy . . . would come steaming over the horizon at any minute.

"Well, they didn't. And those assholes in the Hawaiian National Guard went on a rampage and destroyed every workable piece of military equipment on the islands. Sank all the ships in port. Pranged all the airplanes. Busted up all the radios. I've been stuck inside here ever since."

"You mean you never leave the base?" Hunter asked.

"I mean I never leave the building," McDermott answered. "The Tribes—the *Tau Fin*—rule this island, and me and the twenty-five guys I got left are all mainlanders. We're lucky they don't burn the place to the ground."

"Where are you from, Commander?" Hunter asked.

"Rhode Island," McDermott said, pouring another drink. Then he looked up at Hunter and asked, "Is it still there?"

Hunter slowly shook his head. The man laughed

bitterly. "Then why should I complain? I'm better off in the sun and fun of Hawaii."

Hunter wanted to get out of the place. He started to get back to business and ask the officer if he'd mind helping him search the *Arizona*, when he felt a very familiar feeling.

"Commander, are you sure you don't have any aircraft operating here?" he asked.

"Are you kidding?" McDermott laughed. "There hasn't been an airplane on any of these islands in three years."

Hunter's senses were tingling.

"Well, there is now," he said, concentrating. "Heading this way. A lot of them."

"Ah, forget it," McDermott said, pouring his third drink. "No one within a thousand miles of here can fly a kite, never mind an airplane. Besides, it's Sunday . . ."

Hunter walked to the window and rubbed off some of the grime. He looked out to the northwest. Twenty, thirty of them, he thought. Slow. Low. Carrying something. Bombs, maybe.

He turned and looked McDermott. "Got any enemies, Commander?"

The officer pondered the question. But Hunter didn't have time to waste. "Get the hell of of here," he yelled to the man. Then he was out the door, down the stairs and running toward the *Arizona* Memorial. As he ran he could see the faint outline of a chevron of tiny dots approaching the island from out over the ocean. They were old airplanes, he knew. Prop jets.

He bounded down the pier next to the sunken battleship and up the gangplank. If the airplanes were coming to attack, he couldn't take the chance of the black box being destroyed. The message that Josephs left behind said the box was stashed in the base of the flag pole that sat at the very top of the partially-submerged ship's conning tower.

Hunter scrambled up the ladder to the conning tower and was next to the flagpole just as the airplanes were turning toward the harbor. Two by two, the airplanes broke off and raced in low. They were old, but powerful A-1 Skyraiders, similar to the ones back at PAAC-Oregon. The airplanes were dangerous. They were known for being able to carry more ordnance than B-17 bomber, yet were only slightly larger than the big fighters of World War II.

The first two airplanes streaked right over his head and released two bombs each. As if in slow motion, the four bombs slammed into a warehouse-like building two down from the dirty white officer's building. Four individual balls of smoke and flame erupted from the structure. The two A-1s peeled off to the right together.

Suddenly, two more attackers were over his head. They too let go a total of four bombs, theirs falling short of the first group and hitting the little used docking area nearby. He could see that other pairs of Skyraiders were attacking other targets in the base and in the city nearby.

Hunter knew it was a matter of time before the unknown assailants attacked the Memorial. He kicked out a panel at the bottom of the flagpole base and looked inside the small, wooden base.

Just like Josephs promised, there was a gray safe-like box inside the hollow base. Hunter dragged it out. A padlock was squeezing the lid shit. If the contents weren't so valuable he would have shot the lock off. But he chose to simply pick it instead. Using the stiletto he always kept with him, it twisted the padlock off and opened the box.

"Jesus Christ!" he had to exclaim. "It's here!" The box was black—shiny black. He could tell by the various connections and receptacles on its side the box was the genuine article. It had a tiny red light on its top and it was blinking. It was then he realized that for the first time in his trip, he really believed that the long-distance recovery operation might just work.

His excitement was cut short. He heard the unmistakable whine of a propeller airplane as it was turning to attack. He looked out and saw an A-1 coming in at wavetop level, heading straight for the Memorial and his position.

He was up and firing the M-16 in less than a second. The A-1 was fitted with a Vulcan cannon, which now opened up. A rain of shells exploded around him. Hunter kept firing away trying to puncture the engine beyond the whirling prop enough times to make it stall. But the airplane was on him. Two bombs released from its wings and seem to hang in the air. With quick precision Hunter pumped four shots into each bomb, exploding one in mid-air and deflecting the other to fall short of the Memorial and into the water.

He knew he'd just made two of the luckiest shots in his career. He couldn't duplicate them if he tried. That's why he didn't want to be in the conning tower when the airplane came back. He quickly slammed the safe shut again and slipped it into his backpack. Then he was back down the conning ladder and running down the ship's deckways toward the gangplank.

The entire base and city were now under a crushing attack. It seemed like the entire sky was filled with airplanes—bombing, strafing, twisting, turning, diving. Another swarm of A-1s had joined the attack and they were mercilessly pounding everything from the dock to the skyscrapers nearby. He could see people running in terror through the streets outside the base. But no one was rushing to mount a defense from the inside.

He remembered the APC he'd seen near the base's main gate and ran toward it. There were a few sailors—all in the dirty, unpressed uniforms—running about, looking confused. Their commander—McDermott—was nowhere to be found.

Christ, where are the officers of these sailors? Hunter thought. No matter where he looked, he saw only enlisted men. It quickly became apparent that he would have to rally a defense.

He grabbed a sailor and pointed toward the APC.

"Can you drive that thing?" he yelled to him. The man nodded uncertainly. "Then let's go!"

Hunter dragged the man with him toward the tankish-looking personnel carrier. There was a .60 caliber machine gun mounted on it with a belt of ammunition hanging off its side. Hunter crossed his fingers and hoped the gun would work.

Zig-zagging through the rain of exploding bombs and fiery debris, he and his reluctant ally reached the vehicle and climbed on-board. Explosions were going off all around them. A huge fire raged just 20 paces from the tracked vehicle. Some of the attacking Skyraiders were strafing the APC, trying to take out what they had identifed as the only formidable piece of gunpower on the base.

Hunter knew he had to move fast.

The sailor crawled down into the driver's seat, while the airman positioned himself behind the big gun. He squeezed the .60's trigger. The gun bucked. He squeezed again, it bucked once, then twice. "C'mon you mother . . ." He squeezed again. This time the gun kicked and a short burst streamed out of the muzzle. "Solid," Hunter yelled, turning to the man at the controls. "Get me down to the pier!"

Slowly the APC creaked to life and right away Hunter knew the thing was a shitbox. Black smoke was belching out of the back, nearly choking him and making them a perfect target for the angrily buzzing Skyraiders. The engine sounded like it was going to throw a rod. The nervous sailor was driving like he'd just drunk a fifth of bad scotch. Somehow they dodged the shrieking bombs, the building fires and the smoking debris and rolled out onto the pier.

Despite the absolute lack of return groundfire, the A-1s were relentlessly pressed home their attack. Hunter had no idea who the attackers were, but they were polished airmen, he knew that much. The attack was being conducted in a very effective workmanlike manner. They had done this kind of thing before. The airplanes were all painted in the same uniform gray color, too, indicating some kind of organized force, as opposed to just a pirate gang. The only insignia he could see was three small red dots painted on the tails. Where the attackers came from or why they would choose to strike at the defenseless base and city was a mystery. But it made no difference to him. He didn't really care who they were. One of America's most precious memorials was in danger of being destroyed and he refused to let it happen without firing back.

He had the sailor drive right past the *Arizona* on out toward the furthest point on the pier which ran about a hundred yards out into the harbor. The bombs were falling uncomfortably close to the Memorial. At least he could draw some of the fire from it. As the APC bumped its way along, Hunter spotted his first target. It was a rogue A-1 sweeping in from the north, just 10 feet off the water. The attackers had become emboldened and were now flying slow and easy, routinely depositing their bombs.

It was their mistake. Hunter lined up the first A-1 in his sights and opened fire on it, no more than 50 feet away from him. A stream of shells walked up the surface of the bay toward a rendezvous with the Skyraider. Unlike his M-16 bullets, the .60 shells were able to rip into the airplane's fuselage. Hunter moved the stream of fire up to the airplane's canopy. The pilot, finally realizing he was under attack, tried to accelerate. But Hunter saw his bullets hitting the plane's bubble-top and, just as it was passing out of his range, the airplane's canopy shattered and exploded. Its pilot mortally wounded, the A-1 turned up slightly, then twisted and plunged into the water, exploding on impact.

He thought he heard his cohort let out a cheer, but Hunter didn't have time to celebrate. Another A-1 was bearing down on them from the south.

"Back up! Back up!" Hunter yelled to the driver. He had to stay moving or the Skyraiders would eat him up. The APC slammed into reverse just as he unleased another burst at the A-1 coming in at him about 300 feet away. This time he aimed at the Skyraiders' external belly tank. The shells hit home and the fuel inside the teardrop shaped tank exploded, obliterating the airplane just a hundred feet away from them.

Suddenly, a stream of cannon shells raked the APC from the rear. Hunter swung the big gun around to find another A-1 bearing down on them. But before he could squeeze off a burst at the attacker, the vehicle was buffeted by a second accurate barrage, this one coming from his left. It was another Skyraider, sneaking in low and from the west. Hunter knew in a matter of seconds, the APC would be caught in a deadly crossfire.

He yelled at the sailor to bust the thing into forward and the driver rammed the APC into drive. The transmission screamed. Hunter was nearly knocked out of the turret and off the back of the vehicle. Recovering, he swung the gun around did some instant calculations then took careful aim on the first A-1's starboard wing. He counted to three, then pulled the trigger and a two-foot section of the airplane's steering control ripped away. This caused the big prop plane to bank suddenly to the right and directly into the path of the second attacker. The two A-1s hit head-on a few seconds later. The sound of the blazing collision was tremendous. A rain of smoking debris fell all over the APC. This time, Hunter didn't have to yell to the driver, he had already jammed the APC back into reverse. The two Skyraiders, now strangely joined, plunged to earth, striking the pier near where the APC was seconds before. The airplanes exploded again, then kept right on going, taking out a large section of the dock and sinking into the harbor.

Hunter whistled. That was *too* close. A momentary break in the action let him take stock of the situation. He was glad to finally hear some return fire—feeble as it was—coming from the city itself. Probably Tribesmen firing their small arms at the attackers. He could see a few sailors were up and about and doing the same thing.

The attack was gradually winding down. In twos and threes, the A-1s were dropping the last of their bombs and turning away off to the west. He told the driver to stop. No more Skyraiders came within his range. Within a minute, the attackers were gone.

They spun around and rolled forward again, back toward the base. Nearly half its buildings were in flames, as was a good portion of the city. Survivors were staggering about the docks, some still in their sleepwear. Those few who had taken part in the defense were half-heartedly celebrating. Some of them rallied around the APC.

But Hunter knew the celebration was premature. High above the harbor he saw a single Skyraider slowly circling. He knew it was a spotter plane, charged with assessing the damage of the sneak air attack—and identifying targets for a second strike.

"They'll be back within two hours," Hunter told the ragged sailors around the APC." Get your asses in gear and find your CO. Get something coordinated with the people in the town and be ready when they come again."

He then climbed down from the APC and clasped the hand of the sailor who did the driving. "Thanks, pal. What's your name."

"Murphy, sir," the sailor said. "Mark Murphy."

"Well, Murph, you done good." Hunter told him. "Hang in there."

"But where are you going, sir?" the sailor asked, nervous that the man rallied the small but effective defense was now heading off. Other defenders started to air the same view.

"Don't worry, guys," Hunter said, "I'll be back."

With that, he was sprinting for the base's main gate, the precious black box firmly in his grasp.

It was close to noon when the second wave of 12 Skyraiders appeared over the western horizon and bore down on the base again. But things would be different this time.

The A-1 flight leader looked over his shoulder and caught a glint of reflection coming out of the sun. It was moving too fast to be one of his Skyraiders. In fact, it was moving too fast to be any other kind of prop airplane. It must be . . .

Before the pilot could get his thought out, his airplane exploded into a thousand flaming pieces, the victim of one of the three Sidewinder missiles heading toward his formation. As soon as the other A-1 pilots saw the explosion they began to react. But just as quickly, two more of their number fell victim to air-to-air missiles.

Before the Skyraider pilots knew it, a red-white-and-blue F-16 was spinning wildly through their formation. It came out of nowhere. A thick, steady cough of flame was coming out of its nose. Pieces of Skyraiders were flying everywhere. Not one of the A-1 pilots thought of shooting back. The F-16 pilot was acting like a wild man behind the controls. Every time the jet fired, its cannons hit something.

The would-be attackers tried to scatter. The F-16 launched another Sidewinder. The heat-seeking missile was attracted to a hot-running Skyraider piston-driven engine, slamming home just below the pilot compartment. The A-1 flipped over and went down. Another Sidewinder clipped the tail portion of an A-1, splitting it in two before carrying on and impacting on another luckless Skyraider nearby. A third missile managed to lodge itself into the underbelly of another airplane, pausing a few frightful seconds before exploding.

Its six missiles spent, the F-16 roared after a group

of three retreating A-1s, cannons blazing. One by one the airplanes dropped into the sea. By the time it was over, only two of the 12 Skyraiders escaped, and that was only because the F-16 broke off the attack. The last they saw of the jet it was streaking off to the east and climbing. Whoever the hell the crazy man in the F-16 was, he had singlehandedly prevented the second wave of attackers from going in and finishing off the targeted base and harbor.

The A-1 pilots knew their employers were not going like the story they would have to tell them . . .

Back on the ground at Pearl, a combined sailor-tribe gunmen force had watched the spectacular air battle off in the distance. They cheered as the surviving A-1s scurried away. They would not have to fight off another attack. Then, they saw a lone airplane was criss-crossing the sky high above them, leaving behind long, white contrails that eventually took the shape of a huge "W."

Chapter Seventeen

Hunter returned to his base in Oregon only long enough to turn over the black box to Jones, get a quick briefing and make preparations to take off again. This time, he was flying the captured Yak. His destination: Devil's Tower, Wyoming.

Jones had filled him in on the situation in the Badlands. Another convoy had been attacked; this time 31 airliners were shot down passing over the northern top of South Dakota. This was the last convoy to attempt to fly over the middle of the continent. By now, every convoy jockey knew that someone was shooting at them from the Badlands. It would still be a matter of days before they knew just who it was.

Jones told Hunter he had ordered both PAAC-Oregon and PAAC-San Diego on to a First Class Red Alert. The Texans had taken the same action. Dozer and some of his airborne troops were at the moment flying in the Crazy Eights and scouring the western edge of the Badlands, looking for an acceptably large place where the PAAC jet fighters and other aircraft could set down. Once this forward base of operations was found, Jones planned to start sending elements of PAAC aircraft east.

On the other side of the Badlands, St. Louie was organizing an airlift evacuation of Football City. Huge C-5 transports, courtesy of the Texas Air Force, began shuttling in and out, their routes being covered by Texas jet fighters. It was a strategic and intelligent retreat. The two Circle army divisions closing in on the city were too big and too well-equipped to try to fight off, especially since Football City was still recovering from its massive war against The Family. Instead, St. Louie sent his squadron of elite F-20 jet fighters to harass the advancing enemy, giving him enough time to lift out his small civilian population and his well-equipped army.

Mike Fitzgerald of the Syracuse Aerodrome was also forced to bug out. He knew it was a matter of hours before The Circle would be at his southern flank. Although his famous F-105 fighter-bombers could have inflicted much damage on the advancing army, he agreed with Jones, in a scrambled conversation they had had the night before, that the splendid Aerodrome Defense Force would be needed in the effort to take out the Soviet SAMs in the Badlands. Early that morning, a long convoy of Free Canadian army trucks and buses arrived at the Aerodrome and started loading on anyone at the outpost who wanted to get to the relative safety of the country to the north. Most of the people at Syracuse took advantage of the offer. As soon as the non-combatants were evacuated, Fitzgerald ordered his regiment-sized ADF armored unit to head out in their own trucks, driving east toward Lake Erie, warning and picking up civilians along the way before diverting into Free Canada by way of Buffalo. A contingent of Fitzgerald's ground troops—the World War II GI-clad Border Guardsmen—were the last to go. As ordered, they had destroyed anything valuable they couldn't carry, burned all the left-behind food and poisoned the water and liquor supply. After detonating huge blockbuster bombs along the center of the Aerodrome's runways, the soldiers jumped in their big Chinook helicopters and flew away. When The Circle Army reached the Aerodrome less than a day later, they found the place smoking and empty.

Long before he evacuated Syracuse, however, Fitzgerald had dispatched a large contingent of his undercover agents into areas coming under control of The Circle. These spies would be the eyes and ears of the democracies—first-hand witnesses to the madness that was sweeping the continent east of the Mississippi.

Already their reports were filtering in . . .

All across the eastern half of the continent, they said, regular army units loyal to The Circle were sweeping through small towns and villages, signing up eager recruits and impressing the not-so-enthusiastic, to fight in "The War Against the West." It was a road show rivaling the fervor of a religious revival. Walls and billboards were painted and posters plastered up anywhere and everywhere—all proclaiming the righteousness of attacking the governments of Texas and west of the Rockies. *"Manifest Destiny!"* one poster read, *"Recover our profitable lands! The oil of Texas, the mineral rich mountains of Colorado, the beachfront property of California are being held unfairly by the greedy governments of the West."* Only by war could the people of the East claim what was "rightfully" theirs.

The rallying cry was all that was needed for the thousands of rogue soldiers who had been wandering the countryside, especially in the south ever since the break-up of the Mid-Aks and the destruction of The Family. Making war was their trade. Most of them carried a festering hatred for the forces that now made up the armies of the West, for it was these same warriors who had defeated them in the North-east and at Football City. Along in the ranks with these veterans were the raiders, bandits and outlaws who knew it was more profitable to fight with an army than on their own. Many grounded air pirates—no longer able to keep a working jet fighter in order—joined up too, a number of whom became officers in the ever-expanding army.

But it was the raw youth of the East—teenagers who were too young to fight in the big war and had grown older in New Order America—who filled the infantry ranks of The Circle Army. Living a hand-to-mouth existence for several years made these recruits particularly vulnerable to Viktor's brand of adolescent propaganda. It was widely rumored that, per Viktor's orders, the chow at the recruiting camps was liberally sprinkled with feel-good drugs. Long hours of indoctrination followed for a new recruit, along with rudimentary military training and a promise of a bag of gold once The Circle captured California. In six weeks, The Circle had its "perfect grunt": drug-addicted, brainwashed, armed and foaming at the mouth.

So with this unhealthy mixture of cynical battle-hardened veterans, whipped-up teenage fodder and many freed prisoners, habitual criminals, psychotic murderers thrown in, the Circle Army could boast close to 180,000 men under arms. All under the tight control of the minions of the mysterious Viktor—a man they had never laid eyes on in the flesh.

And conveniently unmentioned in all the hoopla was that the Russians would be providing air defense cover over the frontline in the catastrophic war to come . . .

Hunter started to get shivers about a hundred miles south of Devil's Tower.

The sun was just setting on the day he began in Hawaii. His body was pumping with adrenaline. The news of the frenzy sweeping the East was upsetting, but he couldn't let it get to him. The importance of the recovery mission had long ago overridden the less human concerns, such as peace of mind, eating a good meal or sleeping. His concentration had to remain focused on retrieving the second black box. The massacred convoys. The retreats from Syracuse and Football City. The Russian SAMs. The Circle. The slaughter that was about to begin. Dominique. Everything had to become secondary. Just get the box, he told himself.

Yet it was the spookiness of the landscape below

him that was nearly overwhelming. The fact that the rugged countryside of Wyoming was now supposedly the home to many renegade Indian gangs did nothing to lighten up the situation. If he believed just half the stories going around, then were he forced down here for any reason, his chances of getting out were just as bad—if not worse—than being stranded in the Badlands.

Devil's Tower was a conical mountain with a strangely flattened-out summit, located in the northeast corner of Wyoming. Theories ranging from a backfired volcano to an ancient landing site for UFOs were thrown out as explanations for its unusual shape. Whatever the reason, Hunter's own deep psyche and extraordinary senses all signaled that strange forces resided near the place. Airline as well as service pilots avoided going near the remote area whenever possible, pointing to screwed up instruments and incorrect readings any time they had to overfly the place. And reports of strange lights in the skies had become routine over the years.

And once again, no one could ever accuse General Josephs of not having a vivid imagination: The second black box was reportedly hidden in "an altar-like stone at the very center of the Tower's flat peak." For Hunter, the whole thing was like something out of a science fiction movie.

He brought the Yak because he knew a vertical landing on the Tower's flat peak was the only way he could retrieve the black box quickly. But as the airplane drew closer to the place, it started acting up. At first he thought it was just the shitty Russian cockpit instruments. The airplane was so crude by American jet fighter standards, even he had a hard time figuring out just what every button and lever was really for.

But now everything seemed to be going haywire at once. Lights flashed on his panel simultaneously indicating that he was out of fuel, half full and at full fuel maximum. His altimeters—one electric, one pressure-driven—told him he was 10 feet off the ground or at 87,400 feet, take your pick. At one point, his "Missiles Away" indicator light came on, went off, came back on then started to blink as if to mock him.

He decided to ignore the airplane's wacky instruments and fly it on instinct. He climbed to 30,000 feet and started to widely circle the mountain. Right away he knew there was trouble below. He could see lights—red, yellow, green—ringing the top of the Tower. Some were blinking, others not. Immediately the "landing site" theory leaped into his mind. The way the lights were laid out, it did look as if whoever installed them expected something to come out of the sky and set down there.

He lowered down to 30,000 then 25,000. All the while he had the airplane on a portside bank, allowing him to focus in on the lights and the Tower below. Down to 20,000, then 17,000. At 15,500, he flipped the switch which started the jet's thrust turning from the horizontal to the vertical. It allowed him to slow down and finally hover long enough to take photos with the infrared camera he brought along. The Russian fighter had nothing even approaching the sophistication of an outside infra-red camera mounting. This one he'd have to do the old-fashioned way—by hand.

He stayed hovering just long enough to snap a picture and then he sped away. He realized it had been wishful thinking to expect the top of the Tower to be deserted. The lights meant people and he instinctively knew those people wouldn't provide him with a friendly welcoming committee.

Hunter set the airplane down at a remote location about five miles from the Tower. Using a flashlight and a small bag of chemicals he'd brought along, the pilot quickly developed the photo he'd taken. Just as he suspected, the picture revealed about 25 individuals on top of the Tower. They didn't have anything heavy—the photo showed no heat emissions indicating missiles or serious anti-aircraft guns. But Hunter had to assume they were carrying personal arms; weapons that could damage the Yak.

He had no choice. He would have to climb the Tower and recon the top up close. He sandwiched the Yak between two trees. Then with his M-16 in hand, he set out for the strange mountain.

Hunter didn't believe in ghosts, per se. And he was aware that at night, in an unfamiliar location, the human senses reacted in such a way as to heighten the intensity of the slightest potential of strangeness going on around them. An owl's call might sound as if it were being broadcast from a loud and deep echo chamber. The wind might feel like it's whipping by at

90 MPH. The moon may appear twice as large as it really was. A simple shooting star might look like an inter-galactic starship streaking overhead. The mind plays tricks on the body, and the senses short-circuit as a result.

But as much as Hunter tried to convince himself of all this as he scrambled across the plain approaching the Devil's Tower, there was some pretty strange shit going on around him that he couldn't explain away. The wind *was* blowing so hard it nearly yanked his flight helmet from his head. And that *was* the loudest owl he'd ever heard—at least he thought it was an owl. And that Goddamn moon was so big, it was taking up half the sky!

And if that thing that flew over his head really was a meteorite—it was the first one he'd ever seen that was shaped like a cigar and carried a bunch of blinking lights underneath it.

He pressed on, the M-16 now off his shoulder and in his hands, the safety clicked off. The Tower loomed ahead, bathed in the incredibly bright light of the oversized moon. Again, he grudgingly admired General Josephs for selecting this area to hide the second black box. He vowed he would never return here without anything less than a couple of the Crazy Eights and about 100 of Dozer's best troopers.

He saw more lights in the sky—initially these looked like genuine shooting stars. First one, then another, then another. Soon they were falling in twos and threes. Then fours and fives. Inside of two minutes, they were coming down like raindrops in a summer shower. Hunter was baffled by it—sometimes the sky in August was lit up with meteorites—but this was only May.

He came to almost ignore the strange falling lights and finally reached the base of the Tower. That's when he heard the voices . . .

At first it seemed as if someone was standing right over his shoulder, talking into his ear. He instinctively spun around, but no one was there. Then it sounded as if the voices were farther away. Then he heard a shout—echoed like the owl's hoot. Then more voices. They were jumbled up, making no sense, and in no particular language, more like a murmuring. First in front of him, then off to his left. Then to his right, then behind him. Then from all directions at once.

"Fuck this," he muttered. He didn't have time to pay attention to all the weirdness around him. If someone—or something—approached him, he'd just empty the M-16 into them. Simple as that.

He soon located the most climbable section of the mountain and started to scramble up.

It took him nearly two hours to reach the Tower's summit. Throughout his trip, the voices got louder. The shooting stars waned, then returned. And the moon got even bigger. It all became secondary—he was concentrating on how he would deal with whoever the hell was living on top of the Godforsaken place.

Chanting. That's the noise that stuck out most. Chanting at the top of the Tower. He double-checked the M-16 magazine. There were no signs of sentries or a defense perimeter, nothing which would indicate the people at the top were snuff military types. That was fine with him.

Finally he reached the top. Looking over a mound of boulders he could see right down onto the leveled section of the mountain. It was about the size of a football field, he determined, but round, almost like it *was* a volcano at one time but the lava had barely reached the top when it coagulated and formed the platform.

There were people down there. Indians. Not like the Native Americans he had come to know and admire back in Oregon. These people were dressed and painted just like Indians he'd seen in the movies. They were also armed to the teeth. He spotted rifles, shotguns, and at least two machineguns set up on the edge of the platform.

The Indians were chanting and whooping it up in a primitive-looking war dance step, circling a huge bonfire they'd built. The lights he'd spotted were anything but primitive—they looked to be arc lamps of some kind. Color filters—red, green, yellow—like the type used on searchlights, covered about half of them. The others were bare white.

Then he saw the box. It would have been hard to miss. Right at the edge of the Tower's platform there was what could only be described as "an altar-like stone." And, sure enough, there on top of it was the small black box, its small red light obediently blinking away.

But there was also a photograph on top of the altar. Hunter was astonished to see it was a picture of a B-1. Then he started to notice other things. One Indian had what looked like a B-1 painted his bare back. Another carried a spear that had a small B-1 shape carved out at the top. Then he saw a half dozen Indians appear, carrying crudely carved pieces of wood that resembled the distinctive shape of the B-1.

The study of primitive religions had always fascinated him, and this one would probably fill a textbook. The warriors were *worshipping* an idol shaped like a B-1. He had heard of a similar case reported during World War II in the South Pacific. Natives on an out-of-the-way island had never seen a white man before until the Marines landed and started hacking away at the jungle to make landing strips. The natives had never seen airplanes before either. When the landing strip was finished and the supply airplanes came, some of the barter—cigarettes, chocolate, whatever—was given to the natives as goodwill presents. The more airplanes that came, the more presents they got. Soon enough, the natives came to worship the airplanes. And why not? The big birds brought them good things from the sky. For their culture, that was as god-like as you could get. When the war moved on and the Americans moved out, the airplanes stopped coming. Confused, the natives built crude wooden airplane-shaped idols and set them up all over the island, as if displaying something that looked like an airplane would cause one to swoop down and land.

Hunter was convinced that same kind of idol worship was in force on top of the Tower. Somehow, these Indians—probably one of the more isolated tribes—knew there was a connection between the black box and the B-1. By displaying the box and carrying airplane-like shapes, the Indians were praying, chanting, almost pleading for a B-1 to come down out of the sky.

Hunter had to shake his head. With all the weird stuff flying around the skies near the Tower, the Indians chose a B-1 to pray to. He sniffed the air. Well, he thought, maybe all that peyote he smelled had something to do with it.

The air was thick with it. He could see the warriors ceremoniously passing a pipe around, and he could tell by the distinctive yellow curling smoke that they were inhaling a form of *ka-rac-hee*, or smokable peyote.

He would have loved to have stayed and observed the dancing and chanting all night, but he had a job to do. Get the box. And now, he thought as he scrambled back down the mountain, he knew how he was going to do it.

The night sky was spinning . . .

"See the stars fall from the sky!" the Indian named Katcheewan chanted. He raised his arms over his head, one hand holding an M-16 decorated with tribal feathers and ornaments, the other holding a rattle-like instrument called a *wan-tauk*. "Hear the owl!" he bellowed. "The wind sings! The voices of the dead are with us!"

The other 24 Indians sat transfixed, their eyes cast

deep in the shaman's hypnotic spell.

"Tonight!" Katcheewan whispered dramatically, pointing the *wan-tauk* first at the blinking black box that sat on the stone before him, then to the crystal-clear full moon directly above them. "The moon fills up the sky!"

The sweet smell of peyote smoke was everywhere, swirling with the winds that sporadically buffeted the top of the Devil's Tower. The brightness of the moon and the light of the raging bonfire combined to cast the most eerie of shadows around the band of warriors.

Katcheewan—himself into a peyote-induced trance so deep, his eyes had turned red—slowly began to rattle the *wan-tauk*.

"Tonight!" the shaman yelled, his voice rising an octave and startling the other Indians. "The wind tells me it comes!"

As one, the group raised its eyes and stared out into the night sky. Shooting stars were falling everywhere. Never had they'd seen a night so fantastic.

Off in the distance a rumbling sound deeper and louder than the wind arose. It was coming from the east. The noise slowly turned to even deeper thunder as it drew closer to the Tower.

Katcheewan saw it first. It was just a speck with a faint thin flame spitting out beneath it. The object moved slowly into silhouette in the large white moon, at which time all the Indians saw it. A gasp ran through the warriors.

"It comes . . ." one warrior shouted out in awe. The other Indians instinctively started chanting in low, moaning voices. Katcheewan himself felt paralyzed. He was unable to take his eyes off the strange flying object.

It moved to the center of the moon, then seemed to stop. The flames emitted underneath it turned from yellow to bright white and grew in intensity. The object hovered for a moment. Then it started to move toward them.

A chorus of frightened yelps came from the warriors, some breaking from their cross-legged sitting positions. Katcheewan wanted to yell to them to stay where they were and to not be afraid, but he could not speak. The words would not come out. The object grew larger as it came closer. The noise was getting very loud, by now drowning out all evidence of the high wind. Not one of the warriors thought to raise his M-16.

Now the object was directly above them, no more than 200 feet away. Katcheewan—his mind swimming in a mixture of surprise and shock—could not even shake the *wan-tauk*. He watched as the intense white flame took on a tinge of deep blue. By now the noise was a thunder, never ending, getting louder. Some of his warriors fled to the nearby rocks; others sat like stones, unable or unwilling to move. They had come south to the Tower 12 seasons before from deep in the Caribou Mountains of northern Alberta. Of them all, only Katcheewan had ever seen an airplane, and that was only once.

But he had never seen anything like this. The object was very close. So close, they could make out its silver color and the large red star bordered in yellow painted on its side. As many as ten blinking lights flashed from its wings and tail. The power of the flame was kicking up dust and stones on the platform as the craft hung barely 100 feet above them.

Suddenly its nose burst into flame. Streaks of light shot out from it, adding the combined sound of hundreds of explosions to the already excruciating noise of its whining engine. The craft started to turn slowly, streams of tracer lights still emitting from its snout. Another half dozen Indians jumped up and fled to relative safety of the rocks. Still, Katcheewan could not move.

The craft completed its circle and the firing from the nose ceased. The engine noise now reached its peak and the downward wind thrust was like a hurricane. It was coming straight down. Still a few die-hard warriors stayed in their places, their peyote-resin soaked blood pumping rapidly through their bodies.

Somewhere deep in his diaphragm, Katcheewan found the strength to scream: "It comes!" Then his eyes rolled up into the back of his head and he collapsed in shock. Seeing their leader fall was all it took for the rest of the Indians to scatter. From their ledgework hiding places they saw the craft come down and land next to the stone altar where the blinking box lay. They could see a figure, wearing a strange white headpiece sitting inside a glass bubble at the front of the strange craft.

Suddenly the bubble burst upward and the man stood up. He raised his right hand, causing some of the Indians to cower behind the rocks in case the god was going to strike out a lightning bolt in their direction. He did not. Instead the figure climbed out of the broken bubble, stepped onto the craft's wing, then leaped to the ground. The light from the still raging bonfire reflected off his suit.

Thankfully, he didn't approach the warriors. Instead he walked to the altar, picked up the black box, then quickly returned to the craft. Sitting back down inside, the figure somehow made the bubble top come together with the rest of the craft.

Then with a roar and a flash of fire, the craft started to shake, then move. Slowly it began to ascend into the night sky. Some of the Indians stood now and watched as the craft rose high above them. A reassuring chant rose up from them as the object climbed back into the light of the moon, getting smaller by the instant.

When the craft was as small as when they first spotted it, they heard one last burst of noise and saw another long streak of flame come out of its tail. Then it suddenly shot forward and was gone . . .

the Indian [illegible] expect him to make [illegible] was going to strike out a lightning bolt in their direction. He did not. Instead the flame climbed out of the [illegible] and [illegible] dropped onto the [illegible] then seemed to the ground. The [illegible] from the still gazing [illegible] collected all the way.

Thankfully, he didn't approach the warriors. Instead he walked to the altar, picked up the black box, then quickly returned to the craft. Sliding back down inside, the figure squeezed inside the bubble top cover together with the rest of the craft.

Then with a roar and a flash of fire, the craft started to shake, then rose. Slowly it began to ascend into the night sky. Some of the Indians stood now and watched as the craft rose high above them. A reassuring chant rose up from them as the object jumped back into the light of the moon, getting smaller by the instant.

When the craft was as small as what they had spotted it, they heard the last burst of noise and saw another long streak of flame come out of its tail. Then it suddenly shot forward and was gone.

Chapter Eighteen

Jones was waiting on the tarmac when the Yak landed.

Two runways over, a pair of A-7 "Strikefighters" roared away on take-off. Almost immediately, two more taxied out onto the strip and awaited permission to go. In back of them waited two F-106's. Then another pair of A-7's.

The VTOL craft settled down and Hunter jumped out. Jones saw the box and shook Hunter's hand. "All right, Hawk," he said breaking out in an appreciative grin. "How to come through, buddy."

"Two down, three to go," Hunter said, taking off his helmet for the first time in what seemed like days. He ran his hand through his long, sandy hair and looked around the base. The place was jumping with activity.

"You've found a forward base?" Hunter asked the general, correctly interpreting the reason behind all the hustle.

"Yes, old Denver airport," Jones replied, leading the pilot toward the base's all-purpose mess hall/

saloon. "The city is deserted, of course. But the airport's big and it's got good mountain cover all around. We've found places to stick our mobile radar units and our own SAMs. The runways are still in good shape as are the maintenance shops."

"What's the word from Fitz and St. Louie?" Hunter asked. He was anxious to find out about his two friends.

"All reports are go," Jones told him. "Everyone got out clean in both Syracuse and Football City. The F-20s are down in Dallas and Fitzie's '105s are sitting up in Winnipeg, waiting for us to tell them where to go."

"Anything else from the Texans?" Hunter asked as they reached the mess hall.

"They were raided again during the night, I'm afraid," Jones said, claiming the first table they could find. "They hit a place called Pampa, up near Amarillo. Really tore it up."

"Same pattern?" Hunter asked.

"Yep," Jones said. "Cavalry. Yaks. Hit and run. The town is fairly large, so they would seem to be getting bolder. More willing to take on big targets."

"This is not good news," Hunter said, reaching for the coffee pot a waitress had produced.

"It gets worse," Jones said grimly. "The Texans did a photo recon overflight of New Orleans harbor this morning. The place is lousy with Russian subs."

"Holy Christ," Hunter said softly.

"And they weren't little tin cans either," Jones continued. "Those were big boys. Nuclear jobs. They took a shot of them hauling long metal cylinders out of the missile tubes. They're probably bringing either more mean high-explosive, or SAM fuel."

"Probably," Hunter agreed. "They figure the tubes would protect them if something went unstable."

"There is some good news," Jones said. "Word's getting around pretty quick. Not just about The Circle, but about the Russians, too. We have guys—volunteers—pouring into San Diego. Small militias and stuff, looking to sign up. And, the Texans tell us that people are crossing over from Louisiana and Arkansas who want no part of the Reds, or The Circle or Viktor. Canadians say the same thing. To make it easier, we've agreed to be known as the Western Forces."

"Well, every last guy will help," Hunter replied. "What about the regular Free Canadian Army?"

"Frost is up in Montreal right now," the general told him. "The Canadians want to help—but they can't send their entire army down. It would leave them too unprotected."

"I can understand that," Hunter agreed. "There are a lot of people from the USA up there. It's risking too much."

"They did say they'd have two divisions waiting at the border near Winnipeg. They'll intervene if we need them. They'll also 'encourage' volunteers and they'll take up our Northwest Approach air patrols."

Hunter was glad to hear that. With the Free Canadians watching over the territory from Alaska over to Siberia, more PAAC aircraft would be freed up to join the fight over the Badlands.

Their waitress reappeared with a bowl of scrambled eggs and a string of sausages. Hunter immediately dug in.

"How are things at Eureka going?" he asked between mouthfuls.

"Slow," Jones said, lowering his voice a meter. "They finished all the engine work, no problem, and began to work on the avionics. But it's so complicated they have to start at square one just about. We have some great guys working on it. Wa and Twomey are there, as you know, plus a lot of former CalTech people. But they're expected to figure out in a matter of weeks what it took the U.S. Government years to put together."

"I don't envy them," Hunter said. "Compared to what they have to do, I've got the easy job, just getting the boxes."

Jones nodded gravely. "All we can hope for is that you get Boxes three, four, and five and when it gets down to the nitty-gritty,—the final battle, so to speak—we'll have the B-1s up and operating."

Hunter wolfed down the rest of the eggs, drained a cup of coffee and prepared to leave. "Well, I'd better get the '16 up and running. I'd like to be down by the Grand Canyon by noon."

He looked at the general and was troubled to see an especially grim look come across his features. "There's one more thing, Hawk," Jones began. "You'd better sit down."

Hunter was back down in an instant.

"Hawk, Dozer and his guys ran across a plane wreck out on the border of Colorado and Kansas, near the Smoky Hill River," he told him.

"One of ours?" Hunter asked, mystified.

"No," Jones said. "One of theirs. Looked like an L-1011 converted for cargo. It was an accidental crash. They found one of its engines first, about fifteen miles from the rest of wreckage. Dozer figures the engine probably came off in flight. I don't imagine The Circle has high air maintenance standards, so the thing probably ran out of oil."

"So?" Hunter said. "What was it carrying?"

Jones looked at him for a moment, then took off his cap and scratched his wiffle-cut head. He slipped an envelope out of his pocket. "This," he said, handing it to Hunter.

Hunter took the envelope and ripped it open. He felt a lightning bolt come up his spine and explode in his brain. It was yet another photo of Dominique. Same shot, same pose.

"It's weird, Hawk," Jones said. "The whole God-damn airplane was filled with them!"

Hunter looked at him. "What does you mean, sir?"

"I mean there were crates of them," Jones said, leaning forward and speaking in an urgent whisper. "Thousands—tens of thousands of copies of the same picture."

"This is crazy . . . " Hunter said.

"Hawk, I can't imagine what the hell is going on," Jones said. "The Russians, The Circle, this Viktor guy—these things I can understand. But what the hell is it with these pictures? It looks as if they were going to drop them. Spread 'em around like propaganda leaflets or something."

Hunter could only shake his head and stare at the photo. Would he ever know?

Chapter Nineteen

The Grand Canyon black box was hidden in a very unusual place. Yet Hunter had been there several times before.

It was a secret airstrip that the CIA had built years before the Third World War; a place where ultra-sensitive aircraft could land and take off from without anyone outside The Company knowing about it. Hunter knew the place existed during his Thunderbird days at Nellis Air Force Base at Las Vegas not a hundred miles to the west. At that time, he was asked to fly "special" visitors to the secret base on occasion. The approach to the strip was very tricky by design and thus, the best Thunderbird pilot was always asked to go.

He'd been to the secret base—code named Phantom Ranch Ringo—a half dozen times. Yet he'd never actually met anyone who was stationed at the secret base except for the ground crew. His missions had called for him to fly in the "guests"—always in the jump seat of a specially-equipped F-5—drop them off then *vamoose*. Because the strip was so short, a launch-and-recovery arrangement—taken right off an aircraft carrier—was installed. It involved an arresting gear setup which would catch the hook especially attached to the bottom of the F-5 allowing it to come to a dead stop very quickly and a very powerful catapult system that launched him for the return flight. How the CIA got all the equipment to the bottom of the canyon and working was beyond him.

Now he knew that black box 3 was hidden at the base, specifically in a laboratory that was built right into the solid rock wall close by the landing strip. In theory, he would fly into the canyon, check to see if the arresting gear was still in place, set down if it was, then get the box and leave by way of catapult. The alternative would involve a long, time-consuming climb down.

He and Jones had discussed this part of the recovery mission at length. Really it was a job for a helicoper strike force—and they would have sent one, except for one thing. While no one really knew what the hell was going on in the Grand Canyon these days, the rumors were that right-wing fanatics—mostly from Utah—had retreated to the canyon after the war. The stories went on to say that these fanatics were well-armed and had adopted a "shoot first" attitude. Several small airplanes had been shot down around the canyon in the past two years and not just with small arms fire. A convoy airliner that had run into fuel trouble a year before had to fly low over the canyon while attempting to land at the deserted Nellis. Someone fired a small surface-to-air missile at the airplane, just missing it. Jones and Hunter were aware of the incident at the time, but in the wild and wooly New Order America, they couldn't go around wasting valuable time, men and equipment chasing down every radical with a SAM launcher.

But now Hunter had to go back and he had to do it in the airplane which would give him maximum maneuverability, firepower and escape potential. There was never any question that he'd take his F-16. In fact, while he was recovering the black box 2 from Wyoming, the PAAC monkey crew had worked round the clock and installed a Navy-style arrester hook on the belly of his jet.

It was uncommonly overcast above the canyon when he arrived around noontime. He knew that ever since the Soviets had nuked the Badlands the continent's weather patterns had changed—still a foggy cloud bank enveloping the crevices of the canyon was highly unusual.

He brought the jet fighter down to barely 1000 feet and located the western mouth of the canyon near Lake Mead. Dropping even lower, he found the clouds ended completely at 500 feet.

The secret base was cleverly hidden about 100 miles east of Lake Mead, in an extremely narrow and isolated part of the canyon. Built near an outcrop of rock that was nearly inaccessible by foot, when viewed from the air, one could only see canyon walls and the Colorado River snaking its way through. The buildings, the arresting gear and the catapult were all hidden from casual view. Only someone flying low off the river and expertly following two very hairy miles of the twists and turns of the canyon floor could reach the place. It was so well hidden that only a handful of the many excursion pilots that had flown the canyon before the war had tripped over the installation. When they did, the CIA tracked them down—then offered them a lucrative flying job. Only the most courageous or craziest of pilots would dare to fly the narrows that led to the base. But those were two qualities in demand at the CIA any time.

Hunter located several landmarks and slowly brought the F-16's airspeed down to barely 150 knots. Just off Steamboat Mountain, he carefully descended until he was below the rim of the canyon. Further down he went, gingerly edging the '16's right side control stick back and forth, staying with the twists of the river below.

Soon he was just 50 feet off the water and his airspeed was down to 120 knots. He started to pick up some more fairly familiar landmarks. A cliff here, a set of rapids there. Although he'd had only flown the secret missions here years before at night, he had guided his way in then using a helmet-attached "NightScope." The device made the flights seem like flying in the clearest of daylight.

He recognized a bend in the river ahead as the two-miles-to-go landmark. He applied his airbrakes and lower his landing gear, reducing his speed to just 110 knots. He inched his way down to 40 feet off the deck. Above him he could see the outcrops of rocks jutting out this way and that. This was the hairy part. If any trouble developed, he could not pull up without smashing into one of the overhangs. All he had to do was keep it slow and steady and hope that the arresting cables were still there . . .

Bang!

Suddenly something hit his starboard wing. He turned to see a hole had drilled clearly through and a wispy stream of fuel starting to leak from the wound . . .

Bang!

Something—probably a .20 mm cannon shell—went through his port wing, just at the tip, close to his wingtip-mounted Sidewinder . . .

Bang! Bang! Bang!

In a matter of seconds the air around him and in front of him was filled with streaks of anti-aircraft fire. He reacted quickly: he couldn't go up, so dropped down, all the time trying to identify the source of the gunfire. Then he saw puffs of smoke—hundreds of them coming from guns hidden in every crevice and crack on both sides of the canyon wall. Only by his rocking of the F-16 in the narrows did he avoid getting hit.

Up ahead he could see the firing was even more intense. But at the same time, it was sporadically placed. The gunners—whoever they were—weren't aiming at him as much as setting up a wall of lead, which made it impossible for anything to get through. Bullets were glancing off the wings and body. He had no choice. He put the '16 into a 180-degree roll—the tightest he'd ever performed. As most of the gunfire was coming from above him, he'd much rather take some hits on the bottom of the airplane than the top.

But the maneuver was not enough. He still had at least a mile and a half to go. He had to fight back . . .

He couldn't imagine this many gunners were hiding in the canyon just waiting for some airborne intruder to pass through. Then he got an idea. He immediately punched his Electronic Counter Measures console and heard the reassuring whine as the variety of radio jamming equipment came on.

Suddenly the firing stopped. His gamble worked. He realized that these weren't humans shooting at him—they were robot-controlled anti-aircraft guns. The CIA must have installed the things to finish off anyone—like a single fighter or even a cruise missile—they judged hostile before it even reached the base. His ECM equipment was effectively jamming the signals, confusing the guns' automatic fire system and bringing the attack to a halt.

But Hunter felt far from secure. Someone had activated the robot-controlled gauntlet—someone who didn't want anybody getting into the base. The fact that his airplane was equipped with ECM counter-measures was the only reason he was still in one piece. Most of the aircraft flying around these days considered ECM equipment as an expensive and hard-to-maintain luxury.

He could see the secret base less than a mile ahead of him. In an instant he knew that the arresting gear was still in working order, because there was another jet—a banged-up Lear—sitting next to the midget runway. The only way it could have landed safely was to use the arresting device. He switched on his forward-looking topographic infra-red radar system and got a clear TV picture of the base. He could see at least seven individuals running about the installation. Obviously, they knew they were about to have some uninvited company dropping in.

Suddenly, a warning light flashed on his control panel. Someone had launched a small SAM at him. His ECM was still working, but it wasn't needed. Whoever fired the missile was an amateur—and that was being generous. The SAM—it looked like a Stinger—bounced off the canyon wall about a quarter mile from his position, exploded and fell into the river causing a minor avalanche in the process.

He pressed on. He had two options and he was running out of time. One choice was to rip up the base with his Vulcan cannon six pack then pull up, go around again, survey the damage, before going around a third time and trying to land. He didn't want to shoot up the place for fear of destroying the precious black box . . . Suddenly he knew he didn't have time to consider option one. The fuel leak from the hit on his starboard wing had just gone from bad to worse.

He had no choice but to set the F-16 down.

He cut back his powerful engine to almost nothing, lowered the specially-installed arrester hook and crossed his fingers . . .

The F-16 hit the arresting wire at 105 knots. With a great squealing of tires and a cloud of dust, the airplane jerked to a halt in less than two seconds. It was more of a controlled crash than a landing. Now Hunter knew why the Navy flyboys described carrier landings like "having sex in a car wreck."

When the smoke and dust cleared he saw he was on a small stretch of sandy beach, no more than a quarter mile long. The escape catapult was about 300 yards directly in front of him. A dangerous set of Colorado River rapids cascaded nearby. The base looked the same as when he flew the secret missions in some years before—nothing more than four concrete bunkers built into the side of the canyon wall.

He immediately popped the canopy and leaped out of the jet fighter, his M-16 up and ready.

That's when he saw the naked woman . . .

She was tall, thin with blond hair flowing almost to her waist. On second look, he realized she wasn't completely naked—she was wearing the thinnest of bikini bottoms, but that was it. She was standing about 25 feet away next to one of the concrete bunkers. She was also aiming an M-16 at him . . .

He held his hand up to a gesture of peace.

"How!" he called to her. "Friend . . . "

She lowered the gun slightly. Then another woman appeared from behind the bunker. She was smaller, a brunette with shorter hair, but besides an even skimpier bikini brief, quite naked, too. She was carrying a shotgun.

He clicked the safety off his M-16, though he would never use it against the women. Slowly he walked toward them, his right hand still raised.

"Go away," the blonde yelled.

"I need fuel," he told them. "Your robots back there are pretty good shots." He was having a hard time keeping his eyes on their weapons and off their beautiful, bare breasts. Both women were gorgeous.

"Who are you?" he heard a third voice call out. Off to the left of the two women, a third emerged from behind a large, arrowhead shaped boulder. She was a redhead, clad in cut-off dungarees, but also naked to the waist. Her breasts were, in a word, enormous.

Hunter felt like he had dropped in on an X-rated Amazon movie.

"I'm Major Hawk Hunter," he called out. "From the Pacific American Air Corps. I'm a friend, if you are. I took a hit back there on my gas line."

He was walking slowly toward them all the time and could see they were slowly relenting to him. The closer he got, the younger he realized the women were. The blonde couldn't have been 23, the brunette and the redhead even younger.

He finally stopped about ten feet from them. "Who are you, girls?" The question came from nowhere. He just had to know.

"We're members of the Church of the Canyon," the redhead said to him as she walked over to join the others. "You're trespassing on our property."

"Well, I'm sorry, ladies," Hunter said. "But I'm on a very important mission. I have to retrieve something—a black box—that I've been told is hidden here. Have you seen such a thing here?"

The women looked at each other. The redhead seemed to be the spokesperson for the group. "Maybe," she said, her interest growing. "What do you need it for?"

Hunter wanted to keep it simple. "My commanding officer needs it to get an old airplane of his back up and flying."

The redhead smiled at him, while the other two

girls broke into a giggle. "You mean the B-1s Project Ghost Rider of Eureka?"

Hunter was startled. How would she know that?

"Surprised, flyboy?" the redhead asked. She nonchalantly cupped her huge breasts in her hands and gave them a seductive scratch. Hunter felt his biological juices starting to act up.

"How do you know about 'Ghost Rider' " he asked.

The women laughed again. "That's all we hear about," the blonde said.

"From whom?" Hunter was determined to get to the bottom of this one.

"From our 'high priest,' " the brunette said, lowering the shotgun completely.

" 'High' is right," the redhead said with a laugh. She walked forward and extended her hand. "My name is Tracy," she said, shaking his leather-gloved hand. "This is Stacy and Lacey."

Tracy, Stacy, and Lacey?

"Or at least those are the names he gave us," Tracy said.

"Who's 'he'?" Hunter asked.

"Our fearless leader," said Stacy, the blonde. "Come on, we'll show you."

They led him to the door of the first bunker. The place looked like someone had jammed a concrete quonset hut into a wall of sheer granite. Hunter knew the bunker was built that way by the CIA for one reason: It was nuke proof.

Stacy opened the door and the three women allowed Hunter to go in first. It was dark inside, the only light being provided by about a dozen candles. The air was thick with a sickly sweet smell of incense mixed with the unmistakable scent of marijuana. There was music playing somewhere—a prickly, sour pinging that Hunter recognized as an Indian sitar. He had once owned one.

He was aware of several bodies moving at the far end of the bunker's first room. Stacy closed the heavy metal door behind them and Hunter's eyes instantly adjusted to the darkness. He saw a man, dressed in dingy white robes, sitting on a large chair in the bunker's far corner. He had shoulder-length scraggly brown hair, a long, apparently unwashed beard, a headband and rose-colored sunglasses. He was drowzily smoking an elaborate looking water pipe.

Around him were four more girls. All of them absolutely naked—Hunter was sure of it this time. Water pipes lay strewn around the floor near them. One of the women had her head on the man's right knee, her hand buried in his crotch. It didn't mater; she was asleep. Another woman lay at the man's feet. She, too, was out like a light. The two other women were embracing and kissing each other. Amidst the cloud of reefer smoke, Hunter thought he detected a whiff of opium.

"Major Hunter," he said, hoping to wake the nodding man. "P-A-A-C."

The man looked up. "Hunter?" he said, barely mumbling the name. "Hawk Hunter?"

The pilot was surprised. Did this man know him?

"Yes," he replied. "Hawk Hunter."

The man took off his sunglasses and even in the flickering candlelight, Hunter could see his eyes were bloodshot beyond recognition. He shakily pointed at Hunter and managed to wheeze out: "Eur-ee-ka!"

This was not some ordinary kook. Hunter took a good look at the man. Despite the long hair and beard, he knew he'd seen the man somewhere before.

"How do you know about 'Ghost Rider' and Eureka?" Hunter asked him.

"Ha! I know all about it," the man said. A smile washed across his face, revealing a jagged set of teeth. "And I know all about Hawk Hunter."

Then Hunter knew where he'd seen the man. It was in a photograph Jones had showed him. The man was Captain Travis, General Josephs' aide-de-camp! This was the very man who, at Josephs' direction, hid the black boxes.

"Hawk Hunter," Travis said. "I saw you fly in an air show at Nellis. It was incredible, girls. I didn't think an airplane could move like that."

"What the hell is going on here, Travis?" Hunter said sharply, and loud enough to wake up the woman at the man's feet.

"I am holding my position, Hunter," Travis said with an air of woozy importance. "I'm guarding the black box. Following orders."

"Whose orders?" Hunter demanded. The man was a disgrace. Hunter would never condemn anyone for partying every once in a while, but the self-indulgence here was a joke.

"Josephs," the man blurted out, a stream of drool oozing out of the side of his mouth. "My general."

"Who are these girls, Captain?" Hunter asked.

"Believe it or not," the man said, another gross-out smile spreading across his face. "They used to be my secretaries. And look what I've done with them. They are now my goddesses. I am their priest. We are the Church, Major Hunter. The Church of the Canyon."

Tracy came up and stood so close to Hunter he could feel her massive breasts brush against his flight suit. "Some priest," she laughed. "He so zonked out all of the time, he couldn't get it up on a bet. Look at Teresa and Isabelle. They have to make it with each other they need it so bad."

Hunter couldn't help but watch the two girls passionately kiss each other. Suddenly he though of Aki and Mio back home in Oregon.

Hunter couldn't waste any more time. "Look Travis, where's the Goddamn box?"

The man looked at him. "What's the rush, Major? Stay here with us. Hang out for a while. Lookit these girls, we got plenty go round . . . "

Hunter started to boil. "I know you haven't the faintest idea of what the hell is going down in the Badlands right now, Captain. And I'm not about to explain it to you. Just give me the box and I'm gone."

"It had better be for a good reason," Travis blathered out, a gooey thread of spittle spilling out of his mouth. "The general didn't want . . . just any bozo . . . to get into . . . Ghost Rider." With that he slumped in his crude throne, and lapsed into a drug-induced blackout.

Hunter was tempted to slap the man awake. It was the continent's most critical hour and here he was, dealing with a konked-out, drooling idiot.

He turned to Tracy. "What exactly did he tell you about Ghost Rider?"

She thought a moment. "He was always claiming that he was on this big deal secret mission. We were secretaries at the Eureka base, but we didn't know what was going on, of course. He says his commander told him to hide four black boxes and bring the fifth one here. He was flying all over the place when the war broke out. Hawaii, Wyoming, somewhere. New York City."

"Did he ever say *where* in New York City?"

She nodded. "He sold it to some guy named Calypso."

Hunter was shocked. *"Sold it?"*

"I'm afraid so," the pretty redhead replied. "He used the money to buy all the drugs you see around here."

Calypso. Well, thought Hunter, at least he had some kind of clue to go into New York City with.

"How about the box in New Mexico?" Hunter asked. "Did he ever say where that one went?"

"I'm not sure," she answered. "Some little dinky town in New Mexico."

"Pecos?" Hunter asked.

"That's the place," Tracy confirmed. "That's the last place he landed before coming here. Said it was really scary. That he had to—get this—fight a huge monster to hide the box. That's also where he picked up all the dope.

"When the New Order came down, he had already told us about this place. Things looked hairy, so we bribed a chopper pilot to drop us here. By that time, the CIA boys were long gone. And they left the place unlocked! Travis landed in the Lear a few days later, stoned on his ass. Cracked up the airplane for good. Told us we were all under orders to protect the box until the right someone came for it. I guess that someone is you . . . "

"Can you get it for me?" Hunter asked, an element of charm sneaking into his voice.

She looked him straight in the eye. He realized she was very pretty and no more than 21. Her body was in great shape; her breasts being nicely out of proportion. "You do me a favor, Major," she cooed. "And I'll do you a favor."

She took his hand and led him to another chamber, away from the marijuana smoke and sitar music. This room too was lit only by candles, but it was neatly kept. A large mattress covered with pink blankets took up half the space.

She turned and cupped her breasts again. "I haven't had a real man in two years," she said in all frankness. "Not since that fool out there told us the Russians were about to bomb the West Coast and tricked us into following him here."

She came closer to Hunter. Now he could feel the full impact of her large breasts on his chest.

"Take me," she said softly. "Take me and I'll give you the box."

Hunter looked at her. The candles were highlighting her fiery red hair. She had movie star looks and beautiful green eyes.

"Please?" she asked, pressing against him.

Hunter had little choice. He had to retrieve the box and this appeared to be the easiest way.

He took her in his arms and kissed her. "Duty calls," he said smiling.

The next morning he was attached to the catapult waiting to bring his F-16's engine up to trim. The fuel leak only took an hour to patch and the base was stocked with leftover barrels of JP-8 jet fuel, which he used.

It had been quite a night. He got to know Tracy very well. Also Lacey and Stacy, who joined them later on. They hadn't been with a drug-free male in many months either. Hunter did everything he could to make them happy. He felt sorry for them. They were stranded just like thousands of other Americans were when the war broke out. But in a way, they'd been lucky. Sure, they were stuck with the drug-soaked Travis, but they also had plenty of food, water and booze. In fact the secret base was stocked with enough food and libation for 100 people for 10 years. The Colorado River provided the fresh water.

And, at least at first, Travis had provided the entertainment. Tracy had told Hunter that the officer had used his New York City money to buy 200 pounds of marijuana in Pecos, along with several pounds of opium. The canyon hideout was to be his own little harem, under the guise of some crazy religion. A dream world of nude women, smoking dope and serving his every whim. It worked for a while. At one time all of the girls were smoking opium and Travis was firmly in command. But gradually he sank into his weirdness. Tracy, Lacey and Stacy knew there was life beyond endless drugs and orgies, so they gave up the dope and had been living straight for the past year.

They asked Hunter to get them out, but he couldn't. Not right now anyway. The Lear jet was beyond repair, even for him, and the F-16 was strictly a one-man ship. With all-out war imminent to the east, he could think of no better place to be safe than in the impregnable bunkers. He told them to sit tight for the time being.

As promised, they gave him the black box. Then while Tracy cooked him a meal, Stacy and Lacey turned the dials and pushed the buttons that activated the catapult system. Three hours of boiling water and there was enough steam for a launch.

Now, as he gave them the thumbs up signal, the three were waving to him sadly. Travis and the others would continue their druggie ways, he knew. But these girls were smart. And pretty. And—for reasons he still couldn't figure out—still bare-breasted. They'd make it, barring unforseen circumstances.

He felt the steam pressure build up under the F-16.

A massive cloud of steam rose up underneath him. He took one last look at the girls as the catapult activated. "Stay safe, girls," he said as the F-16 rocketed forward.

Then he was gone . . .

Chapter Twenty

Time was running out . . .

General Dave Jones sat alone at the enormous lighted table in the War Room at PAAC-Oregon. Before him were stacks of intelligence reports and more than five hundred recon photos including all of the pictures Hunter had taken of the Badlands SAM sites. Other photos were high altitude jobs, shot at great risk by the Texans, on the very edges of the Badlands where the perpetual haze that hung over the placed thinned out enough to take an occasional photo.

The officer had spent most of the past day and night correlating the information with previous intelligence reports—all of which were indicated on a lighted map of the continent that stood in the center of the room. Green cubes represented the Circle Forces, red blocks represented the Russians. The Pacific American armies—the newly dubbed Western Forces—were coded blue with their various volunteer allies colored white. At the moment, the green and red blocks outnumbered the blue and white by a 2-to-1 margin. The wizened officer looked at the photos on the table, then at the map stretched out before him and felt a chill go up his spine.

War was fast approaching. He knew it. True soldiers sensed when the real thing was coming, and Jones' body hadn't stopped buzzing since Hunter returned from his one-man mission into the Bads. Now the combatants were making their final preparations. Two great armies—one marching east and the other marching west, were getting ready to collide head on. Soon enough, the land would be covered with the blood of its own. It seemed like such a waste . . .

Just about all the intelligence reports he had were bad news. The Circle armies had solidified their occupation of The Aerodrome and Football City and in doing so, now controlled all the free territories east of the Badlands. The Texans were really feeling the heat. There had been no less than a dozen raids along their border the night before. Once again the Mongols selected isolated townships as their targets, overwhelming their defenders at first, then counting on the air cover by their Russian cohorts for the second fist of a one-two punch. This time the Texas Air Force tangled briefly with the Soviet Yaks over the Red River before driving them away. But 12 more Texas towns lay in ruins, causing the Texans to speed up their full-scale evacuation of their border area.

The Western Forces were desperately trying to mobilize. Those already in the service were being sent east to the Denver forward base by any means possible. Some were riding in converted tractor trailer trucks, others on the one rail link still operating over the Rockies. Still others were flying. In all, Jones knew he had to move close to 45,000 men as quickly as possible.

Jones was also arming and equipping thousands of the volunteers who were flooding into Oregon and San Diego bases. Many of them were good fighters—militia men and free-lance border guard troops—and some of them were just able-bodied men who wanted to fight for the cause. Normally Jones would never have considered using them. But the situation was critical and he had no choice. If they were willing and could aim a gun, they were transported to the front.

And, as always, there were secrets . . .

Ghost Rider was really their only hope, but very few people outside of the PAAC High Command knew of its existence. The team of PAAC scientists and engineers—most of them CalTech people with a few former employees of the pre-war West Coast aircraft manufacturers like Boeing and Lockheed helping out—were working around the clock on the five extraordinary B-1s. Integrating the Ghost Rider system was a bitch, but early on the team had agreed that the one thing they *couldn't* do was duplicate the five missing black boxes, because each one was different in its own right.

That's why Hunter's mission was so critical.

But one thing bothered Jones even more than the impending war situation. Something that nagged him, gnawed at his stomach and his psyche. It was one photograph set aside from the others. One of Dozer's guys had found it tacked on the wall of an abandoned building they'd searched near Hot Springs, South Dakota. Others began turning up almost immediately.

Jones reached for it again and held it in front of him. It was the damndest thing. He was almost considering not showing Hunter. The photo was the first glimpse they'd had of this mysterious Viktor, yet Jones had immediately recognized him. Quite simply, the man looked like the devil incarnate. He was sitting in a chair in a bare room, leering at the camera. Thin face, pointed beard, strange slicked back hair, dressed entirely in black. Very military. Very dangerous. Jones knew the evil contained in the man's eyes was without measure. This was the man behind it all. Was he a Russian? Was he an American? Jones didn't know, and at that point, couldn't have cared less. This was their enemy.

But the strangest thing of all was that sitting beside this Viktor in the photo was none other than Hunter's girlfriend, Dominique.

And she was smiling . . .

Chapter Twenty-one

Pecos, New Mexico was like a living hell.

The highway outside the small town was jammed with refugees from Texas fleeing the butchery of the Mongol raiders about a hundred miles to the east. Inside the typical throwback Old West town, a huge gun battle had been raging off and on for the past five days. New Order New Mexico was a so-called Free Territory—no central government, just every town for themselves. So an occasional gunfight was nothing new in Pecos. But this one was turning into a small-scale war.

It started with the local sheriff and his small deputized force shooting it out with a band of local criminals, troublemakers and looters. Then everyone who had a gun and a grudge to settle began to take sides. By the end of the second day, it had become impossible to tell who was shooting at whom and why.

The town's two banks had been long ago robbed and many large buildings burned to the ground. The small airport had been bombed, the water supply destroyed and about half the high tension wires bringing electricity into the city had been dynamited. What was worse, someone had blown up all seven of the town's gas stations and also a half dozen small oil derricks on the east side of town, leaving blazes that would take weeks to burn out. It made no difference in one respect, though; most everyone owned a horse and soon the equine was the preferred mode of transportation.

And the two Main Street saloons and the whorehouse on Gowano Avenue were still opening and holding packed houses. Liquor seemed to be in unlimited supply as was ammunition. Card games were going on everywhere, a few of which escalated into smaller gunfights. When the bullets started flying, the nonparticipants nonchalantly took cover, waited for the lead to stop, then returned to their drinking and poker and whoring.

Hunter was an odd sight when he first appeared at the swinging doors of the Pecos' Double Star Cafe. Most everyone at the bar and at the card tables turned to look at him, clad in a black flight suit, carrying an M-16 in his hands and his flight helmet on his belt. He purposely strode into the saloon, staring down the few who chose to look at him for longer than three seconds.

Don't fuck with me, his eyes said. No one dared to. The card playing and the drinking started up again almost immediately. Outside another gun battle was in full fury.

Hunter leaned up against the bar and ordered a whiskey, throwing down a dozen real-silver quarters. The bartender, aware that Hunter had overpaid for his drink by about five times, quickly recognized the bribe and asked: "What do you want to know?"

"Scary Mary," Hunter said. "Who or what is it?"

"Depends on which one you mean," the barkeep said in a voice drenched in Western twang. "Got two of 'em. One in town, the other outside."

Hunter downed the whiskey and motioned for another. It was late afternoon. Several hours before, he had successfully catapulted out of the Grand Canyon and, instead of flying back to PAAC-Oregon, he had moved immediately to Location No. 4. He set the F-16 down on a desert strip near the town and had walked in, ducking bullets and dodging running gun battles all along the way. According to notes left behind by General Josephs, the box could be found "under Scary Mary." Adding this clue to what Tracy had told him about Travis' adventures in Pecos, Hunter had to put the pieces together.

"What's the one outside of town?" Hunter asked, swigging the cheap bourbon.

"A big rock," the bartender said, pouring himself a drink. "About 20 miles to the north, near a village called Mary de Vista. Biggest chunk of stone you'll ever see. Mile and a half if you walked around the thing. Might be a meteor, people say, dropped in long time ago from outer space."

"What's so scary about it?" Hunter said, dropping a few more quarters on the bar for a third.

The bartender leaned over to him and poured. "The rock is filled with sink holes and blind cliffs," he half-whispered. "And pumas. And buzzards. And rattlers. And bad spirits. Some people go in, some don't come out again. It's dangerous. The Indians used to call it *chimiyo chimayo*. Means like 'no hope' or 'no way out'."

Hunter thought it over for a moment. He didn't have the time to go crawling all over a chunk of desert rock—never mind one that was infested with vipers, cougars and vultures and was haunted to boot. And he doubted that Travis did either.

"Where's the other one?"

"The 'other' Scary Mary?" the bartender laughed. "Watch out, pal. It's *much* more dangerous. Over at the whorehouse. Room 333."

The door to Room 333 burst open, courtesy of Hunter's powerful flight boot.

He was ripping mad. It took him four hours to get the three blocks from the saloon to the whorehouse, so intense was the gunfire in the streets. He had to take a dozen detours and spent most of the time ducked in doorways waiting for the bullet-happy party to pass by. He wound up shooting his way out of a couple tight spots. Luckily his M-16 qualified as heavy artillery in a battle that contained mostly .22s and shotguns.

It was dark by the time he reached the cathouse, and he immediately ran up the stairs to Room 333. A dim bulb provided the only light in the room. He saw only a bed, a dresser, a mirror and a night stand. On the bed was a huge, dark complexioned woman, naked except for a cheap garter belt and stockings. An old cowboy—shriveled up, on his last legs and drinking his way through it—was trying his best to get it on with the tubby prostitute. But from what Hunter could see, their size difference made it a physical impossibility.

Not only were gun battles raging outside the whorehouse, people were shooting at each other inside the place as well. It was total bedlam. Just the noise of all the guns going off made it hard to hear anything. Hunter knew he'd have to hurry, before the next gun fight passed through. He had to announce himself quickly so he fired a burst from the M-16 which ripped away a large section of the room's shabby ceiling. Immediately, the woman sat up, knocking the elderly rustler clear off the bed.

"Well what the fuck do you want?" she screamed at Hunter. He instantly knew how she'd earned her nickname. Her hair was dyed a terrible fright yellow, her eyes sported massive fake eyelashes and her chubby face was painted in gooey make-up. She must have weighed in at 400 pounds.

"Few years ago. An Air Force guy named Travis came through here," Hunter said sternly. "Gave you a black box . . ."

The woman looked at him strangely. "Travis?" she asked, reaching for a bowl of multi-colored pills that sat on the nightstand. "You mean that crazy flyboy guy with all the weed?"

"That's the guy . . ." Hunter said quickly. Outside the particularly intense gunfight was going full tilt.

"God damn asshole he was!" the woman shouted. "Owes me money. He comes into town a few years back. He buys dope. He takes his piece of me. He doesn't pay. Instead, he gives me this box, with a red light blinking on it. Then he's gone. Vamoosed. So I got this box with a red light. Hey that's my business, so I put it in my window. To help my customers know I was . . . available."

Hunter had guessed right. *This* was the monster Travis had wrestled with.

Suddenly the gunfight outside got louder and closer. He could hear several explosions going off just a few blocks away and screams coming from the street outside the room's window. Inside the house, bullets were ricocheting off the walls down the hallway. Scary Mary however seemed oblivious to it all.

"So where's the box?" Hunter said.

"Well, Jesus, aren't we in a hurry?" she quickly lit a cigarette, swallowed a handful of pills then pushed herself up off the bed. Unlike the scenery in the Grand Canyon, Hunter had no trouble averting his eyes as the big woman bent over and reached underneath her mattress. Seconds later she came up with the box, its red light still blinking.

"Here you go, fella," she said, handing him the precious black box. "That's been holding up this bed for more than a year now. Don't need no sign anymore. Everyone knows where I am."

Hunter took the box and for the first time smiled. He reached into his pocket and gave her a handful of real quarters. "See ya, Mary. Take care of yourself," he said.

She looked at him as he was about to turn and leave. "Hey, hold on," she said, squinting her eyes to get a better look. "Aren't you that 'Wing Man' fella everyone's always talking about? The guy with the famous airplane? You look just like him."

Hunter smiled again, leaned over and gave her a kiss on the cheek. Then he was off, running down the hall, dodging stray bullets as he went.

Hunter landed at the Denver airport early the next morning after being directed there from New Mexico. Jones met him in the base's makeshift situation room, taking possession of the two additional black boxes and making arrangements to get them to Eureka immediately.

Then they sat over a pot of coffee and talked. Both knew instinctively it was the last time they'd be able to have a normal conversation for a while.

"We know we can't destroy all the SAMs right now," Jones told him. "But we have to act, to get them to start thinking defensively."

Hunter's mind flashed back to the Big War.

"We're up against the same type of thing as in Western Europe," he said. "The Soviets had superiority in men and weapons, just like now. But we beat them not so much on the front line, but *behind* the lines. We went after the rear echelons. Their supply dumps. Their means of communications. There wasn't a bridge left standing between Paris and Moscow by the time we were through. They definitely had the quantity but we had the quality. We forced them into a fight near Paris and they had no back-ups. No supplies. No way to get their reserves through. We kicked their asses.

"It's really no different now. Between them and the Circle ground forces, they've got us on numbers. But all the time I was flying over the 'Bads, I kept thinking: 'Where the hell are their rear areas?' The answer was, they didn't have any. Nothing between the eastern edge of the SAM line and the Circle troops moving east.

"That area is like a limbo now. No civvies, that's for sure. But plenty of bridges, highways, railroad tracks. Lines of communications they're counting on to move the Circle troops on."

Jones thought for a moment, "What you're saying is that if we can get in there, behind the SAM line and in front of the advancing ground troops, we can make it difficult for them."

"Exactly!" Hunter said. "We'll force them to fight somewhere, but only after we've taken our measure of them."

Thus, the strategy for beating the Circle was born . . .

It was time to go. Hunter had to load up his F-16 and make arrangements to meet a Free Canadian Air Force tanker plane over Saskatchewan to get the fuel needed to make the long trip to New York City.

But Jones had one more subject to discuss. He pressed the photograph of Dominique and Viktor into Hunter's hand, expressing total mystification of what it all meant. But Hunter seemed to totally block out everything. Jones would never forget the transformation that came over the pilot as he studied the photograph. Hunter's mouth narrowed and his fists clenched in rage. A new color roared into his face—a crimson associated with an adrenaline rush. His whole body began to vibrate, as if some inner strength was threatening to burst out of him. But it was Hunter's eyes that got to the senior officer. Normally blue, they seemed to turn almost white with anger . . .

What seemed like an eternity later, Hunter looked up from the photo and said to Jones: "I'll be back . . ."

Then he walked briskly from the room and toward his F-16, carrying the crumpled photograph in his hand . . .

Chapter Twenty-two

Dawn broke unevenly over the Badlands that next day. There were rain showers extending from central Nebraska on up to the Canadian border. At the same time, Kansas and Oklahoma had clear, if typically hazy, skies.

For the Russian soldiers stationed at the large missile site concentration near Broken Bow, Nebraska, the day began as any other. They were on the edge of the bad weather; it had rained during the night, but had stopped just before first light. This meant that all the tarpaulins that had been placed over their missiles when the rain started the night before had to be taken off and the missiles literally wiped down. But this would not happen before a dull hour of calisthenics at five in the morning, followed by an even duller fare for breakfast. Then would come the daily political lecture that followed the morning meal—an assembly that all the soldiers loathed. Most of them had been hidden away in the Bads for nearly a year and thus had been hearing the same boring Marxist indoctrination day after day, week after week. But in the lock-step regimen of the

Soviet Armed Forces, the daily speech would be held as planned. Only after that would the missiles be attended to.

The soldiers—SAM technicians mostly—were filing into the briefing tent when six PAAC A-7 Strikefighters suddenly burst through the permanent smoky haze. The jets came in very low and two abreast, covered from above by Captain Crunch and the F-4Xs of the Ace Wrecking Company. Before any of the Russians could act, one of the lead A-7s deposited a laser-guided anti-personnel missile directly in the center of the briefing tent, destroying it and everyone inside. The second lead Strikefighter took out the missile installation's all-important communications hut, before streaking away off to the east.

The next pair of A-7s concentrated on two of the six SA-2 missile launchers at Broken Bow. Again using laser-guided munitions, both pilots fired at the same time, and watched as their missiles smashed into the sides of two rocket launchers, each hit creating an enormous explosion. These two airplanes then also disappeared to the east. The tail end pair of attackers each deposited a missile into two further SA-2 sites, again scoring laser-guided direct hits.

By this time, the lead jets had circled back around and commenced to strafe the remaining two SA-2 sites with their Vulcan cannons. The second pair of A-7s followed their leaders in, cannons blazing. First one, then the other SA-2 launcher took hits and exploded. By the time the tail-end of the flight returned, all of the installation's missile launchers were in flames. Each of these trailing jets made a strafing run on several support buildings before linking up with the rest of the strike force and heading back to their Colorado base. During the lightning attack, the Russian soldiers failed to fire a single shot in defense of their tarpaulin-covered missiles. And the F-4 pilots of the Ace Wrecking Company saw nary a Yak in the area.

The attack on the eight SAM sites near Dodge City, Kansas also came as a complete surprise. Not expecting any enemy action, these Russian missile handlers had neglected to leave on their low-altitude phased radars during the night. Thus, when four PAAC A-10s appeared out of the morning sky, the Russian defenders didn't know what was happening until the first A-10 dropped a 2000-pound blockbuster right on the installation's central radar house, creating a huge fireball and leaving nothing in its wake except a smoking crater half the size of a football field.

As two PAAC F-106 "Delta Daggers" watched from above, the A-10s swept in one at a time and deposited a potpourri of bombs and missiles onto the eight SAM sites. Again, the Soviets had no time to mount a defense. Those who found cover simply hunkered down as the A-10s swept in again and again, taking a deadly toll on the SAM sites. With most of the targets destroyed or burning, the attackers finished up the strike with two strafing runs apiece, then broke off and streaked off to the west.

At about the same time, a makeshift squadron of PAAC fighter-bombers with fighter protection attacked a string of Russian missile installations set up along the Smoky Hill River 50 miles north of Dodge. There were 22 missile sites altogether. The strike group—made up of eight PAAC San Diego A-4 Navy Skyhawk attack aircraft, and a half dozen souped-up PAAC-Oregon T-38s—was being covered by four PAAC-Oregon F-104 Starfighters. As soon as they arrived over the target, the strike force was met by a barrage of heavy anti-aircraft fire thrown up by Soviet troops along the river. One A-4 and a T-38 were shot down immediately. The Starfighters' flight commander—who also acted as the strike's overall leader—ordered the attackers to clear the area, then led his F-104s in to take out the ack-ack battery with missiles and napalm. But this time, the SAM sites were going hot and missiles were launched at the attacking A-4s and T-38s loitering nearby. Two more T-38s were shot down within seconds.

While the Starfighters destroyed the anti-aircraft position, one of their group was lost to a SA-7 shoulder-held missile fired by someone on the ground. Ten minutes into the attack, five of the PAAC jets were downed and not a single missile site destroyed. At this rate, the attacking force would be decimated before anything on the ground could be hit.

That's when the Starfighter flight commander

called in the Spookys . . .

The C-130 gunships were on station above the Colorado-Kansas border ready to be vectored wherever needed. The two big airplanes arrived near the Smoky Hill River within ten minutes of receiving the call from the strike leader.

As the gunships started a wide arc around the target area, the strike leader coordinated a second attack on the objective. Once again coming in low to best avoid any SAMs fired at them, the remaining A-4s and T-38s as well as the three F-104s, concentrated on the missile batteries located on the far flank of the positions. At this altitude the major threat from the ground was from the shoulder-launched SA-7s and the mobile anti-aircraft batteries. One by one, the attackers braved the withering fire being sent up at them and came in on the target, each dropping a single bomb or firing a single missile, then streaking away. The action caused the Soviet troops to concentrate their missiles—and their undivided attention—to their northern flank. That was their mistake; the second attack was simply a feint.

Just as the last of the attacking jets dropped its single token bomb and cleared the area, the Spookys had completed their wide turn. Now they approached the riverside base from the south, practically unseen. Each airplane sported three GE Gatling guns poking out of its port side. Each gun was capable of firing 6000 rounds per minute and was equipped with a computer aiming-and-firing device.

Like most Spooky attacks, this one nearly defied description. With a total of six powerful Gatling guns firing at a rate of 3600 rounds *a second*, the two planes swept over the missile installation pouring out a curtain of flaming lead that cut through Soviet positions like a sickle. Secondary explosions followed in the wake of both airplanes. Buildings around the central command center of the missile base—mobile trailers mostly—were sliced in two by the awesome gunship barrage. Fuel supplies were hit, adding to the conflagration. Anyone unlucky enough to be caught in the path of the gunships was perforated with bullets where he stood.

By the time the two gunships completed their run, half the missile base was in flames. Once again, the strike leader brought his remaining aircraft around and went in on the missile sites. It was a bold move, sending in gunships to attack SAM sites—a tactic worthy of a court martial in the normal earlier times. But these weren't normal times. These were the times to innovate, to use whatever was at your disposal. And the idea worked. While the Soviets were still reeling from the unexpected barrage by the Spookys, the attack jets swept in and laid down their ordnance all around the target area.

With the majority of the targets destroyed, the strike leader ordered his airplanes to return to their Denver, Colorado base.

Later that morning, F-105 Thunderchiefs from the Aerodrome squadron led by Mike Fitzgerald himself and flying out of a secret base in Manitoba, destroyed six missile sites near the Black Hills in South

Dakota. Two squadrons of mixed Texas Air Force F-4s and exiled Football City F-20s bombarded 10 more Soviet sites around Oklahoma City and Tulsa. However, this time, the Russian missiles were waiting for the attackers. In a swirl of laser-guided bombs and flying SA-3 missiles, three F-4s and a valuable F-20 were downed.

By noontime, 15 separate attacks were launched against the Russian SAM installations. More than 50 SAM launch sites were destroyed or heavily damaged at the cost of 14 attacking aircraft. But the grim total was just the tip of the iceberg. The commanders of the Western Forces estimated there were still as many as 2000 to 3000 more operational missile sites scattered throughout the Badlands. And there would be no more "sneak" attacks—the Russians would be waiting for the attackers from now on.

But the air strikes were serving one part of an overall strategy. They were meant not to destroy the entire SAM wall, but simply to poke a few holes in it . . .

Chapter Twenty-three

It was the last night of the full moon and the yellow lunar glare threw a freakish light and shadow display across the battle-scarred skyline of Manhattan. About half the island's skyscrapers still had working lights, some were even equipped with large searchlights on the roofs. Many bristled with machineguns, rocket launchers and heavy artillery pieces on their top floors, where they could be easily positioned to fire at enemies in any direction and any number of blocks away.

Other tall buildings were dark, burnt-out skeletons of twisted metal and dangling concrete. Nearly four years of sustained warfare had turned downtown New York City into a bizarre urban battleground.

It was a war of territory that was being fought not only on the streets but in the skyscrapers. There were as many as a hundred different groups formed after the original combatants—the National Guards of New York and New Jersey—had fought themselves to a standstill a few years before. With the break-up of these two armies, other smaller militias proliferated. Street gangs, organized crime families, religious fanatics, even Nazis operated in the dense urban sprawl. Not a day went by when one faction was not fighting another. And frequently, groups of different factions would join together to battle a common enemy only to fight each other at some point down the line.

What was everyone fighting for?

Gold. There was plenty of it floating around the city. New York had become the ultimate Black Market, its main occupation was trafficking in dangerous and hard-to-get items. With enough money and the right contacts, anyone could buy anything—from a pound of cocaine to a thousand M-16s to a small tactical nuclear weapon—in New York City. But to make it work, ships had to dock, bridges had to work, streets had to be secured, protection had to be provided. This meant territory had to be conquered—property in midtown and down by the East and West Rivers was at a deadly premium—and the best way to hold an area was to utilize the buildings contained within it.

So the measure of power in New Order Manhattan was how many skyscrapers your groups held, where they were located and how tall they were. Some smaller group held just one or two skyscrapers. Others claimed dozens of buildings as their own, fortress-like blocks of territory and power. Most of the fighting was done between one group seeking to take over another's skyscraper. A key 'scraper on a key block of buildings meant more money into the coffers of the turf masters—payment for passing through. Also, the taller a building, the better line of sight and, therefore, fire one had. The fight for turf was just not concentrated on level areas but had evolved to vertical conquests as well.

The balance of power shifted daily.

One group's attack on another's skyscraper could be compared to the great ocean battles fought in the 17th and 18th centuries between the navies of Great Britain and Spain. First the enemy would maneuver as close as possible to its intended prey, moving guns in and out of the many abandoned downtown skyscrapers. Then, when their position was right, the attacker would put guns in every floor possible and blast away at the desired prize. The defenders would inevitably fire back, leaving the two buildings to pound each other like two man o' wars.

Once it was determined that the target building was sufficiently softened up, the attacking troops would move in. Some were experienced ground fighters, others earned their keep by scaling the sides of buildings like human flies, leading attacks to the higher floors. The outcome could take days or even weeks to be determined—rarely was a takeover bid successful without many bloody hours of floor-to-floor, room-to-room fighting.

Like magnets to steel, Manhattan attracted every sort of low-life, criminal and soldier-for-hire. It was a place so dangerous, even The Circle had decided to leave the New Yorkers to their own devices, for the time being, at least. In fact, The Circle found it very convenient to deal with the New York power brokers—many top-shelf combat weapons systems, technologies and ammunition were bought by Viktor's minions sent to Manhattan with bags of gold and promises of more. Not surprisingly, the city was also crawling with leftover Mid-Aks, air pirates, Family members, Russians and other representatives from "eastern" European countries.

And somewhere in the morass lay the fifth black box.

Punk 78 and Iron Man were two soldiers in the Power Systems Sector. Theirs was one of the top five largest groups in Manhattan—its territory stretched from the southeast corner of the obliterated Central Park to Park Avenue and down to the border of 42nd Street and Fifth Avenue. Along with the The Wheels, The Corporate Cats, Maximum Army Inc, and The House of David, Power Systems ruled the very profitable center of Manhattan. That there was a perpetual war going on between the five groups had little or no bearing on the huge profits they reaped. Battles or not, each group pulled in hundreds, if not thousands of pounds of gold and real silver each week as a result of their various gun-running, drug-pushing, protection and prostitution enterprises.

On this particular night, Punk 78 and Iron Man were serving as lookouts. They were stationed on top of a 'scraper on Madison Avenue, near East 52nd Street. Just a few blocks away, a battle royal was raging between the CorpCats and MaxArmy Inc. The two groups, deadly enemies despite their common border along the Avenue of the Americas, were blasting away at each other along adjacent buildings near the old Rockefeller Center. The flash of the artillery and the glare of rocket fire brilliantly lit up the night sky. The PSS soldiers were watching the engagement with glee. The more these two mortal enemies battered each other, all the better for Power Systems. The job of Punk 78 and Iron Man was to report the outcome of the battle to their superiors, The Chairmen, as soon as it was decided.

Iron Man was about to break open the pair's second bottle of crack juice when something caught his eye high above the 55-story 'scraper where they were stationed.

"What the fuck was that?" he yelled to 78 over the noise of the battle a few blocks away.

Punk looked up from his infra-red NightScope. "What the fuck was *what*?" he yelled back, grabbing the bottle from Iron Man.

"I don't know," Iron Man replied. "A flash of light in the sky. Strange looking."

"Yeh," Punk '78 spat out, swigging the crude cocaine-derivative liquid. "You're the only thing that's strange looking around here."

The Punk turned his attention back to the Night-Scope and did a long sweep of the city. There were some heavy duty fireworks up around West 83rd Street—probably The Yankee Machine and the Zebras, two of the smaller militias, punching it out. A section of Central Park up near the lake was blazing like a forest fire. Turning east he spotted a battle between two unknown groups around the Queensboro Bridge. Looking south, the nightly pall of smoke was rising from Times Square, but nothing much was happening toward Wall Street.

No doubt the battle between the CorpCats and MaxArmy Inc. was the best show in town tonight, and Punk 78 turned back to see what he'd missed. "Jesus Christ will you look at that!" he yelled. "Those guys are using incendiary mortars, flame-throwers, .88s, the works on each other! We haven't seen a rumble like this in months . . ."

He turned to get the crack juice from Iron Man, but found his companion was nowhere to be seen. In his place stood a man, dressed in black, wearing a flight helmet with the visor pulled down. He was pointing an M-16 right at the Punk's nose.

"Hey, who the fuck are . . ." Punk yelled at the stranger. But before he could spit it all out, he felt the stranger's heavy boot crash into his right cheekbone. Punk 78 went reeling across the tar-and-stone roof of the 'scraper, losing his .357 Magnum in the tumble. The stranger retrieved it, then lifted him up and forced him halfway over the edge of the building.

"Jesus! Jesus!" the Punk screamed, terrified at dropping 55 stories to the concrete pavement below.

"Listen you fucker," the stranger said, his helmet's closed-tight visor weirdly muffling his voice. "I ain't got the time to fuck around with a little scum like you. Where's this guy Calypso?"

"I don't know no Calypso!" the Punk yelled, only to have the stranger push him even far over the edge.

"Don't bullshit me," the man said. "I'll drop you so hard they'll hear the splat all the way over in New Jerk."

"He'll kill me if I tell you!" Punk screamed.

"I'll kill you if you don't," the stranger said, his hands tightening around the Punk's throat.

"Okay! Okay!" Punk 78 gurgled. "I'll tell you!"

The stranger released his grip only slightly. "Where?" he asked.

"Down at the Twins," Punk said, tasting blood from the cracked vessels in his throat. "The WTC. The old World Trade Center. He lives down there. But you can't get at him."

"Why?" the stranger asked angrily.

"Because he's high up, man," Punk answered. "He's higher than anyone. He sees everything. And he's got enough firepower to knock out anything up to 14th Street. He's got big stuff on every floor and soldiers everywhere. Don't you understand? He's King of Lower Manhattan. *We* don't even go down there . . ."

The stranger let go of Punk's throat, then knocked him sideways with a slap aside the head. The Punk hit the roof hard only to see the unconscious body of Iron Man lying 20 feet away. Somehow the stranger had taken out his partner without Punk hearing a sound.

Punk sat up and watched as the man stuffed his pockets with .357 ammunition. He took a good look at the man. "How the fuck did you get up here, man?" he asked.

The man quickly grabbed the soldier's throat again, brought his helmet visor to within an inch of the Punk's face and said: "I flew . . ."

The man they called Calypso sat on a leather couch in front of the huge window on the 110th floor of what once was the World Trade Center's easternmost building. Before him stretched the island of Manhattan. From Wall Street to 14th Street was his. A buffer zone of allies—the Combat Lawyers, the Asbadah Holy Militia and the Laser Razors—held parcels of territory right up to Madison Square Garden and the Empire State Building. The further away from those assholes uptown, the better, Calypso always said.

He was the most powerful man in New York City. So powerful that when the Mid-Aks came to Manhattan to shop for everything from small arms to .88 artillery pieces, they came to Calypso. When the air pirates wanted to buy a couple of tons of smack, they came to Calypso. Even the Russians brought him a present every time they passed through.

And now, The Circle had asked to pay their respects, at a party Calypso would host later that night. They wanted something from him—something they knew he had. Good, he thought, watching a battle off in the distance up near Rockefeller Plaza. Because The Circle had something Calypso wanted, too.

He clapped his hands and two young girls appeared. One carried a martini pitcher filled fresh to the brim with the champagne-cocaine mix that Calypso enjoyed so much, the other an extra large NEW YORK GIANTS glass, also one of Calypso's favorites. The shitty little wine glasses others used couldn't quench his thirst. He wondered if these girls could. They were barely sixteen and seventeen—a present of a Soviet general who stopped by a few months ago.

He motioned one to pour him a drink and the other to stand in front of him. He was getting old, he thought as he looked at the young girl. She was blonde, small, shy, dressed per his orders as a cheerleader. He was bald, graying on the sides and fat. And perverted.

"Strip . . ." he said to the cheerleader, taking an enormous swig of the drug-soaked bubbly. The girl immediately obeyed, lifting off her sweater, tugging at her socks, pulling down her skirt and revealing her pert, little breasts.

He turned the other girl and said: "You, too." The second girl, a brunette, was dressed as a schoolgirl. She slowly removed her nylon stockings and her dress and slip, then had her companion undo the snap on her bra.

"Come, sit with me," he said, taking the two naked girls on to the couch with him. "Drink, drink up, girls and get me in a good mood. I have a party to do tonight."

He was getting old, he thought, as he casually fondled the young girls' bodies. He was getting sick of this kid's stuff. His friends and "business associates," knowing his taste in "developing" women, were always dropping off two or three young ones, just to keep in his good graces. But although it was tough to admit it, he now realized he needed maturity in his playthings. He wanted something unattainable.

That's why he was especially looking forward to

meeting Viktor . . .

The submarine surfaced just off Coney Island. From here, it would ride quietly on the dark surface of the water right through Lower Bay off Brooklyn, up The Narrows and into the Upper Bay off the southern tip of Manhattan. The trip would take less than a half hour; there would still be a good four hours of night left when it arrived at its destination near Liberty Island.

The five men crowded in the sub's conning tower all wore black combat fatigues. Their faces had been charcoaled, as were their hands. Each man carried a silencer-equipped M-14 rifle. The sub's captain managed to squeeze his way up through them and quickly went over their coordinates one last time. Their pick-up point would be Ellis Island, the rendezvous time exactly three hours and 10 minutes after the time they left the boat. Miss the time or the location, same thing 24 hours later. Miss it again, and they would be on their own.

The submarine was from Free Canada; four of the charcoaled soldiers were Free Canadian commandos. The other was an American—an intelligence agent from Mike Fitzgerald's Syracuse Aerodrome. The tiny group had planned and trained extensively for this mission for the past two weeks. Now that D-Day had come and the tides were finally running right for them, they were anxious to get on with it.

The sub slowed to a halt just off Liberty Island. The captain called down a warning to his steering crew that the massive severed head of the Liberty Statue sat in ten feet of dirty water right off the sub's bow. The sub obediently backed-up for 20 feet then steered around toward deeper water.

The captain wished the men good luck as they scrambled down the tower's ladder and into a large rubber raft they had inflated. The captain looked up at the full moon. Smoke from a fire way uptown was drifting in front of it, giving everything struck by moonbeams a dark orange tinge. It took five brave men to go into that city alone, the captain thought as the men paddled away. He hoped they were being well-paid.

The Lincoln Continental gun wagon roared through the abandoned intersection of West 41st Street and Broadway. The noise of the relentless explosions coming from the CorpCats and MaxArmy Inc. battle six blocks back, drowned out the car's own, muffler-free racket. Inside the car sat five soldiers plus a tail gunner. The powerful beams of the six modified headlights provided a path of light through the darkened streets. The gunmen were from The House of David; every man wore gray camouflage fatigues, long shoulder-length hair and a beard. Their squad commander—a former Israeli Army lieutenant—sat behind the wheel, careening the big car through a routine patrol of the southern edge of their territory.

If there was a moderate force in New York City, it was the House of David. They were into diamonds—

buying them, selling them. Most of their members were former Israeli soldiers who headed for America after parts of the Middle East were obliterated during the war. Through their leadership, the House Army was tough, well-trained and very dangerous in a fight. Although the smallest of the big league groups, no one on the island wanted to tangle with the House if they could at all avoid it.

The Lincoln screamed around the corner of West 38th Street and turned onto Eighth Avenue. That's when they saw the bodies. The squad commander—a young man called Zack Wack—stood on the brakes as his troopers readied their weapons. The car screeched to a halt and the five soldiers leaped out and assumed defensive positions. The rear gunner, working a M60 heavy machinegun out of a small turret placed where the car's trunk used to be, covered their tails. The men watched and waited.

Slowly, Wack moved forward. The heavily-littered avenue was completely deserted except for the eight bodies that were lying in the middle of the block. Wack didn't like the looks of it. It appeared the men had been ambushed. But if that was the case, it must have been a quick fight. All eight men went quickly, even before they were able to get to cover. Either that or someone had lured them out into the open.

He reached the first body and pulled the man over. Wack thought it might have been a soldier from Adzubah—the House of David's mortal enemy—but he knew right away this was not the case. This man was Nordic and new in town; his uniform was still creased and his hands were clean. He carried no papers but Wack knew right away what the man's nationality was. He could tell by his boots. Only one army in the world issued black leather ankle-boots as standard equipment. The man was a Russian soldier.

Wack knew that Russian soldiers sometimes passed through New York, but this was the first one he'd seen up close.

He moved on to the next man, then the next. It appeared as if each was wearing a .357 Magnum bullet wound somewhere on his head or neck. Strange, Wack thought. It was as if they'd all been shot from above . . .

Chapter Twenty-four

The wind was cold and blustery at the tip of Manhattan. Despite the spring season, the four Calypso sentries were bundled up in their winter gear, standard equipment for anyone pulling duty outside and on top of Calypso's WT buildings. It galled them that while four squads of Calypso's personal security guards lounged around in comfort inside one floor below them, they, being lowly grunts in Calypso's street army, had to freeze their asses off, sitting 112 stories high, exposed to the elements and watching for God-knows-what.

The men sat huddled around five cans of Sterno and killed time by rolling dice. All they had to drink was a bottle of Harlem Juice—powerful, but terrible stuff. Downstairs, inside the once famous restaurant called Windows of the World, they knew the security guards were taking turns on the two young things Calypso just used . . .

"But do we see any of that stuff way the fuck up

here?" one of the men grumbled.

"No fucking way," another answered.

"And that asshole Calypso give them to those pansy security guys," a third said, taking a swig of the Harlem Juice. "You know, what's the big fucking occasion that he's treating those shitheads so good?"

A fourth man—the group's sergeant and leader—grabbed the bottle and said: "No wonder you guys are all asshole privates. Don't you know what's going on here tonight?"

The three soldiers shook their heads.

"You ever hear of this guy Viktor? The leader of the whole fucking Circle? He's coming here. Tonight," the sergeant said.

"Here?" one of the men said. "You got to be shittin' us."

The sergeant took another long, slow swig and wiped his mouth. "What the fuck do you think all these heavyweights are here for?" he said. "The place is triple-decked with security guards and the whole Goddamn Battery company stationed up here tonight."

"They are?" a soldier asked. "Then who the fuck's watching the Battery?"

"Who the *fuck* cares?" the sergeant drunkenly screamed at the man. "This place is crawling with celebrities. Not like those assholes up town. I mean big shots. Top Mid-Ak guys. Air pirates. I hear some Family guys are in town. Even a bunch of Russians. They're all here to see this Viktor guy."

"Well just as long as Calypso don't volunteer us to go fight out in the 'Bads," one man said. "That's the baddest shit that's going down today, brother. I mean, they was recruiting up in Times Square three months ago. These dudes is signing up like they'd never seen a new suit of clothes before. They just say: Gimme the gun. Gimme the gun. These guys are dedicated, you understand? But they go out to the Badlands, I say half of them don't make it back."

"None of them make it back," another soldier said, spitting out some impurity his teeth caught in the Harlem Juice. "There's some bad ass flyboys out on the coast. And that's who they is fighting out west. And you don't never want to fool with these jet fighter guys. I mean, these guys are fast and they can drop some very big bombs on your ass. I know, I was there when The Family tried to take Football City. These fucking Free Forces guys in their airplanes kill about half the Family guys before they even cross the fucking river. Then, when they do get across, the Football City guys run back into this big motherfucker stadium and this dude Hunter—the famous guy—he calls in a B-52 strike! And when the dust cleared, there ain't no Family no more. They're ain't even a fucking city left!"

"Fuck it man," the sergeant said. "This guy Viktor is clutch. If anyone can bump off those jets, it's The Circle. They say he even bought off the Russians to sneak in every fucking SAM they had left. You can't fly over the Badlands any more. Fucking Russians will shoot you down."

"They say he's got a bunch of Chinamen riding around on horses out there, too," another said.

"You bet your ass," the sergeant said, grabbing the

bottle again. "And he's got a huge motherfucking army. So it's all these people and rockets and cavalry and things against a bunch of jets fighters and about six divisions. Circle will kick their ass!"

The sergeant took the bottle, wiped the top and put it to his lips. He took a gulp and in doing so, raised his eyes to look directly at the full moon above him.

That's when he saw the man fly by . . .

The commando team from the Free Canadian submarine landed on a small beach near the Battery on the very tip of lower Manhattan. They ditched the raft, checked their maps and confirmed their location. Each man fitted his M-14 with a NightScope. Then, in precision pattern, they moved into the streets using every alley and doorstep to their advantage.

Silently, they headed for the World Trade Center.

Normally they knew the area would be crawling with Calypso troops, but tonight the streets were nearly deserted. Their intelligence proved correct; most of the soldiers usually assigned to guard every street corner on this end of the island were all assigned to the Trade Center tonight. The commandos avoided an artillery 'scraper on the edge of Wall Street, then circled around a machinegun checkpoint near West Street. When the reached the edge of WTC plaza, they split up, found individual hiding places. The first part of their plan went off without a hitch. Now, they settled in to wait.

One hundred and ten stories above them, Calypso was swallowing a handful of amphetamine pills, washing them down with a swig of his cocaine cocktail. He had long since finished with the young girls. His personal security forces were now having their way with them. He could hear the troopers in the next room, yelping and screaming like a bunch of dogs in heat. Calypso only smiled. He would never have condoned this type of bullshit if he wasn't in such a good mood. But this was a special night.

It was nearly 2 AM, and his guests were begining to arrive. He stayed in his room, waiting for everyone to show up before he made his entrance. Tonight would be *his* night. Nothing could ruin it.

He had quintupled the guard, but it was more for show than anything else. He expected Viktor would arrive with about a hundred of his top security troops—Calypso had at least 500 troops somewhere inside or close by outside the building. At least he could beat Viktor in numbers.

He opened his walk-in vault and stepped inside. The shelves were stocked with boxes of diamonds, gold and real silver, but there were only two items that he considered of real value. One was a small black box with a tiny blinking red light on top. Some Air Force guy had sold it to him a few years back right before the war. Calypso had no idea what it was, but he knew it was some kind of top secret thing and that someone would come looking for it someday.

It was his second valuable item—a small gold box—that he retrieved. Inside was a map. A map that the Circle wanted. And Calypso would give it to Viktor, but only when Viktor gave Calypso what he wanted in return.

A short time later, five faint red lights appeared out on the eastern night sky. Gradually the lights got larger and larger and a loud chopping noise could be heard accompanying them.

The lights turned into three Russian-built Hind helicopter gunships and two big Chinook choppers, all five painted entirely black. The aircraft landed on the WTC plaza which was bathed in the light of a dozen high powered searchlamps, giving the whole affair the look of a Hollywood premiere. As soon as their blades stopped rotating the choppers were quickly surrounded by Calypso's troops. The door on the first Chinook slid open and a contingent of black uniformed Circle Special Forces leaped out and elbowed the Calypso soldiers for positions around the other big helicopter. The two groups of soldiers eyed each other nervously, they were jittery allies at best. The Hind gunships didn't stop their engines—all the better to clear a way with their twin cannons and rocket launchers should they have to make a quick exit.

Watching from their hiding places nearby, the Free Canadian commando team saw the door to the other Chinook finally open. A dozen more Circle soldiers—elite storm troopers—jumped out. They formed a human phalanx, surrounding two more individuals who slowly alighted from the chopper. The commandos couldn't see the faces of the people being escorted toward the entrance of Calypso's buildings but they didn't have to—they knew who they were. As the entourage disappeared into one of the building's elevators, the Circle troops snapped into a frozen line of attention and didn't move a muscle. Though not as practiced, the Calypso soldiers did the same thing. Together, they stood on uneasy guard over the plaza and the entrance to building.

The main room of Calypso's suite looked like a who's who of New Order American terrorism. Five Mid-Ak officers, the last of a shrinking corps, were gathered in one corner locked in an animated discussion about how they won, then lost control over the entire eastern seaboard of the continent. A contingent of Family members had arrived—five thugs in three-piece suits, each with a blonde bombshell on his arm, and a stooge carrying a machinegun at his back. Seven leather-clad air pirates sat on Calypso's favorite couch, sloppily eating appetizers by the handful and drinking liquor straight from the bottle. A dozen or so partially clad young women and girls circulated about the crowd, serving drinks and cocaine and letting any guest who wanted to fondle their private parts.

Watching it all from a far corner were three plainly worried Soviet Army officers. Their discussion dwelled on the whereabouts of the rest of their group. It had been planned that eight special bodyguards were to have accompanied them to the gathering. But these men were nowhere to be seen, leaving the Soviet officers virtually defenseless should any trouble break out.

Suddenly the huge glass doors to the suite opened and twelve Circle Storm Troopers walked in. They eyed every guest suspiciously, paying particular attention to the rowdy air pirates. Finally satisfied the room was secure, one of them returned to the suite's elevator and gave a thumbs-up signal. With a rush of excitement, the infamous Viktor strode into the room. The woman on his arm, dressed in a stunning low-cut black evening gown, was Dominique.

Calypso made his entrance almost simultaneously. He was dressed in a flowing white robe, bedecked with jewels and gold medallions. He looked like a huge, post-modern Caesar. In contrast, Viktor was dressed in a tight, black military uniform, apparently of his own design, but looking suspiciously Nazi-like. He was thin, tall, remarkably devilish-looking.

Calypso walked over to the door and greeted the Circle leader, as the rest of the gathering watched in hushed silence. It was like two heads of state meeting.

"Welcome to my city," Calypso bellowed. "We're honored to have someone of your stature here with us."

"Thank you," Viktor said in a vaguely accented voice, adding, "We must talk."

"Talk?" Calypso asked, handing Viktor a cocaine-laced cocktail. "Surely we will talk. But first, let me introduce you to my guests. Then, you can introduce me to this lovely creature with you . . ."

Meanwhile, in the corridor outside the function room, a disturbance was taking place. The sergeant who was stationed on the top of the WTC building now found himself pinned up against the wall by four Circle storm troopers, four Uzi barrels pointed at his head. The sergeant had foolishly burst into the corridor right after Viktor had entered the function room, and the Circle soldiers were on him in an instant.

"I tell you, there's a guy flying around outside!" the sergeant tried to tell the storm troopers. But they were looking at him as if they didn't speak the language.

The sergeant tried to wiggle free but the Circle soldiers didn't flinch. A number of Calypso's personal security guards were looking on, but no way were they going to buck the Circle storm troopers.

"I'm trying to tell you," the sergeant pleaded. "There's a guy—he's in a little airplane—a rocket jet or something—flying around outside! I saw him!"

A Circle major appeared and leaned into the man. "He's drunk," the officer whispered sternly.

The man tried a third time. "Look, we're up on top of this 'scraper to be on the lookout, right? Well we've seen something!"

"A man in a 'little jet?' " the major mocked him. Then, he motioned the four soldiers to take care of the man.

The storm troopers hustled the now-screaming and

kicking man out the exit door he'd come in through, and back up to the roof. They didn't stop until they reached the edge. Without a moment's hesitation, they threw the struggling man off the roof and watched as he plunged 112 stories to his death.

The three other Calypso grunts had watched in terror as their boss was pitched over the edge. One of the Circle troopers turned his attention to them. He was dressed entirely in black and looked like a vision of death to the Calypso soldiers. "Anyone of *you* assholes see a man in a little jet?" he asked.

Inside, Viktor had already tired of Calypso and his crude excuse for a party. But he was here to deal.

He pulled on the obese man's robe. "We must talk, Mr. Calypso," he said.

"Yes, talk!" Calypso said loudly. "Let us talk. Here. In front of my friends. I have no secrets."

Viktor shifted his eyes around the room. Mid-Aks, Family, air pirates. All losers. Even the Russians were cowering in the far corner as if they had left home without their guns. He decided to show them all how a *real* winner operated.

"Very well. I call for a toast to you, Mr. Calypso," Viktor said loud enough for all the guests to hear. "To a man of real courage. A man who knows wealth and how to use it!"

"Hear! Hear!" the crowd laughed.

"Now, let us make a deal," Viktor said. The crowd gathered in a little, forming a loose circle around the two men. "I understand you have a map. A very valuable map."

Calypso smiled broadly and nodded.

"I am prepared to pay you one hundred million dollars for that map, Mr. Calypso," Viktor declared.

An audible gasp ran through the crowd at the mention of the large amount of money.

Calypso laughed again, this time louder. "I don't want your money, Mr. Robotov," Calypso said.

"Two hundred million in real silver," Viktor said quickly. He enjoyed the bargaining.

Calypso shook his head. "No, not money," he replied.

"Three hundred million dollars . . ."

"Please!" Calypso said, drunkenly looking for his cocaine cocktail. "I have enough money."

"Then what *do* you want, Mr. Calypso?" Viktor asked, showing some authentic curiosity.

Calypso smiled and reached inside his pocket. He drew something out and slowly unfolded it. It was the photograph of Viktor and Dominique, the same one found all over the Badlands. He handed the photo to Viktor, then set his eyes on Dominique.

"This, sir," Calypso said lecherously. "This is what I want."

The partygoers were on the verge of shock by this time. It took a few seconds to sink in that Calypso had turned down $300 million in real silver.

Viktor looked at Dominique. Her eyes had been cast down since they had entered the party. She had fulfilled her role nicely over the past several years, he thought. A student of mass hypnotism and propaganda, Viktor knew that Dominique's mysterious sexual allure would serve to increase his control over the vast Circle Army. Carefully staged photographs, released only sporadically at first, were the vehicle used to introduce her to the troops, while their field commanders were under strict orders not to let them near anything even resembling a woman. Thus, Dominque became the pin-up girl for this war—an X-rated queen in a land that hadn't seen a nudie magazine in more than five years. It was that "something about her" that got to them all. She became New Order America's fantasy girl, at least in the Circle lands east of the Mississippi. "People will fight for a king," Viktor was fond of saying. "But they will die for a queen." And that she was Hunter's love made it all the more appealing to Viktor.

Dominique had been his prisoner since the day two of his agents kidnapped her right after she stepped off the plane in Montreal a few years earlier. Hunter had put her on that flight shortly before the Mid-Aks put Hunter's former employers—the Northeast Zone Patrol—out of business. Some way—she never found out exactly how—Viktor knew of her close relationship with Hunter. His agents knocked her out with a drug, then she was shipped to some unknown country—possibly Switzerland—where she was held against her will in a huge chalet. She was confined to a suite of rooms, though she never wanted for anything. Except her freedom.

Viktor would sometimes come in the middle of the night and take photographs of her, frequently drugging her food beforehand. Sometimes, he'd take her. She resisted at first. But he had convinced her of one thing which made her give up hope. Hunter was dead, he told her, over and over. Killed during the Battle for Football City. Viktor even went through the trouble of showing her photographs of a crashed F-16, the bloody remnants of the pilot clearly visible through the wreckage. She didn't want to believe him at first, but he broke her down. And although she never really accepted in her heart that the man she loved was really dead, she frequently questioned whether it was true.

And that's all Viktor needed.

"But, Mr. Calypso!" Viktor said. "This is my queen . . ."

Calypso took Dominique's hand and kissed it. "Yes, he said. "And this is what I want."

Viktor laughed. He owned her. He could give her away.

"Granted." he said.

Another gasp ran through the captivated crowd. Even the air pirates—slugs who worked hard at maintaining their reputation—were fascinated at the ritual of high shelf white slavery.

Calypso held up his hand. "Wait, Mr. Robotov," he said. "You have only heard half my offer."

Viktor looked at him curiously. "I have given her to you, Mr. Calypso. What more could you want?"

Calypso leered at Dominique. The cocaine had his hormones boiling. She looked so innocent, standing there, shy, like a schoolgirl, yet dressed in a gown so low, he imagined he could see the outline of her nipples. Her long blond hair was curled so seductively. She reminded him so much of Bridget Bardot.

A soft little sex kitten, yet really a mature young woman. This is what Calypso knew he needed.

"I want her," Calypso said. "Here. Now." With that, he clapped his hands. Some one of his aides, off in another room unseen, pushed a button and two fur-lined chains slowly descended from the ceiling. The room doubled as Calypso's sexual playground. For the first time, Dominique looked up. She felt a shiver go through her. Did the man *really* want to chain her up and force love on her? In front of the crowd?

"Wait!" Viktor said, bringing a quick end to the hushed conversation that had rippled through the guests. "My queen is one thing. To expose her is another . . ." He bit his lip in thought, then said: "What else do you have to offer, Mr. Calypso?"

The man had not taken his lusting eyes off Dominique. "Name it, Mr. Robotov. It's yours. Jewels. Gold." Calypso started to undo his toga's belt.

Viktor countered. "I have jewels, Mr. Calypso. And I have gold. I want something of *value*."

Two words popped into Calypso's head. "The black box," he said, smiling at the black uniformed, goateed man. "It belonged to the U.S. Air Force before the war. God knows what it does. But I'm sure you—or your allies—would want to disassemble it. Study it, perhaps." With that, the big man clapped his hands and a moment later, another aide appeared, carrying the black box.

The Russian officers looked on enviously as Viktor took the box and examined it. He was smart enough to know it was more valuable than all his money. Or his queen.

He looked at Calypso, then at Dominique. He ran his hand through her blond hair and laughed.

"Take her . . ." he said finally. "Do what you want with her."

Chapter Twenty-five

It took Calypso's men just a minute to secure Dominique to the fur-covered chains. The drug-induced guests cheered as she hung helplessly, her arms stretched out, her feet barely touching the ground. Calypso undid his tunic to reveal his lardish plump body, grossly clad now only in briefs. Once Dominique was secured, he ripped off the front of her dress, exposing her pert breasts to the crowd. She gasped and moaned: "No . . . please. No." But her pleas only brought laughs and jeers to the crowd. Even the paranoid Russians seemed to be enjoying the spectacle.

Viktor laughed as Calypso stepped up and roughly fondled Dominique's beautiful body. He ran his hands down her breasts to her exposed soft stomach, then down one of her black-stockinged legs. He tried to kiss her, but she spit at him, much to the crowd's delight. He then slapped her cruelly and removed his briefs to reveal a stubby erection.

"I am the king of New York City!" he proclaimed, drunk and drooling. "What I want . . . I get!'

With that, he charged forward and attempted to

enter her.

One of the Russian officers saw it first. A flame, outside one of the huge plate glass windows, clearly reflecting against the night sky. It was getting closer—moving very fast . . .

"What the fuck is . . . " he began to say in Russian. But before the words came out, he had his answer.

There was a mighty crash, ear-splitting with the sound of exploding glass, as one of the huge windows near where Dominique was about to be raped exploded inward. The glass, shattering into pebble sized shards, flew all over the room like a million diamonds, reflected in a ball of flame.

Behind the smoke and the shower of the glass was the minijet—with Hunter behind the controls.

The hole in the huge window caused a violent whirlwind around the room. The lights flickered, objects were flying everywhere. The noise was tremendous. Things began getting sucked out as the difference in air pressures caused a great vacuum effect. One of the air pirates went first, screaming as he was unwillingly drawn out into the night. A Family thug and his moll went next, their desperate attempts to grasp on to something—anything—failing. Calypso was the next victim of the vortex—his large frame slamming against the jagged edges of the glass, ripping his jugular as he went out the window and plunged to a bloody death. Dominique, although close to the hole, was prevented from being drawn to it as she was still secured to the rape chains.

Everywhere in the room, people were screaming,

holding on for their lives. Other windows started bursting. Two of Calypso's men were slowly drawn out a new, smaller hole, though the slow suction made it a long and painful prelude to death. One of the storm troopers, vainly holding on to the edge of the sill, finally weakened and allowed himself to be sucked out, but not before letting out a chilling scream. Another Family moll followed right behind him.

The minijet sat in the middle of the confusion, its jets still smoking and sparks from its engine starting small fires around the room. The canopy popped and Hunter came out, his helmet visor down, his .357 Magnum blazing. He took out two of the Circle storm troopers first, then spun around and shot a Family goon right between the eyes. Storm troopers out in the corridor had recovered from his bursting in and started to return fire, but they were shooting so wildly, they were hitting some of the guests instead of Hunter.

The noise inside the room was like a tornado. More windows were exploding. More people, some no more than bloody masses of pulp, were being sucked out. Glasses, bottles, lamps, ashtrays were whipping around the room like missiles, striking people before disappearing out of one of the broken windows.

Hunter quickly jumped down from the minijet and made his way toward Dominique. She had fainted by this time. Hunter reached her by carefully crouch-running from one secured object to the next. Another couple of windows exploded, showering the already bloody guests with more sharp pieces of glass.

Hunter knew that every window that exploded served to balance the air pressure, reducing the danger of being sucked out into the night. He had to move quickly. Rescuing Dominique was his first priority, but getting the black box ran a close second. He was also looking for Viktor, but in the darkness and confusion, the man was nowhere to be seen.

Hunter reached Dominique and two quick blasts from the Magnum busted her chains. She fell into his arms, and at that moment, in the swirl of blood, flame of death all around him, he tenderly held her close to him. "I've got you," he whispered to her.

Her eyes opened weakly and she saw him for the first time in years. "Hawk?" she cried faintly. "Is it really you?"

He momentarily opened his helmet's visor. "The original, honey," he said, winking.

Hunter had flown to New York in the F-16, carrying the collapsible mini-jet on one of the jet's underwing "hard points," the place where weapons would normally be attached. He had landed at the abandoned JFK airport, hid the '16 in a remote hangar, then had taken off in the minijet for Manhattan. He was armed only with his sophisticated electronic eavesdropping device, the one he carried in the U-2 and later into the Badlands. He had adjusted it so as to listen in to conversations anywhere within a 50-foot radius of his position—even through building walls. This was how he had planned to recover the fifth and last black box. Eavesdrop on the whole fucking Manhattan until he tripped over a clue.

It had been a bold plan—an improvised, one-in-a-million shot. But it had gone better than clockwork. Using the tip from Tracy back in the Grand Canyon, he had nailed down who Calypso was. After Hunter had iced the Russian patrol he happened upon, he spent the good part of the night floating around Calypso's 'scraper, monitoring everything the decadent slob said and did. But, as always seemed to happen to him, Hunter was really in the right place at the right time, almost as if he sometimes forced fate to take over. The fact that the night he picked to take on Calypso also happened to be the night that Viktor was in town with Dominique was another in a long line of complete flukes. His life had been full of them. Bolts of divine intervention? Incredible coincidences? Synchronicity? Hunter preferred to think of it as something in the middle—maybe someone, somewhere in the ether, was pulling for him. What ever it was, he was the first to admit that at crucial times in his life, he was the luckiest bastard on earth.

But now he still had to get Dominique and himself out of the skyscraper in one piece. She had thankfully lapsed back into unconsciousness as he gathered her up and started to plot his escape. Then luck hit again. Next to where she had been chained lay the black box. He would never have seen it except for its tiny blinking red light. And beside it was the gold case which held Calypso's secret map. Having listened in on Calypso for the past few hours, Hunter knew about the map's existence, although he didn't have any idea where it led or what would be found once a person got there.

But he was going to try like hell to find out . . .

He draped Dominique over his shoulder and started for the door. The inside of the room was quickly filling with smoke. Human shapes were moving through the flames. His wrecked mini-jet being the center of the conflagration. He hated to see it go—it had served him so well. But he had no time to get sentimental. It was getting too fucking hot!

He made it to the corridor and found that whatever guards had been stationed there had long since fled. Smoke was filling the top floors of the sky-high building. He had to get out—quick. He pushed the elevator button and crossed his fingers. Instantly no less than 10 of the available twelve doors slid open, amidst of great ringing of bells. He wasn't all that surprised—the elevator call button was activated by heat—the slight amount on the tip of a person's finger normally did the trick. But the heat of a fire ironically called all the available elevators to the scene of the blaze. "Ah, technology," he said, stepping into the lift.

He took one last look into the devastated room for Viktor. Did he get sucked out into the night? Did he perish in the flames? Did he escape? Hunter had no time to ponder the questions. He pushed the down button.

He didn't know what to expect when the elevator reached the bottom floor. Dominique was still out, her face oddly showing a slightly contented look. He watched the floor numbers slide by. He saw other elevators were also descending from the top floor—

possibly containing some surviving guests, possibly some storm troopers as well. Maybe even Viktor himself. But Hunter's elevator would win this race, but he still had to worry about what—or who—would greet him when the lift stopped at the bottom. By the fifth floor, he had Dominique back over his shoulder and his hand cannon up and ready for gunplay. But when the doors opened he was surprised to find the gunfight had started without him.

It was confusing at first to determine who was fighting whom. The whole bottom floor of the building, as well as the plaza outside, was being raked with rifle and automatic weapons fire. He saw some Circle storm troopers, plus a very few Calypso soldiers firing in the direction of some darkened buildings near by. Hunter took advantage of the confusion to run out behind the enemy troops, and leave the building by a side door.

Dominique was coming to and, though woozy, she was able to stand on her own feet. She refused to let go of him however, as he hurriedly moved in the shadows toward the front of the WTC. Whoever was fighting against the storm troopers was getting the worst of it. "My enemy's enemy is my friend," he thought. He had to help out.

Despite all the flying lead, the glass front of the building's lobby was still intact. But not for long. Assuming a classic firing position, Hunter popped off six rounds from the powerful Magnum, each one taking out an enormous plate glass window. The resulting crash of broken glass—a sound he'd been hearing a lot lately—served to divert the storm troopers' attention. Hunter knew if the people hidden in the building had any smarts, they'd be leaving *tout de suite* right about now.

Sure enough, he saw one, then two figures emerge from the rear of the building across from the WTC. Two others quickly followed. Somewhat recovered, the Circle troops began firing at the building once again, not realizing that their quarry had escaped.

Hunter moved down the block toward the five running people. He felt more than compelled to link up with them—he was drawn to them. He just hoped they wouldn't shoot back.

There was a brief lull in the action as the Circle soldiers realized they weren't getting any return fire. Hunter saw his chance.

"USA!" he yelled into the night. "Hey, USA!"

The five figures stopped in their tracks then hit the pavement. They were only a block away from Hunter by this time. He tried again: "Hey, USA here!"

This time a reply came back: "Keeping talking, pilgrim!"

"Major Hunter, Pacific American Air Corps!" he called back.

"Hawk?" a familiar voice called out. "Is that you, buddy?"

Jesus Christ, Hunter thought, who the hell would know him out here?

"It's Zal!" the voice called again. "From the Aerodrome!"

One of Mike Fitzgerald's boys? Out here? Slowly Hunter moved toward the voice. Finally a face appeared from out of the darkness and smoke. It *was*

Zal. He was one of Fitzie's best fighter pilots. In fact, Hunter and Zal had been captured by a gang of air pirates name The Stukas a while back, only to escape via a hot air balloon.

They hugged each other like long lost brothers.

"What the hell are you doing here, Hawk?" Zal asked.

Hunter looked at Zal's commando clothing, up to his blackened face. "I have to ask you the same question," he said. "You're a long way from flying one of Fitzie's F-105s."

Just then Zal's attention was diverted over Hunter's shoulder. "Jesus, Mary and Joseph," Zal said in such a tone Hunter thought his friend was going to make the sign of the cross. Hunter turned around to see that Dominique had groggily moved into the faint light. "We're looking for her!"

Hunter put it all together in an instant. As a favor to him, Fitzie had had his intelligence people looking for Dominique since she had disappeared. Zal was one of those guys.

"We've been tracking her—and Viktor—for two weeks," Zal explained. "Ever since those strange pictures of her started showing up. We haven't been able to contact Fitzie since Syracuse was evacuated. But we went undercover and spotted her near Boston, traveling with the big creepo. We grabbed one of his guards, beat the shit out of him and found out he was due down here tonight. That's when we called in some help from Montreal. The guys with me are Free Canadian Sea Commandos. The best in the business. We were going to rescue her, Hawk. Been looking forward to it, in fact."

"Well, thanks, Zal," Hunter said, shaking the man's hand. "But right now, I think we'd better figure out how to get the hell out of here."

As if to emphasize his point, a burst of gunfire coming from the WTC plaza ripped the concrete above their heads.

"We're with you, Hawk!" Zal said, waving his arm at the rest of the group. By this time, Hunter was already running down the street, supporting Dominique with one arm, and trying to reload the .357 with his free hand.

Chapter Twenty-six

The House of David gun wagon moved cautiously down Canal Street. Zack Wack was still at the wheel, his troopers, their guns at ready, checking every window, every doorway, for anyone hostile. They were way out of their territory—further out than Zack Wack could remember. But he was taking advantage of an unusual situation.

The House of David's southern border ended where Calpyso's empire began. An unwritten, uneasy truce of sorts was in force between the two groups, though firefights erupted occasionally. But now, tonight, there wasn't a Calypso soldier to be found. Wack knew that in the ever changing fortunes of living in New Order Manhattan, intelligence was the best weapon. He was a highly-trained Israeli soldier. Back in the Middle East, a smart soldier took advantage of everything. Wack knew something weird was happening on Calypso's turf. It was worth the risk to find out what was going on.

They had just entered what was left of the old Chinatown section of the city when he first spotted fire coming from one of the WTC buildings. His hunch was right; there *was* trouble in Calypso's paradise. He called back to his men to up their vigilance another notch, then turned onto Chambers Street. That's when he saw the group of seven individuals running toward them.

It was an odd collection. Five guys dressed in black, their faces blackened; one guy dressed like a pilot and a girl, the front of her dress in tatters. "Now what the hell is this?" Wack asked.

He screeched on the car brakes and turned the wheel to the left. The resulting skid brought the car perpendicular to the street, allowing the rear gunner to swing his big .50 caliber around. Wack reached for his own M-16.

Suddenly, there were explosions right in back of the group running toward him. Then he could see other individuals—soldiers—were chasing the first group. Wack knew he had three choices. Do nothing. Take off. Or help the people being chased.

Screw it, he thought. He'd been saddled with compassion all his life. Also there was a woman with them. He stood up in the car and started yelling: "Come on! Come on!" By this time the group was nearly in front of them. Wack looked at the pilot—strange, he seemed familiar. But it was no time to exchange greetings. Urging them on with his arms, the seven people piled into the gun wagon and Wack floored the gas pedal. With a great amount of smoke and tire squealing the big Lincoln roared away into the night, leaving nothing for the pursuing Circle troops to shoot at.

Chapter Twenty-seven

The city block where the temple was located was surrounded by a variety of heavy machine guns, rocket launchers and other defensive weapons. Its perimeter was patrolled by heavily-armed soldiers, many of them wearing original pre-war uniforms of the Israeli Defense Forces. At strategic points, tall, recently-erected towers served as lookout stations and gun posts. The block—home of headquarters of the House of David and located right in the middle of their 14-block turf—was probably the best protected, best secured area in Manhattan.

The overcrowded gun wagon rode through a checkpoint, past the perfectly preserved temple and pulled into a warehouse-turned-barracks next door. The group piled out and followed the House of David men into the building. Inside was a table with a meal already cooked and waiting for the patrol. Several elderly women wearing homespun aprons and wide smiles greeted the House of David men like family. Word was passed that there would be seven more eating, and within a minute, seven more meals appeared.

As they all sat down to the late-night meal, there were grateful handshakes all around—both Hunter and the commando team members knew the House men had saved their asses from a very dangerous situation.

Hunter was especially grateful to Zack Wack, the patrol leader.

"I feel I know you from somewhere," Wack told the pilot as they sat and ate together.

Hunter looked at the man. He seemed familiar too. He was about 35, rugged, slightly balding, with a full black beard.

"Your name is Zack Wack," Hunter said. "Could that be short for Zachariah Wackerman?"

Wack looked surprised. "Yes, it is," he said.

"Was your father's name Saul Wackerman?"

Now Wack looked absolutely astonished. "Yes, it was," he replied. "But how would you know?"

Hunter's mind went into instant flashback. When he and Dozer and the 7th Cavalry first arrived in New York after the war, Manhattan was in the midst of a battle between the National Guards of New York State and New Jersey. Dozer's men had rescued a bunch of civilians, but one of them—an elderly man who had been proudly displaying the American flag—was shot in the back by a sniper. He died in Hunter's arms, still clutching the small Stars and Stripes. This was the same flag Hunter carried with him. The man who died holding it was named Saul Wackerman. A picture in the dead man's wallet showed a son who was in the Israeli Army.

Hunter reached into his pocket and pulled out the

neatly folded, slightly tattered flag.

"Do you recognize this?" Hunter asked. "Could it have belonged to your father?"

Wack took the flag and felt it. "Yes, he said almost immediately. "My father was a tailor. He made this himself. I know his work. But how did you get it?"

Hunter took a deep breath, then said: "I was there when your father died."

Hunter then told the man the entire story, much to the astonishment of the others who couldn't help being caught up in the moving tale.

"So you're the famous Hawk Hunter," Wack said after a while. "We've heard of you, even in this place. We always admired you ZAP guys, then when we heard about Football City—well, we were ready to pack up and come out and join you."

"I think your father would have told you to stay here," Hunter said. "From what I can see, you guys are the only ones trying to preserve what this city once was."

Wack shook his head. "It's a crazy place," he said, pouring out grape wine for all at the table. "We're a small group. We're doing okay now, but one never knows what tomorrow will bring."

Hunter felt Dominique lean on his shoulder. She was more interested in sleeping then eating. He put his arm around her and she immediately dozed off.

"We're in a lot of trouble out in the Badlands," Hunter said, draining his cup of wine. "While we were busy fighting the Family, the Russians infiltrated six or seven SAM divisions. Brought in a whole cavalry unit, too. Apparently they've been in league with Viktor for quite some time.

"We hear bits and pieces of it here," Wack said. "It seems like this Viktor came from nowhere. When we first heard of him, it appeared as if he were a chairman of the board type—The Circle was supposed to mean an alliance between the Mid-Aks, The Family, the air pirates. But it's Viktor who's behind it all. He *is* The Circle. His boys have been sneaking around down here for a while, buying weapons and paying for them with drugs, or gold or young girls."

Wack shook his head. "The worst thing about it all is that Viktor knew there were still a lot of crazies on the continent who would fight—for any cause—just as long as they were fed. They're his puppets. Like Germany in the Thirties."

"True," Hunter said. "But puppets hang by thin strings. Break a string here and there and the whole thing tumbles down."

Hunter left the thought hanging. He reached in his pocket and pulled out Calypso's gold box. For the first time since he recovered it, he took out the map that Viktor had deemed so valuable, quickly explaining how he got it to Wack and his men. Hunter unfolded it, expecting an elaborately detailed plan. But he was in for a surprise. It was a simple drawing showing—of all places—*Yankee Stadium*. An "X" indicated somewhere near the left field wall.

"What the hell does this mean?" he asked aloud, as the commandos and the House of David soldiers crowded around.

"The Stadium?" Wack asked. "That area has been abandoned for years. Nothing there. No people. No buildings of value. It's a No Man's Land."

"Well whatever this 'X' is, Viktor was willing to pay three hundred million in real silver for it," Hunter said.

He looked up at Zal, who was standing next to the Canadian commando commander, a man named Norton Simmons. "I'm going to see what this is," Hunter said, pointing to the "X" on the map.

Zal looked at Simmons. "That means he's looking for 'volunteers,' " Zal said wryly, but with a hint of a smile.

"So I gathered," Simmons said. He checked his watch. It was nearly 5 AM. "Well, we missed sub rendezvous anyway."

He turned to his men. "What do you say guys? We in?"

The team nodded as one. Simmons turned back to Hunter. "For anyone else, I'd tell them to send me a postcard. But for Hawk Hunter, you can count us in."

"Us, too," Wack added. "If it will help in fighting The Circle. Because if they win in the 'Bads, sure as hell they'll be here next—coming down on us."

Hunter felt a warm feeling spread throughout his body. Courage. Dignity. Pride. Patriotism. Resolve. Democracy. All of these things and more were alive and well and dwelling in this place.

Hunter pulled Dominique's naked body closer to him. The world was still spinning, but he had become used to the feeling by now. As always, his days seemed to last for years. Time moved in slow motion when he was in overdrive like this. Even now, lying in bed with her in a spare room that Wack had provided, sleep defied him. Instead he felt surges of power, anger, love, determination pump through his body. That he was in Hawaii only a few days before, then Wyoming, Arizona, New Mexico and now this—it was all too dreamlike. His senses rippled with electricity, his mind was racing. Calculations, permutations, probability quotients, the measurable effect of coincidence—they all had to add up if he was to be successful.

Going after whatever was hidden at Yankee Stadium was an unexpected yet calculated risk. He knew it meant at least one more day that PAAC and the others would have to carry on without the crucial fifth black box, but from the deepest part of his gut instinct, he felt he was making the right decision. Something so valuable to Viktor would also be valuable to the Western Forces, even if all they did was destroy it. So Hunter and his new allies were lying low during the daylight hours and planned to drive to the stadium as soon as night fell. Then Hunter knew he would have some tough decisions to make. And the first one would be what to do about Dominique.

He turned to look at her. Life was *so* strange and he knew it better than most. In all that time that she was missing, he had always felt like she was alive—somewhere. And he had vowed to find her. Now she was with him again. The woman who had haunted him since the first time they met was beside him, in the flesh. He had her again. Would he be foolish enough to let her go?

A wave of doubt clouded his mind. Why shouldn't he just take her and take off? Go to Free Canada, live as normal a life as one could in the New Order world. Just what the hell was he running around the whole Godforsaken continent for anyway? This dream—this Goddamn myth—that somehow, some way, he could magically put the United States back together again? He had to laugh. It was a joke. Imagine carrying around such an impossible dream of reuniting America again when there were thousands of Soviet missiles sitting in the middle of the country, a huge hostile army holding more than half the territory of the former U.S., and, thousands of Mongol warriors roaming the countryside, terrorizing, murdering, raping.

So why fight it? Why not just chuck it all, leave the wars to someone else? Grab Dominique and take a sub ride back to Canada and become a fisherman. Or a farmer? Or a crop duster?

There were plenty of reasons to do it.

But there were more reasons why he couldn't. Sure, he could leave the U.S., but he couldn't leave it behind. And he could live with Dominique, but he couldn't live with himself. The whole idea—the whole concept—of the United States of America was alive just as long as one person believed in it. Fought for it. Died for it. He was one person. But there were thousands, tens of thousands, hundreds of thousand, even millions, of people who still believed in the dream. Still would fight for it. Die for it. Tell their children about it. The difference between him and all those people was that he—by a fluke of nature—could have a direct bearing on the outcome. That twist of fate—that he was the best fighter pilot ever born. He knew it. But far from being a glamorous calling, the responsibility was awesome—to the point that sometimes, in his darkest and deepest recesses, he resented it. And the life that went along with it was too hard for him to carry any false modesty about what he was.

So he could flee to Canada and be comfortable, even wealthy. But he wouldn't be free. And neither would his country. And that made all the difference . . .

Dominique turned to him, her eyes open only wide enough to let her tears flow out. She knew what he was thinking. They were psychically linked—probably she more to him than the reverse. He felt the pain well up inside his heart and catch him in the throat. Here she was, in his arms, after all that time. And yet he knew, that all too soon, he would have to let her go again.

They made love again, then they fell into a tightly locked embrace and finally went to sleep.

One hour after the sun set, two House of David Cadillac gunwagons passed through the last friendly checkpoint and started north. The first car—a converted hearse—featured an oddly-sized .35 mm cannon mounted on its hood and twin .50 caliber machineguns hanging off its sides. A small but powerful rocket launcher was installed in a home-made turret drilled into the center of the car roof. This car was filled with House of David night fighters, the best the group had to offer. Car Number Two, a converted limousine with Wack behind the wheel, carried Hunter and Dominique in the front seat with Zal, and the rest of the commandos riding in back. This vehicle was a land version of a recon aircraft. Its only "weapon" was a large camera mounted on the dashboard.

Both cars were heavily armored on the sides and the roof, wore metal skirts to protect the tires and featured cloudy, but secure-looking bullet-proof glass. Each was equipped with a CB radio, and as soon as the nine-mile journey to Yankee Stadium began, a non-stop racket of radio chatter commenced between the cars.

The route to the stadium that Wack had selected was the least treacherous of several. The two cars would move up Sixth Avenue, cut through Central Park, emerge at about 110th Street then cut over to what remained of the Henry Hudson Parkway. From there it was a straight line—more or less—to Yankee Stadium.

Wack and his crew were old hands at what they called "turf-busting." That was, driving as fast as possible through another groups' territory, zig-zagging so no one could get a clear shot at you. It was an acceptable practice in New York City these days, to a point approaching sport. But only the fastest survived. Helmets were required, as were elaborate seat harnesses. And, of course, no headlights could be used.

The two cars took off and soon enough, they were skirting the edge of CorpCat country at close to 60 MPH. Only a few shots were fired at them, and to no effect. Wack yelled over to Hunter that the Cats were too blown out from their 'scraper battle with Max-Army the night before to worry about the two House gunwagons.

Once off Sixth Avenue, the cars roared through Central Park, which to Hunter resembled nothing less than photographs he'd seen of the Ardenne Forest during World War I. In the intense moonlight, he could see the ground was churned up like a massive plow had worked it. Acres lay bare of trees or any vegetation. The various ponds and lakes were bone dry. Destroyed military equipment—tanks, personnel carriers, even a few downed helicopters—lay rusting; relics from the war between the New York and New Jersey National Guards. Beside many of the wrecks lay skeletons and parts of skeletons, their bones long ago licked clean by dogs, rats and other vermin.

After passing through the nightmare landscape of the park, the cars began picking up sporadic fire courtesy of soldiers of the Gwanda Nation. Their turf covered the area from West 110th Street to the George Washington Bridge, a critical long stretch of the journey. Wack expertly wheeled the big car back and forth, as Hunter shielded Dominique. The two gun wagon cars were moving at 70 mph, and all the weaving was causing a racket of squealing tires and burning rubber. With little damage done, Wack followed the lead car onto the Cathedral Parkway.

That's when they saw the roadblock . . .

It was straight ahead of them, right at the entrance to the Hudson Parkway. There were four vehicles—two cars on the outside and two jeeps on the inside—parked in such a way as to block off the entire roadway. The roadblock looked to be manned by at least 20 Gwanda Nation warriors, fierce-looking men in jungle fatigues. Hunter pushed Dominique all the way down to the floor, then checked his .357 Magnum.

"Don't worry, guys," Wack said confidently. "We've been here before."

Hunter saw the gunner in the car in front of them slip into position behind the turret-mounted rocket launcher. The driver of the first car called back to Wack: "Stay on my tail, Number Two. This is a Red Sea. Repeat, Red Sea. Sam's aiming for the middle."

"Roger," Wack yelled into the radio, then back to his passengers. "Okay, guys, hang on!"

About 50 feet out the first car stopped swerving. The rocket gunner lined up a shot and hit his launch button. A wire-guided missile leaped from the turret and instantly hit square in the middle of the two center vehicles. The powerful rocket exploded in a ball of orange flame, lifting the first jeep up and off the ground, and knocking the second one back a good 10 feet.

Before Hunter knew it, the two House of David cars were speeding through the burning hole created by the missile. He could hear a few thuds against the cars as the Gwanda Nation soldiers fired at them. But the armor on the doors prevented any of the bullets from getting through.

Wack laughed as they burst onto the relatively safe Hudson Parkway. "Just like Moses, it works every time!"

The two car caravan reached Yankee Stadium without further incident. Outside, the huge bat that marked the stadium entrance for years now lay broken in several large chunks, as if a giant had smashed it. Slowly, the gun wagons circled the stadium, looking for a means of entry.

There was a garage door to the rear of the place which was both locked and rusted in place. A shot from the rocket car's cannon took care of it, snapping its springs and causing the door to rise high enough for the two cars to sneak through.

They drove out onto the field, the high stadium walls giving them the feeling that they were in a dark valley. The place had fallen into disrepair, yet oddly, the bases were still in place, as was the pitcher's mound. Hunter had been to the stadium as a boy, on all occasions watching the Yanks beat his hometown Boston Red Sox. Now it was as dreary as a place could be, another rusting symbol of a faded American dream.

They drove right out to the left field wall where they found another garage door, an entrance way that maintenance vehicles used to access the field. Another burst of cannon fire opened this door and soon the tiny band found themselves walking in a large, pitch black room.

Hunter was directing one of two high-powered flashlights Wack had supplied, Dominique glued to his side.

"What could be here, Hawk?" she asked. "Why would this place be so important to Viktor? He never mentioned it in all the time I was with him."

"Beats me," Hunter said, playing the flashlight beam over racks of old grass rakes and bags of baseline lime. "But he knew that Calypso had hidden something here, something he was willing to pay big numbers for. Something he must have thought would help him in winning the war in the 'Bads."

Suddenly they heard Zal call out: "Hunter! Over here!"

They rushed to his side and saw that he had found yet another door, this one smaller and apparently installed fairly recently. A computerized combination lock held the folding door shut.

Hunter made short work of the combination, finally getting the computer to show three red indicator lights in a row. With the entire force standing around him, he pushed one final button and the door slowly began to rise.

"Well, Jesus Christ!" Zal was the first one to speak.

"Ditto," said Wack, pointing his flashlight beam onto the object inside. The rest of the group could utter no more than a chorus of "Oohs" and "Aahs."

For the first time in a long time, Hunter was speechless. So *this* is what all the fuss was about, he thought. He had had a clue even before the door opened, detecting a whiff of aviation fuel. Now he knew why.

It was an airplane hidden in the secret room. But not just any airplane. In fact, it was probably the only one of its kind.

"What the hell kind of jet is that, Hawk?" Zal, the experienced F-105 Thunderchief pilot, asked. "Those curves, that material, that design. It looks more like a kid's toy."

Hunter ran his flashlight beam the length of the small aircraft. Ah, yes. Those curves. That material. That design. He couldn't contain his smile.

"That, ladies and gentlemen, is called 'Stealth.' "

Chapter Twenty-eight

The Stealth airplane was probably the most closely guarded secret the U.S. Government ever had, before the lid came off when one of its models crashed in the California highlands back in the early 1980s. Oddly enough, just like the Ghost Rider Project, the object of Stealth was radar avoidance. Ghost Rider deflected radar waves through an ultra-complicated, electronic jamming system. Stealth was invisible to radar primarily because of its design and what it was made of.

Even Hunter wasn't entirely sure how it worked—not yet anyway. It looked like a flattened-out teardrop with French curve wings and tail section. It was about two thirds the size of an F-16, small for a military jet. It was painted dull black. But it was because of this small, curving design and the use of mostly non-metallic building materials and paint, that U.S. aeronautical engineers were able to get the Stealth airplane's radar signature down to nothing. Unlike the five Ghost Rider B-1 bombers, this airplane was designed as a fighter. It sported two .20

mm cannons and also hardpoints on its wings to carry missiles or bombs. Hunter instantly knew that if he could get this airplane back to the Badlands, along with the fifth Ghost Rider black box, then the Western Forces would be nearly invincible against the Russian SAMs.

No wonder Viktor wanted it so much.

"We've got to get it out of here," Hunter said. With that, the group took positions around the wing and fuselage and started to push. The airplane was lightweight by design so it was fairly easy to get it rolling. Once it was out on the field, Wack produced a length of chain and worked on setting up a makeshift towing line.

Meanwhile, Hunter had popped the airplane's canopy and had climbed inside. How the airplane got into Calypso's hands and into Yankee Stadium, he would never know. But he could tell by one sniff that at some point recently, the airplane had been expertly maintained, right down to clean oil in the engine, and fresh fuel in the tanks. Its battery was still charged, and Hunter was glad to see that like his F-16, the Stealth was equipped with a self-starter.

By this time, they had towed the airplane out into the stadium's enormous parking lot. Hunter had everyone stand clear as he flipped a barrage of preliminary switches. Then, he crossed his fingers and hit the start button . . .

Without an instant's hesitation, the engine sprang to life.

He quickly adjusted the fuel mixture and activated the computer. Then he climbed out.

Zal met him. "Jesus, Hawk," the ADF pilot said. "If that thing can penetrate their radar net, their aircover will be zilch. Once the word gets out and you show up over the battlefield in that, and you'll have half of them turning tail and running back home."

Just then an idea flashed through Hunter's mind.

"Wack," Hunter yelled to the House leader. "You got film in that camera?"

Five minutes and 20 high-power strobelight flashes later, Wack was removing a roll of film from the camera and handing it to Hunter. "I'll be sure to send you prints," Hunter said, jokingly.

But it was the last laugh he'd have for a long time. For now it was decision time. The others wisely stood off to the side as Dominique stood by him. He turned to her and opened his mouth to speak. But no words would come out.

She did all the talking necessary. "Oh, Hawk," she sighed as she held him. "I know what you have to do." She was crying. He felt a heaviness in his chest. Before they had departed House of David territory, Wack had made arrangements for two of his fighters to meet the Free Canadian sub at its rendezvous point and direct it up the Hudson River to a point off the Hunter's group's position. The plan had been for the sub to carry the commandos out, head for JFK where only Hunter would be dropped off to pick up his F-16, and bring the rest of the group—Dominique included—back to the safety of Free Canada. Wack and his guys would then make their way back to safer ground.

Now there was a slight change in plans. Hunter

was determined to fly the Stealth back to the war zone. This would mean leaving behind two of his greatest loves—Dominique and his F-16.

"Come for me darling," she said, kissing him hard. "Come for me when the war is over. I'll be waiting, like I always have."

He looked at her. She was beautiful. "I love you, honey," he said, hugging her tightly. He didn't want to let go. "Someday . . ."

He could say no more.

Suddenly, he saw a muzzle flash off in the distance. Wack and Zal saw it to. A shell came crashing into the parking lot, landing nearby. A check of Zal's NightScope confirmed their worst fears.

"Christ!" Zal yelled. "It looks like an armored column coming our way."

Hunter took a look through the scope. He counted at least twenty vehicles, all gunwagons of some sort, including several tanks.

"Who the hell are they?" Simons, the Canadian commander asked, taking the scope from Hunter.

"Probably some 'instant allies,' " Wack told them. "If Viktor is still alive, he could have rounded up some heavy metal from the other groups. Either that or word got around real quick as to what we found here."

"Whoever they are, they're coming to claim this package," Hunter said referring to the Stealth. Suddenly a tank round landed even closer to them, causing the group to hit the pavement. "And they ain't going to be friendly about it," he finished.

Another round came in, and landed dangerously

close to the Stealth. The column was about a half-mile away, traveling quickly up the Hudson Parkway. At this rate, Hunter's tiny army would soon be overwhelmed.

Suddenly they saw another muzzle flash—this one coming from the blackness of the nearby Hudson. A shell landed right in front of the column hitting squarely on the lead gun wagon.

Hunter took the NightScope and peered in the direction of the latest gunfire. "It's the sub!" he yelled.

Hunter could see the definite outline of the submarine as it sat in the middle of the river. Several figures were scurrying around its deck, working the gun installed there.

"Come on!" Hunter yelled. "They're giving us the cover we need . . ."

He turned to look at the parking lot. It was only about 1800 feet long and he calculated the Stealth would need at least 2500 to take off. Still he had to try it.

The enemy column was recovering. It had stopped but now was returning fire toward the sub as well as toward the stadium parking lot. Hunter grabbed Dominque one more time. She hugged him and then squeezed his hand and whispered: "I'll always be with you . . ."

Then she was gone, hustled off into Wack's gunwagon. Zal rushed up to Hunter and quickly shook hands.

"Don't worry, Hawk," he said. "We'll take care of her. We'll get her to a safe house in Quebec. Fitz will know where she'll be."

"Thanks, Zal," Hunter told his friend. "Thanks for coming to the rescue."

"Good luck, buddy," Zal said, as they both ducked away from another enemy shell explosion. "I hope I get a chance to get back into my F-105 and join the party out in the Bads."

"Great!" Hunter yelled over the noise.

With that Zal jumped into the House gun wagon. Wack wheeled the big car back toward Hunter. The fighter reached his hand out the window.

"See ya, Hawk," he said. "Take good care of that flag."

"You know it," Hunter told him. "We'll meet again."

The gun wagon roared away, followed by the rocket car that was firing as it went. The last Hunter saw of Dominque, she was waving to him through the bullet-proof glass. "Goodbye," he said, to no one but himself. Suddenly, he was alone. He couldn't remember ever being so devastated.

Another shell hit nearby, *too* close to the now-warmed up Stealth. He turned his attention to the troops firing at him from the highway. His sadness turned instantly to anger. A fire was lit in his heart that wouldn't go out for a long time. He clenched his fists. His eyes began to burn. These troops. The Russians. The Circle. The Mongols. Viktor. All of them were marked. He felt himself go a little bit crazy. Another shell landed nearby, but he didn't even bother to duck.

"Fuck around with me, will you?" he screamed,

climbing into the Stealth.

He spun the jet around and pointed it toward the longest part of the parking lot. There was only one way the jet would get airborne. He simultaneously engaged the air brakes and gunned the engine. Higher and higher the RPMs climbed. The engine was roaring, smoking, straining. Like a coiled cat, it was ready to leap. Yet he held back, waiting. Two more shells landed nearby. He could see the deck gun of the submarine go off again. The House of David rocket car fired once more. There were tracer bullets flying everywhere. All the while, the Stealth's engine was screaming for release.

"Okay," Hunter said after checking the instruments. "Time to go . . ."

With that he snapped off the air brakes. Like a dragster starting out down a quarter mile, the jet's tires squealed and smoked. The airplane catapulted forward, going from zero to 100 mph in less than three seconds. At 125 mph, Hunter coolly brought up the landing gear. Now the airplane was airborne whether it liked it or not. At the same time he yanked back on the controls and turned the nose of the airplane straight up. He felt the tail end of the ship smack into the far parking lot fence. No matter. Scratched paint he could live with. He was flying.

Higher he climbed, until all the lights and the omni-present fires of New Order Manhattan came into view. He quickly checked his instruments. Everything looked good. The airplane was very smooth flying and easy to handle. And the controls were so standard, any military pilot could have figured them out eventually. It took Hunter approximately four seconds.

He test-fired the cannons. They too worked perfectly. Then he turned the airplane around and dove. Below him was the enemy convoy. He could see the sub still firing off shore. Somewhere down there he knew that the Canadian commandos were scrambling aboard a rubber life raft and paddling like hell toward the sub. Wack and his fighters, vastly outnumbered, would soon be drawing all the fire from the enemy column. Hunter intended to even things up.

He came in low and fast on the line of trucks, tanks and gunwagons. With the press of a button, the two cannons opened up and a deadly spray of fire rained down on the column. One truck, then another went up in flames immediately.

He flipped the airplane over and bore down on the enemy again. The cannons routinely chopped up vehicle and body alike. More explosions followed as the shells hit gas tanks and ammunition boxes. Best of all, no one was shooting at him.

By the end of his third strafing run, all firing from the column had ceased. He pulled up and slowed down. After a few seconds he spotted the two House of David gunwagons sprinting across the George Washington Bridge. They would temporarily retreat into New Jersey then sneak back into Manhattan when the time was right. Hunter was glad to see the brave fighters make it out in one piece.

He turned again and came down low over the river. A light was flashing at him from the sub's conning tower. It was blinking: "A-OK. A-OK." One more pass over the river and he saw the sub was submerging. He knew it would glide just a few feet below the surface until it got out into deeper water. Then it would be off to the sanctuary of Canada. He felt his heart lighten just a notch. For the first time in a long while, he felt that Dominque was finally safe.

He climbed and turned the jet west. Already he could fee the sting of the battle in his bones.

Chapter Twenty-nine

The flight of 20 B-52 Stratofortresses were still 30 miles from their target when the SAMs first appeared.

"Take evasive action!" each bomber pilot heard simultaneously. "We got company coming up at five o'clock!" The familiar voice belonged to General Jones. Flying the lead bomber, he was the first to pick up the Soviet anti-aircraft missiles. The general hit a button on his control column which activated a chaff dispenser at the rear of the airplane. Immediately a long stream of radar-reflective tinfoil squirted out of the B-52. The other bomber pilots did the same. The tinfoil cloud would serve to confuse the on-board radar homing devices on the SAMs. But not by much.

Within 10 seconds the early morning sky was filled with SA-2 missiles—the same type American pilots dodged over North Viet Nam years before. One missile found its target with deadly accuracy, hitting one of the big bombers on the port wing, severing it from the fuselage. The airplane immediately flipped over and began a long plunge to earth. There were no parachutes.

"Group, break!" Jones yelled into his radio. Immediately the Stratofortresses peeled out of their closed formation and went to pre-assigned staggered altitudes. At the same time, each pilot switched on his airplane's Electronic Counter-Measures devices designed to confuse the enemy missiles. But Jones knew that this would provide only minimal protection at best.

"Jesus, this one has our name on it!" Jones yelled to his co-pilot, as they could see a missile's trail of smoke rising up toward them. Jones pushed down on the controls and put the B-52 in a harrowing dive. The missiles whooshed by them dangerously close to the starboard wing. They had hardly recovered when another missile just missed impacting on their nose.

"Christ, there are hundreds of them!" the co-pilot yelled, looking down at the multitude of tell-tale smoke trails rising up out of the clouds.

Jones yanked back on the controls and put the bomber into a steep climb. Back in Viet Nam, a bomber force such as this would have had the luxury of dozens of fighter aircraft as escorts, as well as many fighter-bombers sweeping in on SAM sites before the big boys arrives. But not so here. With the exception of a half dozen fighters looking out for the Yaks, the B-52s were on their own.

Jones had ordered the big bomber strike on the most formidable targets in the Badlands: the Soviets' castle-like main base near Wichita and the nuclear power station nearby, both of which Hunter had identified during his foray into the forbidden zone. The pre-dawn bombing raid was timed to catch the enemy off-guard. But still, Jones knew his losses to the SAMs would be high—probably no other target in the 'Bads was so protected as these two were by the deadly Soviet missiles.

Time was running out for the Western Forces. Jones's intelligence people told him that the Circle Army would be in place and linked-up with the Soviet forces in the Badlands in a matter of days. Once that took place, the Western Forces would be facing an organized, fully deployed enemy. It would be next to impossible to fight them even up at that point. The democracy's only hope harked back to Jones's conversation with Hunter several days back. Increase the air attacks, disrupt the enemy's lines of communication, hit important targets, keep them guessing.

Which is why Jones knew this bombing mission was so necessary. Air strikes on SAM sites up and down the Badlands had continued unabated for the past several days, with thankfully low loss rates for the democratic air forces. These attacks served two purposes. They kept the enemy off-balance, and they punched holes in the SAM line, very important passageways that the Western Forces would soon need critically.

But Jones needed time. Time for the armies of the west to fully mobilize. Time for all of the available air units to get operational. Time for all the Free Canadian "volunteers" to get in position. And time for the west's best weapon—Hawk Hunter—to return, ideally with the fifth black box in hand. Then they might have a chance.

A missile explosion off to his left jarred Jones's thoughts. He saw another one of his bombers get hit; a long fiery trail spiraling down was all that was left of it. He put his airplane into another dive, and yanked it hard to the portside, just in time to avoid two missiles that were rising up toward him, side-by-side.

"I've never seen anything like this," he called over to his co-pilot. The sky all around them was filled with powerful explosions and white streaks of exhaust contrails caused by the seemingly endless barrage of SAMs.

And they were still 20 miles from the target . . .

Still the bombers pressed on. Jones's navigator called out the coordinates of the "castle" target, now 10 miles ahead. Jones radioed for his bombardier to make his final adjustments, then he ordered his remaining bombers to quickly form up again. One group would divert to hit the nuke station; he would lead the others to hit the Soviets' main base.

They were going to use an old World War II tactic called "bomb-on-leader." This meant when Jones's B-52 started dropping its bombs, the rest of the bomber group would follow suit. It was up to Jones and his crew to pick the absolute correct time to order their bombs away.

Seven miles to target and amazingly the SAM fire increased. Two more Stratofortresses were hit; one right behind Jones took a missile hit direct on its bomb bay door. The big airplane was immediately obliterated. The other airplane got its wing clipped. Jones watched as most of its crew bailed out and the pilot steered the ailing bomber into a suicide dive directly into a SAM concentration just outside the castle base. The airplane slammed into the enemy position with a tremendous explosion.

Soon Jones's bombers were only seconds from the target. The general's bombardier called up his ready signal and Jones acknowledged it. He waited for a three count, gritted his teeth then yelled, "Bombs away!"

He immediately felt the aircraft go lighter as the 30 tons of bombs fell away from the bomb bay. The other B-52s dropped their bombloads at exactly the same times. As Jones watched out of his window, he could see the first string of bombs landing right in the middle of the walled city. Then another string hit. Then another. The resulting explosions were so powerful and concentrated, a fiery mini-mushroom cloud rose up over the city.

Just as the last bomb was dropped, Jones ordered the entire force to immediately climb. Then the survivors turned for home. The B-52s had battled their way in and now would have to battle their way out. But they had delivered 400 *tons* of high explosives right on top of the main command center of the enemy.

Jones figured the destruction of the enemy HQ would give the west another few days of valuable time. Off in the distance, he could see the nuke station was also enveloped in flames, courtesy of 50 additional tons of bombs. Suddenly, there was a green flash of light, followed by a king-sized mushroom cloud. Jones knew that was the nuke's reactor going up. Anyone left alive on the ground would now have even radiation to contend with.

Jones figured the destruction of the enemy HQ and the nuke would seriously disrupt the Soviets' command structure and give the west another few days of valuable time.

Now if only Hunter would show up . . .

Chapter Thirty

One by one, the surviving B-52s approached the Denver air station and began their landing descent. Jones was stationed toward the end of the pack as several of his ships had been damaged and had fallen behind the main group. Suddenly the pilot of the last trailing bomber—code named Caboose—called ahead to Jones with an urgent message.

"Sir, we got a bogie back here!" the pilot radioed. "He's right off our tail!"

Jones yelled back to his own radar man. "What do you show back there?"

"Nothing sir," the answer came back. "All I got is '52s."

Jones radioed back to his tail pilot. "What do you have? Visual sighting? Or a blip?"

"It's a visual, sir," the pilot replied. "I've got no radar signature. My set must have caught some damage over the target."

Jones was worried. The bogie might very well be

a Yak recon ship, following the stragglers back to their home base in preparation for an air strike of their own. But why didn't the aircraft show up on radar? He quickly radioed all the other airplanes ahead of him to drop down and land as quickly as possible.

"What's his airspeed and altitude, Caboose?" Jones then radioed the last ship.

"He's at 450, and about 2000 feet above us," came the reply. "He's keeping pace with us, sir."

There was a crackle of static. "Stand by sir," the pilot called out. "He's booted it sir, coming down fast."

"Can your tail gunner get a fix on him?" Jones radioed back.

"Negative, sir," the pilot said, his voice raising a notch in anxiety. "He's going right by us . . . right now!"

Jones turned around in his seat and looked back toward the Caboose. Sure enough, a small, strange-looking fighter streaked by right underneath him. His co-pilot saw it oo.

"What the hell kind of airplane is that, General?" he asked.

"Beats the hell out of me," Jones said. Just then, his B-52 entered a low hung cloud bank. Jones had to concentrate on landing the airplane. He activated his landing gear and deployed his tail chute to further slow down the big bomber.

When he broke through the clouds, the landing strip was directly ahead of him. And so was the mysterious fighter!

"The Goddamned thing has landed!" co-pilot called out. "Jesus, he walked right in without the tower or the scramble jet picking him up? He's got to be friendly or crazy . . ."

"Or both," Jones said, looking at his co-pilot.

By the time Jones taxied his Stratofortress into its holding station, a crowd of armed guards and curious monkeys had surrounded the strange jet. The general quickly shut down the big bomber's engines and climbed out of the access hatch. He wasn't totally surprised to see Hunter standing on the wing of the oddly-shaped black fighter, coolly discussing something with the group of onlookers.

Hunter jumped off the wing and walked quickly to meet Jones. He was holding the fifth black box.

"Am I glad to see you," Jones said. "And that black box."

The general put his fingers to his mouth and let out a long, shrill whistle. Immediately a jeep filled with military police appeared. Jones handed the precious black box to the sergeant of the group, saying: "You know what to do."

The jeep sped off to a pair of F-104s waiting nearby. The two planes were already warmed up and ready to go. The MP passed the box to a monkey who gave it to one of the pilots. Immediately the two Starfighters taxied out onto the runway and began their take-off roll.

"They've been waiting to scramble with that box for the past three days," Jones told Hunter as they watched the scene. "It will be in Eureka within three hours."

The recovery mission was now complete. But there would be no time for celebration. No round of welcome back drinks.

"Sorry for sneaking in unannounced," Hunter said, his voice slightly distant. "I was down to two pounds of fuel when I touched down. I had to cut off everything, lights, radio, radar, everything except the flight controls."

Jones scratched his wiffle haircut. He looked at Hunter. He looked different. He could tell his pilot was burning inside. "Is this what I think it is?"

"Yes," Hunter confirmed. "It's a Stealth fighter. A warlord in Manhattan named Calypso got a hold of it somehow. He was about to . . . well, trade it . . . to Viktor, when I upset their plans."

"Viktor himself? Sounds interesting," Jones said.

"I'll tell you all about it sometime," Hunter said soberly, choosing his words very carefully. "But it will have to keep for now."

Jones looked at him again. This man, his friend, had changed. Something, almost imperceptible, yet very obvious had come over him. He *looked* different.

"Hey, Hawk," Jones told him. "Grab some chow and shut eye. You'll need it."

"Chow, yes," Hunter said. "Sleep, no. I've got a lot of work to do, and this airplane is going to come in handy."

For the first time in what seemed like years, Hunter chowed down, showered and climbed into a fresh flightsuit. A few hours later, he was sitting in the operations room at the air station. The usual group of PAAC principals was there, gathered around an enormous map of the mid-American continent. Jones laid out the strategy for the crucial days ahead.

Western Forces recon teams had located three major concentrations of Circle troops making their way toward the Badlands. One army, dubbed the Northern Group, was made up of two divisions or 30,000 men. It had been gradually moving across the north central states, and was now on the border of old Minnesota and Wisconsin.

"This army is probably going to link up with the northern part of the SAM line in the Dakotas," Jones told them.

The Circle's Southern Group, made up of three divisions, or 45,000 men, had swept through the southern states and now was encamped in northern Louisiana.

"These guys are getting a lot of heavy equipment and supplies from New Orleans," Jones continued. "They've got a major concentration at Shreveport, and it's a good guess they're going to get into Oklahoma or possibly invade Texas when the time is right."

The third and largest Circle Army group—this one containing as many as 105,000 men in seven divisions—had formed up near occupied Football City and would soon embark across Missouri, heading for central Kansas and Nebraska.

"This has been their plan all along," Jones said, moving colored indicators representing the enemy troop movements. "Link up with the Russians, use the SAMs as an umbrella and just keeping on coming until they meet some opposition. And we, gentlemen, are the only opposition that they *can* meet."

He pointed to the area around the Dakotas.

"We've got to rely on the Canadians to deal with this Northern Group," he said. "The idea will be to isolate them in Minnesota. Fitzie's ADF F-105s will help out there."

He shifted his attention to the southern part of the map. "The Texans and the exiled Football City troops will take charge of stopping this Southern Group. The key here is to grease New Orleans. That port had been lousy with Russian subs for weeks now. The Texans have one hell of a bunch of F-4s down there, so that will be their job. St. Louie's F-20s will support the action near Shreveport."

Jones paused and turned his attention to the center of the map. Then he said soberly: "Gentlemen, I'd be less than honest if I didn't say we've got the toughest job facing us.

"I've got to figure that this middle group will move right through the Badlands in Kansas and southern Nebraska. They're the ones we need to worry about. They're more than three times as large as the other two groups, so they represent their major thrust. They've got the most transport—trucks, railroad, boats.

"So they're very mobile. And they're heading right for us."

He turned his attention to the markers representing the middle positions of the democratic forces. "Here are our lines," he said, indicating a long stretch that roughly coincided with the borders of Colorado and Kansas-Nebraska. "This is where we've got to meet them. We're digging in. All of our ground troops will be in this trenchline in the next two days. And, frankly, we'll be lucky if we get sixty thousand men in place."

Jones turned and addressed the group directly. "They've got us by about two-to-one as things stand now," he said earnestly. "If they break through, they'll be unstoppable."

There was a deadly silence in the room.

"So what are we going to do?" Jones asked. "Well, three things . . .

"First, you're all familiar with the so-called "Land-Air Battle" strategy. Anyone who fought in Europe knows it well. This will be *our* plan of action. We've got to hit their supply lines, their lines of communications and their means of transportation. Fitzie's got to do it in Minnesota. St. Louie and the Texans have to do it in Louisiana. And we've got to do it in Kansas and south Nebraska.

"We've *got* to break through the SAM line using the holes we've punched in it before they seal them up. We've got to take out every bridge, highway and railroad line in Missouri. We've got to isolate those troops from their reserves and their supply lines.

"Second, once we've done that, we go after the troops themselves. Bomb the shit out of them wherever they are. And we can't be timid. Napalm, antipersonnel stuff. Whatever it takes. And anyone we miss in Missouri, we catch on the roads and rivers in Kansas and south Nebraska. The harder we hit them and the longer we delay them, the better our chances in the trenches will be."

"As for strategic bombing . . ." Jones produced a large photo of the Soviets' castle-like main base, with the still smoking nuke station nearby. "This was taken just a couple of hours ago, right after we went over. We lost five airplanes and crews to accomplish this, but I have to say it was worth the price. You can see both targets were hit hard.

"We have to assume they're now trying to operate without electricity, which, if anything, will screw up their radio communications. Plus we're banking on some of their top people being stationed at their HQ when we hit it. Also, I wouldn't want to buy any property real soon near that bombed out nuke station. It'll be hot there for a while."

Once again, there was a stark silence in the room.

Then Dozer spoke up: "You said we have to do three things, General."

Jones nodded. "That's right. Missions one and two—hitting their lines of communications and blasting their troop concentrations—these things we can do.

"But we have to do one more thing—and it may be the hardest mission of all."

He paused, looking several of the principals straight in the eye. "We've got to remember that Viktor—wherever he is—assembled The Circle Army the same way Hitler assembled his. By deceit, propaganda and hero-worship. First he gathered together all of the riff-raff, leftovers, anyone who could aim a gun. Then he 'recruited' some young blood. Teenagers. Filled them with a bunch of bullshit and pointed them in the direction of the front. From what we hear from Fitzie's spies, a *lot* of these soldiers are really young kids, sixteen, seventeen, eighteen years old. They're heavily indoctrinated. Brainwashed. Fanatical. They look to Viktor as their leader, their general, their god.

"So what does this mean? Well, for one thing, I think we can expect human waves once we meet them on the battlefield. We'll see suicide squads, human booby-traps, things like that. At least with these young grunts.

"But remember, Viktor's army is really made up of two kinds of soldier. These young radical kids and the old vets—the 'Aks, Family guys, whatever—that are just along for the ride. They *know* what's ahead of them. We have to assume these guys are very tightly-strung. Whatever Viktor has buzzing around *their* heads—probably drugs—they're close to the edge at any given moment. They're one step away from snapping out.

"So, the third objective I spoke about is to *get* to these guys. Zap them. Demoralize them. Drive 'em crazy. Force them to go over the brink. You can be sure that Viktor and his guys are not leveling with them. Not telling them we've got more than one hundred fighters and fighter bombers and heavy bombers ready to unload on their asses. You know they haven't told them about our hitting the SAM line or flattening their HQ. But you know the army. You can be sure that rumors are flying through those camps. I'm sure Viktor's told them all it would be a cakewalk. Well, some of them have got to be questioning that right about now.

"Now most of the crazy kids will believe the Party line, no matter what. But the vets won't, if we show them different. They remember the battle for Football City and what happened to the 'Aks. I think Viktor's empire is a house of cards. And, from what Fitzie's spies tell us, we're not even sure if he's still alive. I think one or two good slaps in the face and half these veterans do a one-eighty and starting walking back east. For every guy that deserts, that's one less that we have to waste fuel and airplanes and bombs and bullets on. We've got to be *economical* with our firepower. It's not a bottomless pit.

"But we have to light that fuse. Get into the minds of these guys, just at the right moment. Just when they're wondering just what they hell they're doing. The question is, how do we do it? How do we spook these guys?"

Suddenly someone spoke loud and clear from the back of the room. "Leave that to me."

It was Hunter.

An hour later, Hunter was strapped inside the refueled, rearmed Stealth fighter, warming up its engines for take-off.

Jones and Dozer watched from the flight line as the radar-proof airplane took off and disappeared into the clouds.

"I've known him for what seems like a long time now," Dozer said. "I've never seen him like this. He's like a quiet madman. That look in his eyes is terrifying. He's carrying around some emotional baggage with him. And it's so typical that he won't talk about it."

"Maybe it's his F-16," Jones said. "That was a bold move leaving it behind in New York City. There's a good chance he'll never see it again. And he knows it's probably the only F-16 left in the world."

"Or it could be the girl," Dozer theorized. "All he told me was that he found her in New York. Rescued her. But I guess he had to leave her behind too."

Jones lit a cigar. "Or, then again, maybe it's the Russians. The Circle. Viktor. Maybe it's the whole fucking mess."

"Well, whatever it is," Dozer said. "Someone's made a big mistake messing around with him."

Jones paused for a moment. "He says he wants to operate on his own for this one," he said finally. "Wants to be the unpredictable driver. Operate independently. Be what he called 'the uncalculable equation.' I can't stop him. I wouldn't want to. But we'll miss him . . ."

Dozer nodded in agreement, adding: "Yes. But we don't have to worry too much. He knows what our strategy is. He'll be on top of every move we make."

"I'm glad he's on our side."

Chapter Thirty-one

The war began in earnest the next day.

Using the narrow "holes" in the SAM shield cleared by the surgical air strikes of the previous days, PAAC fighters and fighter-bombers swept through the central Badlands just as their allies were doing in the north and south. Bridges, roads, communications stations, fuel dumps and other targets were attacked up and down the Circle areas. More than 80 missions were flown. The strategy of hitting the enemy's rear echelon was put into full effect.

The day was not without its losses. While the heavy duty SAMs were fixed in the Badlands, many of the rear units of the Circle Army were equipped with Soviet-made SA-7 shoulder-launched SAMs. Two of Fitzgerald's Thunderchiefs met their end this way while attacking an ammo train near Mankato, Minnesota.

But the Aerodrome Thuds took back their measure of revenge. One flight, led by Mike Fitzgerald himself, caught a converted AMTRAK train moving south from Minneapolis, carrying ten cars of Circle troops. The four F-105s attacked the train just as it was going over a bridge which spanned a gorge near Springfield, Minnesota. Using rather dated, but still deadly TV-guided bombs, both the bridge and the train were completely destroyed.

In the south, St. Louie's famous F-20 Tigersharks attacked a number of Circle targets around Shreveport. Oil storage tanks and pump houses were high on the priority list. Some of the F-20s were carrying 500-pound "iron" bombs, ideal for busting the sides of oil tanks and igniting the precious fuel inside. The Tigersharks were also successful in severing two major highways leading out of Shreveport, roads on which Circle troops were already moving toward the Texas border. Using laser-guided bombs, the F-20 pilots were able to collapse overpass structures which fell and crushed hapless troops who had sought shelter underneath them. By the time the Tigersharks broke off the attack, a 15-mile span of Interstate Route 20 was rendered useless and dripping with Circle blood. Not one of the ultra-sophisticated F-20 jets was lost.

The Texas Air Force launched a bold air strike on the port of New Orleans, the major staging area for the Circle Southern Group and their Soviet allies. Sweeping in off the Gulf of Mexico, the Texans bombed and strafed the city's docking facilities and managed to sink two Soviet subs. More oil storage tanks and volatile liquid natural gas facilities were also hit. The city was well-defended and returning pilots told of a sky filled with SAMs of every size and power. Four of the 16 F-4s were lost.

By the end of the day, Jones knew the plan to hit the enemy's rear echelon was a sound one. Even if half the reports of bombing damage were true, the first 24 hours of his counter-offensive were a success. He ordered the same strategy for the next day.

But two things bothered him. One was that despite all the air activity, not one pilot reported spotting any of the enemy Yaks. The other question was: where was Hunter?

Jones had his answer several hours later.

The pilot of a C-130 cargo ship flying over the Rockies to deliver the supplies to the Denver air station, reported seeing the Stealth fighter streaking over Idaho just at sunset. Around midnight, Jones received a coded telex message from the commander of the Free Canadian Forces stationed in the Dakotas. He said that a heavily fortified Soviet radar station located in the Black Hills was attacked and destroyed earlier that night by a single "top-secret type aircraft."

A few hours later, Jones heard from one of Fitzgerald's ADF Thunderchief pilots, via a scrambled radio message. The pilot, flying a night recon mission over Bismarck, North Dakota, was attacked by several hidden radar-controlled anti-aircraft batteries guarding a top priority target just outside the city. The pilot said the fire was so intense, his airplane was hit more than a dozen times within a half minute. With his radio and some flight controls knocked out and the enemy fire getting worse, the pilot was looking for a place to bail out when a "dark, mysterious-looking fighter" came out of nowhere and blasted the AA batteries. "Whoever it was," the pilot told Jones. "He saved my ass."

Early the next morning, before PAAC fighter bombers went into action again, pre-strike recon airplanes found that a few of the "holes" that were opened in the SAM line several days before were now closed up, by the Soviets redeploying their mobile SAM batteries. But what the recon airplanes also found was many other Soviet radar stations destroyed or burning up and down the Badlands SAM line. Without radar, the SAMs were blind. Where there were a half dozen large "holes" in the Soviet wall the day before, now there were upward of twenty, smaller ones, especially around the northwest section of Kansas. The information was flashed back to the PAAC attack craft even as they were taxiing for take-off from their bases.

"It's Hunter," Jones told Dozer as they sat in the Denver Air Station situation room sifting through the reports of the "radar-busting" the night before. "He's giving us a lot of leeway to get in and out."

Dozer shook his head in admiration. "Just as we expected. Where the hell is he fueling up? Or getting his ammo?"

Jones shrugged. "Who knows? But at this point, I don't care. He's gone after the radar stations. I wonder what's next on his list?"

Due to Hunter's night work, Western Forces' fighters and fighter-bombers were able to get in behind enemy lines quicker. Once over The Circle's rear areas, the attackers roamed free, hitting targets of opportunity everywhere except around major cities, where SAM sites still made flying very dangerous. Once again bridges, highways and railroads were the main targets. Transportation lines from The Circle's weapons factories in the east were especially hit hard.

And once again, no Yaks appeared to challenge the attacking aircraft . . .

Meanwhile, activity was stepped up on the Western Forces defense line near the old Colorado-Kansas border. A long and elaborate series of trenchworks had been in the works for several weeks, with soldiers and volunteers using equipment ranging from heavy machinery to picks and shovels. Mine fields were laid, anti-personnel traps were built. Gun emplacements were installed, interlocking fields of fire plotted. Artillery bases and surface-to-surface rocket platforms were activated. It was here—on the sandy hills and open range land of Eastern Colorado—that Jones and the other Western Forces leaders were gambling the final confrontation between East and West would take place. The circle Army's Central Group would move forward.

The Soviet SAM line—most of which was on wheels—would be right behind the ground troops.

It was shaping up to be a monstrous battle . . .

Chapter Thirty-two

The four Yaks rose one at a time from their hidden base in North Dakota and headed south. It was dusk—the only time the Soviet commanders would dare move the precious jets. With reports of a second day of numerous air strikes by the West behind the SAM line still coming in, the Soviets were banking that most of the enemy airplanes had returned to their bases by now. The last thing they wanted was for their Yaks to get in a dogfight situation with the more skillful Western Forces' pilots.

The Yaks were deploying toward the center of the SAM line. They would be needed there when the bulk of The Circle Army's Central Group finally arrived. The Soviets' plan all along was to use the VTOL fighters in a ground attack role—thus the

Soviet commanders had kept the jets out of the recent murderous air action. They had already suffered a serious blow when their HQ and power supply near Wichita was destroyed by PAAC's big bombers. Now they knew they couldn't afford to lose a single Yak before the big ground battles began.

But even under the cover of the gathering darkness, the Yak pilots were jittery. It wasn't the free-roaming fighters that bothered them; it was this strange airplane—this secret weapon of the Western Forces—that had the Soviet pilots concerned. Word had spread quickly about the black jet fighter that was invisible to radar screens and therefore attacked without warning. It was an old U.S. Air Force Stealth, the Soviet version of scuttlebutt had it, being flown by this legendary fighter pilot named Hunter.

So the Yaks were ordered to play it cautious. Flying at 40,000 feet in single file, separated by a mile between them, the Soviet jets proceeded toward their destination, a battered yet still working airport near Dodge City, Kansas. As planned, the four pilots were maintaining strict radio silence, their only communication being the sequential clicking of their cockpit microphones every 15 minutes. Two clicks meant "Okay."

The Yaks had just passed over the Nebraska-Kansas border when the flight commander—a Russian colonel—routinely pressed his microphone button twice. His Number Two man, flying exactly one mile behind, responded quickly with two clicks. Number Three did the same.

But when it was Number Four's turn, there was nothing . . .

The Soviet colonel initiated the pattern a second time. Numbers Two and Three responded immediately, but still no sign from Number Four. After a third attempt failed to raise the Yak, the Soviet flight commander began to sweat.

He slowed down, letting Numbers Two and Three to catch up to him. A wag of his wings and a flick of his landing lights was enough for them to know they were to proceed with caution. Then the Soviet colonel doubled back to look for his stray.

Five minutes into his search he found the missing Yak. Pieces of it were lying on the side of a Kansas foothill, burning uncontrollably. One look told him that the pilot could not have survived. And the airplane did not simply crash, either. The wreckage had all the earmarkings of an airplane destroyed in flight.

The Soviet commander made a note of the location, opened his throttle and nervously sped up to rejoin his flight. His fourth man's fuel might have blown up, or perhaps one of his weapons had malfunctioned.

Or maybe an air-to-air missile did the job . . .

The commander linked up with his two remaining jets and they fell back into the same mile-spread pattern. The Soviet colonel now started clicking his microphone button every five minutes, an action which drew instantaneous responses from his equally-nervous Number Two and Three pilots.

It was twenty minutes later when the commander heard his Number Three man start clicking his microphone not twice but a rapid-fire 10, 20, 30 times! The colonel knew his pilot was panicking. Something was happening. He immediately yanked back on his stick, did a wide loop and headed back to investigate. He arrived just in time to see Number Three take an air-to-air missile right on its exhaust nozzle. The Yak burst into a ball of flame and smoke.

The Russian colonel instinctively looked to his radar screen. There was nothing there except the scattered blips of the Yak wreckage as it plunged to the ground. The deadly missile had come from nowhere. He wheeled the Yak around and armed his own weapons, four Aphid air-to-air missiles. The night was virtually cloudless with moderate light from a waning moon. Yet someone out there had shot down a second Yak.

The colonel was gripped with fear when he realized it had to be the Stealth airplane tracking them. He jerked his head from right to left, up and down, vainly looking for the airplane. He started zig-zagging, diving, climbing, trying to deny a clean shot at him by his unseen enemy. Dogfights, the Soviet commander could handle . . . maybe. But fighting a ghost, he could not.

He booted his throttle and sped ahead to link up with his Number Two ship. He knew his commanders would not want him to stay and fight whatever had knocked down the two Yaks. In the Soviet scheme of things, airplanes were more valuable than people. The Soviet colonel quickly planned to bring the flight down to the lowest possible altitude and make a run for it.

Just as he was getting a radar reading on Number Two, he saw a brilliant flash light up the night sky up ahead of him. He desperately reached for his microphone and started clicking frantically. He got no response. In seconds he was flying through the area of the flash, just in time to see the severed front portion of his Number Two ship tumbling to earth, leaving a trail of fire and smoke.

Now he was alone. He immediately brought his Yak down to tree top level and headed south with all due haste. He knew the ghost jet was somewhere nearby. It *had* to be. Something up ahead caught his eye. A glint of light. In a complete panic, he launched one of his air-to-air missiles only to see it impact on a radio tower—its red light blinking—standing on a hill a mile in front of him.

Another light, right ahead of him. He wildly opened up with his cannons, only to realize he was shooting at a truck,—it had to belong to The Circle—moving along the top of a ridge. The Soviet had been flying so low, he thought the faint spark of the truck's headlights was coming from something airborne. He was in such disarray he wasn't even reading his instruments. He felt a wave of vertigo—the nightmare of all pilots—overcome him. He sharply pulled back on his control stick and yanked the Yak back up to a higher altitude.

Now he saw something for real. It was a dark shape, barely visible in the faint moonlight. It was moving fast and heading right for him.

"He's going to ram me!" the Soviet's panicking reflexes told him. He momentarily froze at the controls. Then he saw the tell-tale burst of flame which indicated cannon fire. A split second later a small chunk of his canopy glass shattered and broke away. He could feel cannon shells perforating the Yak's fuselage and engine intakes. Still the black shape was streaking toward him, licks of flame protruding from it. He lamely tried to fire his own cannon, knowing full well an air-to-air missile would do no good in a head-on meeting. But his shells seemed to go haywire. No doubt his gun muzzle port had caught some of the enemy's well-placed opening shots.

The Soviet was just about to finally react and pull up when a burst of cannon fire found his cockpit. He was shot first in his shoulder then through his throat. Everything went from black to red. His uniform was soaked with blood. In his last conscious moment, he realized his whole airplane was aflame. His own body was on fire, yet he couldn't feel any pain. Grabbing his throat, and squinting before his eyes closed for the last time, he saw the mysterious black fighter bank to the left and streak by him, its pilot invisible through the dark tinted canopy.

Ten hours later, General Jones was awakened from a restless sleep by a loud buzzing noise. It was one of his lieutenants, calling him on the intercom set up next to his bunk.

"Sir?" the younger officer called. "Sir, we have someone here who wants to talk to you . . ."

Jones's eyes barely opened. He was still dressed in his flight suit, not having the time to peel it off in the past two days of intense action. He had finally caught some shuteye a few hours before, buoyed only by the fact that the second day of air strikes had gone better than any of them had hoped—thanks in good measure to Hunter's single-handed work on the enemy SAM lines.

"Sir?" the lieutenant repeated, his voice crackling over the intercom. "One of our PAAC cargo pilots is here. He says he spoke to Hunter a few hours ago . . ."

Jones was up in an instant. He fell into his boots, zipped up the front of his overalls, and ran out of the makeshift barracks toward the air station's flight ops building. It was still dark out—there was still an hour to go before sunrise—and it was raining ferociously. Jones was in the situation room in less than a minute, dripping wet.

"Captain Robinson reporting, sir," the pilot said, jumping to attention when Jones walked in.

"At ease, Robinson," Jones said, waving off the military formality. "You've just got in from Oregon? Must have been a hell of a flight in this weather."

"A little bumpy, sir," Robinson said.

"Well, we'll get you some grub and coffee," Jones told him, signalling to one of the night watch lieutenants.

"You spoke to Hunter?" Jones said, plopping down in to a chair. "When?"

"A few hours ago, General," Robinson said, finally sitting down. "He was at PAAC-Oregon."

"Really?" Jones asked. The general wasn't surprised that no one from PAAC-Oregon had radioed him about Hunter's presence there. They were just following orders. With the exception of emergency transmissions, there was a strict radio silence order in effect between Denver and the PAAC installations in Oregon and San Diego. It was standard for wartime footing. Jones was certain the Russians were monitoring every radio signal west of the SAM line, and they would have certainly picked up critical intelligence—especially about Ghost Rider—if the radio waves between the air station and the coast were used.

"Yes sir," Robinson replied. "That strange jet of his was there and he had a bunch of monkeys going over it."

"What was he doing?" Jones asked. He was intensely curious. "Plotting bombing patterns? Loading up with additional guns for his airplane?"

Robinson hesitated for a moment. "Well, no, General," he finally said. "In fact, he was working in the photo lab."

Jones looked up in surprise. "The photo lab?" he asked. "What the hell was he doing in there?"

"I'm not sure, sir," the captain answered. "I was there to pick up a barrel of photo developing wash. You know, for our photo recon boys here? So I went to the photo lab's dark room to get it and there was Hunter, working over a photo printer."

"He was developing pictures?"

"More accurately, he was developing a negative, sir," Robinson answered. "It was kind of funny talking to him, because the only light in the room was the red safety light they use so as not to screw up the developing. All he asked me was how it was going here in Denver, and I said it looked good what with the air strikes and all.

"Then he just said something about it was still a long road to go, and everyone had to pitch in. He was real busy. Very intense. So I got my developer and left."

The junior officer arrived with a pot of steaming coffee and a plate of sandwiches. Both Jones and Robinson immediately dug in.

"Any idea what kind of negative he was developing?" Jones asked. "Recon mission stuff? Bombing targets?"

"No way of knowing, sir," Robinson said.

Jones scratched his head. "Is that it, Captain?" he asked.

"Just about, other than that one of the photo lab guys told me that Hunter wanted them standing by because he would need a lot of photos in a hurry. They had one of their big printers warmed up and ready to go. You know, one of those high speed jobs that can print a couple of thousand photos at a whack."

Jones thought about it for a moment then wondered out loud. "What the hell is that boy up to?"

"Beats me, sir," Robinson said. "But whatever it is, he was sure serious about it. If you could have seen the look in his eyes, you'd know what I mean."

Jones nodded his head slowly. "I know *exactly* what you mean, Captain."

The day dawned cold, wet and miserable. Jones knew a big weather front that stretched back across the Rockies was due to pass through the Badlands during the daylight hours. That was fine with him. It would give his pilots a breather, allow maintenance crews to do necessary work on PAAC's aircraft and would also give the ground forces another day—though a wet one—to continue work on the defense line.

At least two airplanes were flying though. One was an ADF F-105, its pilot carrying a secret pouch from Fitzgerald. It was a videotape the Irishman had just recorded of himself. Because of the strict radio silence order, videotapes were the means of communication the Western Forces allies had agreed on to keep in touch.

Jones slipped the tape into the situation room's video machine and the TV screen slickered to life. It was Fitz himself, giving the latest situation report from the northern front.

"We have our friends pretty well bogged down," the Irishman reported, sitting behind a desk somewhere at a secret base in Manitoba, a huge painting of a shamrock hanging on the wall behind him. "Ain't a bridge standing between Minneapolis and Sioux Falls. We go after the railroad lines today."

"The Canadians have their guys ready to strike, should we need ground forces. We hope it doesn't come to that. Good luck down there, General."

Thirty minutes later, a Texas F-4 streaked in from the south under the weather to deliver another videotape, this one from St. Louie. It was shot out on a runway near Dallas and the white cowboy suited St. Louie looked more like a used car salesman than a leader in exile.

"Howdy, Dave!" the old ex-bomber pilot began. "Our buddies here are about to launch another air strike on the port of New Orleans." As if to confirm it, two Texas Air Force F-4s taxied by in the background.

"My flyboys plan to continue hammering the troops of the Circle Southern Group around Shreveport today.

"We have four teams—two Texan, two of my guys, waiting at the border, Dave," St. Louie continued. "We're waiting for whatever comes across. We figure we'll be seeing the whites of their eyes in two days. Good luck, buddy . . ."

The tape flickered and ended.

What characters, Jones thought. He was about to watch both of them again when he was surprised to hear the situation room's scramble radio crackled to life.

"Denver, Tango-Six-Maxwell calling . . ."

Jones instantly recognized Hunter's radio call sign.

He immediately picked up the radio microphone. "Hawk?" Jones answered. "That you, pal?"

The transmission was very faint, so much so, it sounded like Hunter was calling from another planet.

"General, got to be . . . fast," the static filled voice said. "I put a convoy together. I'd like to take them through tonight. Right over you. As soon as that weather front clears . . ."

"Do I copy, 'convoy,' Hawk?"

"That's . . . a . . . roger . . . sir," the voice faded in between annoying bursts of static. "Out . . . of Oregon. Request top priority radio boot."

Jones was twisting dials and punching buttons in an effort to clear up the signal, but to no avail. He knew a request for top priority "radio boot" meant absolutely no radio contact from here on in, even in an emergency. Even this call from the coast, scrambled as it was, was risky.

"Understand and copy, Hawk," Jones said as slowly and distinctly as he could. "What's the mission . . . ?"

"Psyche-Ops . . ." came the reply. "Repeat Special . . . mission."

Then the radio signal went dead.

The weather cleared just as night fell. Jones and Dozer stationed themselves out on the air station's tarmac, with a pair of NightScopes and a radio phone hook-up. Crunch was in the control tower, at the other end of the radio-phone watching over the shoulders of two radar operators.

Nothing happened until 10:30. Then one of the operators spoke. "We're getting blips, Captain," he told Crunch.

The Phantom pilot watched the screen as first one, then two more radar blips appeared, indicating aircraft approaching from the west. He immediately called down to Jones and Dozer.

"Here they come, General," he reported. "One big boy riding out front. Two more, also heavies, right on his tail. You should see them soon, your north-by-northwest."

Both Jones and Dozer craned their necks, scanning the now-cloudless sky with the infra-red NightScopes. After a few minutes, they both saw the three faint lights at the same time.

"That front one looks like the B-36!" Jones exclaimed as the light started to take shape in the Scope. "Jesus, don't tell me he got that shitbox running . . ."

"Those look like the C-141s coming next," Dozer

said, focusing on the trailing images. "He must have bribed a bunch of our cargo flyboys to follow him on this one."

The radio crackled once. It was Crunch. "Picking up three more, medium size, right behind them," he reported.

Sure enough, Jones picked out three more aircraft, moving silently across the star-studded sky.

"Those are the old 727 cargo ships," he said, directing Dozer to the three other lights.

Jones noticed a small, barely visible object bringing up the rear of the air train, an object that Crunch would never see on the radar screen. Jones knew this had to be the Stealth with Hunter behind the controls.

By this time, many of the people at the air station were outside, looking up at the strange menagerie of airplanes 60,000 feet over their heads.

"Well, he was right," Jones said. "He's heading directly into the 'Bads. Probably through that SAM hole near Oakley. That's probably another reason why he really squashed them in that area the other night."

They watched as the airplanes passed directly overhead. Then, on what had to be a pre-arranged signal, all six airplanes flicked their wing lights three times.

A spontaneous round of cheers went up from observers at the airport. "Hunter's way of saying 'Hello,' " Jones said, laughing for the first time in days.

They stood and watched until the convoy disappeared from view. "He's got something in that mind of his," Dozer said. "God only knows what."

"I have a feeling we'll know soon enough," Jones said.

Suddenly the radio-phone crackled. "General," they heard Crunch say. "We're getting small outline readings in the trail of those airplanes, sir. It's like one of them dropped something."

Jones looked up and could barely see a bunch of tiny white specks falling from the sky. They also looked like snowflakes for a moment. Then, as they got bigger, he saw they were leaflets of some kind.

About 100 of the sheets fluttered down. "Talk about a precision drop," Dozer said. "It's like a phony war bombing." He was referring to the time early in World War II when the Allies faced the Nazis in a six-month, non-shooting 'phony war,' when propaganda leaflets were the heaviest ordnance the enemies dropped on each other.

Jones grabbed the first one that blew his way. It was a photograph—taken in the correct and simple, propagandistic style. But it was very strange . . .

It showed Hunter's long-lost girlfriend, Dominique. She looked as beautiful as she did in the other mysterious photos that the Circle had been circulating of her earlier. But in this photo, she was standing next to the Stealth fighter, holding Hunter's small American flag in one hand, and pointing à la Uncle Sam with her other. There was a printed message at the bottom of the photograph.

It read:

"VIKTOR IS DEAD. LAY DOWN YOUR ARMS NOW AND GO TOME. REMEMBER THAT YOU ARE AMERICANS. YOU HAVE BEEN TRICKED BY THE RUSSIANS. EVERY AIRPLANE YOU SEE WILL BE DROOPING BOMBS ON YOU. DON'T DIE AS RUSSIAN PUPPETS. THE WAR WILL SOON BE OVER.—QUEEN."

"I guess this is his way of telling us what he's up to," Jones said, studying the leaflet. "Well, at least now we know what he was doing in the photo lab."

"I thought I'd seen everything," Dozer said, reading his own. "But this has to be the wildest stunt he's ever tried . . ."

Jones read the message over and over. "Wild, yes," he said. "But also quite effective, in a crude sort of way.

"If I'm guessing right, he's got those big airplanes loaded with these things. He's going to drop them all over the Circle's Central Group troop concentrations. Shit, if it works on one tenth of those guys—that means they'll be ten thousand less of them shooting at us."

"Well, it's worth a shot," Dozer said. "He did say he would take care of 'spooking' the bastards. I guess every 'Psyche Ops' plan is a little weird."

Then the Marine captain looked at the photograph even closer. "But I do have one question . . ."

"What's that?" Jones asked.

Dozer pointed to the photo. "Is that really Yankee Stadium in the background?"

Chapter Thirty-three

The rain had finally stopped. But in the muck of the 9th Circle Regiment's camp, it didn't matter. The ground around the encampment was so soaked, many of the soldiers had abandoned their tents and were trying to sleep in the back of trucks, or on top of the group's few tanks. Any place that was solid and could be made dry. Still, these places were at a minimum, so many of the men simply huddled together in the wet mud, and stayed awake all night, sharing cigarettes and what little whiskey they smuggled in.

To a man, they were cold, tired and mad. Their anger was directed toward the dozen "special" soldiers attached to their regiment. Rumors were rife that the "specials" were really Russians. And while The Circle troops shivered in the damp after-rain, they could also see the lights from the large, well-heated house trailers that served as the special troops' bivouacs nearby. They also knew when chow came, these troops would be the first to eat.

It had been getting worse since they marched out of Football City. Before then, things hadn't been as bad. Most of the men in the Circle 9th were former Mid-Aks soldiers from the West Virginia area. Before Viktor's recruiters appeared, they had supported themselves by raiding small towns and hamlets in the Wheeling area, sometimes bringing their booty—young girls mostly—up to The Pitts for resale. With promises of gold, new weapons and conquest in the west—especially against the same hated democratic forces that had brought down their Mid-Atlantic Empire—the members of the 9th had greedily enlisted.

Most of them had managed to put up with the strange ways of The Circle. The "re-education sessions" during training—where they watched countless videos detailing the outlandish heroics of Viktor—were bearable because the food was plentiful and it was occasionally spiked with some kind of "feel-good" drug. While the good old mountain boys of the 9th quietly snickered at the suggestion that the "Video" Viktor was "the Cosmos Chosen Leader," they knew many of the other recruits—especially the young ones in their teens—bought the foolishness lock, stock and barrel.

What the Circle recruiters never told them was signing up in the Army of the East meant a long separation from what man needed most—sex. No women were allowed in or anywhere near Circle

Army camps. No Circle soldiers were allowed the wanton rape and pillage that had been the trademark of the Mid-Aks. Photos of women and girls were banned. Whoring was punishable by firing squad—several public executions drove the point home quickly enough. The life of The Circle grunt was one of enforced abstinence.

Except for The Queen . . .

She was beautiful, even the men of the 9th agreed. And she was the only woman they ever saw—and then only in carefully distributed, carefully staged photographs. They were passed out like medals—rewards for good duty, and then only rarely. Photos of the Queen quickly became status symbols. Soldiers in favor carried them proudly. They became items for trade, like cigarettes in a POW camp. How valuable was determined by The Queen's varying states of undress. The more she showed, the more precious the photo. It was said that some officers possessed photos of the Queen partially nude and given to them by Viktor himself. But these photos were as rare as diamonds and never filtered down to the enlisted men. Not unless it was planned that way. It was all very controlled, just as the portions of "feel-good" slipped into the troops' meal rations. The Circle ruled its soldiers with an iron fist tightly wrapped around their libido. The erotic photos of the unnamed, beautiful Queen were the only release. They became as valuable and as guarded a commodity as The Circle's guns, and rockets and bombs.

But now even that had ended, at least for the 9th. Rumors had been sweeping the troops' encampments for days before they marched out of Football City that Viktor was dead and The Queen was missing. Something big had gone down back in New York City. They were heading for a bloodbath in the Badlands.

And worst of all, the camp food didn't taste as good as it did before . . .

Now, on this cold, wet night, new rumors were sweeping the 9th's camp. They would start on a new march route the next day because a major bridge they had been slated to cross had been destroyed by an enemy air strike. Wild stories about the West's aircraft bombing targets *behind* their column were running rampant. Some soldiers who had been up to the front claimed the skies were filled with enemy aircraft. Yet Viktor's officers had told them there would be no enemy air force by the time they reached the front. There were SAMs installed at the front, which made flying anywhere east of the Badlands impossible.

Even worse were the stories about the West's "ghost" jets. Supposedly they could appear or disappear on command. Foolish as the story was, many of The Circle soldiers suspected there was something to it—and they sensed their superiors were taking the claims seriously.

So when the soldiers of the 9th Circle Regiment heard the rumbling of aircraft approaching from the west, they were quick to find shelter. But they found it was no easy task. Their encampment was set up out in the open of the Missouri plain. There was no place to hide. As the sound of the airplanes got louder, there was much confusion as the soldiers ran around in the dark, sloshing in the mud, looking for a hole to jump in or a rock to cower against.

"How did those airplanes get through!?" was the cry through the camp as the PAAC aircraft passed overhead.

"What happened to the SAMs!"

So it was a complete surprise to the men of the 9th Circle Regiment—as well as to thousands of their comrades camped nearby—that the high-flying airplanes didn't drop bombs on them. Instead, thousands of leaflets floated down out of the sky. Leaflets showing the woman known to them only as The Queen, carrying a message that Viktor was dead and that they should give up the fight. Gone were her slinky black pornographic costumes. She looked all-business in the combat-style coveralls.

But many of the soldiers were startled more by the fact that she was holding an American flag. The symbol—and any talk of it—had been banned long ago by the New Order. It was the first time in years that many of them had seen the flag. Something stirred deep inside of a few of them. The picture of the Queen holding the stars and stripes was enough to kick some out of the hazy drug hangover they'd unknowingly been suffering from.

Still others wondered what the strange craft in back of her in the photo represented. Was this one of the "ghost jets" they'd been hearing about?

The leaflet drop added weight to the rumors that had swept the camp. If these airplanes got through the SAM line, what was to prevent others, carrying more deadly payloads from getting through? Maybe Viktor *was* dead. Maybe enemy aircraft *were* bombing positions behind them in the rear areas. Maybe there *was* a bloodbath waiting for them up ahead.

It was enough for many of the veteran soldiers of the 9th. They quickly packed their meager belongings and started marching again—this time toward the east, back to the the West Virginia hills. When their officers appeared and ordered them to stop, they ignored them and kept moving. And when their officers shot a few of them, the members of the 9th, returned the fire, killed the officers then fled.

The scene was repeated all over eastern Kansas and Missouri. Wherever the leaflets fell, the "borderline" Circle troops—veteran Mid-Aks, Family soldiers, mercenaries mostly—began questioning their resolve. Scattered mutinies, uprisings, and random defections started to take place. More than a few Circle commanders resorted to force to keep their soldiers in line. By morning, The Circle High Command estimated that they'd lost anywhere from 10 to 15 percent of their troops. The Russians believed even more had deserted. How this would affect the planned link-up of their forces was anyone's guess.

What they didn't know was the worst was yet to come . . .

Back at the Denver Air Station, General Jones studied a video tape shot by an A-7 Recon Strike-fighter and rushed to the situation room. Taken only an hour earlier, the tape clearly showed small groups of Circle Army deserters moving east along highways and secondary roads. Most were walking, some riding in commandeered trucks. Everywhere—blowing in wind, or scattered amongst the trees—were Hunter's propaganda leaflets. The Wingman had succeeded in covering most of eastern Kansas and Missouri with them.

Jones turned to the principal officers who had also gathered to watch the tape.

"Well, it looks like Hunter's brainstorm worked as well as could be expected," the general said. "It's certainly not a rout, but they are losing at least some of their paycheck soldiers."

"And those are the guys who are their veterans," Dozer added. "Most of them have been in combat before, some of them would have been tough nuts to crack. Leave it to Hunter to push the right buttons in them, and at the right time."

The others agreed.

"We can probably expect more of this after we hit their troop concentrations—with real bombs—today," Jones said. "But there's another certainty we have to be prepared for from this, and I'm sure Hunter is as aware of it as we are.

"That is, as The Circle loses their veterans, only

the die-hard fanatics will remain."

A grim silence descended on the room.

Jones continued. "When that Central Group hits our defense line, we can expect everything, even kamikaze attacks. That means we'll have to kill every last one of the bastards . . ."

Chapter Thirty-four

The two F-4X Phantoms known as the Ace Wrecking Company swept in over El Dorado Lake without warning. Coming in side-by-side, each jet deposited a fat napalm cannister right into the heart of the Circle encampment. A tidal wave of murderous burning jelly washed across the camp in an instant, igniting trees and flesh alike. For the thousands of Circle troops just waking up to the first light of dawn, it seemed as if they were still locked inside a horrible nightmare. Everywhere they saw their comrades running in panic, with their clothes, hair, faces on fire. Blood-curdling screams echoed throughout the old state park camping area. The flames reached ammunition stores, blowing them up and causing additional carnage. Many soldiers fled from their tents and leaped into the nearby lake.

The Phantoms pulled up, banked to the left and bore down on the encampment again. Two more large napalm cannisters were dropped. Another wave of fire tore through the camp. More screams.

More burning flesh. More horrible death.

By the time the Wrecking Company made its third and final bombing run, a small firestorm was sweeping the encampment. Huge trees were exploding from the heat alone, perforating any soldiers nearby with thousands of searing deadly splinters. The heat from the gasoline-jelly flames now threatened those soldiers who had sought refuge in the lake. The temperature had become so unbearable near the shoreline, those troops who could had to swim for it. Those who couldn't were forced back into the deeper water until they drowned.

Eventually, the fires became so hot, the lake itself began to steam . . .

High above, watching the action, was a small, dark, mysterious-looking fighter plane.

Thirty miles west of Topeka, a convoy of small boats was making its way on the Kansas River. The vessels—work barges, pleasure ships, fishing boats—were carrying an elite brigade of Circle Army sappers to Manhattan, Kansas, where they would be dispatched to the front. Moving the 2,000 troops by water had become necessary after an entire 20-mile stretch of the division's original route—Route 70—had been destroyed by Western Forces aircraft two days before.

Despite some grumbling from their soldiers after many had read the leaflets dropped by the enemy the night before, all was going smoothly for the

Circle commanders charged with sailing the make-shift fleet to Manhattan. The sappers were a cut above the ordinary Circle Army soldiers, therefore their resolve was more reliable. And now, with only ten miles to go to the landing port at Rocky Ford, the commanders were confident the force would arrive intact and on-time. Some were even beginning to enjoy the view along the pleasant, tree-lined river bank.

Suddenly, from out of nowhere, they heard a loud chopping sound. There was a flash of smoke and flame from the northern shore treeline, and one of the boats—a huge commandeered yacht traveling third in line—exploded with a horrendous sound. The yacht went under in a matter of seconds.

The overall Circle commander, riding on a fishing vessel safely placed in the middle of the pack, leaped to his feet to see an Apache helicopter rise above the treeline. It had fired the missile that took out the boat, and was in the process of firing another one. The commander's eyes were diverted to the southern shoreline where another Apache had risen up just over the treeline. It too was firing at the boats. Then another Apache rose up beside it. Then another and another. All were firing TOW rockets into the tightly packed line of boats. All were hitting their targets.

In a matter of 20 seconds, the air was filled with buzzing Apaches, strange-looking bug-like choppers, that were loaded with cannons and TOW missile launchers. The Circle commander realized they had foolishly sailed right into an ambush. They were literally sitting ducks for the Apaches. He could only watch as the helicopters methodically rocketed and strafed the boats. There were explosions everywhere. Bodies and pieces of bodies were being flung high into the air as it seemed like every TOW missile launched founds its mark. Some of the sappers gamely attempted to return the fire, but most were only armed with M-16s and hand guns and their effort was useless in the face of the vicious onslaught.

Then, in the middle of the battle, a small, black jet fighter swooped down over the river, strafing the boats, sinking two before disappearing over the western horizon. The Circle commander knew he had seen such an airplane before. It was the same as the one in the propaganda leaflets dropped by the Western Forces the day before.

One by one, the Circle boats went down. Some troopers tried to swim for it, others were caught up in the many gasoline fires raging on the surface of the water. The commander's boat took a TOW right on the bridge, killing him and everyone stationed there. Now leaderless, the boats were twisting and turning in every direction. But the fire from the squadron of Apaches was so intense, it seemed useless to even attempt an escape.

Within five minutes, the Apaches' deadly work was complete. Every one of the boats had been hit, more than three quarters of them sent to the bottom. The sapper unit was destroyed.

Back at the Circle stronghold in Topeka, troops guarding the city's bridges noticed the swift moving Kansas River had turned red with blood . . .

The 40-mile stretch of Kansas Interstate Route 135 between Salina and McPherson was the scene of an incredible traffic jam. . . .

A convoy of 300 trucks, carrying six battalions of Circle ground troops, was traveling south on the highway when it met a large column of Circle tanks and armored personnel carriers moving in the opposite direction. Someone had screwed up. Strange radio reports had reached both commanders earlier in the day, countermanding their previous orders. The armored column was trying to get to Salina to get on Route 70 heading west. The infantry convoy had been directed south—off Route 70—and toward McPherson to take Route 56 west. Both of the column commanders used all four lanes of the abandoned interstate to get where they were going. They had met roughly halfway, near the small town of Bridgeport, Kansas and had been stalled, in place, while the Circle High Command tried to figure it out.

It didn't matter. The Western Forces were about to do that for them.

The first PAAC aircraft to arrive on the scene was a pair of C-130 Spooky gunships flying 10 miles south of Salina. Each one was equipped with three rapid-fire GE Gatling guns poking out of its portside. The Spookies overflew the area once. Then while one headed south to ascertain the length of the exposed enemy, the other climbed and went into an orbit 1000 feet above the stalled infantry column. Before their commanders could order their troops to scatter, the C-130 opened on the trucks, its gun spitting out bullets at an incredible rate of 6000 rounds a minute.

Next on the scene were four aging PAAC B-57 bombers. The pre-Viet Nam era, two-engine jobs had been outfitted with deadly array dispensers. Fitted beneath the belly of the airplane, each dispenser contained hundreds of small, globe-like bombs. When released, the hand-sized bombs—which packed the punch of ten hand grenades—floated to earth via small parachutes. Exploding on impact, they would burst with a scattershot of deadly shrapnel going highspeed in all directions. The dispensers were originally designed to destroy an enemy's crowded runways. They would work just as fine on the traffic jam . . .

The B-57s came in low and streaked just above the tops of the trucks, trailing a small cloud of little parachute bombs. The deadly globes slowly sank to earth, then started exploding as they landed on the tops of trucks, jeeps and people. A five mile stretch of the highway was soon the scene of incredible carnage. The small bombs tore up metal and flesh. Even the soldiers who were able to take cover at the side of the road were sliced up by the flaming pieces of bomb fragments.

But the Circle troops were not defenseless. A Stinger missile flashed up from the truck column, catching the starboard engine of one of the B-57s. The small jet bomber lost its wing immediately, and went into a freakish cartwheel above the crowded highway. It finally slammed into the traffic jam, exploding on impact and destroying a dozen more trucks in the process.

Their work done, the surviving B-57s turned west and headed back to their base. Meanwhile, the two C-130 gunships had moved south and were firing on the tanks and APCs of the armored column.

Then two PAAC A-10 Thunderbolts appeared on the scene. The C-130s again backed off and let the small, squat Thunderbolt "Tankbusters" do their thing. Carrying a powerful cannon in their noses, the A-10s swept up the highway, further chopping up the column and adding to the destruction. Several small SAMs rose to meet the 'Bolts, but the PAAC pilots were able to maneuver their rather slow-moving but effective ground attack airplanes out of harm's way.

But there was trouble ahead for the A-10s.

A Russian general and his entourage had been unlucky enough to be caught in the deadly traffic jam. He had seen a number of his command staff shot to pieces in the first pass of the gunships. By the time the B-57s had wreaked their destruction, the Russian was on the line to his headquarters, demanding that air support come to the aid of the beleaguered column.

Ten minutes later, six Yaks appeared.

Three of the Yaks went after the gunships, the other trio pounced on the A-10s. Neither the Yaks nor the Thunderbolts were built for dog fighting but the Russian jets had it all over the slow, ground attack PAAC airplanes. The A-10s split up and attempted to flee, but one was quickly overtaken by two Yaks and mercilessly gunned out of the sky. Even after the airplane skidded to a fiery crash landing, the Yaks strafed the wreckage, just to make sure.

Meanwhile, the three other Russians attacked the prop-driven C-130s. Although the gun crews gamely tried to shoot it out with their Gatling guns, it was not even a close match. One gunship took an Aphid air-to-air missile on its starboard inside engine, destroying it and setting the wing on fire. The C-130 pilot ordered his crew to bail out. Rapidly, the five airmen went to the silk and watched as their pilot put the airplane in a steep dive, pulling back on the throttles to get his air speed down. He was going to try to put the big ship down, but a Yak was right on his tail. Another Aphid missile finished it. The Soviet air-to-air caught the airplane's port wing, its explosion severing the wing from the C-130's body and killing the pilot. The gunship never pulled up. It plowed right into the ground, exploding on impact.

The parachuting survivors, watching their airplane go down in flames, never saw the other two Yaks. The jets systematically and ruthlessly strafed the airmen as they descended helplessly in the parachutes. All five died horribly before they reached the ground.

Feeling smug in their cruel victory, the three Yaks climbed to join the uneven chase for the other two PAAC aircraft.

They found the second A-10 had been disintegrated by a barrage of Aphid missiles. But they soon realized their comrades had forced the second C-130 down on a plain ten miles from the highway. The airplane had landed more or less intact, but now the Yaks were playing a cruel game. They were hovering over the big airplane, taking turns dipping their noses and puncturing the fuselage with cannon fire. For the crew members still trapped inside, it was leading up to a particularly slow death.

That's when the Stealth appeared . . .

It came out of nowhere, without any warning. Now the hovering jets were the hunted. As the Soviet pilots scrambled with their flight controls to get their airplanes moving forward again, the Stealth ripped into two of them with its powerful cannons. Two Yaks immediately exploded in mid air.

The Stealth did a screaming loop and was soon on the tail of a third Soviet jet. One push of the button and a Sidewinder flashed from underneath the wing of the strange-looking airplane. Scratch one more Yak.

Wanting no part of the Stealth fighter, the three remaining Yaks made a break for it. Not quick enough as it turned out. The Stealth was on the tail of one Yak in 30 seconds, pumping cannon shots into its rear quarter until its fuselage broke up and its fuel supply exploded. The Stealth never stopping shooting—its shells were now licking at the wing tips of another of the fleeing Soviets. One pilot attempted to slow down by punching in his VTOL control to hover, hoping the strange airplane would overshoot him. Not a chance. The Stealth delivered a well-placed shot underneath the Yak's belly, igniting its fuel tank, flipping it over and causing it to plunge straight down at full throttle. The Yak impacted on the side of a butte, and exploded.

The Stealth caught up with the final fleeing Yak over the burning highway. Once more a Sidewinder flashed out from beneath the mysterious black fighter. It caught the Yak as it was trying to perform an outlandish maneuver. The missile bounced off the underside of the Soviet jet, exploding a split-second later. The force of the blast knocked the jet sideways then down. It slammed into the already burning wreckage of a group of Circle tanks.

The Stealth then strafed the entire length of the wreckage-strewn highway, then disappeared over the western horizon.

Chapter Thirty-five

Word of the bloody highway battle reached the Denver Air Station very quickly. PAAC fighter-bombers, returning from air strikes deeper in Kansas, reported seeing the long stretch of burning vehicles, with wreckage of ten aircraft—both Soviet and Western Forces—scattered throughout the combat zone. A rescue helicopter was able to lift out the survivors from the second downed C-130 gunship. Jones requested to see the men as soon as they arrived and they told him the incredible story of how the Stealth came out of nowhere to blast the Yaks from the sky and save their lives.

"Hunter again," Jones told Dozer and Crunch, as they grabbed a quick bite in the situation room. "He's been like our guardian angel up there."

The men discussed the combat reports of the day. Their plan appeared to be working—large concentrations of Circle troops were hit repeatedly. The Western Forces attack planes were squeezing all the Circle ground troops into Kansas and toward the relatively narrow front line on the Colorado border. Jones was certain that after word got around about the additional PAAC victories on the Kansas River, at El Dorado Lake and elsewhere, would only add to the Circle's defection rate.

Jones showed the two officers two additional videotapes he'd just received from Fitzie and St. Louie.

Fitzgerald's ADF fighters were roaming the skies of Minnesota at will, blasting everything that moved. At last report, the Circle Northern Group had completely stalled, and the Irishman vowed to keep the pressure up.

St. Louie reported that his F-20s had succeeded in driving most of the Circle Southern Group back into Shreveport. Round-the-clock bombing raids on that city were continuing. And St. Louie also reported the brazen Texans were still battering the key supply port of New Orleans.

But not one of the men felt anything approaching over-confidence. The battle on the highway had cost them two A-10s, two C-130s and a B-57, and a number of valuable men. Five additional PAAC aircraft were lost in other scattered actions around Kansas that day. All were shot down by SAMs.

"The Russians are finally getting smart to us," Jones said. "Their moving the SAMs around like crazy."

"Plus they committed the Yaks for the first time since our air strikes began," Dozer pointed out.

"Ten airplanes in one day," Crunch said grimly.

"At that rate, we'll be out of aircraft in a month."

Jones ran his hand through his close-cropped hair. "We're winning the opening battles, but we need help, boys," he said. "And soon . . ."

Fifty miles to the northwest, a lone figure stood atop the mountain known as Comanche Peak. The snow cap was blowing, giving the summit a misty collar. The sun had long set and the sky was dazzling with stars.

Hunter pulled his jacket collar tighter around his neck. He faced the west and closed his eyes. He was tired. Cold. Hungry. He'd spent more time in the air in the past few days than he had on the ground. He was beginning to think that *too* much adrenaline was bad for his body, his mind, his psyche. He'd been on combat binges before, but nothing like this. He was pulling out all the stops—the night of destroying SAM radars, the leaflet drop, the round-the-clock air missions—anything and everything to keep the superior Circle Army off balance.

But he knew the war was entering a critical phase.

He opened his eyes. The night sky was now lit up with brilliant crimsons. It was the *Aurora Borealis* again, flashing across the sky. How strange they were. Arching. Streaming. Disappearing here, only to reappear there. Like a rainbow, yet so completely different. Electricity swirling in the atmosphere. Memories swirling in his head. His lonely arctic overflights. Discovering the Yaks. The strangeness in the Oregon mountains, and off the coast, and around Las Vegas. Pearl Harbor. Devil's Tower. The girls in the Grand Canyon. Scary Mary. New York City. *Dominique.* All during it, these strange lights had followed him. Lighting the way. *Aurora Borealis!* He could feel their electrical charges in the wind . . .

Then, deep down inside him, he now felt something else. It shot up and out of his soul, through his heart and into his brain. He closed his eyes again. Slowly, surely as the wind-blown snow touched his face, it was coming to him. *The Feeling!* That undescribable beautiful feeling. It was the fix he needed. He let it wash over him, immerse him, soak him through to his spine and bone.

They were coming. He could sense them. Feel them in his soul. Smell them. And finally, hear them. Approaching from the northwest. Five lights, dim now against the Milky Way, but getting brighter. He felt his body recharging. *Are you ready?* he asked himself. *Are you ready to fight harder, faster, stronger?* He felt his breast pocket. The flag was still there. It was always there. Not just to comfort him, but to strengthen him.

This is for you, Seth Jones! his mind shouted. *Your wingman is still on the job.*

This is for you, Saul Wackerman! Your flag is still here and so is your spirit!

This is for you, Dominique, honey . . .

He opened his eyes. The lights had grown larger and brighter and they were heading right for him.

The noise filled him. He threw his fist up in the air. The Russians have dared invade his country? The Circle has dared to enslave its citizens? Viktor dared to take his woman? They had yet to taste his full wrath.

He looked up as the formation of five beautiful white B-1s streaked directly over his head.

"That's just what I need . . ." he said.

Chapter Thirty-six

The five B-1s touched down at the Denver Air Station less than a half hour later. They did not radio ahead, so to those few monkeys and ground personnel who first saw the airplanes in the still-dark early morning, it was quite a shock.

"General!" Jones's situation room intercom crackled to life. It was the watch officer in the air station's control tower. "You've got to see this, sir. Coming in on runway-two-right . . ."

Jones, Dozer and Crunch hurried out of the situation room, just in time to see the B-1 known as *Ghost Rider 4* touch down. All three men felt a thrill shoot through them.

"Hallelujah!" Crunch yelled.

"You mean, Eureka!" Jones said.

"They even look good to a Marine," Dozer added. "But can they do what we hope they can do?"

"Only one way to find out," Jones said, heading back to the situation room and calling the air station control tower.

A few seconds later, he was talking to the tower's radar operator.

"I can't understand it, sir," the somewhat confused young radarman told him. "Five big airplanes—B-1 bombers no less—and they didn't make so much as a blip."

Jones smiled for the first time in days. "That's okay, son," Jones said. "That's exactly what I wanted to hear."

A half hour later, Jones was sitting in the cockpit of *Ghost 1* talking to the B-1 group commanders, Ben Wa and J.T. Twomey.

"The system works, General," Twomey told him. "But we couldn't have done it without all five boxes. We found out the Goddamn things were designed to self-destruct if anyone tried to pry 'em open. We still don't fully understand what makes them tick."

Jones looked around inside the ultra-sophisticated bomber. It was crammed with so much electronic gear, he was surprised it could get airborne.

"You got here just in time," Jones told him. "We had a hell of a day yesterday. Ten airplanes shot down. We put a lot of hurt on The Circle and the Russians—but it was a costly couple of victories."

Jones led the two men out of the airplane and toward the air station's mess. They had been isolated from the battlefront since the war began. Jones quickly updated them.

"Here's the situation, guys," Jones began after they sat down to a pot of coffee and a large bowl of morning stew. "We've been able to divert the main

Circle Forces into Kansas. Right now, they're about a day away from our lines. And they've finally linked up with the Russians."

"So the unholy alliance is complete," Wa said.

Jones nodded. "They're coordinated now. They finally got smart and started their SAMs rolling. So the SAM line as we knew it is no more."

"How many enemy troops are we talking about," Toomey asked.

"Well, we figure they lost about fifteen thousand guys thanks to Hunter's Psyche-Ops plan," Jones said. "And we've greased a lot more. But they still have about five divisions—seventy five thousand men—heading our way. And they're bringing the SAMs with them. Anywhere between two and three thousand launchers, each with four missiles on its back."

"Jesus Christ . . ." Twomey said softly, trying to imagine what three thousand SAM launchers in one concentrated area could do.

"We've got to hit them hard and quick, boys," Jones said defiantly. "Just as soon as the sun is up, we have to get airborne and plaster the shit out of them. If we don't then they'll run over the fifty-five thousand men I have waiting on our defense line without even stopping."

"What do we have for air support?" Twomey asked, pouring himself another coffee.

"Well, Mike Fitzgerald is sending down a squadron of his Thunderchiefs," Jones said. "They should be here any time now. He has The Circle's Northern group so screwed up in Minnesota, it'll take them a week to figure out how to get out.

"St. Louie promised us six F-20s and the Texans are sending a squadron of their F-4s along with them. They wanted to send more—but they still have their hands full, hitting New Orleans everyday while trying to keep Circle Southern Army from crossing their border."

Jones paused to light a half-burned cigar. "As for us," he said, through a cloud of stale smoke. "I sent back word to PAAC Oregon and San Diego. Anything that can fly, and carry a gun or a bomb will be here by noon."

Wa shook his head. "Even the World War II stuff?"

"You bet," Jones said. "The Mustang. The P-38. Everyone's coming to the party. Choppers, too. Any that we can spare, that is. We got the Crazy Eights and the Cobra Brothers working the defense line. God help them when the SAMs start flying."

"Seems like you've done everything you could, General," Twomey concluded. "By the book, too."

"Well, we're still missing one piece," Jones said, chewing the end of his cigar. "One very *valuable* piece . . ."

Chapter Thirty-seven

"Does anybody here remember the movie, 'High Noon?' " Jones asked.

It was still a half hour before dawn and the situation room at the Denver Air Station was crowded with pilots on hand to receive their pre-mission briefing.

"Well, that's what it's going to be like out there today," Jones told the assembled airmen. "More bad guys than good guys."

He displayed a photograph of a large portion of the encamped Circle Army taken just after sunset the day before. It showed tens of thousands of tiny lights, like a galaxy of candles in the night, dotting the west Kansas plains. They went on and on for miles.

"Those," Jones said grimly, "are campfires . . ."

A wave of low volume swearing and whistles of amazement passed through the room.

"If we figure at least five men to a campfire,"

Jones said. "Then we're talking about a lot of bad guys. And they've been on the move. They're only about fifteen miles away from our lines now."

Now there was a deathly silence.

"We've been chipping away at them every day," Jones continued. "And between defections and our air strikes, we figured The Circle lost close to two divisions and a hell of a lot of equipment.

"But . . . we estimate they've still got five divisions to throw at us. And these guys are the hard-core radicals. They're like the Shiites back in the 'I-ah-toll-lah's' heyday. Anyone remember that old goat? Fanatics. Ready and willing to die for the cause. These bastards still believe that Viktor's in charge. A lot of them were probably too blitzed to read the words on Hunter's propaganda leaflets."

He paused again.

"What kind of shape are these guys in?" Jones asked. "Bottom line is, we don't know. Our plan all along has been to hit their supply lines, cut them off, starve 'em. They've been through bad weather, their food supplies should be running low. They've been bombed every day, without so much as a single Yak to defend them. We'll know whether our strategy has worked or not as soon as we see the condition of the first Circle soldier who hits our defense line."

A slight murmur went up from the assembled pilots.

"But we have to expect the worse," Jones continued. "They have enough guys to hit us on three sides. Our defense line is being compressed. We've got some artillery, howitzers, tanks dug in around the area where we expect them, but all they have to do is hit us with a series of coordinated attacks, and our lines will not be able to hold.

"Now those B-1s you saw out on our runway are part of Top Secret project the Skunkworks cooked up before the Big War. We found them a few years ago. We've just got them working. How they do what they do, I couldn't even begin to explain to you all. Simply put: When conditions are right, and those five airplanes are working together, they're invisible on radar."

Jones waited a few seconds to let the news sink in. "Now that's a big advantage we were sure we could use. But the bad news is, those B-1s alone can't win this one for us. We can't send those airplanes out there helter-skelter, because they can be shot down by visually-sighted heatseekers, manually-aimed AA guns, and worst of all, air-to-air missiles. And there are still some forty-odd Yaks out there, somewhere."

He paused again.

"I don't have to tell anyone of you how serious the situation is. We're fighting for our Goddamn lives. We're also fighting for something we used to call 'democracy.' It's what our country used to be built on. If this is its last gasp, well, so be it."

Jones looked out at his pilots. Fighters, all. Brave men, all. Americans. Every last one of them.

"So, it's going to be up to us," Jones said. "We've got fifty-five thousand guys sitting out there in that trench, with seventy-five thousand guys and a lot of SAM cover, coming at them. Anything we let get through will be going for our guys' throats.

"So we have no choice really. I've ordered all our airplanes to be fitted with heavy bombs. Stuff that can wipe out trucks, vehicles. I know that will slow everyone down and cut down on their maneuverability. But we'll have to gamble. Half of us will have to go after the SAMs and the rest will have to dodge all the fucking missiles and get to those Circle grunts."

"And what about the B-1s?" someone asked.

"At this moment," Jones said slowly. "We'll have to hold the B-1s in reserve. If we were in the driver's seat for this one, I'd send them against the Circle Army right now. But as the last photo shows, they're just too spread out. If they move toward us in a wide range of attacks, they'll be too scattered for the B-1s to do much good. Remember B-1s are strategic bombers. I can't risk sending them on tactical strikes, especially when they have to work together. They'll wind up dropping ten thousand pounds of bombs on a couple of squads of Circle jerks.

"So we have to keep the B-1s here. Have them ready to strike whenever the Circle breaks through. They're the only ace in the hole we have left."

There was another long silence, then one pilot spoke up. "Any chance of more recon photos coming in, General?"

Jones hated to hear the question. "Sorry, guys. The answer is no," he said slowly. "That's the last photograph we've taken of them."

Jones sensed the uneasiness on the part of the pilots in the room. Good recon was the most important element in a successful air strike. Without it, you were flying "dumb."

"As far as recon goes I'm sorry. But that's the best we can do. And, after all our preparation, that's what we need most . . ."

"Jesus Christ," one of the pilots said aloud. "If only Hunter was here with that Stealth of his . . ."

The words were just barely out of the man's mouth when the door to the situation room swung open. A bright light on the other side made it difficult for the pilots to clearly see who was standing in the doorway. But Jones knew who it was.

"Well, Major Hunter," he said with a wide grin. "Nice of you to join us . . ."

Relief swept the room. The star pitcher had just declared himself ready for the Big Game. Hunter bounded up to the front of the room. The assembled pilots broke into a spontaneous round of applause. It was getting to be a habit. With the Wingman on hand, the pilots knew they now had a fighting chance.

"You've got to see this," Hunter said in all urgency, handing a videotape to Jones. "I just shot it less than an hour ago.

"The Circle has just made what might be a big mistake. And if we move fast enough, we can catch them with their pants down . . ."

Chapter Thirty-eight

A sudden jolt of excitement ripped through the situation room. The video recorder and TV were turned on. Jones pushed in the videotape. Instantly the screen flickered to life.

"Holy Christ!" Jones said.

The screen showed long lines of Circle vehicles, headlights blazing in the pre-dawn darkness, all heading west.

"They're moving everything! *In a line!*," Hunter said. "It looks like a Goddamn May Day parade out there. Their infantry is riding on the launchers, trucks, jeeps, tanks, APCs, old cars, buses, you name it. They're jammed up on Route 70 like the LA Freeway at rush hour!"

"The fools!" Jones exclaimed. "Didn't they learn anything when we greased that column a few days ago?"

"Knowing the Russians, they probably hushed it all up. Kept it secret," Hunter said.

"Either that or they're desperate," Jones said.

"Whatever the hell is going on," Hunter continued. "They've closed their ranks. They've been maneuvering all night. They're attacking us with one major thrust."

"But why in hell would they move on us now?" Jones asked.

Hunter shook his head. "Any commander with an ounce of brain would complete his consolidation then dig in and sit tight. But the Russians are so clamped into their command structures that they have no freedom of thought, no freedom of action. If someone in Moscow says attack, they *have* to attack. And now."

Hunter turned to the situation room map. "They know our trenches are just over this ridgeline. They're making a dash for it. They want to get in position between the ridges and our lines, set up their missiles and attack. They're hoping to overwhelm us with numbers. That's why they've suddenly gone mobile. Their commanders are no doubt kicking their butts all along that highway."

Jones had another question. "But if they're moving their guys on the SAM launchers, how are they handling their air defense?"

"That's just it," Hunter said, turning back to the video machine and speeding up the tape. He finally reached a spot that showed a close up, if hazy view, of the front of the approaching army column. "They're trying to leap-frog it. The front of the column has about two hundred SA-2 launchers. Then every mile or so, they got anywhere from twenty to thirty more. These are the dedicated air defense guys. They're not carrying any ground troops. They have their radars on and can go hot quick."

"But when they see anything coming," Jones interjected. "They'll still have to stop their vehicles and start launch procedures."

Hunter nodded. "And that's our chance to get them . . ."

Jones read Hunter's mind. "I get it," he said. "We send in the fighters first. Just blow right over the top of them. Stop the column. That should cause them to dispatch their troops."

"That's right," Hunter said, barely containing the rising excitement in his voice. "*Then* we send in the B-1s . . ."

". . . and even though the SAM radars will be hot," Jones said, finishing Hunter's thought. "They won't be picking anything up on them!"

"Exactly," Hunter said. "And you can be sure that when the shooting starts, those Reds will kick off their valiant Circle allies off their launchers and start firing every Goddamn SAM they have. But by the time the B-1s arrive, they'll be shooting blind."

The pilots were on their feet by this time, crowded around the TV set.

"While the B-1s take care of the SAMs, we'll have to go after the troops plus any Yaks that might show," Hunter said, summing it all up. "If we're lucky, we can cut their ground attack in half before they ever reach our defense line."

The general grabbed a red phone and was soon talking to the commander of the flight line personnel. He quickly told the man that all of the PAAC aircraft should be refitted with anti-personnel weapons and extra ammunition. The B-1s should be loaded up to the maximum with high explosive bombs, appropriately known as "super-blockbusters."

Jones again addressed the airmen. "Okay, that's the plan . . . let's go! Launch now and go. We'll have the coordinates to you while you're taxiing. Good luck guys!"

Chapter Thirty-nine

Roman candles . . .

The sky over the front of the long enemy column looked like the Fourth of July. Hundreds of long, fiery streaks of light and smoke were popping up from the roadway, shooting off in all different directions. Some were exploding in mid-air. Others traveled in smoky corkscrew flight lines, only to fall to the ground and blow up.

Desperation. The Soviets knew their attack had been discovered. They knew the Western Forces' air armada would soon strike. As predicted, they were sending up a wall of panicky SAMs.

Hunter's Stealth fighter was the first one over the scene. Behind him were Crunch's F-4s. Then came the A-7s, the F-104s, the F-106s, the A-10s and the T-38s.

Per Jones' orders, all of the airplanes were carrying not high explosive bombs, but guts filled with cannon shells and air-to-air missiles.

Most of the Circle Army troops riding in the

long column had yet to see an aircraft the entire war. Now suddenly the sky was filled with them. Even the barrage of SAMs being sent up by the launchers at the head of the column offered no comfort. Even the lowest grunt knew you couldn't fire a SAM when it was moving along the highway. The column had quickly screeched to a halt. The ground troops were ordered off the launching trucks and over to the side of the road. They felt helpless. Exposed. Some of them panicked.

Hunter went in first. Twisting and turning to avoid getting hit by a lucky SAM shot, he opened up with the Stealth's powerful cannons. The airplane confidently shuddered as long spits of flame shot out from its nose. The streaks of burning shells found targets immediately on the overcrowded highway. Troop-carrying vehicles, tanks, APCs, fuel trucks, buses, and everywhere, the SAM launchers . . . nothing escaped Hunter's furious barrage.

He could see the hapless Circle troops scattering toward the sides of the highway. It was as if they had already read the script. Strange. He felt for them in a way. They had been taken in by Viktor's mind games, sold a bill of goods that was now going very sour. Now they would die fighting for that madman's twisted plan . . .

Hunter pulled the Stealth fighter straight up and spun around to his right. Looking over his shoulder he could see Crunch's F-4s walking down the column's length, firing their cannons non-stop while dropping anti-personnel bombs all along the roadside.

Behind them came two A-10s. Then two F-106 Delta Darts. Then a pair of A-7 Strikefighters. Then the T-38s and the F-104s. On and on, two by two, the Western Forces aircraft swept down on the column, ripping up both flesh and metal targets, then sweeping away. All the while, SAMs were streaking everywhere—but shooting too late and not hitting a thing.

That's when *the feeling* hit Hunter like a shot out of the blue . . .

Here they come, he thought. Directly over the horizon. To the east. At least 30 of them. The Yaks had decided to join the fray.

"Okay," Hunter called into his microphone. "We've got company."

Many of the PAAC fighters were only now picking up the faint images of the Soviet jets on their radar screens. Immediately the radio traffic between the fighters picked up. Vectors were given, coordinates checked. Enemy targets counted, attack patterns discussed.

"Delta One group, arm your air-to-airs," Hunter called out. "Crunch, you got Delta Two!"

"Roger, Major," Hunter heard Crunch's reply. The Ace Wrecking Company's two F-4s would break off with half the attacking PAAC force and go after the Circle infantry now moving toward the ridges near the Western Forces' defense line. Hunter would take the remaining fighters and go after the approaching Yaks.

As the air armada neatly split in two, a curious calm settled over the stalled enemy column. Just as the sky was filled with jets a moment before, now it was empty. Quiet. Almost serene. A few wisps of smoke rose above the wrecked vehicles. The PAAC attack had been swift, sharp, accurate. Like a long wound delivered, the column was bleeding. But the worst was yet to come . . .

Captain Bull Dozer adjusted his electronic binoculars. He had been warned by radio that the first elements of the approaching Circle Army would be coming into view shortly. Looking out over the Western Forces' defense line, the Marine could see nothing but the ridgeline two miles away. But then, slowly, surely, he saw small groups of soldiers appear on top of the ridge. Within two minute's time, the enemy soldiers were swarming over the ridgeline like an army of ants.

He calmly reached for his radiophone and called up and down the Western Forces' defense line. "Get ready . . ."

A push of another button and he was talking to the Denver Air Station air controllers. "Enemy troops within sight," he radioed. "Entering buffer zone now. No SAMs . . ."

Dozer heard the thunder less than a minute later. Over the top of the hills to their rear came six B-52 Stratofortresses that had been loitering nearby. Now they were flying so low, Dozer could read small lettering on their bellies. The SAM-vulnerable big bombers could only be expected to make one ground-hugging bombing run, then scoot. Dozer knew the napalm bombs they were carrying would further reduce the number of enemy soldiers who would reach the defense line. But, judging by the thousands of enemy troops he saw through the scope, the quick B-52 strike would only serve as a delaying action.

As the Stratofortresses roared over The Circle troops and started dropping their bombs, Dozer was on the phone to his officers up and down the line. The biggest job of the veteran 7th Cavalry Marines was keeping the many volunteer troops on the flank from panicking. Luckily the all-important center line was made up of professional Pacific American soldiers.

All of the Western Forces soldiers could see the great wallops of flame rise above the plain before them, incinerating the lead element of the approaching Circle troops. Suddenly, a shoulder-launched SA-7 flashed up from the mass of enemy soldiers, catching one of the B-52s on its port wing. The big airplane immediately flipped over and plowed into the swarm of enemy soldiers, exploding with a force that shook the ground like an earthquake.

Still The Circle troops kept coming . . .

Their work done, the B-52s cleared the area, just as Crunch's Delta Two group appeared from the east. The fighter jets immediately pounced on the front of the enemy column which was now spreading out into walking lines nearly two miles across. It was an odd way to attack a trenchline. The Circle soldiers looked more like an advancing army of British redcoats than anything else—throwbacks to the set-piece battles of the American Revolutionary War.

One by one, the attacking PAAC jets swooped in on The Circle troops, dropping napalm and anti-personnel bombs then roaring away. But still the enemy troops kept coming . . .

Dozer grabbed his radiophone and was instantly in touch to the artillery commander a half mile behind his line. He yelled one word: "Fire!" On his command, thirty howitzers opened up. The Western Forces troops in the trench watched as the big shells streaked over their heads and slammed into the plain around the advancing Circle troops. For awhile the front of the enemy lines were obscured by smoke and flame. But then, one by one, then by the thousands, surviving Circle troops emerged from the smoke.

Crunch's aircraft appeared again, this time sweeping in in pairs and raking the enemy with cannon fire. More soldiers were hit, ripped up by the cannon shells. Yet still The Circle soldiers kept advancing.

"This is incredible," Dozer told one of his officers nearby. "These guys just don't know how to retreat . . ."

There was something very peculiar about how the advancing Circle lines were acting. They were now just a half mile away from the Western Forces trenches, yet they were still walking, and very slowly. Dozer had told the soldiers in his line to hold their fire until his command. But strangely the enemy was doing the same. Except for the one SA-7 that brought down the B-52, not another shot had been fired by the advancing Circle soldiers.

Dozer zoomed in on the approaching line with his electronic scope. Faces of the soldiers were now becoming clear. He focused the high-power spyglasses, keying in on several Circle soldiers at the front of the advancing line.

"Jesus Christ . . ." he whispered. "They're . . . just kids!"

What Dozer saw was a line of teenagers. Most were not wearing helmets or boots or anything expected of ground soldiers. Many of them weren't even carrying arms! But the Marine captain immediately saw The Circle troops were carrying something more sinister.

Wrapped neatly around the waist of some of the soldiers were strings of sticks of TNT.

"Oh God," Dozer said. "Hunter was right. They're coming at us with human bombs . . ."

General Jones looked at the console of the ultra-sophisticated B-1 bomber. In its center was a flat black panel containing five red lights. Right now only one of the lights was blinking.

Jones had just lifted off in *Ghost Rider 1*, the lead ship of the Eureka B-1s. As he circled the Denver Air Station, he saw the other four B-1s taxi and take off in cool precision. The small armada banded up and then turned to the southeast. "Won't be long now," Jones thought. "Then we'll finally know whether it was all worth it or not . . ."

Ten minutes out of Denver, the B-1s formed up into a diamond pattern. Jones was at the lead point, with *Ghost Rider 2* and *3* taking the sides and *Ghost Rider 4* in the rear. *Ghost Rider 5* took up its position in the middle of the formation. As soon as Jones was sure each of the airplanes was in place, he leveled the flight off at 20,000 feet, and threw a series of switches on his control board.

These signals were instantly transmitted to *Ghost Rider 5*, which carried the bulk of the formation's electronic gear. At the speed of light, the fifth aircraft's computer started printing out computations, calculations relating airspeed to altitude, engine exhaust heat to fuel consumption, bomb load to the rotation of the earth. Slowly but surely, every aspect of the five airplanes' radar "signatures" was identified by the super-computer, and then, carefully masked electronically.

Jones saw one of the red lights on his black panel blink once then stay on. "Ghost Rider 2, on lock," he heard J. J. Toomey, the second bomber's pilot say.

A few seconds later, another of the red lights blinked on, followed by the radio call: "Ghost Rider 3, locked."

Jones checked his location. They were ten minutes from target.

"Ghost 4, on lock," he heard a pilot call while the fourth red light blinked on.

His aircraft would be next. He closed up the formation slightly, giving the tons of electronics on *Ghost Rider 5* every advantage.

Suddenly the red light on his control panel that had been blinking, stopped. It was now burning a bright, constant red. He was in.

"Ghost 1, locked," he called into his microphone. Thirty seconds later, the fifth and last red light came on. He heard the message he'd been waiting for a few seconds later:

"Ghost 5, locked on, sir."

"Verify, Ghost 5," Jones radioed.

"Verified, sir," the pilot of Ghost Rider 5 called back. "We are now 'in system.' "

Jones smiled. They were invisible . . .

The Soviet general stood on top of the roof of his own personal BMP, looked over his column and smiled . . .

Most of his SAM launchers were now in place and ready to go operational when the Western

Forces' jets returned. He knew the Yak fighters would soon arrive. His men had counted only about 30 Western Forces' jets in the brief air attack; he was expecting about 40 Yaks to appear shortly. The combination of his SAMs and the Yaks would make him unbeatable.

Best of all, he was finally rid of the ragged Circle soldiers. He could see the last of their army marching west toward the ridgeline and the Western Forces' trenches that lay beyond. Good, the Soviet thought. Let them all kill each other off. His column, with its professional Soviet troops, the SAMs and the Yaks, were now a self-contained fighting force. Once they defeated the Western Forces' air corps, he would be able to roam the countryside at will. No longer would he be bogged down by the hooligans of The Circle Army. The American word for them was "suckers." They had followed Viktor like a bull with a ring in its nose; fallen for his elaborate "exotic Queen," psych-ops, fallen for his call to arms, fallen for his whole line of Circle bullshit. The Soviet general knew that The Circle soldiers had been just pawns in Viktor's game all along.

He watched as the Western Forces' aircraft streaked over the horizon, bombing The Circle troops. He laughed. The PAAC jets wouldn't dare come close to the column now that the SAMs were "hot." The sounds of the bombing and gunfire coming from the other side of the ridge was music to his ears.

He knew there was never any real plan for The Circle to take over the continent, never any real alliance between The Circle and the Soviets. The whole thing was masterfully staged with just one purpose in mind: destabilization. Keep the Americans fighting amongst themselves, even if it took every SAM trooper the Russians could muster. They had reached their goal with a minimum of effort—the Americans would wipe out each other's army and the Soviets would be the ruling force on the continent. The capitalists had finally hung themselves.

Now if only those Yaks would arrive . . .

The PAAC aircraft of the Delta One group plunged right into the heart of the advancing Yak force. A swirling, twisting dogfight of enormous proportions ensued. The Yaks were at a substantial advantage—their pilots were able to stop their aircraft on a dime, hover in the air as the attacking PAAC aircraft would swoop on by. Then suddenly the Yak would become the hunter.

But the Western Forces' had their own, not-so-secret yet radar-proof weapon. The Wingman was everywhere . . .

PAAC pilots who were there that day told of how Hunter had purposely let several Yaks at once get on his tail, his Stealth fighter moving only enough to the left and right to prevent the Soviet pilots from getting a good missile lock on him. Drawing two or three Yaks at a time, Hunter would lead them on a merry chase, climbing to extreme altitudes, diving at nose-bleeding speeds. More than a few of the Yak pilots passed out from the g-forces, only to awake just as their airplanes were about to smash into the ground. As the other PAAC pilots held their own with the Yaks, Hunter was knocking them off two and three at a time. And all without yet firing a shot.

Finally the Soviet officer in charge of the Yaks realized the insanity of chasing the Stealth and ordered his fighters to attack the other PAAC jets instead. That's when Hunter got down to business.

A Yak had locked onto the end of a F-104 and fired an Aphid air-to-air. Hunter suddenly flashed between the two airplanes blasting the missile with a well-placed cannon burst. He then twisted over backward and locked on his own Sidewinder missile. The Yak pilot pulled back on his controls to attempt a mid-air stop, but he was too late. Hunter went screaming by, and released a Sidewinder as if he was flying a torpedo-bomber. The missile went hot and impacted on the Yak's exhaust tube simultaneously, blowing the Soviet jet to smithereens.

Hunter was now tailing two Yaks at once. They were intent on downing a slow F-106 that was diving toward one of their comrades. The Russians had no idea Hunter was so close—their radars showed nothing but blue sky behind them. Two squeezes of his cannons' trigger and two

Yaks were soon on their way to fiery deaths.

Although the Yaks outnumbered the Western Forces' airplanes, the Soviet pilots were now getting panicky. The crazy man in the Stealth was shooting at them from every direction, or so it seemed. One second he was flying barely 20 feet off the deck. The next instant it seemed like he was diving on them from 40,000 feet. He was taking on everyone. Firing missiles, strafing with cannons. Any Soviet pilot who chose to stop in mid-air risked death by collision. The Stealth was even trying to ram the stationary Soviet fighters.

All the while the other PAAC jets were chalking up wins. Soon the Kansas prairie below was littered with Yak wreckage. Several of the Russians had seen enough and fled to the south. Hunter let them go. He knew they wouldn't get far. Just over the horizon he "saw" a flight of friendly jets approaching. F-20s. F-4s. St. Louie's situation on the Texas border had lessened enough for him to send some help to the major battle area. He learned later that the Yaks ran head-on into the Football City-Texas Air Force airplanes with disastrous results for the Soviet side.

Another group of Yaks also opted to break off the battle and roared off to the north. Their escape attempt too was futile. They met a flight of Fitzgerald's ADF Thunderchiefs over the Nebraska border . . .

Hunter searched the skies above the Kansas battlefield. All of the Soviet airplanes were either shot down or retreating. His mind flashed back to that arctic recon flight so long ago. The VTOL adversaries he had first found hugging the snow-covered ground near Nome, Alaska, had, for the most part, been defeated. It had been a long, tiring campaign, but at last he could say the right side won. He reached inside his flight suit pocket and pulled out the small tattered American flag.

"Okay, old buddy," he whispered. "Make it through another one . . ."

The first bomb dropped from *Ghost Rider 1* landed less than a mile in front of the Soviet general's command car. It was a 10,000 super blockbuster, a huge explosive device that obliterated every truck, tank, APC and SAM launcher on a quarter mile stretch of the highway.

The Soviet general was at first stunned, then angry. He was certain that one of the SAMs had exploded on its launcher. But suddenly another blockbuster detonated. This one barely a half mile from his position in the column. He saw a T-72 heavy tank thrown more than 200 feet in the air so powerful was the blast.

Where were the bombs coming from?

He screamed to his BMP's radar operator to sweep the area. The report came back as a solid *nyet*. There wasn't an aircraft in sight.

Just then a third blockbuster exploded not a thousand feet away from him. Horror struck him deep down. Someone *was* dropping bombs on them, but they weren't being picked up on radar. His first thought was it was the Stealth airplane. But he immediately discounted this notion. These bombs were too large to be carried by the Stealth.

He scanned the crystal-clear sky. Then he saw them . . .

About four miles up. No contrails. No sound. Five jets. Big ones. Flying in a precision formation. Were they B-1s?

He screamed to his radar man again. "We have nothing on the scope!" the man yelled back, realizing just as his general did that they were suddenly vulnerable.

The Soviet officer reached for his microphone even as he heard the next bomb screeching through the air. "Fire all missiles!" he screamed. "All units fire all . . ."

The next blockbuster landed directly on his BMP. His message was cut off by the blast of 10,000 pounds of explosives. In the instant between life and death that seemed to last an eternity, one last thought flashed through his mind. "These Americans . . . you cannot defeat them."

Orders were orders and so the panicking SAM technicians started launching every missile from every launcher, hoping to hit the radar-invisible bombers.

The Ghost Riders were not carpet bombing the

column. Rather they were using their invisibility shield to precision-bomb the highway. One bomb from each plane then the whole formation would swing around and start the whole procedure again.

It was a devastating strategy. The B-1s bombed with impunity. The hundreds of SAMs—their radar-homing target devices rendered useless—were being shot every which way. Many fell back to earth, hitting vehicles in the column. This only added to the fright and confusion of the Soviet troops. They were leaderless yet ordered to stay at their positions. They were being bombed but were unable to fight back. Some ran. Some tried to maneuver their vehicles out of the burning, twisted traffic jam. But it was of no use. The blockbusters were coming down in clockwork precision. The column and all the precious SAMs were being systematically destroyed. Thousands lay dying in the Kansas sun. Russian blood mixing with American soil.

Another Soviet foreign adventure was coming to an end . . .

Chapter Forty

"Sharpshooters! Front and center!" Dozer yelled into his radiophone.

The advancing Circle army was now only a quarter of a mile away from the Western Forces' defense line. He had yet to order his ground troops to fire. The sight of the approaching rabble, most of them young kids with no weapons, was causing his head and his belly to ache.

Up and down the line, the sharpshooters of Dozer's 7th Cavalry got into position. "Pick off the ones they've strapped with TNT," Dozer's order went out.

One by one the crack Marine riflemen aimed and fired at the approaching human bombs. One by one The Circle *kamikazes* were hit by the rifle bullets, exploding in a flash of fire and a spray of bloody guts. Each human bomb that went up killed a dozen of the comrades closest to them.

Yet still the human wave advanced.

All along the defense line, the Western Forces soldiers were getting anxious. They, too, could see the approaching army was little but a rabble, yet, not every human bomb had been destroyed. They were assuming the worst and figuring that many of The Circle troops were also booby-trapped. Yet the trench soldiers would hold their fire until they received the order . . .

Dozer had made his decision. He couldn't risk the lives of his troops in the hand-to-hand fighting that would follow if he had his soldiers hold their fire now.

The Marine captain shook his head. His radioman nearby heard him whisper: "God forgive me . . ." Then the captain grabbed his radiophone and yelled: "Fire!"

As onc, thc entire two-mile line of Western Forces opened up on the approaching horde. The first line of Circle troops fell. Another line appeared. Another volley and these unarmed soldiers were mowed down. Another line, another volley. Line after line of the enemy simply walked into the murderous barrage of lead. Stomachs were ripped open, skulls exploded. The brainwashed rabble kept marching. Over the horribly shot up bodies of their comrades and sometimes crunching right through them. The air was heavy with smoke and the smell of gunfire and blood.

It was a slaughter. Still no Circle soldier fired a shot. Only later would the Western Forces discover that of the few Circle soldiers carrying guns, none of them had ammunition. The Circle commanders and their Russian allies had hoarded it all, preferring to send The Circle grunts into the mouth of death without so much as a bullet.

Two volleys from the trench hit The Circle line just 100 feet away. Several of the enemy troops broke into a run toward the defense line, but they were quickly cut down. One last volley all along the trench and then it was over . . .

The gunfire stopped. The gentle wind blew the smoke away. It was quiet for the first time in what seemed like an eternity. The Western Forces soldiers looked up from over their rifles and took in the carnage in front of them. A few screams and moans could be heard coming from the field of dead and dying before the trench. Tens of thousands of the enemy lay mangled and twisted before them.

Not a single Circle soldier had made it to the defense line . . .

Now, more news was flashed back to the Western Forces' troops in the line. The enemy column on Route 70 had been stopped. There would be no more Circle soldiers charging the trenches. The back of the evil Circle-Soviet alliance was broken.

Although the war was apparently over, the soldiers in the trenches couldn't relax. The anxious hours, days, weeks. Adrenaline pumping. All to end in the slaughter of innocents? The mass killing of the hopped up brainwashed kids. It was disgusting. Death for death's sake.

But the calm did not last too long . . .

Dozer scanned the horizon. He felt something. Out there. Beyond the ridgeline. Something much more dangerous than the helpless troops they had just gunned down.

Then he saw them . . .

"Jesus Christ . . ." Dozer said, blindly reaching for his radiophone to call Hunter. "There's *thousands* of them . . ."

For miles in every direction, on the ridges in front of them, sat the 30,000 men of the 1st Mongolian Cavalry . . .

They had come out of nowhere. The unexpected variable. The troops in the trenches suddenly found themselves alert again. Tense again. It was frightening. The line of the Mongolian soldiers covered the whole horizon.

Dozer radioed all along to his officers. Each report was the same. The Mongol horde stretched for miles. And it was preparing to attack.

Word was instantly flashed back to the Denver Air Station. Most of the jets that had defeated the Yaks had returned and shut down. Now they learned they had to quickly refuel, bomb up and speed back to the front.

Hunter was the first one off the ground . . .

"Here they come!"

The cry went up in the Western Forces' trenchworks. Every soldier stared out on to the flatlands before them.

The Mongols were bringing their horses up to a canter.

"Get ready!" the word passed through the Western Forces' lines.

Dozer's Marines walked among their volunteer troops on the flank, making sure everyone was in position with a full-load of ammo. The regular Pacific American soldiers in the middle of the line waited patiently in grim anticipation—to finally to draw blood from the Asian horsemen.

Two miles out, the Mongols kicked their horses into a fast trot. They fanned out until their line was nearly two miles across. Many of them were wearing uniforms akin to those worn by their ancestors—bright, colorful, evil-looking. Others were simply dressed in used Chinese Army fatigues. Each carried some kind of rifle—the Mongols' proficiency was shooting well from a moving horse—and the mandatory, razor-sharp sword.

The leader of the horde, a man known as the Great Obo, was at the head of the column, dressed to the nines in the ancient oriental costume, riding a tall, pure-white stallion. He would lead his men into battle this time, just as he had done for the past few months. They would move as he moved.

The moments passed tensely through the Western Forces' line. Dozer, the powerful pair of electronic spyglasses pressed against his face, had identified the Great Obo as the cavalry's leader and watched him every step of the way. Even through the scope, the warrior looked fierce, fearless and proud.

When the horse column reached a mile out, Obo broke his horse into a slow gallop. His army followed in kind. Dozer raised his hand. The young Marine radioman stood close by, holding a phone which crackled continuously with static. High above and far away, the sound of jet engines could be heard . . .

Dozer had Obo in full view now. Suddenly the Mongol gave his steed two, sharp cracks with his whip and the horse responded by breaking into a full gallop. Obo, reins and a rifle in one hand, raised his sword with the other and pointed it toward the trenches. Dozer could almost read the man's lips as Obo screamed the Mongol equivalent to "Charge!"

"Now!" Dozer yelled, pumping his raised arm like a trucker pulling his horn. The word was instantly passed a half mile back of the lines to the 30-piece howitzer column that waited there. Almost simultaneously, the big guns opened up.

Dozer grabbed the radioman's mike, nearly strangling the kid in the process. "Now, Hawk!" Dozer yelled. "Now!"

The Stealth materialized out of thin air. One second, the sky was empty—the next instant, the strange black jet was roaring overhead, just 50 feet off the ground, rushing to meet the charging cavalry head-on. Close behind were the F-4X

Phantoms of the Ace Wrecking Company. Behind them were more airplanes—Crunch's F-4s, the F-104s, A-7s, T-38s, A-10s, the old F-84.

Each plane carried a full load of napalm . . .

"So this is what it's come to," Hunter thought as he gripped his weapons' release control. "Jets against horses? *This is the pure insanity of war.*"

"Drop on me," he radioed the planes behind him. A chorus of "Rogers," came back.

The jets fanned out to form a large arrow formation with Hunter in the lead. He aimed the Stealth right at the center mass of the Mongol horde. Even before the first bomb was dropped, he imagined he could already smell the stink of burning horse and human flesh. "Too bad," he thought, punching the weapons control system computer one last time. "You guys should have stayed where you belong."

He was so low and so close to the charging cavalry now, he could see the determination on the faces of the horse soldiers.

". . . three . . . two . . . one . . . now!"

With that, two napalm cannisters dropped from the Stealth's wings and exploded in the midst of the Mongols. Those in the Western Forces' trenches, again holding their fire until the order was given, saw a tidal wave of flame wash over the attacking cavalry. Horses and men were seared through in an instant. Some of the animals were reduced to skeletons before they even hit the ground.

The Ace Wrecking Company Phantoms dropped their napalm cannisters as soon as they saw Hunter drop his. Sixteen additional bombs landed on the horse soldiers, drawing a blanket of fire over the attackers. Then the rest of the air armada unleashed their bombs containing jellied gasoline. At the same time, the howitzer shells started landing among the charging cavalry, sending up great plumes of fire, smoke and deadly shrapnel.

The Mongols were about a half mile from the Western Forces' lines and still they kept coming. Hunter gunned the Stealth into a tight, 180-degree right hand turn, positioning himself above and parallel the leading edge of the charging army. He released two more napalm cannisters which exploded on the ground slightly ahead of the charging Mongols. Unable to slow their steeds, the cavalrymen plunged right into the sheet of flame, some emerging on the other side, still charging, horse and rider horribly engulfed in fire. The other jets followed Hunter's maneuver, relentlessly laying down a wall of flame in front of the Mongols' lead horsemen.

As many as half of the original 30,000 horsemen were now either dead or dying. But still the remaining attackers plunged onward. Hunter did a quick loop, knowing he would have time for one more pass before the Mongols hit the Western Forces' lines. Again parallel to the attacking edge of the cavalry, he opened up with his cannons.

The Stealth shuddered as the shells ripped through the mounted troops and their steeds. He continued to fire across the entire length of the attacker's front line. The howitzer barrage intensified, pounding the rushing Mongols. The trench soldiers now opened up with mortar fire. Next came the shelling from the tanks dug in along the Western Forces' lines. The Phantoms and the other aircraft were also blazing away with their respective machineguns and cannons. Hunter called a predescribed order over the radio. On his command, the Cobra Cousins' attack choppers, hovering nearby, were thrown into the fray and started firing on targets of opportunity.

The remaining Mongols were 100 yards from the Western Forces' lines when Dozer gave the word to his riflemen to fire. At once the entire line opened up on the attacking horsemen. Those riders who had survived the napalm, the howitzers and the strafing were now met by a wall of lead. Horses were hit head on, reared up and then collapsed, causing the steeds behind them to trip and tumble. The mounted soldiers were thrown and trampled by the unstoppable, panicking animals.

Again and again, up and down the line, the defenders fired into what was left of the charging horsemen. Then the first Mongols reached the defenders' ramparts. The fighting became intense in close quarters. The trench soldiers fired away at the attackers' horses, killing the animals, then shooting the displaced cavalrymen. The Mongols were barely able to squeeze off a shot, the fire from the trenches was so heavy. Hand-to-hand combat ensued up and down the trenches. By this time, Hunter had swung the Stealth back around and was strafing the rear elements of the attacking army, as were the other fighters.

The battle pitched back and forth for what seemed an eternity. The fighting was so close that howitzers stopped firing for fear of hitting friendly troops. Hunter was confined to making low passes, the jet's screaming engine spooking the Mongol horses.

From his perspective high above, he could see the bodies begin to pile up. The soil was actually turning blood-red. Fires were everywhere. Smoke was obscuring the battlefield.

Then, the battle began to turn . . .

The Mongols were slowly being drawn into the center of the defenders' lines. Urged on by Dozer's Marines, the volunteers on the flank, bolstered by the air support's decimation of the Mongols and smelling victory, swept out of their trenches and began a pincer movement to contain the horsemen. Many minutes of intense combat followed until the Mongol attack finally ground to a halt. Completely surrounded, the attackers began to panic. They faced the crack Western Forces' troops to their front, the advancing volunteer irregulars on their flanks and, now, to the rear. Helicopters were peppering them from above. Jets continued to streak in low, rattling the horses.

In the middle of the battle, the Great Obo knew he had been betrayed—by The Circle and in turn, by the Russians. "We are like lambs," he thought, as he watched his once fierce army be slaughtered. "We are being sacrificed."

The fighting continued. Obo had his horse shot out from underneath him by one of the attacking Cobras. Unaccustomed to fighting on foot, he emptied his rifle into the Caucasian soldiers, then started flailing away with his sword.

Out of the sea of faces, he saw a powerful-looking, stocky man moving his way. The soldier was wearing what Obo recognized as the uniform of a U.S. Marine captain. The name tag sewn above the man's left breast pocket clearly read: Dozer. They were suddenly face-to-face. The Marine was chopping away with a captured Mongol saber. Obo raised his own blade to deflect the Marine's thrust. The power of the Leatherneck's blow knocked Obo off-balance. The Marine pressed his attack relentlessly. Obo wished he had the time to impale himself on his own sword, but the attacking officer showed no let-up. Another thrust from the Marine. Obo managed to deflect it, but lost his sword in the process and fell backward. On his back, looking up at the American, the fighting swirling around them, Obo reached into his belt for the dagger he kept there. Too late, as the Marine ran him through. A puff of blood exploded from Obo's nose and mouth. The fierce Marine put his boot on the Mongol's chest and brought his face close up to the dying man.

"What the hell are you doing here!" the Marine screamed at him. "What the hell are you doing in *my* country!"

They were the last words the Great Obo ever heard . . .

The battle was over by noon. Every one of the Mongols had died, most at the hands of the Western Forces, some by their own swords.

Hunter had landed the Stealth on a highway nearby. Jones had been airlifted to the site also. Both men met with Dozer on the battlefield.

"We lost about four thousand men," the Marine told them. "Young men, most of them. Good troops."

Scattered from the plateau to the trenches lay thousands of dead Mongols, covering the bodies of the dead Circle soldiers. On the ridges surrounding the valley, huge fires still burned.

Hunter looked out on the battlefield as the victorious Western Force soldiers collected rifles and swords from the dead Mongols.

"This was needless," he said to Jones and Dozer. "It was nothing more than a mass suicide, with these creeps pulling some of our guys into hell with them . . ."

Hunter walked out into the battlefield alone. He faced the east. The sky was turning red. It was not the *Aurora Borealis* this time. The red was in his eyes. They were burning. Burning with hate.

Viktor was responsible for this. The devil himself had gored the American continent and watched it bleed. And for what? Ego? Power? Or was he just following orders?

Hunter was convinced. Viktor's mission all along was twofold: Conquer America at best, keep it destabilized at worst. He would have won either way. It would take the continent years to recover from this. Hunter's dream of reunification—a long shot before—was now even further stalled.

He felt his senses start rippling. Jolts of energy pumped through him. He closed his eyes. He called on *the feeling*. That's when he saw him. Viktor. Alive. He was sure of it. Fleeing. Escaping. Across the Atlantic.

And Hunter was going after him . . .

WILLIAM W. JOHNSTONE
THE ASHES SERIES

OUT OF THE ASHES (#1)	(0-7860-0289-1, $4.99/$5.99)
BLOOD IN THE ASHES (#4)	(0-8217-3009-6, $3.95/$4.95)
ALONE IN THE ASHES (#5)	(0-8217-4019-9, $3.99/$4.99)
WIND IN THE ASHES (#6)	(0-8217-3257-9, $3.95/$4.95)
VALOR IN THE ASHES (#9)	(0-8217-2484-3, $3.95/$4.95)
TRAPPED IN THE ASHES (#10)	(0-8217-2626-9, $3.95/$4.95)
DEATH IN THE ASHES (#11)	(0-8217-2922-5, $3.95/$4.95)
SURVIVAL IN THE ASHES (#12)	(0-8217-3098-3, $3.95/$4.95)
FURY IN THE ASHES (#13)	(0-8217-3316-8, $3.95/$4.95)
COURAGE IN THE ASHES (#14)	(0-8217-3574-8, $3.99/$4.99)
VENGEANCE IN THE ASHES (#16)	(0-8217-4066-0, $3.99/$4.99)
TREASON IN THE ASHES (#19)	(0-8217-4521-2, $4.50/$5.50)
D-DAY IN THE ASHES	(0-8217-4650-2, $4.50/$5.50)
BETRAYAL IN THE ASHES	(0-8217-5265-0, $4.99/$5.99)